Tales
Out of
School

Gervase Phinn

Tales Out of School

HODDER

First published in Great Britain in 2020 by Hodder & Stoughton
An Hachette UK company

This paperback edition published in 2020

1

A CIP catalogue record for this title is available from the British Library

Paperback ISBN 978 1 473 65067 1
eBook ISBN 978 1 473 65066 4

Typeset in Plantin Light by Hewer Text UK Ltd, Edinburgh
Printed and bound in Great Britain by Clays Ltd, Elcograf S.p.A.

Hodder & Stoughton policy is to use papers that are natural, renewable
and recyclable products and made from wood grown in sustainable
forests. The logging and manufacturing processes are expected to
conform to the environmental regulations of the country of origin.

Hodder & Stoughton Ltd
Carmelite House
50 Victoria Embankment
London EC4Y 0DZ

www.hodder.co.uk

For Layla Sheila Elsey Phinn

I

The woman and the boy sat in the front seats of the shiny black Range Rover. The car was parked on a small square of land just off the road. She rested a hand on the boy's shoulder and squeezed gently, then looked out on the scene before her – a vast landscape of rolling hills and rocky outcrops dusted with a covering of snow; the whole area a vast white sea. The rays of a watery winter sun pierced the high feathery clouds, making the snow glow a golden pink. The scene was magical.

'Just look at that view,' she said, turning to the boy. 'It's so lovely, so timeless and tranquil. It's beautiful.'

'I'm cold,' the boy murmured, shivering a little.

He turned and looked through the side window at the building set back from the road: a solid, square single-storey construction with a greasy blue-grey slate roof flecked with snow and small square, windows, enclosed by low, craggy white-limestone walls. It looked like any other sturdy Yorkshire country dwelling. No traffic triangle warned drivers that children might be crossing and there was no board at the front indicating that this was a school.

'What do you think?' asked the woman. 'Is it worth having a look around?'

The boy gave a convincing impression of appearing not to care. 'If you want,' he replied, sighing.

'It's more about what you want, Leo,' she said.

'It looks like the workhouse out of a Dickens novel,' he mumbled.

She gave him a look of patient indulgence. He has had so much to put up with, she thought, things that most boys of ten never have to deal with. 'It is rather grim,' she agreed. 'It's not a good thing, though, to judge by appearances, is it?' The boy knew this only too well. 'Shall we go inside?'

He didn't reply but continued to stare at the building.

'I know it doesn't appear all that promising,' she continued, 'and it's rather isolated up here at the top of the Dale, but now we're here it might be worth taking a look. What do you think?' The boy continued to stare out of the window but said nothing. 'You know, Leo, if you don't want to go inside, I can turn right around and we can leave things for a while and look for another school.'

'I know that,' he said.

'We could think again about you going to Silverdene Lodge.'

'I don't want to go to Silverdene Lodge,' replied the boy vehemently. 'I didn't like the school and I didn't like the headmaster.'

'No,' granted the woman, 'I can't say that I was very impressed with Mr Mountjoy. A bit too full of his own importance, wasn't he?'

The previous day they had visited the private school in Clayton. Mr Mountjoy, headmaster of Silverdene Lodge Preparatory School, had sat behind a huge mahogany desk in his huge leather chair with his hands on the arms, looking like a king on a throne. Not a thing had been out of place in his plush office. There were smart light-wood cupboards and cabinets, a matching glass-fronted bookcase containing a set of leather-bound tomes, all identical in shape and size, an occasional rosewood table, two easy chairs patterned in burgundy and a deep oatmeal-coloured sofa. A shelf displayed a collection of silver cups and shields. The walls were plain and painted in a soured-cream shade. On one were four garish abstract paintings – all coloured blobs and odd shapes – in silver metal frames, positioned at exact distances from one another. Another wall displayed rows of photographs of the school's sporting teams, the children posing serious-faced and cross-armed for the camera. There was a thick shag-pile carpet and long, pale drapes at the window, through which stretched an uninterrupted view over the market town of Clayton, busy and bustling at rush hour. In the far distance were the moors and misty peaks cloaked in white.

Mr Mountjoy was as pristine as his surroundings. He was a tall, angular individual, clean-shaven with short, neatly parted black hair, dressed in a charcoal grey suit, crisp white shirt and college tie knotted tightly at the collar. A black academic gown was draped around his shoulders. He leaned back in his chair and observed for a moment the woman and the boy who sat before him. She was a tall, elegant young woman of strikingly good looks, probably in her mid-thirties, with a wave of bright blonde hair, a streamlined figure and flawless make-up. But her most attractive feature was her eyes: they were almond-shaped and as bright as blue polished glass. The woman was wearing a smart, close-fitting camel-hair coat and matching cashmere scarf. Judging by her appearance she was clearly refined and demonstrably affluent – he had seen the gleaming black Range Rover pull up outside. Here was just the sort of parent he liked: wealthy, stylish and well-connected. He must do his utmost, he thought, to convince her that this was the school for her son.

Since the increase in fees, numbers at Silverdene Lodge had been declining of late and Mr Mountjoy had been under pressure from his governors to do something about it. But it wasn't just the rise in fees that had occasioned the falling off in numbers. It was the fierce competition from the local primary school in the neighbouring village of Barton-in-the-Dale. Once unpopular and moribund, it had recently flourished under the leadership and management of the new head teacher, Mrs Elisabeth Stirling. It was now one of the most successful schools in the county and parents were queuing up to secure a place for their children.

Mr Mountjoy had looked with interest at the boy (for he assumed it was a boy by the clothes the child wore). He was small and delicate as a china doll with his mass of golden curls, his wide, inquisitive blue eyes and his pale unblemished face. The child returned the man's gaze with undisturbed equanimity. He looked disconcertingly self-possessed.

'Let me tell you a little about Silverdene Lodge,' the headmaster had said, giving a dry little smile. He had then proceeded to give a lecture that he had clearly delivered to parents many times before.

'This is a long-established school,' he had begun. 'It was founded in the 1930s by a clergyman with only twelve children on roll. Since then we have grown and now have over a hundred and fifty pupils. This year we celebrate our fiftieth anniversary.' His voice had been doleful and plodding. 'I make no apologies for this being a traditional school. Let me assure you that we don't follow all the modern approaches and trendy initiatives evident in some schools, approaches that unfortunately have led to the decline in standards in education. Here at Silverdene Lodge we teach tried-and-tested methods that have stood us in good stead for many years and resulted in our pupils securing places, many at the top public schools.'

He had sounded as if he were addressing parents at a school speech day and had carried on, getting into his stride. 'Great emphasis is placed here on the academic – we have a rigorous and challenging curriculum focusing on the basics – and upon developing fit and healthy young people. We are fortunate to have a gymnasium, art block, extensive indoor and outdoor pitches and a swimming pool.' He had thought for a moment of the leaking roof in the gym and the urgent repairs needed to the swimming pool. 'You will see from the prospectus,' he had continued, sliding a glossy-backed brochure across the desk, 'that we are fortunate to have excellent facilities.' He had looked at the boy, who had stared back at him, serious-faced. The headmaster had smiled rather like a hungry vampire ready to sink its teeth into a victim. 'I am sure, were your son to come here, he would do very well.' The boy, who had sat up very straight in his chair with his legs together and his hands folded on his lap, had continued to look at the headmaster with a blank expression. Mr Mountjoy had found it rather disturbing and had turned to the woman instead. 'Here at Silverdene Lodge we pride ourselves on turning out hard-working, well-behaved, polite children who value the education on offer. We have very supportive parents who are fully involved in the life of the school and very appreciative of our efforts, and a committed governing body. You will find that—'

'Thank you so much,' the woman had interrupted, giving a polite if forced smile. She had stood and smoothed the creases on her coat before putting on an expensive-looking pair of leather gloves. She had heard quite enough of Silverdene Lodge and the self-important headmaster. 'You have been most informative, Mr Mountjoy.' The boy had jumped to his feet, as keen as his mother to be away.

'B . . . but I was about to take you on a tour of the school,' the headmaster had stammered.

'That is kind of you,' the woman had replied affably, 'but we are a little pressed for time and I am sure that anything further I need to know is in here.' She had picked up the prospectus, tucked it under her arm and, smiling at the gloomy-faced headmaster, had wished him a good morning.

So now they sat in the car looking at the squat little school that was so very different from the one they had visited the previous day.

'Shall we go inside and see what it's like?' she asked.

Leo turned once more and looked through the side window at the building set back from the road and shrugged. 'I suppose so,' he answered indifferently.

'And try and look a bit more cheerful, darling. Don't worry, we will find the right school.'

They climbed from the car and approached the gaunt grey building. The air was icy fresh and the dusting of snow crunched beneath their feet.

At the door of the school, enveloped in a heavy overcoat and sporting a woollen balaclava helmet, thick woollen gloves and enormous green wellington boots, stood a tall individual with dark deep-set eyes and a large nose that curved savagely like a bent bow. He was holding a canvas sack and having a rest from gritting the path. There was a lugubrious expression on his long face, which was red with exertion and with the cold.

'Good morning,' said the woman, carefully stepping up the path.

'Morning,' replied the man. Clouds of vapour rose from his nostrils.

'Dreadful weather.'

'You can say that again,' sniffed the man. He ran a gloved index finger under his dripping nose. 'Are you lost?'

'No, no,' she told him. 'I was hoping I might see the head teacher. I guess I should have made an appointment, so if it's inconvenient—'

'Mr Gaunt, he's the headmaster, is not a one for appointments,' the man told her, sniffing again. 'We don't get many visitors up here so he's glad to see people. I reckon he can spare the time to see you. He don't stand on ceremony, Mr Gaunt. You had better come in out of the cold.' He made no effort to move. 'It's bitter this morning and no mistake, and we're in for more bad weather by the looks of it.' He stared up at the sky, then he pulled a melancholy face and glanced at his feet. 'Every time I clear the path after it's snowed we get another fresh lot. Then when the snow does clear, it's like an ice-rink with kids sliding up and down like there's no tomorrow. I tell them not to go sliding on the frozen water unless it's been passed by the headmaster but they don't listen. I'm Mr Leadbeater, by the way, caretaker, handyman, gardener, snow-clearer and general factotum. If you'd like to follow me, I'll show you in. Watch your step, I've not finished gritting the path yet.' He looked at the boy. 'And you too go carefully, young fella-mi-lad.'

The interior of the building belied its dark and cheerless exterior. The heavy door, painted a bright red and with a burnished brass knocker in the shape of a fox's head, opened into a small vestibule that was warm and welcoming. The school was a clean and tidy building and smelled not unpleasantly of old wood and lavender furniture polish. Paintwork shone, the floors had a spotless, polished look, brass door handles sparkled and there was not a sign of graffiti or litter. The display boards, which stretched the full length of the corridor, were covered in line drawings, paintings, photographs and children's writing. Everything looked cheerful and orderly.

The school had not always looked as it did on that cold January morning. Before the arrival the previous term of the new young teacher, the energetic Mr Tom Dwyer, and the appointment of Mrs Edna Gosling, the obsessively fastidious cleaner, it had been very different. The heavy then mud-coloured door with the tarnished brass knocker had needed a good lick of paint. It had opened with a loud creak into a small lobby, which had been dark and unwelcoming with its shiny green wall tiles and off-white paint. From the entrance had stretched the corridor, which had been lined with old cupboards and shelves and had a floor of pitted linoleum the same colour as the door to the school. The headmaster, the three teachers and the caretaker had been quite happy with the environment in which they worked. The school had remained unaltered for many years and the staff was indifferent to change. With the arrival of enthusiastic Mr Dwyer and fussy Mrs Gosling, the place had undergone a transformation. Of course, the imminent visit of one of Her Majesty's Inspectors of Schools had also focused the minds of the members of staff who liked things to stay as they were.

'A bit of window-dressing won't hurt,' the headmaster had observed.

In the small office the school secretary, a thin woman with a pale, indrawn face and thick iron-grey hair cut in a bob, peered over her unfashionable horn-rimmed spectacles.

'This lady would like to see Mr Gaunt, Beryl,' the caretaker told her. He ran a gloved finger under his nose again.

The secretary frowned and shook her head tetchily. She dug in a drawer in her desk and produced a paper tissue, which she thrust into the caretaker's hand. 'Blow your nose,' she mouthed, like a schoolteacher speaking to an infant. Then she adopted her professional smile and her affected voice reserved for visitors who looked a cut above the usual callers. She looked up at the woman and removed her spectacles. 'Good morning,' she said pleasantly. 'Hif you would care to wait, I shall see hif Mr Gaunt is havailable.'

A moment later, the woman and the boy were shown into the headmaster's study. The room was small and dominated by a huge oak desk with brass-handled drawers. On top was an old-fashioned leather-bound blotter, a large brass inkwell in the shape of a ram's head, an earthenware mug holding an assortment of pens and broken pencils and a jumble of papers and folders. A battered grey metal filing cabinet stood by the window next to a heavy bookcase crammed with books and journals, magazines and files. On the floor was a brightly coloured rug and displayed on a wall was a variety of children's paintings of various animals – black-faced sheep and prancing horses, grazing cows and stout pink pigs on stubby legs, all executed in vivid colour. Propped up in a corner was the strangest-looking contraption: a long, wooden trumpet-like instrument with a cup-shaped mouthpiece.

Mr Gaunt, a tall, lean man with the weathered face of a countryman, rose from his chair and edged around his desk to greet his visitors. He sported a thick crop of greying hair that curled around his collar and wore a shapeless tweed jacket, baggy flannel trousers and a shirt frayed at the cuffs. The woman smiled narrowly as she recalled Mr Mountjoy's meticulous appearance. Here was a rather different character.

'It's very good of you to see me, Mr Gaunt,' she said, holding out a gloved hand, which he shook. 'I appreciate that Friday afternoon is perhaps not the best time to call but—'

'Not at all, not at all,' he said. He straightened his clumsily knotted tie and smoothed his hair before removing a pile of farming magazines from a small spindle-backed chair. 'Do take a seat, Mrs . . .?'

'Stanhope,' she replied, sitting down. 'Amanda Stanhope.'

Mr Gaunt moved back behind his desk and sat down. He gestured to a stool in the corner of the room. 'And you pull that up, young man,' he told the boy, 'and you can sit up here by my desk.'

The woman immediately liked the look of the man. His smile was genuine and there was palpable warmth in the large dark eyes. He had a deep, resonant voice and a kindly solicitous manner.

'Please excuse the clutter,' he said, waving a hand above the desk. 'I mean to tidy the place up one of these days but have never got around to it. Mrs Gosling, the cleaner, and Mrs Leadbeater, my secretary, are always nagging me to do it. Mrs Leadbeater's the caretaker's wife, by the way.' He smiled genially.

Mrs Stanhope took a seat, crossed her long legs and removed her gloves. She rested her hands on her lap. The chair wobbled beneath her weight. The boy pulled up the stool to sit next to her and stared at the headmaster with peculiar concentration.

'Now,' said Mr Gaunt, resting his hands on the desktop and leaning back in his chair, 'what can I do for you?'

'I like the animal portraits,' she said, suddenly pointing to the wall where the paintings were displayed. 'I guess they were done by the children.'

'Oh yes,' the headmaster told her. 'All done by the pupils in the school.'

'They are very good,' she said. She thought for a moment of the children's efforts on the walls in the entrance at Silverdene Lodge. Most were pictures of poor quality and done in pencil, felt-tip pens and crayons. 'Young children paint with such enthusiasm and abandon, don't you think? Their work is so expressive and authentic and soulful. When they are given the opportunity, that is. They can't be bothered with detail and have no concept of perspective at that age. What they produce is so wonderfully bold and fresh and explosive with shape and colour. John Ruskin encouraged artists to represent nature with the freshness and vitality of a child. These pictures are very fine.'

'I guess you are an artist yourself, Mrs Stanhope,' remarked Mr Gaunt, sitting up.

'Yes, I am,' she replied. 'The former Methodist chapel in the village is to be my studio. I've taken out a short lease and it's being decorated at the moment. I've recently rented a cottage in Risingdale village on Rattan Row, just by Church Lane.'

'You are renting the old Primitive Methodist chapel, are you,' said Mr Gaunt. 'I used to attend the Sunday school there as a child. I'm pleased it's being put to some good use at last. The minister has been very particular about its use. Several people have tried to rent it in the past without success. You must have been most persuasive, Mrs Stanhope.'

'Mr Cockburn was most accommodating,' she told him. The woman rested a hand on the boy's shoulder. 'While I am here in Risingdale, I am looking for a school for my son.'

'Well, of course, I should be delighted to have this young man at this school,' said Mr Gaunt. He looked at the boy perched on the stool who was watching the headmaster intently. 'And what is your name, young man?'

'Leo.'

'And how old are you?'

'I'm ten, going on eleven.'

'Well, now, Leo, do you think you might like to come here?' asked Mr Gaunt.

The boy cocked his head slightly to one side, rubbed his chin and thought for a moment before drawing in a breath. He looked to Mr Gaunt like an academic considering a problem. 'The thing is, I'm not sure,' he said. 'It's difficult to say, really. It does look a bit bleak up here although the views are amazing. I should prefer to be in a country school rather than one in a town, but I can't really say that I might like to come here because we've only just arrived and I don't know much about it. I should quite like to look around, if that's all right.'

Mr Gaunt stared for a moment. What an unusual child, he thought, with his head of flaxen curls, large blue eyes and his old-fashioned way of speaking. Perched on the stool, he looked like a little monkey.

'An honest answer,' said the headmaster, stifling a smile. He had assumed when he first saw him that the boy would be shy and nervous. Mr Gaunt soon changed his mind. Here was an unusually confident and articulate young man and no mistake. One should never judge by appearances, he reminded himself.

'Well, let me tell you a little about Risingdale School. As you can see, it's pretty old, built over a century ago, and set high up at the top of the Dale, apart from the village and a good few miles from the nearest town of Clayton. Risingdale has one of the finest views of any school in the county. It was originally built for the children of the estate workers employed by the local squire, Sir Hedley Maladroit.'

'From whom I rent the cottage,' said Mrs Stanhope.

'Yes, Sir Hedley owns most of the land around here and much of the village too,' the headmaster told her. 'He's a very good-hearted sort.' Unlike his wife, he thought. 'Anyway, we don't have much in the way of facilities like some schools – playing fields, football pitches, a swimming pool or a gymnasium. It's a small school but I like to think it has a special character and it's a happy place, and for me that's the most important thing – a happy school. If you become one of the pupils here, Leo, and you are happy, like the teachers and enjoy the lessons, then in my book everything else follows.'

The boy nodded. 'Yes, I think so too,' he said.

Mr Gaunt turned his attention to the boy's mother. 'To be honest, Mrs Stanhope, Risingdale is not one of the county's flagship schools. We don't number amongst the county's highest performing when it comes to academic results but we hold our own compared with other small schools, and we have achieved some success with the sports and in the County Poetry Competition. One of our pupils won the County Art Prize last year.' He turned to the paintings on the wall. 'He painted a couple of those. I think you will find the children are pleasant enough, well-behaved on the whole, but like all growing children they do have their moments. They try their best and enjoy coming to school. There is a wide range of abilities and the teachers try to ensure every child reaches his or her potential. Some of the pupils have in the past gained places at the grammar school but most go on to Clayton Comprehensive. I don't enter the children for the eleven-plus examination unless a parent specifically wishes me to do so. The comprehensive has a good reputation and suits our intake. The children come largely from the surrounding farms and, to be honest, some would prefer to be out and about in the fresh air instead of being stuck behind a desk. Parents are very supportive and the governors let me get on with the job without undue interference. I think that gives you a flavour of the school.'

'And have you children yourself, Mr Gaunt?' she asked.

'Sadly not, I never married.' He was rather startled by the enquiry from someone he had just met.

'And if you had children and were looking for a school to which to send them, what would you look for?'

The headmaster was surprised by such a question. It sounded the sort of request a governor might ask a candidate on interview for a teaching post. Certainly no parent had ever asked him such a thing. He thought for a moment before replying.

'Well, now, let me see.' He tapped a finger on the desk. 'A good school should be a friendly, happy place where children feel safe and secure; a clean, orderly environment where there is good, challenging teaching, strong leadership and management. I think a good school encourages every individual pupil to grow in confidence by success. Of course, none of this can be measured. Because some head teachers cannot measure what is valuable, they value what is measurable.'

'One cannot measure a love of art or an appreciation of music,' remarked Mrs Stanhope.

'Very true,' agreed Mr Gaunt. 'Many schools pursue success in the examination area. Good results are of course important but they are not the be all and end all. It might sound a tad idealistic, Mrs Stanhope, but I think a good school should touch the souls of its children. They should hear stories and poems that make them laugh or feel sadness, listen to beautiful music, watch a play that takes them into another world, look at great paintings and appreciate art and feel a sense of wonder at seeing the vast and awesome snowy landscape and the first blossoms of spring. I'm sorry. I'm rambling on.'

'Not at all,' said the parent. 'What you say is most interesting.' She smiled. 'You are quite the romantic, Mr Gaunt.'

'If you mean by that, Mrs Stanhope, that I am starry-eyed or impractical,' the headmaster told her, 'then I might take issue with you.'

The woman smiled again. Her gaze was appraising. 'No, Mr Gaunt,' she replied, 'I meant you are passionate about what you believe and I very much approve of what you have said.'

The headmaster coloured a little. He didn't usually have this sort of conversation with parents. It was just that this woman, for some reason he could not explain, had triggered this response. He turned to the boy. 'Now, what about you, Leo? Is there anything you would like to ask me?'

'Yes, if I may,' replied the boy, whose face had remained expressionless during Mr Gaunt's speech. He cocked his head to one side again.

'Go ahead,' the headmaster told him.

'Whatever is that strange-looking instrument in the corner?'

'Ah, my alpenhorn. Yes, I saw you looking at it,' said Mr Gaunt. 'I should explain. Now, this winter we have been pretty lucky up here. It's been unusually mild, although as you can see we have had some snow recently and the likelihood is that more is on the way. Some years we do get thick snow, high drifts, very cold winds and sometimes blizzards, and I have to close the school. And that's when my alpenhorn comes in very handy. A few good blows on that echoes down the Dale and lets the villagers and those on the surrounding farms know that the school is closed and there will be no school that day. It warns parents that the school bus is not running and saves them trudging up with their children to find the school is shut. It works very well. I bought it in Switzerland and I caused quite a commotion at the airport when I brought it back.'

The boy gave a small smile for the first time that day. 'That's ingenious,' he said. 'Don't you think that that's ingenious, Mother?'

'Yes, Leo,' she said, smiling. 'Ingenious.'

'Shall we have a look around the school?' suggested the headmaster, hoping that he had succeeded in recruiting a new pupil. He liked the look and the sound of this young man and his mother.

'Yes, I should like that,' replied the boy, jumping down from the stool.

'I wonder, Leo,' said Mr Gaunt, 'if, while I am showing your mother around, you might like to join the top junior class for a short while. If you do decide to come here, this is the class you will be in and you would have Mr Dwyer as your teacher. You can then decide for yourself if you would like it at Risingdale. Of course, if you would prefer to look around with your mother—'

'I think I should like to join the class, please,' interrupted the boy.

'Splendid,' said the headmaster.

Mr Dwyer's classroom was as clean and colourful as the corridor, with children's paintings, poems, posters and collages decorating the walls. There was a small reading corner, a shelf stocked with glossy-backed books and a set of dictionaries and a table displaying shells, coloured stones and fossils. On the high windowsill was a small selection of stuffed birds: a fierce-looking kestrel grasping a mouse in its talons, a wide-eyed owl, a sharp-beaked raven and a magpie. Instead of the melamine-topped tables and modern chairs usually found in most primary schools, the room was furnished with old-fashioned, straight-backed wooden chairs and highly polished wooden desks with lids and holes for inkwells. The ceiling was a pale blue in colour and the beams, with curved wooden supports that stretched across it, were painted navy blue. There was a Victorian fireplace, its mantel of dark slate; the heavy black iron grate was filled with dried flowers in various shades.

Mr Dwyer was a young man with shiny black curls and an engaging smile. When Mr Gaunt entered with Mrs Stanhope and her son, he placed down the book he had been reading to the children. While the headmaster explained to the teacher that Leo might be coming to the school and would like to join the lesson, Mrs Stanhope ran her eyes about the room before settling them on the children. As an artist well known for her portraiture, she took a great interest in people's appearances. Here, she thought, were some most interesting little characters. There were about fifteen children in the class, dressed in a variety of clothes. A range of physical types was represented: a large, rosy-cheeked boy with a runny nose; a small gangly boy with a squint and hair like a lavatory brush; a lean, bespectacled boy with a thick mop of tawny blond hair; a sharp-faced boy with untidy tufts of hair; two spotty boys; a heavily freckled boy and, sitting smiling at the front desk, a plain-looking child, not much bigger than her son, with dark eyes and tightly curled hair. There was a large, ginger-headed girl; a small, pixie-faced girl; twin girls with frizzy blonde hair tied up in bunches; a girl with long black plaits; a pretty girl with mousy-brown hair and pink glasses; and an angelic-looking girl with apple-red cheeks and curly blonde hair sticking out at the sides like giant earmuffs.

'You are very welcome,' said Mr Dwyer to the boy who, like his mother, was scrutinising the children, who stared back, fascinated by the strange-looking newcomer. 'Come along in, Leo. There's an empty desk at the front next to Charlie Lister.'

He pointed to the plain-looking, thin individual. The boy smiled and patted the chair next to his. All eyes of the children continued to focus on the little visitor as he sat down. Leo did not look at all nervous or intimidated.

'Right, back to the story,' said Mr Dwyer.

'He is a fine teacher,' the headmaster told Mrs Stanhope as they walked down the corridor together. 'He came here last term and has made a great impression. It is his first teaching post.'

The parent stopped and faced the headmaster. 'I welcome this opportunity of having a word with you, Mr Gaunt, without Leo being present,' she said. 'You will no doubt have observed that my son looks rather different from other boys of his age. He is small and slight and a rather delicate-looking child. He may look willowy and frail but he is tough and spirited and can be quite wilful and stubborn when he wants to be. People are fooled by his appearance. He has had a difficult time at the schools he has attended. Children can be very cruel, corrosively cruel at times, and there are those who delight in picking on others who are different in some way. Leo has been bullied quite unmercifully.'

'I'm sorry to hear that,' said the headmaster.

Mr Gaunt was minded to ask about the boy's father. Mrs Stanhope had made no mention of a husband. Perhaps growing up as an only child, without a father on the scene and with an apparently overprotective mother, was not the best preparation for the rough and tumble of school life. He felt, however, that it was not for him to pry.

'There is something else you should know,' the parent told him. 'Leo is not a well child. He has a brain tumour, which involves frequent visits to the hospital where he is monitored with scans and treated with radiotherapy. He is also on a programme of medication. Fortunately, the tumour is benign, which means it tends to grow more slowly than the malignant kind. It does, however, put pressure on areas of his brain and cause him a few difficulties. Leo does become tired easily if he overexerts himself and he gets short of breath. He has a problem sometimes with his vision and balance but luckily doesn't suffer with headaches or with memory loss. He manages very well, but, as you might imagine, it is challenging for him.'

'And can the tumour be operated upon?' asked the headmaster, gazing at her with concern.

'The specialist tells me that it would be difficult to remove because of where it is and, in this situation, he suggests other treatments. He tells me that my son can lead a reasonably normal life. Evidently there are a lot of people who have such tumours and manage to live with them so we are hopeful.'

Mr Gaunt thought for a moment. 'And in this situation, Mrs Stanhope,' he said, 'that is all we can do, be hopeful and pray.'

'Leo manages very well,' she continued, 'but it is hard for him. He's such a brave little boy and tries not to let it get him down. He really needs to be in a school where he feels secure and happy and where his teacher appreciates his condition. He doesn't want pity or any special treatment but some understanding and support. He is bright and interested and I think very intelligent and, as you will no doubt have gathered, he has quite a lot to say for himself. I think being rather outspoken at times did not endear him to his former teachers and attracted the attention of bullies.'

'I'm sorry to hear that Leo is not well,' said Mr Gaunt. 'It must be stressful for him and extremely worrying for you, but from what you say he is a very resilient and spirited young man. I cannot guarantee that your son will not be bullied here, Mrs Stanhope. I don't think any head teacher could give you that complete assurance. You are right that children can be cruel and the bully singles out those who are different, but we take a very strong line with those who pick on others. I can assure you that if you send your son here, we will do our utmost to give him the maximum support. The great advantage of a school like ours is that it is small and the teachers and I know each individual child very well.'

Following a tour of the building and the sound of the bell ringing for the end of school, the headmaster and the parent returned to Mr Dwyer's classroom. They stood back as the children, chattering excitedly, hurried out.

'I have been most impressed with what I have seen this afternoon, Mr Gaunt,' said Mrs Stanhope, 'and I very much like what you said earlier. If my son is of the same mind, I should like him to come to Risingdale School. I think it will suit him very well. Of course, it has to be my son's decision.'

'Well, let's see what the young man has to say,' replied Mr Gaunt, as the subject of their conversation emerged from the classroom in deep conversation with Charlie. He broke off speaking when he saw Mr Gaunt.

'So how did you get on, Leo?' asked the headmaster.

'When can I start?' asked the boy.

2

The first staff meeting of the new term at Risingdale School took place later that day. At the end of the afternoon, as the children made their way home, three of the teachers gathered in the staffroom: Mrs Bertha Golightly, in charge of the infants, a plump, cheerful-looking woman with a round face and tiny darting eyes; Mr Owen Cadwallader, teacher of the lower juniors, a tall, straight-backed individual, with silver hair, cropped short and neatly parted and sporting a thin white moustache, and Miss Joyce Tranter, the other teacher of the lower juniors, a woman of indeterminate age with unnaturally shiny raven-black hair, startling glossy-red lips and large pale eyes. The last member of the teaching staff, Mr Tom Dwyer, teacher of the top juniors, was busy outside marshalling the children on to the school bus.

When Tom had started teaching at the school the term before, Mr Gaunt had asked the young teacher how he was getting on with his colleagues. When Tom had replied that he had found them friendly and helpful, the headmaster had looked thoughtful before deciding to take the young man into his confidence.

'I guess they appear a pretty odd bunch to you,' he had said. 'When I say odd, I don't mean that unkindly. Perhaps a better word might be "idiosyncratic". They do what is asked of them without complaint and the children like them. I have a genuine affection for them.' The headmaster had paused, wondering about the best way of saying what he wanted to say. 'All three of your colleagues are not as they might seem. Don't be fooled by Miss Tranter's air of confidence and self-assurance. Joyce is an actress and plays the part very convincingly. She trained at a drama college, made a career on the stage and when that didn't quite work out for her, she took up teaching. She's a good teacher, Tom, and you can learn a lot from her, but she is quite a fragile woman, very sensitive and unsure of herself under all that poise. You may have wondered why someone so outwardly self-possessed and artistic would teach in a school like this.' This had occurred to Tom, for Miss Tranter seemed quite out of place teaching in a small school miles from anywhere. Mr Gaunt had continued. 'Joyce had a very acrimonious marriage. She met her former husband at drama college. He was, by all accounts, a very controlling and sometimes abusive individual who treated her very badly and undermined her confidence. Eventually she summoned up the courage to leave him and get a divorce but he hounded her, turning up wherever she went. On one occasion he interrupted a performance she was giving at a theatre and he had to be thrown out. You can imagine how that affected her. I think that after that she gave up the stage. Risingdale School has become a sort of refuge for her, somewhere he will hopefully not find her. I know she complains about life up here but I think she feels safe and secure and does enjoy teaching.

'Then there's Mr Cadwallader. He's a character, is Owen. He too is perhaps not all that he appears to be, either. He is a good-hearted man but, as you no doubt have gathered, he's a romancer. I am sure you will have been subjected to some of his army anecdotes. They don't do any harm but should be taken with a pinch of salt. He tends to blow his own trumpet to maybe convince himself that he was once a person of some note. Underneath, like Joyce, he is under-confident. He may not appear so, but he is. Owen is, at heart, quite insecure. And then there's Mrs Golightly. Again I think she puts on a show. She appears to the world always cheerful and outgoing, but deep down she's a rather sad and I guess a lonely woman. Her husband was killed in a road accident not long after they were married. She has no children to fill the gap he has left in her life.'

The headmaster had become thoughtful again. 'So that's a potted history of the lives of the teachers here at Risingdale,' he had said. 'I hope you don't feel it is unprofessional of me to talk about the personal circumstances of your colleagues. I just feel you need to know something of their backgrounds and be aware that all three of them are fragile people. I wouldn't want you to go saying or asking things inadvertently that may touch a few raw nerves.'

Although the headmaster was forthcoming about members of his staff, he told Tom nothing about his own life. In fact, few people really knew anything about Gerald Gaunt, for he was an intensely private person. He enjoyed a quiet occasional drink at the weekend but rarely frequented the local hostelry, the King's Head, knowing that if he did he would be cornered by parents wishing to discuss their children's progress at the school, seeking his advice or quizzing him about numerous educational matters. Instead he patronised the Black Pig in Urebank, where he had a certain anonymity and enjoyed his pint of bitter undisturbed.

Mrs Golightly, who had known him and worked for him for many years, knew little about the headmaster apart from the few facts that he lived alone on a smallholding inherited from his father, that he had never married, that he enjoyed long walks and tended a few sheep and cattle on his small farm. It struck her as strange that he never wanted to socialise with his colleagues after school or involve himself in the various events and activities in the village. She was not even aware that in his younger days he had once had a romantic attachment to the young vet in Barton-in-the-Dale.

Mr Gaunt had met Miss Moira Macdonald when he had called her out to look at one of his ailing sheep. He watched the tall, red-headed young Scot with a homely, freckled face and engaging smile deal with the sickly ewe calmly and effectively. He had found excuse after excuse to call upon her services again: his sheepdog was off her food, his cow was out of sorts, the goat wasn't giving much milk. She was astute enough to guess why she was being asked to visit the farm so frequently when there was nothing really wrong with the animals, realising that the young teacher was interested in her.

Mr Gaunt met her again at a dinner in aid of a farming charity. He was plucking up the courage to ask her out when she surprised him by asking him out. They each enjoyed the theatre, music, walking, reading and farming, but neither of them seemed to want the relationship to get any more serious. They had been going out for a year when new job prospects had come up for both of them at the same time. Mr Gaunt, who was a deputy head teacher in Ruston (the youngest in the county to hold such a senior position), was keen to apply for the headship at the village school in Risingdale and Moira to accept a partnership in her native Glasgow. So – decisions had to be made. Should they get married? If so, who would do the moving? Which one would sacrifice job and career? Their relationship had been a strange one in that they were both so busy in their respective careers that they did not see a great deal of each other. Moira worked late and most weekends at the veterinary practice. Gerald was usually occupied at weekends either playing rugby or refereeing, and in the evenings marking books, planning lessons, taking school trips or rehearsing the school play. When they did go to dinner parties together, they were not greatly enjoyable occasions. He would meet her colleagues from the veterinary practice and be bored by the constant discussion over the dinner table of animal ailments, diseases and operations. When she met his colleagues from school, Moira was similarly wearied by the endless conversations about the curriculum and examinations, standards of education and difficult children. They both realised that their relationship could never survive the test of time. On their last evening together, they talked about things honestly and without recriminations before each deciding to go their separate ways. So they parted, on very amicable terms, to pursue their own careers. That had been over twenty-five years ago. Gerald had often thought about Moira and wondered how her life had turned out.

'I must say that Friday afternoons are not the best time to have staff meetings,' complained Mr Cadwallader now. 'You should say something, Joyce.'

'Why me?' she asked. 'Fire your own bullets.'

'And I hope Mr Gaunt doesn't go on too long,' he moaned, dipping his hand for the third time into the biscuit barrel. 'He does tend to ramble on.'

Miss Tranter rolled her eyes heavenwards and then exchanged a complicit glance with Mrs Golightly. Three words came to their minds: 'pan', 'kettle' and 'black'. Their colleague was noted for his long-windedness.

She examined a long red nail. 'Well, I shall have to leave at five-thirty at the latest. I have the auditions for the new play this evening. It's a murder mystery.' She was the producer of the Clayton and Ruston Amateur Players and took her theatrical interest very seriously. 'I'm hoping to persuade Tom to take a part. He was so good as the prince in the Christmas pantomime.'

'And I've got a Women's Institute meeting,' said Mrs Golightly. 'I'm in the chair this evening so I have to be there in good time. We've got Mr Firkin coming to talk about "A Life in the Day of a Funeral Director".'

'That doesn't sound a barrel of laughs,' observed Mr Cadwallader, crunching on a biscuit, 'and for most of your WI members, being rather past the threescore years and ten and about to come to the end of their earthly run in the not too distant future, listening to a talk by an undertaker is not the most suitable of topics, I would have thought.'

'How very tactful, Owen,' remarked Miss Tranter sarcastically.

'Well, I have to admit a few of the members aren't very keen,' said Mrs Golightly. 'Some got a bit upset when we had Dr Stirling – he is the husband of the headteacher at Barton-with-Urebank School – speak to us on "healthy eating" and he told us that the consumption of confectionery was a major cause of obesity. It was a bit unfortunate because we had all made a cake for the competition. I thought it was rather insensitive of Madam President to ask him to judge it.'

'I thought Mr Firkin drove the school bus,' said Mr Cadwallader.

'He does that part time,' Mrs Golightly told her colleague. 'He just does the morning and afternoon runs for our school. The rest of the time he's an undertaker. We were to have Mrs Wigglesworth to speak at the meeting. She's the psychic. She had to pull out because of some unforeseen circumstances. Mr Firkin is stepping in at short notice. I'm afraid it's so difficult to get speakers. We tend to be scraping the barrel these days. And speaking of barrels' – she stared reproachfully at Mr Cadwallader who was extracting another biscuit – 'will you go steady with the Garibaldis, Owen. We've only been back at school a week and you've nearly eaten your way through a full packet.'

'And stop spitting crumbs on the carpet,' Joyce scolded him, 'or you'll have Mrs Gosling to answer to.'

'Don't mention that dreadful woman,' her colleague told her angrily. 'She's a cleaner, for goodness' sake, and she thinks she runs the school.'

'I must admit, the woman is a menace,' agreed Mrs Golightly. 'She spoke to me this morning as if I were one of the infants in my class and said she hoped my New Year resolution was to leave my classroom tidy in future.'

'Mrs Gosling has got to go,' announced Mr Cadwallader. 'She is worse than the bullying sergeant-major we had in the army, ordering everyone about and complaining about the state of the sleeping quarters. He used to march in and throw everything on the floor—'

'I thought you were an officer,' said Mrs Golightly. 'He would hardly be throwing a superior officer's things on the floor.'

'Ah yes, I was speaking about the other ranks,' he replied. It is a known fact that to be a good liar one has to have a good memory. Mr Cadwallader had been economical with the truth when telling his colleagues about his former life in the British Army.

'Why don't you get Owen to speak at your WI meeting?' suggested Joyce. 'He could talk about his army career. Many is the time he's held forth in the staffroom over the years about his time fighting for king and country, up to his neck in mud and bullets.' There was more than a hint of sarcasm in her voice.

'Now that is a good idea,' agreed Mrs Golightly. 'What about it, Owen? I could suggest it to our Madam President this evening.'

'No, no,' replied her colleague hastily. 'I don't think your members would be interested.'

'I'm sure they would,' said Mrs Golightly.

'They will hang on every word,' added Miss Tranter mischievously.

'It's out of the question,' he said stiffly, glancing at his watch. 'Well, I could do with getting home. I don't like the look of this weather.'

'Does anyone know who that woman was who was being taken around the school by Mr Gaunt?' enquired Miss Tranter.

'I don't know who she was,' said Mrs Golightly, 'but she looked very important and when she opened her mouth, she made the Queen sound common. You don't think she was a school inspector, do you? I mean, she reminded me very much of that HMI, Miss Tudor-Williams, who visited us. She was well turned out and nicely spoken.'

'I don't know who she was,' said Mr Cadwallader, 'but she was a damned fine-looking woman and no mistake.'

A smile pulled at the corners of Miss Tranter's mouth. 'Well, our esteemed headmaster certainly thought so,' she said. 'He couldn't take his eyes off her.'

Tom came into the staffroom rubbing his hands vigorously. 'It's beginning to snow,' he said, going to the sink to make himself a cup of coffee.

'Well, that's put paid to my auditions this evening,' said Miss Tranter.

'And I don't think my ladies in the WI will turn out in this weather,' said Mrs Golightly. She saw Tom looking in the biscuit barrel. 'There are no biscuits,' she told him, looking accusingly at Mr Cadwallader. 'You might guess who's been at the Garibaldis.'

'Do you know who that woman was who Mr Gaunt was showing around the school?' Miss Tranter asked Tom. 'He never introduced her.'

'She's thinking of sending her son here,' he replied.

'What, to Risingdale?' cried Mr Cadwallader.

'Why not?' asked Tom. 'Why shouldn't she send her son here?'

His colleague gave a cynical laugh. 'I shouldn't imagine a woman of her sort would want her son to attend a school like this. People like that send their children to some posh independent school, not a little village school like ours, full of farming children. A child like hers would find it difficult to fit in here. I mean, if he speaks like she does, he'll have the devil's own job getting accepted by the others in the class. And there's no doubt in my mind that he'll come in for some bullying, unless, of course, he's a big strapping lad who can handle himself.'

'Actually, Leo's a small and rather delicate boy,' Tom told him.

'Leo!' exclaimed his colleague. 'He's called Leo! Of all the children least like a lion is a small, delicate child. Of course he will be bullied.'

'If he does come here, he won't be bullied,' Tom told him firmly. 'I will make sure of that.'

'Well, if the boy does come here,' said Mr Cadwallader, 'you want to keep a close eye on Colin Greenwood. He might have behaved himself last term, but worms can turn and leopards don't change their spots. Once a bully, always a bully, that's what I think. I recall there was a sergeant-major who took a perverse delight in—'

'You're being unfair on Colin, Owen,' retorted Tom, rising to the boy's defence. 'He has had a lot to put up with, living high up on that remote farm, expected to do all the chores and then losing his mother. Colin's turned a corner. He's no longer a bully.'

'Well, let's hope you're right,' began Mr Cadwallader, 'all I'm saying is that—'

'Colin's been a different boy since Tom became his teacher,' interrupted Mrs Golightly. 'That boy led poor Miss Cathcart a merry dance when she took the top juniors before she had the unfortunate accident. It was tragic what happened to her.'

'Oh please, Bertha,' sighed Miss Tranter emphatically, 'let's not go into what happened to Miss Cathcart. That's all water under the bridge now. I'm interested in this woman who Mr Gaunt showed around the school. So, what was she like, Tom?'

'I didn't speak to her above a few words,' he answered. 'Her son joined my class just after afternoon break. He seems a confident and polite little lad. He's also a very neat and competent writer. When I asked him to write something about himself, he produced this rather fine pen from his pocket.

When I commented upon it, he told me it was his most precious possession having once belonged to his father.'

'Well, young Leo will not be using it for long,' said Mr Cadwallader derisively. 'Some light-fingered little oik will pocket it.'

'Don't be so cynical, Owen,' chided Mrs Golightly. 'First you go on about bullies and now thieves. Occasionally you might say something positive about the children. We're very lucky here. We don't have half the discipline problems of other schools. I for one hope she decides to send her son here. We could do with some more pupils. Unless our numbers increase, I can see the education people closing Risingdale. A lot of small village schools have disappeared in the last few years and ours could be the next on the list.'

'One wonders why a woman like that would want to come and live in Risingdale,' remarked Miss Tranter. 'Up here it's the back of beyond; the residents live in the Dark Ages. There's more life in a cemetery than there is in the village and the school is not exactly at the cutting edge of education.'

Tom, under normal circumstances, might have asked her why she lived in Risingdale if she found it so tedious and unexciting, but he recalled Mr Gaunt's words to him about Joyce, so he said nothing.

'Maybe she's just looking for a quiet life,' remarked Mrs Golightly.

'Or she's trying to get away from something,' suggested Mr Cadwallader, 'an abusive partner or a violent husband, for example.'

Miss Tranter gave a slight shudder. The comment had touched a raw nerve.

'Actually, the boy wrote that his father was killed in plane crash,' Tom said.

'Oh, how sad,' remarked Mrs Golightly. 'It's a terrible thing to lose a parent when you're young.'

'You're right there, Bertha,' agreed Tom, speaking from experience.

Mr Leadbeater appeared at the door.

'You don't need to hang about,' the caretaker told the teachers. 'The staff meeting's off. Mr Gaunt's told me to tell you to get off home. It looks like weather's taking a turn for the worse.'

As Tom drove home that afternoon there were just a few flurries of snow in the air, but by the time he reached his cottage, great flakes had started to fall thick and fast. Soon the whole countryside would be buried in white. He lit a fire and made himself a drink and thought of the farmers rising the following morning at first light, trudging in the cold to feed and care for their animals in such weather. He thought of Mr Gaunt, who had a smallholding and a flock of sheep and would be one of these braving the elements. Tom had seen how severe the weather up at the top of the Dale could be. Last December the entire landscape had been transformed overnight into a vast white ocean, and an icy wind had whipped and raged and packed the snow up in great mounds and drifts, which froze overnight. He had listened to the locals in the King's Head as they had described the weather of earlier years, the treacherously slippery roads under the car tyres, the water in the troughs frozen solid and the sheep, their coats crusted with ice, sheltering against the drystone walls. He had heard how some were buried deep under the blizzard. He watched the falling snow through the cottage window now and hoped that this wasn't going to be a repetition of last year's weather.

It looked unlikely that there would be any school the following week. He smiled at the thought of Mr Gaunt chuddering up to the school on his ancient tractor to blow the alpenhorn and warn parents not to send their children to school that day.

When he had first set eyes upon the school to which he had applied, Tom's heart had sunk into his shoes. He had looked despondently at the gaunt, grey, uninviting building surrounded by endless fields and miles from anywhere. The previous year he had trained at Barton-with-Urebank Primary School and enjoyed every minute of his time there under the guidance of Mrs Stirling, an experienced and dynamic head teacher, and the supportive members of staff. He had learnt a great deal, loved the company of young people, knew teaching was the profession for him and had gained his certificate in education with a distinction. The school was an immaculately clean and tidy building with a warm, welcoming and optimistic atmosphere. The entrance and corridor had a spotless, polished look. Detailed line drawings, charcoal sketches, paintings, photographs and children's writing were mounted on the walls. Each classroom was equipped with tables and colourful melamine chairs and bookcases full of bright modern books. There was a profusion of bright flowers to the front of the school and at the rear there was an attractive and informal lawn area with ornamental trees, shrubs, a small pond, garden benches and picnic tables. There was not a sign of graffiti or litter. Tom could not have trained in any better place. He had hoped there might be a position there for him, but the Education Authority had insisted that the head teacher accept a redeployed teacher from a village school that was closing. Naively, Tom had imagined that his first teaching post would be in a similar school, so on casting his eyes on Risingdale School for the first time, his disappointment had been palpable.

Despite his serious initial reservations, he decided to accept a position at the school. What else could he do? Teaching posts were so very hard to get in the county since competition was fierce; there were many better qualified and more experienced teachers than him who were being redeployed from those small village schools that had been forced to close. An expression frequently used by his Auntie Bridget came to mind: 'Beggars can't be choosers.'

Those initial reservations soon disappeared. Tom knew, after only a week in the school, that he was going to stay. Mr Gaunt, the headmaster, was not the most go-ahead and well-organised of head teachers, but he clearly had a deal of affection for the children. He didn't interfere with what the teachers were doing and remained his easy-going and avuncular self. Tom liked his new colleagues. It was true he found them somewhat eccentric, but they were cheerful and supportive and he could tell that they had a genuine interest in their pupils, although they made few demands upon them academically. But it was the children who finally convinced him that he should remain at the school. They were eager and good-natured and applied themselves to their work without complaint. When he had walked nervously into the classroom on that first morning, it had been like the return of the Prodigal Son. He could not have received a warmer welcome.

Over the next few weeks he started to know and like the children and found a genuine pleasure in sharing his knowledge with them. There was Charlie, bright and affable and always with a ready smile; Carol, the champion shepherdess; and Vicky, bubbly and enthusiastic with a lot to say for herself. There was David, small and gangly, whose writing had improved by leaps and bounds; George, whose only conversation seemed to be about sheep and cattle and the make of tractors; Marjorie, the mathematics whiz; and Simon, the ferret expert and rat-catcher. There were Holly and Hazel, the twins; Judith, the thoughtful girl with the long black plaits and rosy cheeks; and Christopher, a large, ruddy-complexioned boy with a runny nose who seldom smiled and never laughed. Then there was Colin Greenwood, once a sad and angry boy, who at first was a rude and difficult child but, when his talents in art had been discovered and he came to understand that Tom was genuinely interested in him, had become better behaved and more sociable. At college the lecturer had said that teachers take on the most important role in society, for good teachers change children's lives. Tom felt some satisfaction that he was making a positive difference in the lives of his pupils, and in particular in young Colin's.

Tom's first few months in Risingdale had been eventful. His arrival in the village had started inauspiciously. On his way to the interview for the teaching post at the school, he had come to a sharp bend and as he turned, he very nearly collided with a rider astride a large chestnut horse. He had swerved off the road and landed in a ditch.

'Are you out of your mind?' the rider had shouted at him.

The speaker, who he discovered later was Miss Janette Fairborn, daughter of a prominent local farmer, was a striking-looking young woman with green eyes and a mass of unruly red hair that tumbled out from under her riding helmet. Her face had been flushed with anger.

Their relationship at first was prickly – she found him arrogant and annoying; he found her cool and stand-offish. But this changed as they got to know each other. In Joyce's Christmas production of *The Sleeping Beauty*, staged at the civic theatre in Clayton, in which Tom had been dragooned into playing the prince opposite Janette as the princess, he found that he was falling for her and sensed his feelings were being reciprocated. He had determined to see more of her in future.

Tom soon settled in at Risingdale. He bought a small cottage in the village, the former home of Mrs Golightly who was downsizing to an apartment. Mr Gaunt, keen on this young teacher staying at the school, had been most generous in loaning him the deposit. Before buying the cottage, Tom had stayed at the local inn, the King's Head, got to know and to like the straight-talking locals, attracted the amorous attentions of the landlady's daughter, Leanne, and managed to get into a fight with the son of the local squire. He had endeared himself to the vicar when he prevented thieves from stripping the lead from the church roof and impressed the local Member of Parliament with his views on education. He had also come to the politician's aid when the car the MP was driving ran out of petrol. This encounter resulted in a visit from an HMI. Taking the lead as the handsome prince in Joyce's Christmas pantomime had made many a young woman's heart flutter. As many a resident of Risingdale observed, 'This young man is certainly making his presence felt.'

3

The following morning Tom expected to pull back the bedroom curtains to find that the snow had settled in earnest. To his surprise, he saw that the fields surrounding the cottage, rather than being buried under a blanket of white, merely had a light covering of snow. That meant that he could make his usual Saturday trip into Clayton and that the school would be open the following week.

It was his habit on Saturdays to drive into Clayton, visit the supermarket for his weekly shopping, call into the White Rose Bookshop and the library and, before setting off for home, have a coffee at the café on the high street.

It was in the Ring o' Bells café that Tom came across Mrs Stanhope. He found her sitting at a corner table. She was wearing a close-fitting red woollen coat that perfectly showed off her slim figure. What a startlingly handsome woman, Tom thought, as he approached her table.

'Good morning,' he said.

The woman looked up and smiled, revealing a remarkably fine set of even white teeth. 'Good morning,' she replied.

'I don't know whether you remember me,' he said diffidently. 'We met briefly yesterday when you visited Risingdale School.'

'Yes, of course I remember you,' she replied. 'It's Mr Dwyer, isn't it? Would you care to join me?' Her smile could melt snow.

'Well, yes, if I'm not disturbing you.' Tom sat down. 'I often call into the café on a Saturday before setting off for home. They serve the best coffee in Clayton.'

'Leo has his piano lesson with a new teacher this morning,' she said. 'I'm collecting him in half an hour.'

'He's there by himself?' asked Tom, sounding surprised. 'I should have thought that he would have wanted you with him, this being his first lesson.'

She laughed. 'He's a very independent boy, is Leo. I recall on his first day at school I was so upset seeing him head towards the building, thinking he would be so frightened. I saw this little five-year-old figure walking away and my eyes filled up with tears. When he got to the door, he turned and said, "You can go now, Mummy."'

'He sounds a very confident young man,' said Tom. He found he could not take his eyes off her.

'He's very like his father. May I order you a coffee, Mr Dwyer?'

'Thank you, I'd love one,' he said.

Mrs Stanhope raised a hand and a waitress appeared immediately to take the order. The young woman stared at Tom for a moment as if she recognised him from somewhere. Then she remembered where she had seen him before.

'You were the handsome prince in the Christmas pantomime, weren't you?' she asked.

'I was, yes,' replied Tom.

'I thought you were dead good,' said the young woman. 'You stole the show.'

'Thank you,' he replied, colouring a little.

'Are you going to be in another one this year?' asked the waitress.

'No, once is quite enough,' he told her. He changed the subject. 'I don't think I've seen you here before.'

'I've just started,' she told him. 'It's a Saturday job. I'm still at school. My friends thought you were dead dishy in the pantomime.'

Tom looked at Mrs Stanhope, who was clearly amused.

'Do you think we might have the coffees now, please?' Tom asked the waitress.

'No problem,' she said, before returning to the counter.

Mrs Stanhope smiled at Tom and tilted her head as if expecting him to speak.

'I was in a pantomime,' he told her.

'So I gathered,' she said, still smiling, 'and you made quite an impression, from what I've just heard.' She stared at him for a moment. Here was a young man, she thought, who did indeed make an impression. He had the looks of a leading actor with his chiselled jaw, high cheekbones, shiny black curls and long-lashed blue eyes.

'I don't know about that,' he said, still rather pink in the face.

'Well, you certainly made an impression on my son. Leo really enjoyed the lesson he joined. He said you were a very good teacher.'

The coffee arrived.

'Could I have your autograph?' asked the waitress, presenting Tom with a pen and a paper serviette. 'Could you put "To Bianca"?'

'Yes, of course,' sighed Tom, scribbling the message and adding his name.

When the waitress had gone, Mrs Stanhope looked over her coffee cup.

'Do you live in Clayton, Mr Dwyer?' she asked.

'No, I have a cottage in Risingdale. Roselea. It's up from the church. I only moved in last October and there's a lot to do but I'm gradually getting there.'

'I'm renting a cottage in Rattan Row,' she told him. 'Mr Gaunt no doubt told you that I am also renting the former Methodist chapel. It's to be my studio.'

'I didn't have a chance to speak to Mr Gaunt yesterday,' he answered. 'We were to have a staff meeting after school but it was cancelled. We expected a heavy snowfall. Fortunately, it thawed overnight. That's the thing about this part of the world: the weather is so unpredictable. One minute it's bright and sunny, the next it's pouring down with rain.'

'So you say you didn't have a chance to speak to Mr Gaunt?' she asked.

'No, I didn't.'

'Then you won't know about Leo's condition,' she said. 'I was explaining to the headmaster that he's not a well boy.' She became thoughtful for a moment. 'We discovered when he was eight that my son had a tumour. It's benign, thank God, and doesn't cause him a great deal of discomfort, just that he tires easily. He visits the hospital regularly to have the condition monitored and for treatment. It is, of course, worrying, but he has learnt to live with it. Children can be amazingly brave and resilient, can't they?' He heard the tremor in her voice and knew that she was close to tears. 'The thing is, Mr Dwyer, that Leo's teachers need to be aware of the situation.'

'I am very sorry to hear that your son's not well,' began Tom, 'and I hope that—'

'I did say to Mr Gaunt,' she interrupted, 'that my son doesn't want pity or any special treatment, but some understanding and support.' Her eyes suddenly became moist. 'He doesn't want wrapping in cotton wool but to be treated, as much as possible, like any other boy.'

'Of course,' said Tom. There was an expression of tenderness and concern on his face. Seeing that she was becoming increasingly emotional, he changed the subject. 'So, you are to have a studio,' he said.

'Well, I will soon. I'm an artist. I've spent most of my life in the capital but have always intended one day to spend some time in the country away from the crowded tube, the constant noise and traffic, the hustle and bustle of city life. My family originally came from Yorkshire. I used to spend many happy summers in the county when I was a girl. I do love London, don't get me wrong, but I have been given a commission to paint a series of landscapes of the Dales and portraits of some of the people who live and work there. Hence my stay in Risingdale. It seems to me to be typical of a Dales village.'

'Won't you find life here a little quiet?' asked Tom.

'Not at all.' She raised her coffee cup to her lips and took a small sip. Then she stared at Tom for a moment as if wondering what to say next. 'Mr Gaunt spoke very highly of you,' she said.

Tom coloured a little for the second time that morning. He felt the woman's blue eyes on him. He was fascinated by her and felt himself lighting up inside. She had a way with her that seemed to draw him in.

'He was telling me that you have not been teaching for very long,' she continued.

'I'm sorry?' he said, still mesmerised. 'I didn't quite catch what you said.'

'I was saying that Mr Gaunt told me that you haven't been teaching for very long.'

'No, I came into the profession late. I was a professional footballer.'

'Really? Quite a change.'

'It was the best decision I have made in my life, to become a teacher.'

'And you are happy at the school?' she asked.

'Very.'

'And have you a family, Mr Dwyer?'

'No, no, I'm not married.'

'I'm a widow,' she told him. 'My husband was killed when Leo was seven. He was flying a light aircraft. His plane came down over the English Channel.'

'Yes, Leo told me. I'm sorry,' said Tom.

'But one carries on. Of course, it was difficult for my son losing his father.' She glanced at her wristwatch. 'Goodness, look at the time. I must go. Leo will be wondering where I've got to. I'll settle up.'

'No, let me get the bill,' he said. 'You're in a hurry.'

'Thank you, that's very kind of you. Goodbye, Mr Dwyer. I shall see you next Tuesday.'

'Next Tuesday?'

'When I bring Leo to school. He's got a hospital appointment on the Monday.'

'Oh,' said Tom, 'so you intend to send him to Risingdale?'

She smiled, showing the perfect white teeth. 'Why, of course,' she replied. 'I thought I had made that perfectly obvious, Mr Dwyer.'

Tom watched her go and then stared down at the cold cup of coffee before him. Remarkable woman, he thought: beautiful, intelligent, with such poise.

When he came to pay the bill at the counter there stood Mrs Mossup, landlady of the King's Head in Risingdale. She was a round-faced, cheerful-looking, middle-aged woman with elaborately coiffured, dyed-blonde hair.

'Hello, Doris,' said Tom.

'Oh, morning, Tom,' she replied. 'I'm just doing a bit of shopping and fancied a coffee.'

'I didn't see you when you came in.'

'No, I think you had eyes for someone else,' she replied, winking. 'You're a dark horse and no mistake.'

'Pardon?'

'You and your lady friend were chattering away in the corner like a pair of lovebirds.'

'Now don't you go jumping to any conclusions,' warned Tom. 'The woman I was having coffee with is not my "lady friend", as you term it. She happens to be a parent – or soon will be – of a pupil at the school.'

She didn't look like a parent to me, thought Mrs Mossup, or that they were discussing education, but she said nothing and she smiled impishly. 'If you say so, Tom,' she said.

Sunday was a dry, wintry day with a vast pewter-coloured sky swept free of clouds. Tom decided to clear the remains of the snow from the path at the front of the cottage. He liked to be out in the fresh air at the weekends, having been cooped in a stuffy classroom all week. Later he would go for a run. When at home on Saturdays and Sundays, he dispensed with the suit and tie he wore to school and usually didn't bother with his appearance. That morning he hadn't shaved and wore an old pair of baggy corduroy trousers, heavy boots, a jacket frayed at the collar and cuffs and a threadbare overcoat. He would not have looked out of place in a soup kitchen for down-and-outs. Hearing the thump of a horse's hooves on the bridle path that ran down the side of the garden, Tom looked up, hoping it might be the very person he wished to see. A moment later, Janette Fairborn, mounted on her chestnut mare, appeared. She was dressed in cream jodhpurs, brown knee-length boots and a close-fitting hacking jacket. Her red hair fell from beneath her riding helmet. She looked stunning.

On the night of the last performance of the pantomime, Tom had summoned up the courage and had asked Janette out to a concert at the town hall in Clayton for the following evening. His mind had not been on the music that night but on the bright and beautiful woman who had sat next to him. There had been a strange, dull ache deep in the pit of his stomach. He had never felt like this about any other woman. He had driven her home and kissed her goodnight at the gate to the farm where she lived. Her hair had shone golden; her jade green eyes had sparkled like emeralds in the moonlight. She had looked like a movie star. Later that evening, back at his cottage, Tom had stared at the wintry scene through the window and felt sure he was falling in love with her.

'Oh, hello,' she said now when she saw Tom. She reined in the horse, patted its neck and looked down, smiling.

'Good morning,' he replied. His heart began to thump in his chest. Over the Christmas break he had thought about her often and what he might say when he saw her again. 'So, you're back from your course, I see.'

'Finished yesterday, thank goodness,' she replied.

'I phoned earlier in the week and your father told me you were away. So, how was it?'

'Oh, you know, rather tedious. I could think of better things to have been doing than spending a week with other assistant bank managers in a hotel in York.'

'I phoned to ask you out,' Tom told her. 'I wondered if you might like to come out for a meal one evening. I've heard that there's a rather smart restaurant in Clayton, Le Bon Viveur.'

'I'd like to,' she replied, 'there is something I need to talk to you about, but could we just go for a drink, perhaps at the King's Head?'

'A meal would be nicer,' said Tom.

'Maybe another time.'

'All right. What about this evening?'

She smiled. 'That's fine if you smarten yourself up.'

'I thought you liked the rugged, rustic look,' he quipped.

'I'll see you about seven,' she said laughing and, digging her heels on to the horse's flank, she trotted off.

Tom wondered why Janette should decline the chance of an expensive meal at a smart restaurant in favour of a drink in the village pub and what it was she needed to talk to him about. He would soon find out.

The King's Head, an inhospitable place at the best of times, was frequented largely by the local farmers who, like most of the residents in Risingdale, disliked change of any kind. There had been loud protests when the brewery proposed a thorough refurbishment and the pub's regulars threatened taking their business elsewhere if the suggested renovations should go ahead. The landlady had added her objections to the planned changes and the brewery had finally given in.

The inn was not an attractive place but did have a certain old-world rustic charm, which appealed to the few ramblers who called in. A selection of sticky-topped round tables with wrought-iron legs were arranged on the grey flagstone floor with an odd assortment of uncomfortable and unstable spindle-backed chairs and wobbly stools. The one attractive feature of the hostelry was the large and very old inglenook fireplace that took up most of a wall. In winter a great blazing fire burned in the grate, illuminating the room, puffing out wood smoke and giving off a prodigious heat.

When one of the Methodist chapels in the village closed, the landlady had bought a job lot of pews, which now lined the walls. She had also salvaged a large lectern, which stood incongruously in one corner. The departing minister, who had not approved of the 'noisy carryings-on and drunken revelries' (as he put it) at the inn, was none too pleased to see much of the contents of the chapel ending up in the pub.

That evening Tom arrived at the King's Head a little before seven o'clock. The place was crowded and noisy. He edged his way through a throng of farmers commiserating about the recent dreadful weather, arguing about the price of cattle feed and the recent sheep auction, and arrived at the bar.

One of the men, catching sight of him, approached. 'Naah then, lad,' came a voice from behind.

Tom recognised the deep, low throaty voice of one of the nosiest and most vociferous (and meanest) of the farmers and turned to find a grizzled old man with a wide-boned, pitted face the colour and texture of an unscrubbed potato, a long beak of a nose with flared nostrils and an impressive shock of white hair.

'Mr Croft,' he said. 'I thought I recognised the voice.'

The farmer's usual attire consisted of a grubby, long-sleeved, collarless shirt, a waistcoat that had seen better days and ancient wellington boots turned down at the top. His threadbare corduroy trousers were invariably held up by a piece of twine. This being Sunday he was dressed in a tweed suit and tie and sported a pair of brown brogues.

'Are tha all reet?' asked the farmer.

'I'm fine,' replied Tom, 'and how are you?'

'Oh, fair to middlin', tha knaas,' he answered, holding an empty beer glass ostentatiously before him. 'Not best time o' year but I'm not complainin'.' He tilted the glass suggestively.

'That'll be a first, Toby Croft,' observed the landlady, coming to join them. 'Now then, Tom,' she said smiling, 'what can I get you?'

'A pint, please, Doris,' he replied, 'and you had better get another one for Mr Croft.'

'That's very decent of you, Mester Dwyer,' said the farmer. It was a rare occurrence for him to buy anyone a drink; indeed, it was unusual for him to pay for his own when the young teacher from the school was at the bar.

'One of these days you'll surprise us all, Toby Croft,' said the landlady, 'and buy your own ale. Tight as a miser's purse, you are.'

At the sight of Tom passing the landlady a twenty-pound note, a small, wrinkled individual with wisps of wiry white hair combed across his otherwise bald pate, pendulous ears and a dimpled, veined nose approached the bar. He was holding an empty glass.

'Evenin', Mester Dwyer,' said the man.

'You had better make that another pint, Doris,' Tom told the landlady.

'That's very charitable of you, Mester Dwyer,' said the wrinkled man, smiling to show largely toothless gums.

'You'll have a stampede in a moment if you're not careful,' she said. 'You know what they say about Yorkshire folk – "short arms and long pockets".' She started to pull the pints. 'And there's no prizes for guessing who's got the shortest arms and the longest pockets.'

'I 'ope tha's not referrin' to me, Doris,' said Toby.

'Who else could I be referring to?' asked the landlady. 'I can't recall the last time I saw anything of your wallet. You're so mean you'd pinch a penny 'til it screamed for mercy.'

'I don't come in 'ere to be abused,' said Toby, sounding affronted. 'I can allus tek mi custom elseweer, tha knaas.'

'You're welcome to do so,' retorted the landlady, continuing to pull the pints.

'Now look 'ere, Doris—' began the old farmer.

Mrs Mossup ignored him. 'She seemed very nice, that parent you were talking to in the café,' she said to Tom.

'Yes, she's just moved into the village. Her son starts school with us on Tuesday.'

'Where's she living then?'

'She's renting a cottage in Rattan Row.'

'Who are you on abaat?' asked Toby, nosy as ever.

Mrs Mossup tapped her nose. 'Never you mind,' she told him. She placed the pints on the bar and went to get Tom his change.

'She gets worse, that woman,' grumbled Toby, reaching for his pint.

'So, 'ow's that new sheepdog o' yourn doin' then, Toby?' asked his wrinkled companion.

'I was sold a pup, Percy, that's what,' growled the farmer. 'I gorrer off of Clive Gosling an' she's goin' back. Useless, she is. Teks not a blind bit o' notice when I calls 'er, waint go out in t'cowld, eats like there's no tomorra and runs away from t'sheep. I tried to get 'er to round up flock an' move 'em from one field to t'other an' she stands theer waggin' 'er tail an' lookin' at me as if to say, "Tha's no chance." 'As thy hever 'eard of a sheepdog what's frit o' sheep? My lad Dean stands theer laughin' 'is 'ead off. Anyroad, in t'end I says to 'er, "Yer daft 'apeth. Come an' 'old t'gate oppen, yer dozy mutt, an' I'll round up t'bloody sheep missen."'

Mrs Mossup came down the bar and gave Tom his change.

'Aye, well,' observed Percy. 'Tha's 'appen not treated 'er reight. Tha's got to handle yer beeasts proper.'

''Andle 'em proper!' exclaimed the farmer. 'I'll tell thee this, I've been practisin' hanimal 'usbandry fer more years than thy's 'ad 'ot dinners.'

'Until you were caught at it,' remarked the landlady, chuckling.

'I shall hignore that comment, Doris,' said Toby. He took a quick dissatisfied gulp of his beer.

'Anyroad, tha wants to stop complainin',' his wrinkled companion told him, reaching for his pint. 'Tha'd soon 'ave summat to complain abaat if tha were Clive Gosling.'

''Ow come?' asked Mr Croft before taking another enormous gulp of beer.

'Well, from what I've 'eard, t'poor chap's lost three of 'is prime yows in all this bad weather.'

'Tha dun't say,' said the farmer, cheering up. 'Aye, well, mebbe things aren't as bad as I thowt.'

'I 'ear somebody's rentin' yon Methody chapel,' remarked Percy.

'Aye, so I've 'eard.'

'And I suppose you know who it is then, Toby,' said the landlady.

The farmer bristled. 'Why t'devil should I know?' he asked.

'Because there's nothing much that you miss,' she answered. 'You've eyes like chapel hat pegs.'

'Well, as it 'appens I do know,' the farmer told her. 'I were speakin' to one of t'decorators an' 'e telled me it were a woman, some southerner who's turnin' it into a sooart o' studio.'

'She must 'ave a fair bit o' brass,' observed the wrinkled man. 'There's a deal wants doin'.'

'Tha reight theer, Percy,' agreed the farmer. 'Anyroad, I can't see as 'ow there'll be much call fer a studio up 'ere.'

'It depends on what sort of studio it is,' observed the landlady. 'People might be interested in a dance school or a fitness centre.'

'What, up 'ere!' exclaimed Mr Croft. 'Aye, an' pigs might fly. Anyroad, I can't see as 'ow t'minister will tek kindly to t'chapel being turned into some sort o' dance 'all or gymnasium.' He reached for his pint and took another great mouthful of beer.

'Well, it's better than what happened in Urebank when they converted that redundant church into a discotheque,' said Mrs Mossup.

'Well, you mark my words,' said Mr Croft, 't'minister won't be too chuffed abaat it. 'E were none too pleased as I recall when tha put all them pews in 'ere, Doris. Gev you a real earful, 'e did. From what I recall—'

'That were last chap,' interrupted Percy.

'Eh?'

'That were t'last minister,' his wrinkled companion told him. 'T'new preacher, Mester Cockburn, is a nice young fella.'

'So does tha know who this woman is who's bought t'chapel?' Mr Croft asked Tom, who had remained quiet but interested in the conversation of the two farmers.

'Oh, just someone from London,' he replied vaguely. He decided to keep the information regarding the new tenant of the Methodist chapel to himself. He had learnt early on that anything said would be repeated, often exaggerated and circulated around the village like wildfire.

'Well, I can't figure it out, why someone from London should want to live up 'ere,' declared the old farmer.

'Perhaps because she's taken with the beauty of the place,' Tom told him.

'Aye, well,' grumbled Mr Croft, 'she wun't think that if she 'ad to farm it.'

Tom turned to the landlady, leaving the two farmers to speculate on what sort of studio it might be.

'How's Leanne getting along?' he asked, lowering his voice.

'She's doing very nicely,' replied Mrs Mossup quietly. 'Thank you for asking.' When Mrs Mossup's unmarried daughter had announced that she was pregnant, she had been packed off to Scarborough to stay with her aunt. At first the girl had been tight-lipped about the identity of the father, but she finally admitted that it was the profligate son of Sir Hedley Maladroit.

'We'll have to decide what to do when she's had the baby,' continued the landlady. 'She's all for keeping it but it's a big thing bringing up a child on her own. If she does, she'll have to live with me, of course, and a pub's not the best place to raise a kiddie.' She thought for a moment. 'Leanne's not a bad lass, you know, just very impressionable and easily led. She was taken advantage of, but least said about that.'

'Well, I hope things work out for her.' Tom glanced at his watch. 'I'm supposed to be meeting someone,' he told her.

'Stood you up, 'as she?' said Mr Croft, who had been eavesdropping.

'Looks like it,' replied Tom.

Mrs Mossup gave a small smile as she caught sight of Janette, who had just entered the inn.

'I think your date has arrived,' she said.

'I could think of better places to go out for the evening,' Tom told Janette as he went to meet her and steer her to a corner table.

'By the 'eck,' grunted Mr Croft, to no one in particular, 'yon schoolmaster dun't let t'grass grow under 'is feet. Din't tek 'im long to gerrem under t'table. Only been in t'village a few months an' 'e's runnin' t'school, bought hissen a nice little cottage, got well in wi' t'local MP an' vicar an' now 'e's courtin' John Fairborn's lass.'

'Leave t'lad alone,' Percy told him. ''E's a decent young chap, is Mester Dwyer, an' 'im an' John Fairborn's lass mek a champion couple.'

''Aye, 'appen they do,' conceded Toby begrudgingly.

He might have other irons in the fire, reflected Mrs Mossup, thinking of the woman she had seen with Tom in the Ring o' Bells café in Clayton the previous day.

Having got Janette an orange juice and collected his drink from the bar, Tom returned to the corner table. He was aware that he and his 'date' were the centre of attention.

Mrs Mossup, not wishing to spend any more time in the company of Toby Croft, waddled off to serve another customer.

'I'm sorry I'm a bit late,' said Janette. 'There was quite a lot for me to do at home. I lost track of the time.'

'That all right,' he told her. 'I've not been here that long.'

'I'm afraid I have to get back,' she said.

Tom was surprised. This wasn't the sort of date he had in mind.

'It's just that I wanted to see you, to explain things.' She thought for a moment and took a sip of her drink. 'We started off on the wrong foot, didn't we? I think you thought I was stuck-up, sitting on my high horse, and bossy as well, and I thought you were arrogant and pushy, but when we got to know each other, well, we changed our opinions.'

'Yes, we did,' he agreed, sensing that there was more she wanted to say, something he really didn't want to hear.

'I am fond of you, Tom, you know that,' she began.

'But . . .'

She took a deep breath. 'But I don't think there's a future for us.'

'I see.'

'I mean, it's not as if we are going out or anything, is it?'

'No,' he conceded. He felt crestfallen. What he imagined was going to be the first date of many was now not going to happen.

'Things might have been different if I were staying in Risingdale,' she said.

'You're leaving?' he asked.

'Yes, I'm moving to Nottingham tomorrow. The course I went on last week in York was for assistant managers at the bank, as I mentioned. Well, it wasn't really a course as such. It was more of an assessment to see if those invited had managerial potential. I had an interview.'

'And?'

'To my surprise, I did quite well. In fact, I have been offered a branch manager's position. It's in Nottingham. It's very short notice but they need somebody there quickly. There's lots to do.'

'Congratulations,' said Tom, feeling deflated.

'It's an opportunity that I can't pass up.'

'If it's really what you want . . .' he began.

'It is,' she said. 'To be frank, in many ways I'll not be sorry to leave Risingdale. It's so insular and everything is so predictable up here. I've lived here all my life and feel hemmed in. I want something different. The people in Risingdale are pleasant enough but inward-looking and parochial. All they seem to talk about is sheep and the weather or the latest gossip. I'm wanting more out of life, more challenge and more excitement. I'm sure you must find that yourself, particularly after the life you led as a professional footballer.'

'No, Jan, you're wrong,' replied Tom. 'I love it here. I am one of the luckiest men alive, because I get to live and work in the most spectacular place in the country, amongst the friendliest people, doing a job I like. I wouldn't want to move.'

'I'm sure that if you had lived here since you were a child as

I have done and not seen anything of the world, you would see what I mean.'

'Perhaps.'

'Anyway, after a lot of thought, I've decided I'm off to Nottingham. I'm staying in a hotel until I can find a flat.'

'I'll miss you,' said Tom.

She rested a hand on his. 'I'll miss you, too. You are one of the people I'm very fond of, but any sort of relationship, which might have been, just would not have worked out with me miles away. I'm sure you can see that.'

'Nottingham is not the other side of the world, Jan.'

She took another sip of her drink. 'I know.'

'I could come and see you,' he said, 'and you would visit home now and again. It might work if we gave it a chance.'

'I don't think so, Tom.'

There was a moment of silence. They both stared down at their drinks.

'Well, good luck in Nottingham,' he told her, looking into her eyes. 'I know you will be a great success.'

Janette stood, leaned over the table and pecked him on the cheek. 'Thanks, Tom,' she said. 'I must be off.'

'I'll see you to your car,' he said.

'I 'ave to hadmit,' observed Toby Croft as he saw Tom and Janette leave the inn, 'you're reight, Percy, they do mek a gradely couple an' if t'schoolmaster lands that particular fish, 'e'll 'ave fallen on 'is feet. She'll be worth a bob or two when 'er owld man kicks t'bucket.'

'Do you want another pint?' asked the landlady, approaching the two farmers.

Percy held up his empty glass and looked at Toby expectantly.

'Nay, I'll not bother,' replied the farmer. 'I've got t'wife outside in t'van. I don't like to leave 'er out theer too long.'

4

Tom didn't feel like returning to the King's Head. He needed to think. The evening was cold and crisp as he walked through the village. The wind had dropped and the clouds had moved away, leaving a constellation of glimmering stars and a pale wintry moon. At the duck pond, all was silent. He was aware of the stillness of the night as he looked out over the black water at the skeletal trees. The scene reflected his sombre mood. Tom sat on a bench, closed his eyes and thought for a moment. He recalled the time when he had just arrived in the village and had sat on the same bench by the pond wondering whether or not to accept the position of teacher at Risingdale School. He had begun throwing lumps of bread into the water, attracting an armada of hungry waterfowl, when there had come a voice from behind him.

'It's not a very good idea to feed the ducks bread, you know.'

Tom had turned to discover the young woman with the flaming red hair and green eyes whom he had encountered on the road the previous day.

He had not appreciated being scolded again and another fractious exchange had ensued. It had not been a propitious start to their relationship.

Then he had been prevailed upon by Joyce to take the part of the prince in the pantomime and found, to his surprise, he was acting opposite Janette. It was then he got to know her, and over the weeks he found he was becoming increasingly attracted to this striking and feisty woman and he felt his feelings were being reciprocated. It was clear to him now this was not the case.

'Ah well,' he said out loud now. 'It wasn't to be.'

'Talking to yourself, Mr Dwyer?'

Tom opened his eyes to find Charlie Lister sitting next to him on the bench, his thin legs moving backwards and forwards as if he were on a swing.

Tom managed a small smile. 'Oh, hello, Charlie,' he said.

'I often talk to myself,' admitted the boy cheerfully. 'Saying things out loud sometimes helps you to sort out the thoughts in your head, doesn't it?'

'It does,' replied the teacher.

'Are you all right, Mr Dwyer?' asked the boy. 'You look a bit sad.'

'Yes, I'm fine. Now what are you doing out this late?'

'Oh, it's not that late, Mr Dwyer,' the boy answered. 'I'm meeting my mum at the bus stop. She goes into Clayton on Sundays to play bingo. I don't like her walking back in the dark by herself.'

'You're a very considerate young man,' said Tom.

They sat there in silence for a while.

'You remember on Friday that a boy joined our class?' asked Tom. 'He sat next to you.'

'Yes,' replied Charlie. 'His name is Leo and he used to live in London. His mother is an artist. He's got this really classy pen. It's got a gold nib. It used to belong to his father. He was killed in a plane crash. We had an interesting conversation.'

'Well, he is going to come to our school,' said the teacher. 'He'll be starting next week and he will be in our class. I guess he will be rather apprehensive, so could you do me a favour and look out for him, show him the ropes and make him feel at home.'

'It will be my pleasure, Mr Dwyer,' replied Charlie. 'I liked him. Leo's quite a character.'

'He is,' agreed Tom, thinking that the two boys were like peas in a pod – both small for their age, both highly intelligent and old beyond their years.

They continued to sit quietly.

'It's a beautiful night,' said Tom.

'You remember when the class went to the museum last term,' said the boy, 'and we had a chat on the bus on the way back to school?'

'I do,' answered Tom. 'I could tell that you had something on your mind.'

'I told you I had never met my father and that I really wanted to, and that my mother had told me that he was kind and clever and an important man, but that if people found out who he was, it would cause all sorts of problems for him and for us.'

'Yes, I recall you told me that,' said Tom. He wasn't really listening. He was thinking of Janette.

'She said that she would tell me when I was older.'

'I'm sorry, Charlie, what was that?'

'My mother, she said she would tell me who my father is when I was older, but I felt I was old enough to know now.'

'Yes, I remember,' said Tom.

'You said that my mother probably had a good reason for not telling me,' continued Charlie.

'Yes, I did.'

At the time Tom had thought that Charlie was certainly mature enough to understand and that he should be told the truth. It was the right thing to do. He felt it is always best to be honest with children. Charlie should meet his father, Tom believed, but he felt it wasn't his place to interfere so he had kept his thoughts to himself.

'Well, the thing is, Mr Dwyer,' said the boy, an intent, bright look on his face, 'my mum's told me. I've met my father and I really like him. You're the first person I've told. It's just that I wanted to tell someone.'

'That's really good news, Charlie,' said Tom. 'I'm really pleased for you.'

'Of course, I'm not to tell anyone who he is.'

'Then you had better keep it to yourself,' said the teacher.

Charlie nodded and got up from the bench.

'You know, Mr Dwyer,' he said, 'I sometimes wish I could stay young like Peter Pan. Being an adult is such a complicated business, isn't it?'

Tom nodded ruefully. 'You are so right, Charlie,' he replied.

'That was Mr Dwyer you were talking to, wasn't it?' Charlie's mother asked as they walked home that evening. 'I saw you both as the bus passed. You were chattering away like nobody's business.'

'Yes, it was Mr Dwyer,' replied her son. 'He was sitting by the duck pond looking pensive, so I thought I'd say hello.'

'You do come out with some words,' said his mother, chuckling. 'Where did you hear the word "pensive"?'

'It was in a poem we read at school. It was about daffodils.'

'Well, I shouldn't think it will be long before we see a few daffodils. I think spring is around the corner.'

They walked on.

'Strange thing for your teacher to be doing, sitting outside at this time of night and in this weather,' she said.

'I think he has things on his mind,' said the boy.

'What makes you think that?'

'Well, he wasn't his usual self. He seemed a bit down. I hope he's not thinking of leaving. He's the best teacher I've had. I would really miss him.'

'Has he said anything about leaving?' asked his mother.

'No, but there's a rumour that the school is to close. I heard Mrs Golightly talking to the cleaner. Then Mr Dwyer will have to leave to get another job, won't he?'

'If it does come to that, you have no need to worry. He'll have no problem in finding another and you'll be at the grammar school by then.'

'If I pass the eleven-plus,' replied her son.

'You got through the scholarship exam with no trouble,' she said.

'But going to the grammar depends on passing the eleven-plus as well,' said Charlie. 'It's best not to count my chickens. Things sometimes have a sneaky way of not turning out as you want them to.' He sounded so old-fashioned. She wondered where he got it from.

His mother put her arm around her son and kissed his cheek. 'I love you, Charlie Lister,' she said.

'I know,' he said, nonchalantly.

They continued to walk home.

'I don't want Mr Dwyer to leave the village, though,' said Charlie.

'Yes, I guess there is a lot in Risingdale who feel the same,' said his mother. 'He's certainly made an impression since he's been here. So what were you two talking about?'

'Oh, this and that, you know,' Charlie replied.

'That doesn't answer my question.'

'We were talking about the new boy. You met him when his mum moved into the cottage next to ours. He's to start at the school next week.'

'He seems a nice young man and his mother's very friendly. We were chatting over the hedge when you were changing your library books in town.'

'Yes, I think I'll get on with him,' said Charlie.

'Is that all you were talking to Mr Dwyer about?' she asked.

'Just about,' he replied.

Charlie decided he wouldn't tell her that he had told his teacher that he now knew who his father was and that he had met him. He understood that what he had revealed to

Tom would go no further for he trusted his teacher implicitly, but he felt it better not to say anything to his mother. It was just as well, for Mrs Lister lived in fear that one day the identity of Charlie's father would be known and revealing it, even to Charlie's teacher, would have worried her. She knew that if the residents of Risingdale discovered her secret it would cause more than a few problems and not only for herself and her son. The boy's father was the local squire, Sir Hedley Maladroit.

Sir Hedley had met Charlie's mother some twelve years before at the Clayton Golf Club where she served behind the bar. She was popular and vivacious – so unlike his wife. He fell for the tall, pale-complexioned woman with violet eyes and curly black hair and found her lively and interesting. He started spending more time in the clubhouse than on the green. She, for her part, found the baronet charming and good company and, then, as they say, one thing led to another.

Sir Hedley's marriage had never been a happy one after the first few years. The husband and wife soon discovered the only thing they had in common was their son, James, a son who turned out to be a great disappointment to his father. Indulged and overprotected by his mother, the young man had turned out to be lazy and arrogant. He had also been discovered to be a thief, trying to sell one of his mother's necklaces at an auction house. The theft was blamed on the housekeeper, Mrs Gosling, who was summarily sacked. The Maladroit son was also responsible for taking advantage of the naive barmaid at the King's Head, getting her pregnant. Sir Hedley had packed his son off to work in a distillery (which he part-owned) in the Borders in Scotland.

Over the years, Sir Hedley's wife's sharp tongue was like a knife that grew keener with constant use. The marriage began to teeter on the rocks. Their relationship had become a drama of resentments enacted in weary sighs and simmering silences.

Sir Hedley spent less and less time at home. There was always an excuse why he had to be away: dealing with estate matters, his duties as the Deputy Lord Lieutenant and President of the Landowners' Association, chairing the governors' meetings at the grammar school or sitting on the bench as a magistrate. And, of course, there was the golf club. Many a time he had sat in his study and considered divorce, but then decided that it would be such a bother and, of course, a costly business with a good chunk of his estate disappearing with his wife. Best just to put up with it, keep his head down and see as little of her as possible. His wife had contemplated divorce too but then she thought of what she would lose. A snob at heart, she revelled in the position of the wife of the squire and the deference shown to her by the locals. She enjoyed living at Marston Towers with its parkland and spectacular views. She was not going to give up that lifestyle. So she too accepted the marriage of convenience and was not unhappy that she saw little of her husband.

Sir Hedley and Charlie's mother had been very discreet over the years. They were very careful not to arouse any suspicions and were not seen together around the village. Their Sunday-night trysts took place in a hotel well away from prying eyes. They would spend the evening together and then Sir Hedley would drop her at the bus stop in Clayton so she could get the bus back to Risingdale. He made certain that she was very well provided for with a cottage and a generous monthly allowance to pay the bills. When she told him that Charlie was to enter for a scholarship to cover the costs of the grammar-school education, he said he would pay for anything that was needed and there was no necessity for Charlie to sit the examination, but she was adamant that he should not have to spend any more money on them. They managed perfectly well. She made no demands upon him and did not wish to take advantage of his generosity.

Mrs Lister was something of a mystery in Risingdale. She tended to keep very much to herself, didn't shop in the village, mix with the residents or appear to have any friends. No one knew if she was divorced or a widow, or anything about her background. Just after he had started at the school, Tom had asked about Charlie's mother in the staffroom one afternoon only to discover that there wasn't very much information about her. Mrs Golightly had told him that Charlie didn't know who his father was. Then she had considered what she should say next. 'Mrs Lister doesn't work so there's a bit of speculation in the village about where she gets her money from to pay the rent and deal with all the bills. Some say that she's a bit too friendly with the men but I think that's just idle gossip. She's not a bad mother and clearly loves the boy.'

'I met your father in town this evening,' said his mother now. 'He asked after you. He wondered if we might like to spend a weekend together in Scarborough. What do you think?'

'I'd love that!' cried Charlie.

She put her arm around him again and held him close. 'Just the three of us,' she said.

'Just the three of us,' Charlie repeated, 'like a proper family.'

On the Monday the teachers gathered in the staffroom for their morning coffee. Mr Cadwallader crunched noisily on a biscuit and looked across the room to where the young teacher was sitting reading the educational supplement in the newspaper. Tom was feeling down that morning and had barely exchanged a word with his colleagues since entering the room. He was feeling despondent and wasn't in the mood to enter into the usual staffroom badinage. The meeting with Janette was still very much on his mind.

'Is that new boy starting today?' Joyce asked him.

'Tomorrow,' Tom replied, not looking up from the paper.

'Why not today?' she asked.

'He's at the hospital.'

'Has he had an accident?' asked Mrs Golightly.

'He's got a medical condition,' said Tom.

'What sort of medical condition?'

'He has a brain tumour.'

'My God!' exclaimed Mr Cadwallader. 'Poor little chap.'

'When did you find this out?' asked Joyce.

'I met his mother in town on Saturday,' said Tom. 'She told me.'

'Does Mr Gaunt know?'

'Yes, he knows.'

'So, is he very ill then?' asked Mrs Golightly.

'I don't know,' Tom told her, not wishing to start discussing Leo's condition.

'Perhaps he might be better catered for at a special school,' suggested Mrs Golightly. 'It's a big responsibility taking on a sick child like that.'

'Yes, I agree,' said Mr Cadwallader. 'You should have a word with Mr Gaunt, Tom. I think the boy should be in a school for disabled children.'

'Leo is not disabled,' said Tom, 'and I am perfectly happy that he should be in my class, so could we change the subject, please?'

He returned to his paper.

His colleagues chatted on as they normally did, talking about what they had done over the weekend, the places they had been to and the television programmes they had watched. Tom continued to read his paper.

'You're not searching for another job, are you?' Tom was asked by Joyce.

'No, I'm not looking for another job,' he replied.

'I wouldn't blame him,' commented Mrs Golightly. 'I mean, it won't be long before our school will go the way of all those other small rural primaries. I heard that children's numbers at Skillington are dropping like flies and the school there is on the cards to close. There's no doubt in my mind that Risingdale will follow suit.'

'You do tend to go on about it, Bertha,' Joyce told her, looking at herself in a small mirror and applying some lipstick.

'So, what's so interesting in the paper?' asked Mrs Golightly.

'I'm reading an article,' said Tom.

'I don't read the educational press,' Joyce declared to no one in particular. 'There is never any good news. It's all about what teachers aren't doing and should be doing, with articles about the decline in standards, poor examination results, dreadful behaviour in schools and details of yet more government initiatives. There's never anything positive or helpful or amusing.'

'It's all gloom and doom,' said Mrs Golightly, agreeing with her colleague.

'So what's this article about?' asked Mr Cadwallader. It was clear to Tom that he was not going to get any peace.

'It's about the selection of books for schools – which are the most appropriate and those that the writer deems unsuitable.'

'And what books are deemed unsuitable?' asked Joyce.

'Oh, there's Noddy, for a start.'

'I loved Noddy!' exclaimed Mrs Golightly. 'How could Noddy be thought to be unsuitable? He's such an innocent little chap.'

'It's not Noddy himself, but the books in which he appears. The writer feels that golliwogs and Big Ears are undesirable characters.'

'I've still got my golliwog,' said his colleague. 'My mother knitted it for me when I was a little girl. He's cute and cuddly and always smiling. When I moved out of the cottage into the apartment, there were a lot of things I threw away but I have kept Gladstone.'

'Gladstone!' exclaimed Mr Cadwallader.

'That's the name of my golly. He sits on my dressing table.'

'I can't see what's wrong with golliwogs,' said Mr Cadwallader.

'I can,' said Tom. 'I can quite understand in this day and age why the golliwog is thought to be unacceptable. The word has become a term of racist abuse and the illustration is a crude stereotype of a black person. I think it is offensive.'

'There's telling you,' said Joyce.

'Well, I'm not getting rid of Gladstone,' said Mrs Golightly determinedly.

'So, what's wrong with Big Ears?' asked Mr Cadwallader.

'Ear-shaming,' replied Tom.

'What the devil is "ear-shaming"?' asked Mr Cadwallader.

'Making fun of others who have big ears,' Tom told him.

'Give me strength,' muttered the teacher.

'The writer also feels strongly about nursery rhymes that encourage violence and animal cruelty, such as "The Three Blind Mice", and she's got it in for some fairy stories as well because they depict a negative attitude to women.'

'I came across this attitude when I was deciding which Christmas pantomime to produce. I think I told you that I had first considered *Snow White* but was told it is politically incorrect to use the term "dwarf" these days because it's regarded by some as an offensive word. The correct term is "vertically challenged". I mean, you can't have *Snow White and the Seven Vertically Challenged Men*. Of course, *Mother Goose* was out because of Simple Simon. We couldn't stage *Babes in the Wood* or *Hansel and Gretel* because it involves child abduction and *Robinson Crusoe* was out on race grounds because it featured Man Friday and cannibals. Then I thought of *Cinderella* but came up against the same obstacle.'

'What's wrong with *Cinderella*?' asked Mr Cadwallader.

'I did tell you,' Miss Tranter told him. 'You were probably too busy rootling in the biscuit barrel. You can't describe people as

ugly any more, that's why. *Cinderella* wouldn't be the same without the Ugly Sisters. This undue interference is ridiculous. I can
see, by the look on your face, that you don't agree, Tom.'

'No, I don't agree, as a matter of fact,' he responded vehemently. 'Terms such as "dwarf" and "ugly" are derogatory.
We are trying to get children to treat each other with kindness
and respect.'

'I think you've got out of the bed the wrong side this morning, Tom,' said Mrs Golightly.

'Anyway,' said Joyce, not wishing to argue the point, 'I was
on safe ground with *The Sleeping Beauty*.'

'Not according to this writer,' stated Tom.

'What's wrong with *The Sleeping Beauty*?'

Tom consulted the article. 'Well, a strange man – that's the
prince – sees this attractive young woman asleep in bed –
that's the princess – breaks into her bedroom and, without her
consent, proceeds to kiss her on the lips. That could be
construed as a sexual assault.'

Joyce gave a resounding laugh. 'I don't think Janette thought
it was a sexual assault when you kissed her in my pantomime,'
Joyce told him. 'She enjoyed every minute.'

'So how is the romance going with the delectable Miss
Fairborn?' asked Mr Cadwallader.

'It's not,' replied Tom sharply, returning to the paper.

At lunchtime, when Tom didn't appear in the staffroom, Mr
Cadwallader sought him out. He found his colleague in his
classroom staring out of the window at the children playing
noisily in the school yard. He wore a sad expression.

'May I come in?' he asked.

'Yes, of course, Owen,' replied Tom. 'Look, I'm sorry I was
a bit short with you this morning.'

'Don't give it another thought.' He went to join Tom at the
window. 'We could see that there was something on your

mind. We are worried about you. What's wrong? Does it concern Miss Fairborn, by any chance?'

Tom nodded.

'I gather from what you said that you and she are not as close as we all thought you were.'

'No, it appears not.'

'Do you wish to talk about it?'

'There's really nothing to say.'

'You know, when I went through that bad patch last term, you were there for me. I remember I told you when you asked if I was all right, that there was nothing you could do. I had to sort things out myself. You said to me that it is sometimes good to get things off your chest and talk it through with somebody. A trouble shared. I know that confiding in you helped me greatly.'

Tom looked at him. He was fond of Owen. Of course he rambled on and liked the sound of his own voice, but his heart was in the right place. As Mr Gaunt had said, Mr Cadwallader was a welcoming and good-hearted man. So he told him how he felt about Janette, that he had never met any woman who had affected him so much, that he had fallen in love with her.

'But she has made it clear,' he told his colleague, 'that she doesn't feel the same way about me and is to start a new life away from the village where, I guess, she will find someone far more exciting than I am.'

'If she does, then she's a fool,' said Mr Cadwallader. He thought for a moment. 'You know, Tom, there are some people in life that you thank God you have had the good fortune to come across. As far as I'm concerned, you are one of those people. It's a privilege to know you. Now, I cannot speak from any personal experience, but I should not give up hope. All your friends here at the school feel that you and Miss Fairborn are made for each other. "Faint heart never won fair lady", as the saying goes.'

'Maybe you are right,' said Tom.

*　　*　　*

After school the headmaster appeared in Tom's classroom.

'Could I have a quick word?' asked Mr Gaunt.

'Yes, of course,' replied Tom.

'I've received a letter from a Ms Babcock of the Education Office. She's the newly appointed Information Technology Adviser with the job of developing something called "computer literacy" throughout the county. She says that every school is to receive a computer and is asking each head teacher to nominate a member of his or her staff to take a lead and be responsible for increasing pupils' awareness and use of computers. She's organising a series of training courses and has invited me to send a representative. I imagine you can guess where this is leading.'

'I'd be pleased to do it,' said Tom. 'Computers are the future in education.'

'You think so?' the headmaster asked, frowning.

'I think we have to move with the times,' said Tom. 'It's the 1980s. The sooner we learn how to use modern technology, the better.'

I can't see Mr Dwyer's colleagues sharing that view, thought the headmaster, but he said nothing.

The following week the computer arrived, along with a manual of instructions as thick as a telephone directory, and was installed in Tom's classroom.

5

The following Tuesday morning was bright but cold. A gusty wind bent the treetops and tugged fretfully at the window frames making them rattle. Tom was the first to arrive at the school, for it was his custom to get there just after eight before the other teachers, to prepare his lessons for the day and mark the children's exercise books. As had been their routine for many years, the caretaker and his wife arrived at eight-thirty, Mr Gaunt and the other teachers got to school at a quarter to the hour and the children turned up for nine o'clock or thereabouts depending on the weather. When he arrived that Tuesday morning at his classroom, Tom found the cleaner (or, as she liked to style herself, 'the assistant caretaker') singing to herself as she vigorously polished his desk. The room, immaculately tidy, smelled of lavender furniture polish.

Mrs Gosling was a small, plump woman with darting, judgemental eyes; her handsome features were buried in a broad face. She was large and motherly in appearance but not in personality. That morning she was wearing a pink nylon overall over a thick knitted cardigan and a red and white gingham frock that reminded Tom of the tablecloth in his aunt's house. Her hair, the colour of purple broccoli, stood up on her head in a frizzy mass. It looked as if she had struggled up the embankment after a road crash.

'Hello, Mrs Gosling,' Tom said, approaching her. He resisted mentioning her bizarre hairdo. 'Hard at work, I see.'

'"The devil makes work for idle hands", Mr Dwyer, that's what my sainted grandmother used to say. I've been giving your room a good going-over. Mind you, there wasn't much to do in here, unlike the other classrooms. It'll take me twice as long to fettle the other rooms, and the staffroom is in a right state, papers everywhere, unwashed crockery, biscuit crumbs on the carpet and Mr Gaunt's room's not a whole lot better. I ask the other teachers to keep their rooms tidy but it doesn't make a blind bit of difference. I might as well talk to a brick wall. I mean, it doesn't set a very good example to the kiddies, all that clutter and jumble, how does it?'

Tom decided not to respond. 'I'm surprised to see you here so early, particularly in this weather,' he remarked.

'My son, Clive, dropped me off,' she said. 'He was after buying some sheep and has gone into Urebank this morning. He's had a terrible time of it in this bad weather and lost three of his best ewes. Poor lad is in a right state.'

'I'm sorry to hear that,' said Tom. 'It's a hard life farming up here and no mistake.'

'It's a hard life cleaning this school, Mr Dwyer,' retorted the cleaner. 'I mean, I don't wish to speak out of turn, but Mr Leadbeater never stirs himself. If there was work in bed he'd lie on the floor. It's left to yours truly to get this school shipshape. When I worked as housekeeper at Marston Towers, I didn't have half the work to do and the place is twice the size of this school.'

'Ah, but there are children here, Mrs Gosling,' Tom told her. 'You have to expect a bit of a mess.' Before she could respond, he moved on. 'And you have to admit you weren't happy up at the big house.'

'That's true, not after being accused of thieving by Lady High-and-Mighty. I could have taken her to court for defamation of character but I didn't want to stir up any trouble for Sir Hedley. He's always treated me well. How he puts up with her, I'll never know.'

Tom decided not to go down that road and kept quiet, hoping Mrs Gosling would go about her work, but he was disappointed.

'Anyway, as I was saying, I hitched a ride and had to brave the snizy wind. That's why my hair's like a haystack and I'd just had it permed.'

'A snazzy wind?' Tom repeated.

'Snizy,' the cleaner corrected him. 'Bitterly cold.' She shook her head and hair and smiled. 'How long have you been in Yorkshire now, Mr Dwyer?'

'Clearly not long enough to know all the dialect words,' he told her.

'You want to ask the kiddies,' she said. 'They'll give you a lesson in speaking Yorkshire.'

'Well, you seem to be done in here,' said Tom, 'so I won't keep you.'

'I've brought you something,' Mrs Gosling told him, ignoring his hint for her to get on with her cleaning. She dug into a large canvas bag and produced a long scarf in the most startlingly gaudy colours: sickly greens, garish yellows, scarlets and bright blues, pinks and purples, a veritable multiplicity of hues. She draped the multicoloured article around Tom's neck and stood back to admire it. 'This is for you,' she said. 'I saw you last week in the playground in all this bad weather without a scarf. I thought to myself, that young man will get his death of cold not covered up.'

'It's well, it's . . .' began Tom.

'A scarf,' she said.

'Yes, I see that. It's very, er . . . very striking.'

'I like bright colours. It suits you. I knitted it myself.'

'In a week?' he asked.

'Gracious, Mr Dwyer,' she chuckled, 'I can knit a scarf in a night, never mind a week. I come from a long tradition of Dales hand-knitters. I don't suppose you've heard of them.'

'No, I haven't,' admitted Tom.

Mrs Gosling placed her duster in the pocket of her overall and folded her arms across her substantial bosom. Tom sighed inwardly, knowing that he was in for one of the cleaner's long accounts.

'People have been knitting in the Dales, Mr Dwyer, for centuries – men as well as the women, and children too,' she told him. 'They were all at it, making garters, gloves and large high stockings, which they sold for only a few pence. Course, when they arrived in the York or London shops they cost an arm and a leg. It was the only way they could make a living in those days – to knit. My sainted grandmother, Martha Gosling, God rest her soul, was a notorious knitter and known as "the demon knitter of Risingdale". She started knitting at four years old. Happen you've heard of her?'

'No, no, I'm afraid not,' replied Tom, wanting to get on with his marking. 'The thing is, Mrs Gosling, I have quite a lot to do and—'

'She never stopped knitting,' continued the cleaner regardless. 'Do you know she could knit in the dark with four needles and go to bed and knit under the blankets?'

Tom pictured the bedroom scene and wondered how the cleaner's sainted grandfather put up with a wife clacking away with four sharp needles under the bedclothes.

'She would even sit on the outdoor privy in all weathers knitting.'

'Fancy that,' remarked Tom, picturing the scene.

'Never missed an opportunity for getting out her needles,' said Mrs Gosling. 'She got her reputation not only because of the speed at which she knitted but also because of the quality of her work. Her Fair Isle gloves were the talk of the Dale and in great demand. They were very popular with the gentry. Old Lady Maladroit, Sir Hedley's grandmother, would wear no others. Course, old Lady Maladroit was a different kettle of

fish to the one who lives in the big house now. She was a real
lady, not like that stuck-up mare who nobody likes and who
gave me the sack. Sour as a crab apple, is that one. "All fur
and no knickers", as my sainted grandmother would say. I
don't forget the way she treated me when I was housekeeper
at Marston Towers, accusing me of stealing her necklace and
then it turning up and not a word of apology.'

'Yes, that was unfortunate,' said Tom, 'but—'

'Anyway, as I was saying, my grandmother used to knit
gloves for all the well-to-do people. She made gloves for the
local parson until they had a fall out. She never missed the
opportunity to get out her needles and, on one occasion,
continued knitting during the vicar's sermon, which he didn't
take kindly to. He leaned over the pulpit, pointed a bony finger
at her and told her in front of the whole of the congregation to
stop it. "I can knit and listen," she told him. She wasn't backwards in coming forwards, my grandmother.' Rather like the
speaker, thought Tom, and her granddaughter Vicky, who was
a pupil in his class. 'Parson was not best pleased, I can tell you,
and told her after the service to stop clacking away with her
needles beneath the pulpit and that she sounded like a character in a Dickens novel. I forget her name.'

'Madame Defarge,' Tom told her. 'She sat knitting by the
guillotine as she watched the aristocrats have their heads
chopped off.'

'Anyway, as I was saying,' continued the cleaner, 'parson
told my grandmother he was not prepared to put up with her
knitting in church. "Well then, Reverend," she told him, "I'm
not prepared to put up with any more of your long-winded
sermons and that's the last pair of gloves you're getting off of
me." Like a lot of his flock, she went over to the Methodists.
Oh, and speaking of gloves . . .'

She delved into her bag and produced a kaleidoscopic pair
of matching gloves. 'These are for you as well,' she said.

'That's very thoughtful of you, Mrs Gosling,' replied Tom, staring at the dazzling articles. 'Well, I must get on.'

'Anyroad, my grandmother joined the Prims and they held their meetings in the upper floor of Isaac Catchpenny's outbuilding. The minister, a Christian soul called the Reverend Wiseman, was quite happy for her to knit and listen when he was preaching.' Tom looked at his watch. When would the woman shut up? 'They had to move premises after an unfortunate incident. The minister had just announced the hymn, "Vain, delusive world, adieu", and the floor gave way and the congregation found themselves on the floor below. Thankfully no one was hurt, but my grandmother lost her precious needles. She was convinced the parson had put somebody up to it because the beams holding up the floor had been nearly sawn in two. Well, I can't stand here nattering all day, Mr Dwyer,' said the cleaner, reaching for her duster. 'Some of us have got work to do.'

That morning, to Tom's surprise, Mr Gaunt arrived before half past eight.

'Good morning,' said the headmaster, poking his head around the classroom door. The shapeless tweed jacket, baggy flannel trousers and shirt frayed around the cuffs had been abandoned in favour of a smart pinstripe suit, crisp white shirt and college tie. He had also had his hair cut and smelled strongly of a pungent aftershave.

'Good morning,' Tom replied. He had an idea why the headmaster had changed his usual routine and why he had made such an effort with his appearance. 'Do you have an important meeting today, headmaster?'

'No, no,' said Mr Gaunt airily. 'I thought I'd get here a little earlier than usual.' Mrs Stanhope had told him before leaving on Friday that, having spoken to her son and looked around, she would like Leo to attend Risingdale School and he would start on Tuesday.

Mr Gaunt was here that morning, dressed up to the nines, thought Tom, to meet the new pupil and, in particular, the boy's mother.

'I'll let you know when Mrs Stanhope and Leo arrive,' he said. 'I guess you will want to see them.'

'Yes, yes, of course,' said the headmaster, colouring a little. 'Nice scarf, by the way. Very fetching.'

At just after nine o'clock the school bus rumbled to a noisy stop at the road outside, belching an evil-smelling smoke. The driver, a cheerful-looking individual, climbed out, stretched and yawned. Catching sight of Tom, he gave a smile and a slight nod of the head. The children, chattering excitedly, clambered off the bus and each one wished their teacher a cheery 'Good morning, sir'. One of the first down the steps was a large, ginger-headed girl. This was Vicky, Mrs Gosling's granddaughter.

'Hello, Mr Dwyer,' she said, sniffing noisily.

'Good morning, Vicky,' Tom replied.

'That's the scarf my gran knitted for you, isn't it?' asked the girl.

'Yes, it is,' he replied.

'That the latest fashion then, sir?' asked a heavily freckled, red-headed boy as he jumped down the stairs of the bus laughing.

'Shurrup, Simon!' snapped Vicky. 'I think Mr Dwyer looks dead trendy.' The girl sneezed loudly and sniffed.

'Bless you,' said Tom.

'I always get a cold at this time of year,' said Vicky.

'Have you taken something for it?'

'My mam gave me an onion lemon this morning,' the girl told him.

'An onion lemon?' repeated Tom. 'I can't say I've ever heard of that remedy. I do remember my grandmother cutting up an onion, putting it in a bowl with hot water and getting me to breathe in the fumes. It cleared my nose but, my goodness, it made my eyes water. I can't recall her putting any lemon with it.'

'She gave you an onion?' asked the girl, sounding baffled.

'Yes, like your mother.'

'My mam didn't give me an onion, Mr Dwyer,' said Vicky laughing. 'She gave me an 'oney an' lemon drink.'

'You know, Vicky,' said Tom good-humouredly, 'you always manage to make me smile. Off you go, get in out of the cold.'

When the children had gone into the school, the bus driver approached Tom. Mr Firkin had a broad face with a ruddy complexion and tufts of sandy hair that retreated from a red dome of a head. He was popular in the village, for he was a jolly, good-humoured man with a chuckle that had a way of making other people smile and chuckle too.

'I was wondering, Mr Dwyer,' he began, scratching his head.

'Yes?'

'Could you tell me, am I right in thinking that the infant teacher is a widow?'

'Yes, she is,' said Tom.

'Aye, I thought as much. She's a fine-looking woman, is Mrs Golightly, and no mistake.'

'Yes, she is and a very nice person too.'

'Aye, I thought as much.'

'Was there something in particular you wished to ask me, Mr Firkin?' asked Tom.

'Well, the thing is, Mr Dwyer, I was wondering if she has any . . . well, any connections like?'

'Connections?' repeated Tom. 'I'm sorry, Mr Firkin, I don't follow.'

The bus driver coughed. 'Any romantic connections – if there's anyone, any gentleman friend, that is, on the scene.'

Tom tried not to smile. 'No, no, I don't think there's any gentleman friend on the scene. Not as far as I know, anyway.'

'Aye, I thought as much. Well, the thing is, I was wondering if you might put a word in for me.'

'Put a word in,' repeated Tom.

'Aye, mention that I'm disposed should I be given the nod.'

'You're disposed?'

'Aye, disposed if she gives me the nod.'

Tom bit his bottom lip to suppress a smile. 'I'll be certain to put a word in, Mr Firkin,' he said.

'You might mention that I own my own house and run my own funeral business as well as driving the school bus.'

'I'll be sure to do that,' Tom told him.

The bus driver's face broke into a great beaming smile. 'I'm much obliged to you, Mr Dwyer,' he said and, with a jaunty step and whistling to himself, he headed for his bus.

Before he jumped in the cab, he turned. 'Nice scarf!' he shouted.

Bertha Golightly had been the infant teacher at Risingdale School for all of her career. She had been born in a small cottage a little out of the village, attended the school in which she would later teach and gained a place at Clayton Grammar School for Girls before it became the comprehensive. She had achieved moderate success in her examinations, trained as a teacher of the early years at St John's College and had then moved back to live with her parents. She had been appointed to the post of infant teacher at the village school, a position that she still held. She loved teaching 'the little ones', as she called them, and found her fresh-faced charges, for the most part, delightful, uncomplicated, frank, impulsive, excitable and excited individuals. At other times they could be quite discomfiting: those large, questioning eyes, their pure innocence, their vulnerability, their complete trust. She would look at her class and wonder why adults couldn't be more like them. Unlike grown-ups, little children had no conception of race, colour of skin, status, wealth, background; they didn't know how to curl a cynical lip. For them everything in the world was new and interesting and colourful.

Mrs Golightly met Norman, her future husband, at a meeting of the Clayton and District Historical Society. He was a reticent, rather nervous man with a pronounced stutter and she had liked him from that first encounter. In many ways he was like a small child – vulnerable, trusting, one of the world's innocents. He had served in the Medical Corps during the War and attended to the wounded on the beaches at Dunkirk, an experience that haunted him and was something he would never talk about. They had married, moved in with Bertha's parents and looked forward to a long and happy life together, hopefully blessed with children. It was not to be. A month after their marriage, she was called out of a lesson and told her husband had been killed in a road accident. After her parents had died, she continued to live in the cottage.

Tom had visited Mrs Golightly to discuss buying her cottage soon after he had taken up his post at the school. She had decided to downsize and move into the apartment block where Miss Tranter lived. Tom had imagined Roselea to be a small country cottage in honey-coloured stone with a yellow thatched roof and roses around the door, the sort one sees on picture postcards or on the front of a tin of biscuits. He was soon disabused when he saw where Mrs Golightly lived. Roselea Cottage stood at the end of a cracked crazy-paved stone path. There was an ancient, broken stone birdbath, an overgrown rockery and a circular flower bed choked with dying flowers and weeds. A track of beaten mud ran down the side. It was a square red-brick building with a sagging slate roof, peeling paint and a neglected garden. Faded green-painted shutters framed the windows. There was clearly much to do to get it into some sort of shape. However, as he stared at the building, he had seen the potential. He had turned to look at the view, gazing though the trees at a vista of green undulating fields criss-crossed with silvered limestone walls, which rose to the craggy fellside, and he marvelled at the scene before him. In a sky as delicate and clear as an eggshell, a red kite had soared in circles. Somewhere in a distant field, a tractor had chugged. Tom knew he had to have the cottage.

He had been shown into the sitting room, which had smelled of furniture polish and cats. In front of a blazing fire sprawled a fat ginger tom that hissed on seeing him. On the mantelpiece was a photograph in a silver frame of a tall, not unattractive young man posing on a sea wall.

'That was my husband, Norman,' Mrs Golightly had told him, her voice full of wistful sadness. 'Taken on our honeymoon in Whitby. He was killed in a road accident on his way home from work a month later.'

'I'm sorry,' Tom had said.

'He loved it here,' she had told him forlornly, 'the roses round the door, the view up to the hills, the smell of the country. They do say that time is a great healer. Well, not for me. I've never got over losing him. When you are fortunate to find someone to love, to truly love, you imagine that you will spend the whole of your life with that person. For me it wasn't the case.' Her eyes had become blurred with tears.

Hearing that Mr Firkin was now trying to enlist his help in wooing Mrs Golightly, Tom thought that his colleague might well find the cheerful bus driver someone with whom she could share her life and he determined to have a word with her. One afternoon in the staffroom, Tom raised the matter with her about the love-struck bus driver.

'Mr Firkin,' she said casually. 'Oh, he's had his eye on me for a long time.'

Mr Gaunt, having stood expectantly at his study window for the past five minutes, saw the Range Rover pull up on the road a moment later. He quickly emerged from the school to greet the occupants. Straightening his tie and smoothing down his hair, he hurried down the path, a radiant smile on his face.

'Ah, Mrs Stanhope,' he said effusively as the woman climbed from the car.

She extended a queenly hand, which the headmaster shook, and gave him the dazzling smile.

'Good morning, Mr Gaunt,' she said before turning to her son who was clambering out of the back seat of the vehicle. 'Come, Leo,' she said.

The boy was wearing a white shirt and tie, grey pullover and blazer, long grey stockings and, despite the weather, short grey trousers. He could have been a schoolboy of the 1950s.

'I should have mentioned,' the headmaster told the parent, as they approached the school, 'that the school bus picks up the children outside the King's Head just before nine o'clock.'

'I thought I would bring him in, this being his first morning,' she explained.

'Of course, of course,' said Mr Gaunt. 'I thought you might do that.' He looked at the boy and smiled. 'I'm sure you're feeling a little nervous this morning, Leo.'

'Not really, sir,' replied the boy. 'I'm very much looking forward to starting. I think I am going to like it here.'

'Well, that's good,' said Mr Gaunt, surprised at the boy's apparent self-assurance.

Tom was waiting at the entrance to the school.

'And here is your teacher,' said the headmaster. He turned to Tom. 'Perhaps you might like to take Leo into school, Mr Dwyer, and let him settle in. Mrs Stanhope, you might enjoy a cup of coffee in my study before you set off home.'

'That would be lovely,' she said, giving him another dazzling smile. She looked at Tom and gave him the dazzling smile too.

'Good morning, Mr Dwyer,' she said.

'Good morning,' replied Tom, relieved that she had made no mention of the outrageous scarf that was still draped around his neck like some multicoloured boa constrictor.

Mr Gaunt escorted the parent into his room and, on passing Mrs Leadbeater, asked the secretary to provide some coffee and biscuits. 'The best variety, Beryl,' he said in a hushed voice, 'and use the china cups.'

Tom took the new pupil to his classroom and sat him next to young Charlie Lister.

At morning break, he joined his colleagues in the staffroom to make himself a drink before going on playground duty. He was wearing the multicoloured scarf.

'What the devil is that you're wearing around your neck?' asked Mr Cadwallader when Tom walked through the door. 'It looks like some bizarre draft excluder.'

'It's horrendous,' said Miss Tranter. 'I've never seen an article of clothing so unashamedly tasteless. Are you wearing it for a bet or something?'

'It's certainly not my cup of tea,' added Mrs Golightly. 'My mother had a big, shapeless knitted tea cosy in the same colours. She bought it at a WI "bring and buy" sale. It ended up in a charity shop when she passed on and was in the window for weeks. Then I saw it again on top of a scarecrow in one of Mr Sheepshanks' fields and it did a wonderful job scaring away the rooks.'

'It's a fashion statement,' Tom told them, tongue-in-cheek. 'I think it's rather eye-catching. Actually, it's a gift from Mrs Gosling. She knitted it especially for me.'

At the mention of the cleaner's name, the teachers pulled faces.

Mr Cadwallader snorted. 'The only thing that wretched woman would be disposed to knit for me is a shroud,' said Mr Cadwallader. 'I'm afraid she has little time for me and I have no time for her. She's a menace. Nothing in my classroom is where I can find it once she's been in rearranging things. She goes mad with the tin of polish and air freshener. The place smells like a brothel – not that I've frequented such a place,' he added swiftly.

'She speaks to me as if I were an infant,' said Mrs Golightly, 'or like a care assistant in an old people's home talking to a deaf resident and telling her to eat up the rice pudding.'

'Anybody would think she runs the school the way she carries on,' Miss Tranter put in. 'I'm sick and tired of her telling me what I should or shouldn't do. She's a cleaner, for goodness' sake.'

'Assistant caretaker,' Tom told her mischievously.

'I've asked Mr Gaunt to speak to her a number of times,' she said, ignoring the interjection.

'I think Mr Gaunt has got other things on his mind at the moment,' observed Mrs Golightly, giving a small smile. 'I saw the way he went out to meet the new parent with that silly expression on his face when I was looking through the window this morning. He's never done that before. He couldn't take his eyes off her. Clearly he's infatuated with the woman.'

'Mrs Stanhope strikes me,' said Joyce, 'as the sort of woman who is fully aware of her attraction and is able to twist men around her little finger.'

'As I've said, she's a damned fine-looking woman,' said Mr Cadwallader. 'She has what most men look for in a woman – beauty, brains and breeding.'

His colleague could be describing Janette, thought Tom wistfully, and wondered what her life was now like in Nottingham.

To Tom's satisfaction and surprise, Leo settled into life at Risingdale School with remarkable ease. The teacher had imagined that the boy would find things difficult and daunting; he felt a child so very different from the other pupils and starting at a new school would experience problems. When Tom had come to live in Risingdale – an 'off-comed-un', as Toby Croft might say – a stranger with a strange accent, the Dales people had at first appeared reserved, unforthcoming and suspicious of the newcomer. He soon discovered, however, that once they had got to know him and he had made an effort to know them, as well, that underneath their reticence there was an unspoiled humour and friendliness. 'You will find the Dales people are not quite as talkative as the Irish,' The Reverend Pendlebury, the local vicar, had told Tom. 'They can even be a bit stand-offish at first, but they are warm and friendly once you get to know them. They might be economical with words but, when the occasion arises, they are not afraid of voicing their opinions and they do so bluntly.'

The children at the school, unlike the adults in the village, were far from reserved, unforthcoming and suspicious when Leo entered the classroom on Tuesday morning. From the very first day, the pupils made the new boy feel welcome, explaining how things worked in the school, involving him in their games and asking him questions about himself and his background. They seemed genuinely interested in this unusual boy.

Despite Leo's stature, delicate appearance and genteel manner of speech, the boy appeared extremely confident and demonstrative. He was not afraid of giving his opinions, sharing his ideas and taking an active part in the lessons. Charlie, in particular, made Leo feel welcome. It appeared to Tom, as he saw them chattering away at break times and working together in class, that Charlie seemed to have found a kindred spirit.

As Leo waited for his mother to collect him on the Tuesday afternoon, Tom stood with him by the classroom window and asked him, 'So how was your first day at school?'

'I really enjoyed it,' he replied. 'I didn't like my last school. It wasn't just the bullies, there was a teacher. Mr Wright was his name. He used to say, "My name is Wright and I am always right." That was rather silly, I thought. Teachers aren't always right, are they, Mr Dwyer?'

'Well, I'm certainly not,' Tom replied. He recalled Mr Runswick, his tutor at college, telling the students that a good teacher is always prepared to admit to his pupils his or her ignorance and error, for it is a sign of strength rather than of weakness.

'Mr Wright once spelled a word incorrectly on the blackboard and I pointed it out to him,' Leo told the teacher. 'He said I was being impertinent. I never said anything after that.'

'Well, I'm not the world's best speller, Leo,' Tom told him, 'so if I make a mistake, I won't mind at all if you point it out to me.'

Leo thought for a moment. 'You're the best teacher I have ever had,' he said. 'Oh, there's my mother waiting in the car. I must run. Goodbye, Mr Dwyer.'

6

It was during one Friday morning lesson when Leo left the class 'gobsmacked', as they say in Yorkshire. The week before, Tom had told the children about the legend of Boggle Hole, a secluded and mysterious spot on the east coast of Yorkshire, a place he had visited with the children when he was a student-teacher at the school in Barton-in-the-Dale.

'The name Boggle Hole,' he had recounted, 'comes from the word "boggle" or goblin. It was a sort of mischievous elf who is said to live in small caves or holes in cliff sides. In local folklore,' he went on to explain, 'a boggle is a kind of pixie or brownie—'

'Chocolate brownies are my favourite biscuit,' Marjorie had shouted out. 'My gran makes them.'

'Mr Dwyer,' a girl had said, 'I'm a brownie.'

'Ah, but this is a different sort of brownie, Carol,' Tom had told them. 'This is a sort of goblin or elf and it's not a biscuit, Marjorie.'

'I'm in the cubs, Mr Dwyer,' a boy had said. 'I've got six badges.'

'That's interesting, David,' Tom had replied, 'but let me get on with the story. No more interruptions.'

'Yes, shurrup,' Vicky had shouted, 'I want to hear what happens.'

'I can manage without your help, thank you, Vicky Gosling,' Tom had told her sharply. 'Now these pixies or brownies would, if treated kindly, be happy to help with household chores, in return for a saucer or two of milk. Mean and ill-tempered householders would find boggles rather less helpful. Stories have been told of boggles smashing dishes or blowing soot from the chimney all over the house. Boggles were often believed to have healing powers, and sometimes the villagers would bring their sick children to holes in the cliff sides, called "hob holes", where boggles were thought to live, in the hope that the children would be cured. There are some people who believe that boggles were something made up by local smugglers to keep customs officers away.'

Following the lesson, Tom had asked his pupils to talk to parents and grandparents when they got home and see if there were any traditional Yorkshire legends and folk tales of the area they could share with the class. He was more than pleased with the response, for several of the children came back to school with interesting tales and they volunteered to relate them to the others.

That morning, the first speaker, the pretty girl with mousy-brown hair and large pink glasses, came out to the front and announced with great assurance, 'I'm going to tell you about the legend of Gentleman Jack Joiner told to me by my grandfather.' She cleared her throat theatrically and spoke in a loud and confident voice.

'In the seventeenth century, there was a lot of traffic passing through Bloxton and Skillington and this attracted highwaymen. One famous highwayman was called Gentleman Jack Joiner. He was only small and had a posh voice and dressed really nicely.' She glanced for a moment in the direction of Leo, who stared back at her intently. 'Anyway, that's why he was called Gentleman Jack. When he had robbed the coaches, he galloped off on a grey mare, called Lady, to Risingdale and counted his swag at the King's Head. The story goes that he had an argument with the landlord of the inn who knew who he was. The landlord told the soldiers, who came in the dead of night to arrest Gentleman Jack, but he was warned by the landlord's daughter and escaped by climbing through the bedroom window.'

'So Gentleman Jack got away,' said Tom.

'Oh no, Mr Dwyer, he was shot through the heart and they hung his body up on the gallows at Snig Hill as a warning to others.' The girl thought for a moment, peered through the large spectacles and said, 'You may think that this is not a true story, but on some nights, when it's dark and still, my granddad says you can sometimes hear the clatter of horse's hooves and see the ghost of Gentleman Jack galloping out of the mist towards the inn. He said that he once was coming out of the King's Head when he saw the ghost.' She gave a smile. 'My gran said it was probably the drink talking.'

Tom laughed. 'Well done, Carol,' he said. 'That was a splendid effort.' He looked at a heavily freckled boy with a head of shiny, copper-coloured hair, 'Now, Simon, your turn next. Let us hear about your folk tale.'

The boy made his way out to the front and faced the class.

'This is the legend of the Lost Farmer of Hardraw,' he announced. 'Now before I start, I need to warn you it's a really scary tale and it might put the wind up some of the lasses.'

'It'll not put the wind up me, Simon,' Vicky shouted out, 'so gerron with it.'

Tom shook his head and laughed. 'No, I don't expect it will, Vicky,' he said. There was little that frightened that particular pupil, he thought. He recalled the occasion when a dead rat had been removed from the loft above the classroom. 'Crikey, that's a big one,' Vicky had said, not at all fazed by the sight of the fat black rodent. No, like her grandmother, there was little to alarm Vicky Gosling.

'So,' said Simon, 'this is the legend of the Lost Farmer of Hardraw. The story comes from the time of Henry VIII and has been passed down by the monks of Jervaulx Abbey who had a chantry chapel at Hardraw. A farmer murdered another farmer and buried him near the beck, but the body was washed out of the ground when the beck flooded. The corpse, all white and mouldy, was taken to the monks, who thought the dead man had killed himself and had chucked himself into the beck. The body was buried at the crossroads on the moor with a stake through the heart. That's what they did with suicides in those days. Over the years, the murderer felt tormented by what he had done and went to the murdered man's grave to beg his forgiveness. Guess what happened?'

'What?' chorused the class.

'I'll tell you what happened,' said Simon, putting on a spooky voice.

'Well, gerron with it!' Vicky shouted out.

'Thank you, Vicky,' Tom told her. 'We can do without your interruptions. Carry on, Simon.'

'One sunrise a drover and a boy who were taking their cattle across the moor to the fair came across the murderer, stone dead, stretched out over the grave, his face burned to a crisp and the blade of the knife that he held, melted in his hand. He had been struck by a thunderbolt.'

'And I bet that years later, his ghost wanders the moor moaning and groaning and crying out for a proper burial,' said a small gangly boy with a squint.

'Not as far as I know, it doesn't,' said Simon, shrugging.

'It would have been a better story if there was a ghost in it,' remarked Vicky.

'Well, there wasn't!' snapped Simon.

'Let's move on,' said Tom.

Several more children related the tales they had heard from members of their families. Marjorie fascinated the class with the story of the Kelpie or Waterhorse that lived in the weedy depths of the River Ure.

'It appears only a few times in the year,' explained the girl, 'and rises out of the water like a white ghost. Then it sweeps over the meadows looking for its prey. Those it catches will be pulled underneath the water and never seen again.'

Leo, who had been listening attentively, raised a hand. 'This story is probably an invention of grown-ups to frighten children and keep them away from deep water. Don't you think so, Mr Dwyer?'

'Yes, you're probably right,' answered Tom.

Christopher, who was sitting at the back, gave a grunt.

Then it came to the turn of a tall, fat, moon-faced boy with lank black hair. This was Colin Greenwood. When Tom had first encountered this pupil, the boy had been surly and unco-operative. He would sit at the back of the class scowling and doing the minimum amount of work. Over the weeks Tom got to know this angry and unhappy child and began to under-stand why he behaved as he did. Colin had lived on an isolated farm with his father who, following the death of his wife, had let the place go to rack and ruin. He had also taken to drink and became moody and bad-tempered. He had had little time for his son. Like his father, the boy had been desperately unhappy, grieving over the death of his mother. He had hated the cold, dark, draughty farmhouse a good few miles from the village, he had hated school, he had no friends and had told Tom that he was 'no good at anything'. Then it was discov-ered that the boy had a real talent for art and, encouraged by his teacher, he went on to win prizes for his paintings in the county competitions. His self-esteem soared. Then when his father sold the farm and moved into a cottage on Sir Hedley's estate, to become the assistant gamekeeper, the boy's attitude changed for the better. Tom now smiled as he saw the boy, who a few months before had been difficult and disruptive and who had made little effort with his schoolwork, come forward to recount the folk tale.

'This is the story of the black dog of Coverdale,' he told the class. 'I went into the library at Clayton on Saturday and found it in a book. It's the legend of a big black beast, which comes with a warning of death. Sometimes it appears headless and other times it is described as having eyes like pewter dishes. People walk around a barn seven times and make a wish and the dog suddenly materialises. If it turns its back, then you will die within the year, but if it puts its paws on your shoulder, you will get your wish. That's all, really.'

'Well done, Colin,' said Tom. 'That was another cracking tale. Now you have all—'

'Excuse me, Mr Dwyer,' interrupted Leo, raising his hand again. 'May I tell you about a legend?'

'Yes, of course,' said the teacher.

The new boy came out to the front of the room. He looked at the expectant faces before him and then began in a quiet but confident voice.

'This is an old Yorkshire legend and I think it's really interesting. Would you like to hear it?'

'Yes,' chorused the class, sitting up in their seats.

Leo began. 'My grandfather lived in an old house on the North York Moors, a very old house, built hundreds of years ago. It was in the middle of the countryside and was a cold, dark, spooky place and even in summer it always seemed to be chilly and in the shadows. In the house there was a secret room that was very small, almost like a big cupboard really, hidden under a floor in one of the bedrooms. It was a priest hole and at the time of old Queen Elizabeth, when priests were hunted down and those who hid them arrested and killed, the room was a hiding place. It had remained undiscovered until 1950, when my grandfather was having some repairs done and the workmen found it. When they opened up the room, guess what?'

'What?' chorused the children, fascinated by the tale.

'Inside was a skeleton.'

'Oh my God!' exclaimed Vicky.

'Just listen,' Tom told her.

'The skeleton was dressed in tattered clothes and holding a decaying prayer book and a wooden cross,' continued the boy. 'It was the body of a Father Alban who had been hiding there and had starved to death. His name was in the prayer book. It was reckoned that the people who owned the house had been arrested and didn't tell anyone about him.'

'Poor man,' sighed Marjorie.

'Go on, Leo,' urged Simon.

'Well,' said the boy, 'the story goes that on a certain night the ghost of the priest wanders the house. It is on his feast day, which is the twenty-second of June, when he appears. My grandfather has heard strange knockings and creakings in the night on this very day.'

'Mr Dwyer! Mr Dwyer!' interrupted Simon. 'At Halloween I heard some strange knockings and creakings from my mum and dad's bedroom. I thought they were these ghoulies and ghosties and things that go bump in the night, and I went to see what it was and when I opened my parents' door, my mum and dad were in bed and—'

'I think we will let Leo get on with his story,' Tom butted in quickly, not wishing to go down that particular road.

'So once when I was little I stayed at the house . . .' continued Leo.

'Oh my God!' exclaimed Vicky again. 'You actually stayed there?'

'Just listen,' Tom repeated, 'and I don't think the mention of God is a very good thing to do. I certainly don't think The Reverend Pendlebury, who is in school today, would approve if he heard you, and I don't like it either.'

'My dad says a lot worse than that, Mr Dwyer,' the girl answered. 'You should have heard him when he found some of his dead sheep stuck in the snow.'

'Let's get on with the story, shall we,' said Tom, not wishing to go down another particular road.

'I did stay there,' Leo told the wide-eyed children, 'and guess what?'

'What?' chorused the class again.

'It was the twenty-second of June when I stayed there.' The room went completely silent. 'And guess what?' Leo asked the class again.

'What?' shouted out the class.

'I saw something.'

'W . . . what did you see?' gasped Simon.

Leo could be on the stage, thought Tom. How cleverly he had related the tale, quietly and deliberately, adding details and building up the suspense like a seasoned actor.

The boy inhaled deeply. 'Do you really want to know?' he asked playfully.

'Yes! Yes!' cried the children.

'It was a cold, dark, windy night and I was sleeping in the bedroom, the one with the hidden room underneath, when the clock on the church tower struck twelve. I woke up. It was now the twenty-second of June.'

'Oh my g . . . giddy aunt,' cried Vicky.

'I peered above the blankets and there at the bottom of my bed was a shadowy figure.'

Carol put her hands over her ears.

'It was huge and its hands were outstretched as if to clasp me in its ghostly arms.'

'What did you do?' asked Tom, as spellbound as his pupils.

'I buried my head underneath the bedclothes until morning.'

'I'd have wet myself,' said Simon.

'When it became light,' continued Leo, 'I peered over the top of the blankets and the figure had gone.'

'You saw the ghost of Father Alban?' asked Carol in a hushed voice.

'Oh no,' replied Leo, a mischievous expression on his face. 'The figure turned out to be nothing more than the shape of a person. It was the outline of the statue of Jesus with outspread arms that was on the dressing table. The moon must have cast a shadow on it in the night, making it look larger.'

The children breathed out noisily and then clapped.

'Well, that was quite some story,' said Tom. 'Thank you very much for that, Leo. I don't think anyone can better it.'

Vicky waved a hand in the air like a daffodil in a strong wind.

'I reckon I could, Mr Dwyer,' she claimed. 'Wait until you hear the story that my gran told me about the Phantom Knitter of Nether Norton, who murdered her husband with a pair of knitting needles.'

At lunchtime Tom found the local vicar in the staffroom. The Reverend Michael Pendlebury was a plump, cheerful, rosy-faced individual wearing a cassock and a clerical collar. He was in school to take the infant assembly.

'Good morning,' Tom said to the cleric.

'And a good morning to you, Mr Dwyer,' he replied. 'And what a lovely morning it is, too.'

'How did your assembly go?'

'Oh, not too bad,' the clergyman replied, 'although the children can be rather excitable at times, but one has to accept this with young children. Sometimes parents in my congregation apologise about the noise the children make at the services at St Mary's, but I tell them not to worry. After all, it was Jesus who said, "Let the little children come to me, and do not hinder them, for the Kingdom of God belongs to these." To me there is nothing like the sound of little children's voices. Mrs Golightly tells me that you have a new addition to your class.'

'Yes, young Leo. His mother is the artist who's renting the former Methodist chapel.'

'Mrs Stanhope.'

'You've met her?'

'No, no, but I have heard mention of her. I intend calling in to introduce myself. I am told she's a delightful woman.'

'She is,' agreed Tom. He decided it wasn't appropriate to mention the boy's illness.

'So how is the young man settling in?' asked the vicar.

'Amazingly well,' said Tom. 'Leo was entertaining us all this morning with an interesting ghost story. It's a good job you didn't come into my classroom this morning, Reverend Pendlebury. You would have put the fear of God into the children wearing your cassock.'

'I sincerely hope not,' replied the clergyman, looking puzzled.

Tom explained about the topic they had been studying and briefly related Leo's story. 'I guess if you had walked through the door dressed as you are,' he said, 'the children would have thought that poor Father Alban had come back to life.'

'I don't recall a Father Alban,' said the cleric.

'He lived a long time ago,' Tom told him. 'He was a character in an old Dales legend we were hearing about.'

'You should have asked me to speak to the children about ancient Yorkshire folk tales,' said the vicar, smiling with benign pleasure. He rested his hands on his chest and leaned back in the chair. 'I consider myself something of an authority on local legends, you know. My talk to the members of the Hull Literary and Philosophical Society went down very well, even if I do say so myself. Mr Walker, the President, was most complimentary. But that is by the by. As I said, I could have talked to the children and told them about St Alkelda.'

'I can't say that I have heard of him,' admitted Tom.

'Not a man, Mr Dwyer. She was a Saxon princess and a revered nun. The legend is that two Viking women during Danish raids of about AD 800 strangled her to death.' He sighed. 'Terrible times. The church at Middleham is dedicated to St Alkelda and a stained-glass window in the west window of the north aisle shows her martyrdom. The church was a Royal Peculiar until the mid-nineteenth century.'

'What's a Royal Peculiar?' asked Tom. 'I've never heard of it.'

'A Royal Peculiar is a church that belongs directly to the monarch and not to any diocese and does not come under the jurisdiction of a bishop,' explained the vicar. 'The Reverend Harry Topham, the noted cricketer, served as rector at St Alkelda's.'

'Well, I never.' Tom gave a thin smile that conveyed little more than feigned interest. He was ready for a break and his lunch and glanced surreptitiously at his watch. The teachers, as was their custom on Friday lunchtimes, had retired to the King's Head and left Mr Gaunt to 'hold the fort'. Tom was eager to join them.

The vicar once started was not a man to be put off his stride. His sermons were noted for their length and for him sharing with his congregation his considerable historical and biblical knowledge. Once he had a captive audience, there was little chance of stopping him.

'Interestingly, during the restoration of the church in 1878,' he continued, 'female bones were discovered under the floor in the north aisle where the saint was said to have been buried. Near the church is St Alkelda's Well, which is said to have healing powers. People today still visit the well to drink the waters.'

'Fascinating,' said Tom, smiling tolerantly.

'Oh, and there's a tree in the churchyard at Coverdale that is held in awe as sacred. The vicar there was telling me that a man used to come every Sunday morning with his family to pray under the tree. Of course, these old customs and beliefs go back to pagan days. Many were adopted by the early Christian Church. Now the legend of St Oswine of Deira, a greatly venerated Yorkshire saint in the Anglican Communion, is most intriguing . . .'

It was a good ten minutes before Tom could extricate himself with the excuse that he was on playground duty. He then hastened down to the King's Head to join his colleagues.

Tom usually went for a run on Saturday mornings. The day was icily cold but bright and clear, so he decided to take a longer route than usual. He ran by Rattan Row, the terrace of pretty, rose-coloured stone cottages owned by the local squire, and the squat, grey-stone former Primitive Methodist chapel, now an artist's studio. He passed by the Norman church with its spire spearing the sky and the adjacent imposing Victorian vicarage built in shiny red brick with its broad gravel drive curving through an overgrown, untended garden. He ran on by the King's Head and the post-office-cum-general-store and, skirting the village green and duck pond, where a few coots and moorhens paddled at the water's edge, headed up a narrow track, his feet crunching on the frosted grass. A magpie strutted along a white stone wall as he passed and then a fox appeared, stepping delicately across the path ahead of him, his brush down and snout up, unafraid, unconcerned. In the fields, black-faced sheep foraged hungrily, cropping the hay the farmer had spread out before them.

After a mile Tom arrived at a farmstead and caught sight of an old man and a girl leaning on a five-barred gate observing a lone sheep. At their feet was a black and white collie, which looked up at the child expectantly. Tom recognised one of his pupils – the pretty girl with the mousy-brown hair and pink glasses, who invariably had a wide smile on her face. Nobody had a more comprehensive knowledge of sheep rearing than young Carol. When she saw her teacher, the girl waved madly and shouted, 'Hello, Mr Dwyer.'

Tom ran to join her. He bent and panted to catch his breath.

'You're up bright and early,' said the girl. She turned to the old man before Tom could reply. 'This is my teacher, Granddad,' she said. 'You remember meeting Mr Dwyer when we took the tup to Mr Gaunt's farm last year to fettle the yows.'

'How do,' said the old farmer. He was a short, stocky man with a face the colour and texture of leather that had been left out in the rain. His bright eyes rested in a net of wrinkles. The man wore a greasy brown cap as flat as a cowpat, green corduroy trousers tied at the knee with string, a thick tweed jacket with elbow patches and substantial boots.

'Good morning, Mr Midgley,' replied Tom. 'And how are you?'

'All reet,' replied the farmer.

Tom had lived in the Yorkshire Dales long enough to know that when someone asks of a farmer how he is keeping, the reply is invariably, 'All reet.' The poor man might have been pulled out from under a tractor with two broken legs and a fractured skull and, if asked how he was, he would still answer, 'All reet.'

'It's a grand day,' said Tom. 'Makes you glad to be alive.'

'Mebbe,' answered the farmer.

Tom joined them at the gate and looked at the sheep. It had a white head and legs and a blue-grey fleece.

'What breed of sheep is that?' he asked.

'He's a Herdwick tup, Mr Dwyer,' Carol told him. 'He's getting old now, lost a few teeth and his eyesight's not too good, so we've brought him down from the tops.' She pushed the pink glasses up on her nose. 'He thinks he's in heaven after where he's been, up there in the cold and wet with not much to eat, doesn't he, Granddad?'

'Aye, he does, love,' agreed the old man.

'He's called Lazarus,' continued the girl. 'Granddad called him that after a man in the Bible who came back to life. Our tup was buried in a snowdrift for days until our sheepdog sniffed him out. We thought we'd lost him. Most sheep would have died but he came out and trotted off, didn't he, Granddad?'

'Aye, he did, love.'

'You see, your Herdwicks are a very hardy breed, Mr Dwyer,' the young sheep expert told him. 'They're a Cumbrian breed and can withstand the harsh winters better than most other varieties of sheep because their fleece is as thick as a carpet and keeps them warm and dry in all weathers – hail, rain, sleet, wind – and they can live on less than any other breed, can't they, Granddad?'

'Aye, they can, love,' said the old man. He patted her head affectionately.

'Your granddaughter certainly knows her sheep, Mr Midgley,' said Tom.

'Aye, she does that,' responded the farmer. 'Our Carol's been born to this life and knows more about sheep than some graduate with a fancy degree from an agricultural college.'

'Granddad thinks Lazarus deserves a bit of TLC after all the tupping he's done over the years.'

'So he's now enjoying his well-earned retirement,' said Tom. The old farmer suddenly became animated.

'Not ruddy likely,' he snapped. 'T'old fella's still got it in him. He's not past it yet, not by a long chalk. You know what they say: "There's a dreadful sting in a dying bee." In his time, that tup has served over a hundred yows and we've had some of the best lambs we've ever had. That old tup has fathered more show-winning offspring than any tup in this part of the Dale. I reckon come next autumn he'll still be up for it, won't he, Carol?'

'I reckon so, Granddad,' replied his granddaughter, nodding sagaciously. 'This is Meg, Mr Dwyer,' she told the teacher, looking down at the collie.

The animal pricked up its ears as if understanding that she was the topic of the conversation.

'Granddad bought her for me from Mr Gosling. Mr Croft bought her first from Mr Gosling but he took her back because he said she was no good, so we bought her, didn't we, Granddad?'

'Aye, we did, love,' said the old man.

'She'll make a fine pet for you, Carol,' said Tom.

'It's not a ruddy pet!' snapped the old farmer. 'It's a working sheepdog.'

'Granddad's helping me to train her,' said the girl.

'Toby Croft couldn't train a circus flea,' barked the old farmer. 'He wouldn't know a good dog if he saw one and he's so crooked, when he dies they'll put a spanner on his head and screw him into the ground.'

'My granddad doesn't like Mr Croft, do you, Granddad?' said the girl, a pert little smile on her face.

'No, I don't, love,' growled the old man.

'But he's done us a good turn by taking Meg back because now we've got her.'

'She's a fine dog,' said Tom.

'You see, Mr Dwyer,' said Carol, 'you have to train a sheepdog properly. I take Meg for a long walk every day before school, teaching her to come back when called. If she sees a sheep, her tail drops, she crouches down and draws closer. It's her instinct, you see, to round up sheep. To get her to work well and understand what to do, you have to use patience and kindness, teach her to lie down, walk to heel and come back on command. You don't need to raise your voice, do you, Granddad?'

'You don't, love,' agreed the old farmer, smiling and looking at the child with love in his eyes.

'It's all about trust,' said the girl.

Tom recalled what his young pupil had said as he continued with his run. She was right. Teaching was all about patience and kindness and, more importantly, about trust.

On his way home, Tom caught sight of Charlie and Leo in a field. They were running down a slope, laughing and shouting and shrieking with delight, their arms spread wide like the wings of birds in flight; two little boys in the open air enjoying the great sense of freedom; the simple pleasure that generations of children before them had enjoyed. Their hands were muddy, their trousers wet, their faces flushed with exertion. The teacher stopped at the gate and watched for a moment before continuing his run.

7

That afternoon Mr Gaunt decided to take a walk into the village. He had made a determined effort to look smart that day and wore a clean white shirt and green bow tie, a finely cut sports jacket, stylish cord trousers, a heavy tweed over-coat, kid gloves and brown brogues, all of which he had purchased the previous week from the gentlemen's outfit-ters in Clayton. A wide-brimmed hat sat rather rakishly on his head.

Toby Croft, on his way to deliver some sheep to a neighbouring farm, stopped his tractor at the sight of the headmaster striding purposefully down a path leading to the village dressed like the Lord of the Manor.

'Goin' someweer special, Gerry?' he asked, nosy as ever.

'No, no, just taking the air.'

'What are thy all dressed up fer, then?'

It was a very rare occurrence for Mr Gaunt, when not on his farm, to be seen in anything other than his shapeless jacket, baggy flannels and shoes that had seen better days. He was not a man who usually cared much about his appearance.

'It is good idea to get out of the work clothes and spruce oneself up once in a while,' replied Mr Gaunt. 'You ought to try it yourself sometime, Toby.' And, with that, he set off at a brisk pace.

He found Mrs Stanhope, standing, hands resting on her hips, in the middle of the main room of the former Methodist chapel. The door had been left open to disperse the smell of paint. She was dressed in a white cotton blouse, a loose-fitting, very becoming scarlet woollen jacket and voluminous trousers tucked into Russian-style boots. The wave of bright blonde hair was gathered up into a black toque. She was directing two young decorators, who gazed at her like little boys staring longingly at an array of sweets in a shop window. They were hanging on every word. Mr Gaunt stood for a moment at the door watching her. She looked as cool, handsome and exquisitely turned out as when he had first met her.

'May I come in?' he asked.

Mrs Stanhope turned and gave him one of her dazzling smiles.

'Yes, of course,' she replied. 'Do come along in.' She turned back to the decorators. 'Do excuse me for a moment.'

'My goodness,' said Mr Gaunt, looking around, 'I hardly recognise the place. It used to be rather dark and austere when I was a lad.'

The cracks in the plain, off-white walls had been filled in and were being decorated in a buttery yellow. The high cross-beams had already been painted in a pastel blue, the pale wooden floor had been newly sanded and polished and the doors had been freshly varnished. There was a huge easel, two long pine tables and matching bookshelves and cupboards.

'Mr Cockburn, the minister, has been most generous and helpful,' she said. 'He is allowing me to redecorate the chapel as I would like it and he insists on covering the costs.'

'Well, it certainly needed some renovation,' he answered. He was surprised that the minister had agreed to pay for the redecoration. What a persuasive woman she was, he thought.

'You remember the chapel when you were a boy then, Mr Gaunt?' she asked.

'Oh yes,' he replied. 'Every Sunday the whole family would attend the services, come rain or shine. They were never to be missed. The chapel would be packed and the whole village would resound with the singing. My grandfather Nicholas Gaunt was a stalwart here. He was a notable lay preacher who taught at the Sunday school and sang in the choir. I recall one occasion, when he was telling the children to be honest and kind, and a bluebottle landed on the lectern in front of him. My grandfather raised a hand, as big as a spade. "The devil can lead thee into sin," he pronounced gravely, "as surely as I swat this fly." He brought his hand down with a resounding smack and the fly buzzed off. He thought for a moment and eyed his young congregation, who sat open-mouthed. "Aye, well," he said, "I reckon there's 'ope for thee yet."'

Mr Gaunt chuckled. 'He was a remarkable man, my grandfather, with a strong sagacity and a dogged determination, and, like many a Yorkshireman, he was plain-spoken and a bit daunting until you got to know him. I often think about him. He was a significant presence in my young life and it was he who encouraged me to work hard at school and make something of myself. He understood that the only way to advance in life is through education. I'm sorry, I'm rambling on. I do sound like a schoolmaster, don't I?'

'I find it very interesting,' said Mrs Stanhope.

'Perhaps you're just being polite.' He laughed. 'I have been known to pontificate.'

'No, really,' she said. 'I really do find what you say interesting.' She admired the man's inner calm and practical wisdom. 'I can't say that my grandfather bothered much about my education and my school was mostly concerned with deportment and getting us to speak properly. "Straight deeds, straight words and straight backs" was the motto. I did, however, have a remarkable and somewhat eccentric art teacher, Miss Camomile, who encouraged me to pursue my real interest. Speaking of school and education, Leo loves it at Risingdale. He has never felt quite as happy and settled.'

The headmaster smiled. 'We are delighted to have him. He's a bright and well-behaved young man.'

'He's out bird-watching with Charlie, his new friend, this afternoon. They were up and out at the crack of dawn.'

'Ah, young Charlie Lister,' said the headmaster. 'He's a very clever and considerate lad and was awarded a major scholarship to go to the grammar school, which is no mean achievement. He was encouraged and coached by Mr Dwyer.'

'Leo has certainly taken a liking to his teacher,' declared Mrs Stanhope. 'He's a very dedicated young man.'

'Yes, Mr Dwyer is an excellent teacher,' agreed the headmaster. 'We are very lucky to have him. At our recent inspection by HMI he was singled out as being outstanding.'

'Really?'

'Indeed. Well, I mustn't keep you talking to me all day.' He tipped the brim of his hat and wished her a good afternoon.

Soon after Mr Gaunt had left, the vicar arrived.

'Michael Pendlebury,' he said, holding out a priestly hand for her to shake. 'I thought I would call in and introduce myself. Please do not hesitate to call upon me should you need any help or advice. You will discover that we are a close-knit community here in Risingdale but friendly enough when you get to know us. "The Yorkshireman's affections are strong and deep-founded, but well-concealed and those who come to live amongst them must be prepared for certain uncomplimentary comments, pithily expressed." Not my words, Mrs Stanhope, but a paraphrase of Mrs Gaskell writing about Charlotte Brontë. "They are a strong race," she wrote, "in both mind and body."'

Before she could answer, he talked on. 'I do hope you will come to like us here in Risingdale and, as I have said, do not hesitate to call upon me if I can be of any assistance. My door is always open. I should be delighted to show you around St Mary's, our ancient church. It has many fine features, including a quite exceptional and possibly unique Norman doorway in the nave. It has a rare ornamentation, with chevron mouldings in a most lavish fashion, and the chancel is Norman too.'

The vicar, she reflected, looking into the animated features of the cleric, was certainly unlike the Yorkshire folk he so painstakingly described. She had not yet had the opportunity of getting a word in.

'The transept is Early English,' continued the clergyman, his voice becoming even more enthusiastic. 'The altar tomb of Sir Marmaduke D'Arbour on the north side of the chancel is the only one of its kind and in a wonderful state of preservation. It must be numbered amongst the most well-preserved in the country. It escaped terrible defacement by some of Cromwell's soldiers.' He paused to take a breath. 'And I believe you are an artist?'

'I am, and a sculptor,' she told him.

'A sculptor,' he repeated. 'How splendid. We have some most noteworthy carvings and singular statues at St Mary's, which I am sure will interest you.'

The clergyman, perceiving he had a captive audience, continued to give the newcomer the benefit of his extensive historical knowledge until the arrival of yet another visitor. The next caller was a tall young man with high cheekbones and large dark eyes who, like Revd Pendlebury, was wearing a clerical collar. He had a studying look, neither friendly nor unfriendly, as he inspected the room.

'I guess you know the local Methodist minister,' said the vicar.

'Yes, we have met,' replied Mrs Stanhope.

'Well, I should be making tracks,' said the vicar, 'and leave you in the capable hands of Mr Cockburn. It has been a pleasure to have met you, Mrs Stanhope.' With that he departed.

The minister clasped his hands behind his back and looked around, a thoughtful expression on his face. 'I hardly recognise the chapel,' he said after a long pause.

'That is what Mr Gaunt said,' replied Mrs Stanhope. 'He called earlier.'

'I see.' The clergyman stared for a moment at the ceiling. 'Yes, indeed, there has been quite a transformation. It's quite surprising what a coat of paint can do.' There was another long pause.

'Actually, I hope you don't feel that I've changed very much,' she said. 'It was good of you to let me do a bit of decorating and make the place look a little more cheerful. I do hope I have not overdone it.'

'No, not at all,' he answered. 'I remember the chapel when I was growing up,' he continued, echoing the words of Mr Gaunt. 'It was once at the heart of the village, this chapel, and brought together people socially as well as for services and a shared enthusiasm for music and communal singing. Wesley is said to have preached here, and rumour has it he was stoned out of the village by some of those who attended the established church. It was rumoured that they were put up to it by the vicar.' He gave a small smile. 'I am pleased to say that Revd Pendlebury and I get on very well. A regular visitor here was the great Methodist preacher Joseph Bentley, who founded the Bradford coffee houses and wrote the book *How to Sleep on a Windy Night*. Yes, this was once a thriving place.'

'I guess it is rather sad for you, Mr Cockburn, to see what it has become?'

'Yes, in a way, but times change, congregations dwindle and organised religion doesn't have the same appeal. There is the other chapel in the village, of course, and I do have a regular and very active congregation there with a variety of activities – the ladies' fellowship, Bible study meetings, Sunday school, coffee mornings. I am thankful that this chapel is now being put to some good use. I understand you intend it to be an artist's studio?'

'Yes. The space is very suitable. Actually, there was something I was meaning to have a word with you about, so I'm pleased you called in. It concerns the large window at the front with the coloured glass.'

'Methodists don't usually go in for bright-coloured glass in the chapels,' the minister told her, 'but it is rather plain. This window was a bequest from a member of the former congregation. You will see it has a dedication at the base.'

'I don't suppose there is any chance of having it replaced? I would, of course, cover the full cost and arrange for its removal. I should like to change it to plain glass.' Mrs Stanhope braced herself for the disapproving response. 'You see, I do need as much natural light as possible.'

'Mrs Stanhope,' said the minister, smiling widely, 'it has been my intention since becoming minister here in Risingdale of relocating the window and installing it in the other chapel. I just haven't got around to it. It serves no purpose here, in a deserted building, and over time I guess would become damaged. I shall arrange for its removal and have it replaced with clear glass.'

'That's very kind of you, Mr Cockburn,' she said, 'but I must insist on covering the cost.'

'No, no, Mrs Stanhope, that won't be necessary. I am sure the window will be appreciated by my congregation when it is installed in its new home.'

'I am sure it will,' she agreed.

'You know,' said the clergyman, 'I am intrigued as to what appealed to you about our village. It's very isolated and unhurried up here. Very little of any consequence happens and people lead a simple life.'

'That is the appeal, Mr Cockburn,' she told him. 'I wanted to escape London for a while, to get away from all that hustle and bustle, crowds and noise. Travel on the tube and you will sit crammed between miserable, tired-looking commuters going into the city with their pale faces and hollow eyes. I wanted more peaceful surroundings. Up here at the top of the world there is a beautiful natural light, pure colours and unsurpassed scenery, which offer plenty of inspiration for the artist.'

'Someone seeking the solace of a rustic life,' observed Mr Cockburn.

Mrs Stanhope smiled. 'Something like that,' she replied, before adding, 'for the moment anyway.'

The minister smiled back. He had taken an instant liking to the newcomer. She had an attractive quality: an inner grace.

'Well, I hope your endeavour with the studio is successful,' he said. 'I shall let you get on. It has been a pleasure meeting with you and I do hope we might see you at one of our coffee mornings.'

'Yes, I should like that,' she replied.

Some minutes after the minister had left, a portly, red-cheeked individual with a bombastic walrus moustache above a wide mouth, dark hooded eyes, prominent ears and tightly curled hair on a square head appeared. He looked as if he had walked straight out of the pages of an historical novel.

'May I help you?' asked Mrs Stanhope.

'Good afternoon,' said the man. 'Allow me to introduce myself. I am Sir Hedley Maladroit. I just thought I'd show my face and see how you are getting along.'

'Sir Hedley,' she said. 'That's very kind of you. You are my landlord, are you not?'

'Indeed I am, and I hope that my estate manager has sorted everything out to your satisfaction with regard to the cottage?'

'Admirably,' she replied. She approached him and shook his hand. 'I am very taken with it. It is just what I want.'

'Pleased to hear it. Anything you need doing, just get in touch.'

'That is most kind.'

'So how long do you intend to remain here, if you don't mind me asking?'

'Do you know, Sir Hedley, I haven't decided. For the moment Risingdale suits me fine. The area has quite an unusual beauty and a rare atmosphere and the light up here takes your breath away. There is such a wonderful breadth of space and tranquillity about this Dale.'

'You are something of a poet as well as an artist, Mrs Stanhope,' the baronet told her. There was a twinkle in his eye. Like Mr Cockburn, he was very taken with this attractive and articulate woman. 'Yes, you are quite right, there is something very special about the scenery up here: the rich greens of the fields in summer, the russets and purples in autumn and then the vast whiteness when it snows in the winter. I never tire of the changing seasons. I am pleased you like it. I hope you are finding the people friendly.'

'Yes, indeed. I have had so many offers of help: the head-master of the village school, my son's teacher, the vicar, the Methodist minister; they have all been most kind and I have a delightful neighbour in Mrs Lister. I am sure you know her.'

The baronet gave a small cough. 'Ah yes, Mrs Lister, a nice lady.'

'I believe she rents her cottage from you as well?'

'Yes, she does.' He gazed around the room and then, pluck-ing the pocket watch from his waistcoat and checking the time, he gave a small bow and wished her a good day.

'Buzzing around 'er like 'orseflies around a cowpat,' announced Toby Croft to his wrinkled companion with the toothless gums. They were leaning on the bar of the King's Head that lunchtime. The farmer raised his glass of beer, drained the contents and wiped the froth from his mouth with a flourish. 'I'll tell thee this, Percy, they was in an' out o' that studio of 'ers like rats up a drainpipe. Fust it were Mester Gaunt, dressed up like a dog's dinner, then t'parson, then Methody minister and then guess who walked in through t'door as large as life and as 'appy as a clam at 'igh watter?'

'Who?' asked Percy.

'Only Sir 'Edley 'imself, that's who. Like t'Queen Bee she was, wi' them blokes dancin' attendance on 'er. As my old grandmother used to say, "t'sweeter t'perfume, t'greater number o' flies that buzz round t'bottle".'

'And how come you know all this?' asked the landlady, who came to join them. 'Were you one of the horseflies buzzing around the cowpat?'

'I was not,' the farmer answered. 'I 'appened to be talkin' to one o' t'painters an' decorators, if tha must know. 'E were tellin' me who 'er gentlemen callers were. 'E were another who was bespotted wi' 'er. "Oh, she's a luvverly lady," 'e said all starry-eyed, "an' so suffisticated."'

'Well, I only hope she doesn't hear that you referred to her as a cowpat,' said the landlady, 'and the vicar and Mr Cockburn don't get to hear you compare them to buzzing horseflies.'

The farmer had indeed been wishing to meet the newcomer about whom he had heard so much but when he arrived at the chapel to see her for himself, she had gone, leaving the decorators to get on with the refurbishment. Toby had spent a good ten minutes inspecting the renovations before quizzing the two men.

'She sounds a bit of all reight to me,' ventured Percy, rubbing a bristly chin. 'I might drop in theer an' see 'er missen.'

'I can't fer the life o' me see what a woman like 'er is doing up 'ere anyroad,' Toby continued. 'I mean, there's nowt 'ere to suit t'likes of 'er. It's back o' beyond. Seems to me to be a very rum do. There's summat not reight abaat it.'

'Shall we 'ave another?' asked Percy, pushing his empty glass in his companion's direction. It was Toby's turn to get the next round in.

Mrs Mossup smiled. Little chance of that, she thought.

'Nay, I'll not bother,' replied the farmer. 'I shall 'ave to be off.'

'I hope you haven't left your wife out in the cold again,' scolded the landlady.

'No,' Toby replied. 'She 'as 'er chores to do. I left 'er choppin' wood this mornin'.'

'How that poor woman puts up with you, I shall never know,' said Mrs Mossup.

'She never complains,' he answered. 'In my book, women were created for t'comfort o' men. There's an owld Yorkshire sayin' which applies to my missis: "'Tis a good 'oss what never stumbles an' a good wife what never grumbles".'

'Aye and theer's another owld Yorkshire sayin' an' all,' volunteered Percy, staring at his empty glass with a scowl on his wrinkled features, 'an' one what applies to thee: "Let thi pocket be thi guide, an' t'brass last thing tha parts wi".'

While the locals were discussing the new addition to their community, Tom set off to visit his aunt who lived in the neighbouring village of Barton-in-the-Dale. That Saturday he had invited her out for afternoon tea at the Ring o' Bells café but first he needed to call into the village store in Barton for a copy of the *Clayton Gazette*. He was interested in an article in the colour supplement about Marston Castle, the ancient ruin near Risingdale where some unusual coins had been discovered. It had been Colin Greenwood's father who had found the coins – a rare Charles I silver shilling minted in York at the start of the English Civil War and an even rarer and very valuable Scarborough siege piece, a small and insignificant-looking misshapen rectangular silver coin that was now exhibited in York Museum. Mr Greenwood had given the coins to Tom, who had asked Dr Merryweather, the curator of the Clayton Museum, to look at them. Their rarity and value had then been established and Mr Greenwood had come into a not insubstantial amount of money.

The proprietor of the village store in Barton-in-the-Dale was a round, red-faced woman. She was the eyes and ears of the village and was adept at gleaning information from everyone who walked through the shop door. No customer could escape from her premises without being subjected to a thorough grilling. The intelligence, thus gleaned, would then be circulated throughout the village. Anyone in the area wanting to know the latest news or savour a juicy piece of gossip only had to speak to Mrs Sloughthwaite, and should they ask, they would receive a detailed and colourful account of the latest happening or hear a fascinating fact about someone's personal life.

Tom found the woman in question leaning over the counter in the shop and resting her substantial bosom and her dimpled arms on top. She was in intense and hushed conversation with a customer, but she broke off suddenly when he walked through the door. She raised her heavy frame and gave a broad smile.

'Well, if it isn't young Mr Dwyer,' she said good-humouredly, rising from the counter.

'Good afternoon,' said Tom.

Mrs Sloughthwaite turned to her customer, a tall, thin-featured woman in a knitted hat. The woman wore her miserable expression like a comfortable old coat and stood with her arms folded tightly over her chest. She surveyed Tom unblinkingly.

'You know Mr Dwyer, don't you,' said the shopkeeper. 'He's Bridget O'Connor's nephew, used to be a professional footballer until he damaged a cartridge and had to give it up. He now teaches at the school at Risingdale. He trained and got fully matriculated here in Barton at the village school.'

The customer gave an audible sigh. 'Yes, I do know who he is,' she replied testily. 'I don't need you to give me a potted history of his life, thank you very much. I was on the governing body at the school, you might recall, before they kicked me off. I am well aware of who he is.'

'Good morning, Mrs Pocock,' said Tom brightly.

'Morning,' she answered, managing a slight smile.

'Well, what can I do for you, Mr Dwyer?' asked Mrs Sloughthwaite.

'I would just like a copy of the *Clayton Gazette*, please,' he told her.

'Not looking for a job, are you?' probed the shopkeeper.

'No, not at all. There's an article in the supplement about the castle near Risingdale I'm interested in.' He placed the money for the paper on the counter.

Mrs Sloughthwaite left the coins where they were. This customer was not going to escape until he had undergone a thorough interrogation. She was more interested in his personal life than a boring newspaper piece about some old castle.

'So you are still happy teaching in Risingdale then, Mr Dwyer?' she asked.

'Yes, very happy.' He slid the coins nearer to her, keen to be away.

The shopkeeper left the money where it was.

'I guess there's not much going on for a young man like you up there. It's such an insulated place.'

'There's plenty to keep me occupied,' Tom told her.

'I find that difficult to believe,' remarked Mrs Pocock. 'There's nothing up there bar the church and the pub. We don't have any truck with them at Risingdale. I've always found them a funny lot, slow-witted and unfriendly.'

'Actually, I've found them the very opposite,' Tom told her.

He could have informed the customer that the residents of Risingdale had little time for those in Barton-in-the-Dale, who they claimed were inbred and witless.

It was true there was little communication between the residents of Risingdale and Barton-in-the-Dale. The two villages might have been in different hemispheres. Though there was little more than ten miles between them as the crow flies, the two communities had little contact. It was said that this mutual antipathy dated back to well before the last century, over a dispute about sheep rustling. People in these parts had long, long memories. The old saying that 'In Risingdale they put t'pigs in t'church to listen to t'parson' was frequently quoted in the village.

'It suits me,' Tom continued. 'Now if I might have the paper, Mrs Sloughthwaite. I need to make tracks.'

'Not courting yet, then?' asked the shopkeeper, taking no notice.

'No, not yet.'

'I should think that a good-looking young man like you would have the lasses queuing up.'

Tom gave a small smile but didn't respond.

'I guess you're worried that they might close it,' remarked Mrs Pocock.

'I'm sorry?' said Tom.

'The school. From what I've heard, the County Council are shutting the small village schools right, left and centre. I've heard a rumour that Skillington School is up for the chop. I reckon yours might be the next on the list.'

'I think Risingdale is pretty safe,' Tom told her.

'For the moment,' said Mrs Pocock.

'I've no doubt that Mr Dwyer won't have any trouble finding another situation if they do close it,' Mrs Sloughthwaite observed, leaning on the counter. 'I'm sure if a post came up here in the village school he'd be in with a very good chance. I'm certain he'll be given a good testimonical from his headmaster, and Mrs Stirling has always spoke very highly of him.'

'That's as may be,' muttered the gloomy customer.

'I shouldn't be at all surprised if he's been head-hunted already,' said the shopkeeper. She tilted her head as if awaiting a reply.

Tom smiled but didn't say anything.

'Mrs Stirling hasn't mentioned that there might be a job coming up here in Barton then?' asked the shopkeeper.

The head teacher had indeed mentioned to Tom that a post would be advertised in the coming weeks and that she was hopeful that he would apply, but he wasn't going to divulge this to the shopkeeper to be broadcast around the village and beyond. Mrs Sloughthwaite often assured her customers that anything they told her would not go any further, that she was 'the very soul of indiscretion' but disclosures to her had a habit of spreading through the community, and in quick time. 'So, nothing's been said?' she persisted.

'No, no,' Tom told her. 'Well, I should be off.'

Realising that she was not getting any further with the interrogation, the shopkeeper moved on. 'Have you heard about Lady Wadsworth?' she asked.

'No.' He sighed. When would he be released, he asked himself.

'She's reached her final destination,' Mrs Sloughthwaite told him, shaking her head with appropriate solemnity.

'I'm sorry?' said Tom, puzzled.

'Passed on.' She leaned over, rested her bust on the counter and lowered her voice. 'She's now in Abraham's bosom.'

'She means she's dead,' explained Mrs Pocock bluntly.

'I'm sorry to hear that,' said Tom. 'I only met her briefly when I worked at the school here. She was a nice lady.'

'Oh, indeed she was,' agreed the shopkeeper. 'Never put on hairs and graces, always congenious and patronising on the few occasions she called in the shop and was nicely spoken with it as well. Of course you can always tell a person with breeding. They are so gentrificated.'

Mrs Sloughthwaite was a mistress of the malapropism and amazingly inventive non sequiturs. She managed to mangle the English language, often to the amusement of her customers.

'They're no better than anyone else, these titled people,' remarked Mrs Pocock. 'As my mother used to say about the rich and powerful, "It's all very well them acting superior but everyone has to wipe their own bottoms".'

The shopkeeper pulled a face. 'Lady Wadsworth was never superior or supersidious with me and I never went cowtowing to her. I take people as I find them and I found her very friendly.' She looked at Tom. 'Poor woman had these abominable pains in her stomach, which turned out to be appendicitis. Fancy getting that at her age. I mean, she was no spring chicken and not long for the world, but it was not a nice way to go. Anyway, from what Mrs Robinson, who works for the undertaker, told me, complications set in and she got parrotinitis. Well, as they say, she's now gone the way of all flesh. No one can escape the Grim Raper, and that's a fact.'

'Why don't folks say things in plain English?' asked Mrs Pocock. 'People don't die any more, they "pass away" or "go to meet their Maker" or "are in the arms of Jesus" or "up with the angels". Dead people are called "the departed". I've always been one to call a spade a spade. When my husband was taken to Clayton Royal Infirmary with his heart attack, the nurse told me he'd "gone to a better place". I thought she meant they'd moved him to another hospital. I never cottoned on that he was dead.'

'Collapsed in the kitchen, didn't he,' said Mrs Sloughthwaite, shaking her head and pulling a mournful face. 'Came back from the pub with pains in his chest and the next thing, you found him stretched out prostate on the kitchen floor. The paraplegics gave him artificial insemination, but it did no good.'

'I don't wish to be reminded of it,' retorted the customer. 'It was very upsetting – and for your information, it was not artificial insemination, it was artificial respiration.'

'Well, I really must be off,' said Tom. 'My Auntie Bridget will be wondering where I've got to.'

'Her house has been sold,' announced the shopkeeper.

'My Auntie Bridget's?'

'No, no, Lady Wadsworth's,' said Mrs Sloughthwaite. 'Limebeck House. Some distant cousin has come in for the lot.'

'Where there's a will, there's always a relation,' said Mrs Pocock cynically. 'Not cold in the coffin before relatives come creeping out of the woodwork to see what they've been left.'

'From what I've heard,' the shopkeeper went on, 'he's going to turn it into one of those state of the ark hotels.'

'I can't see there'll be any call for a fancy hotel in these parts,' remarked Mrs Pocock.

'I really must go,' said Tom looking at his watch.

Mrs Sloughthwaite scooped up the change on the counter and passed over a copy of the newspaper.

'Give my best wishes to your Auntie Bridget,' she said.

When Tom had gone, the shopkeeper stretched upright. 'It's beyond my apprehension why a young man like that wants to teach right the way up at the top of the Dale at the backside of beyond.'

'He might not be there much longer,' said Mrs Pocock. 'Not if his school closes.'

8

Mrs O'Connor, Tom's Auntie Bridget, was a dumpy, round-faced little woman with the huge, liquid brown eyes of a cow and a permanent smile on her small lips. Her hair was set in a tight perm. Like many of her race, she embroidered the English language with the most colourful and original axioms and expressions, most of which were throwbacks to her old Irish grandmother who had a caustic comment, saying or snippet of advice for every occasion.

'So, what's on your mind?' she asked her nephew as they sat at the corner table in the Ring o' Bells café later that afternoon.

'What makes you think I've got something on my mind?' he asked.

'Now come along, Thomas. I've known you all your life, so I have, and I can see in your eyes that something is bothering you.'

Tom thought for a moment, staring down at his coffee cup. 'Do you remember when we were in this café before? We were sitting at this table and I got up to pay the bill and started talking to a young woman with red hair. Her name is Janette. You asked me who that attractive young lady was and I replied that she was just somebody I had met in the village and that she was nobody special.'

'Yes, I do,' replied his auntie.

'Well, the thing is, she is . . . well, was someone special. We started off on the wrong foot. I nearly knocked her off her horse when I was rushing to the interview for the teaching post at Risingdale. I came a bit too fast around a sharp bend and she was crossing the road and I nearly hit her. She gave me a real earful. Anyway, since then we have got to know each other and I have come to really like her, rather more than that. She's clever, strong-minded, opinionated and independent and I think I was falling in love with her. I thought perhaps that she shared my sentiments.'

'And?' asked Mrs O'Connor.

'Clearly she didn't and felt there was no future in any relationship. She was promoted at the bank where she worked and has been offered a manager's position in Nottingham. She's moved there.'

'And you miss her.'

'Yes, I miss her,' he replied sadly.

'Relationships are like glass,' his auntie told him. 'They are easily shattered, so they are. When they break it's better to leave the broken bits alone rather than hurt yourself picking up the fragments.'

'Easier said than done,' he answered. 'I can't seem to stop thinking about her.'

'You'll never plough a field, Thomas, if you keep turning it over in your mind,' she said.

'No, I guess not.'

'Well, I won't offer you any more advice. As my Grandmother Mullarkey was wont to say: "Hearing other people's advice is like listening to someone singing out of tune. You don't want to hear it." I understand that it must be painful to love someone more than they love you.' She patted his hand. 'Skinned knees are easier to mend than a broken heart.'

'It's not just thoughts of Janette that're on my mind,' he said. 'There are rumours that more of the small village schools will be closing and Risingdale might well be near the top of the list. Last term we had a reprieve after the headmaster spoke to education officials, but it was only a stay of execution and I fear the axe is likely to fall, and rather sooner than later.

I was in the village shop in Barton earlier and Mrs Pocock seemed sure the school at Risingdale will eventually close.'

'Sure, I'd take no notice of Mrs Pocock,' said Mrs O'Connor. 'The woman has awful notions of herself, so she does. She knows just about enough not to eat herself. Don't you worry yourself, Thomas, you'll have no trouble at all in getting another job. Why, Mrs Stirling would have you back at the drop of a hat. She is always telling me that you are greatly missed, so she is.'

'Well, yes, she did mention that there would be a job at her school and thought I might be interested.'

'There you are, then,' said his aunt, 'you don't need to worry your head about getting another teaching post.'

Tom recalled a conversation he had had the previous term with the head teacher of Barton-with-Urebank school, in which she had mentioned that a post would be coming up and he would be in with a good chance – more than a good chance – should he apply. He also recalled Mr Gaunt's words that if he decided to move on and seek another position at a larger and more challenging school, he would not stand in his way.

'The thing is,' Tom told his auntie, 'were I to get another teaching position, I would feel pretty bad about leaving midway through the year. I really like the children, I couldn't work with better colleagues and the headmaster has been more than supportive.'

'Well, Thomas,' said his auntie, 'there's only you can decide what to do. But as . . .'

'Grandma Mullarkey was wont to say,' he interrupted, smiling and knowing that he was in for another aphorism from the old Irish sage.

'"May the most you wish for be the least you get,"' said Mrs O'Connor, completing the sentence and returning the smile.

* * *

On his way through the village later that day, Tom saw the light was on in the former Methodist chapel. He thought he would see how Mrs Stanhope was getting along and was interested to see what changes she was making.

'Hello, Mr Dwyer,' she said when she answered the door. There was the smell of fresh paint.

'I thought I would see if you are settling in and if there is anything I can be of help with.'

'That is good of you,' she answered. 'I have been over-whelmed by well-wishers. I was told that Yorkshire people tend to be a bit stand-offish and suspicious of strangers at first, but I have found everyone so very warm and welcoming. You and Mr Gaunt have both been most attentive. This afternoon I've had visits from the vicar, the Methodist minister and Sir Hedley Maladroit, amongst others, all offering help.'

'Yorkshire people are famed for their friendliness,' Tom told her, minded to add that they are also known for their curiosity. The appearance of this mysterious woman in their midst had undoubtedly caused comment and great interest amongst the villagers. He caught sight of a large sheet of paper on the easel. 'I see that you have started painting already,' he said, walking over to look. He was quite taken aback by the beauty and artistry of the watercolour. The scene depicted was a vast, snow-covered landscape: dazzling, sun-drenched fields and a pale blue sky, sweeping contours to the distant windswept summits and the dark, scattered woodland creeping up the steep slopes. 'But this is amazing.'

'Oh, there's a great deal to do on it yet,' she said.

'It's taken my breath away. It's magnificent.'

'That is most kind of you. It's to form part of a commission of a number of paintings depicting scenes of the Yorkshire Dales,' she told him. 'It's for a book. I also want to include some portraits of the country people who live and work here. In this, you may be able to help me.'

Tom laughed. 'I'm not an artist, Mrs Stanhope.'

'No, I want to represent some interesting characters, people who are close to nature, and I wonder if you might introduce me to some of the locals – the cleaner at the school, for example. She has a most striking countenance and the caretaker, he has very distinctive features.'

'Mrs Gosling and Mr Leadbeater,' said Tom, thinking of the small plump woman with the broad face and darting eyes and the thin man with the wild white hair and bushy eyebrows that met above his beak of a nose, giving the impression of a permanent scowl. 'Yes,' he agreed, 'they are certainly distinctive.'

'And there's a farmer with especially arresting features. He has a long bony face rather like a horse, creased and weathered. He is ideal for a portrait.'

'That would be Toby Croft,' Tom told her, picturing the grizzled old farmer.

'So, I wonder if you might introduce me?' she asked.

'Yes, of course,' he answered, 'but you might return the favour.'

She smiled. 'I was warned that Yorkshire folk never like to do anything for nothing.'

'There's an old Yorkshire saying I was told when I came to live in Risingdale,' said Tom:

> 'Ear all, see all, say nowt;
> Eyt all, sup all, pay nowt;
> And if ivver tha does owt fer nowt,
> Do it fer thi sen.

She laughed. 'So how might I be of help?'

'I have a young man in my class,' Tom told her. 'His name is Colin Greenwood. When I first started at the school, he was a rather rude and uncooperative boy. He had recently lost his

mother and was going through a bad patch, angry at the world
and moody. Anyhow, he changed when it was discovered he
has a talent for art and—'

'I am guessing that you wish me to look at his work and give
him some advice on how he could improve it?' She thought
for a moment. 'I am happy to do this, but must warn you that
I will be honest in my assessment. In the past when I have
been asked to give my views on other artists' efforts, my
comments have not always been well-received. Some people,
I'm afraid, do not take kindly to criticism, however constructive it might be. I think it is unhelpful to tell people that all
their work is very good if it is not, just to boost their self-
esteem. I won't, of course, be unsympathetic of the boy's work
but will hopefully offer him some helpful advice and practical
criticism and ideas for how he might improve it. I think, before
I speak to him, I should look at some of his paintings and if I
feel he does have some talent, then I will gladly give him my
opinion of it.'

'That sounds fine to me,' said Tom. 'Actually, I have one of
Colin's pictures on the wall in my cottage. I could pop back
home and get it, if it's convenient now.'

'Why not call around to the cottage,' she said. 'It's Number
8 Rattan Row. I shall be in tonight.'

Arnold Olmeroyde grazed a small flock of his sheep in the
field that separated his farmhouse from Tom's cottage. The
old farmer had proved an excellent neighbour. He had rebuilt
the drystone wall around Tom's cottage, repaired the gate,
delivered a load of logs and arranged for the chimney to be
swept. Coming back from school, Tom often found a basket
of eggs or a bag of potatoes and onions and sometimes a
pheasant skinned and prepared for the oven on his doorstep.
Mr Olmeroyde's granddaughter, Marjorie, a pupil in Tom's
class, had appeared one Sunday morning with a beautiful

multicoloured quilt that her grandmother had made as a housewarming present.

Arriving back at his cottage later that day, Tom was met at his gate by Marjorie in a state of panic. She waved a small shepherd's crook with a curled horn handle, the right height for a child.

'Mr Dwyer! Mr Dwyer!' cried the girl. 'You have to come!'

'Whatever is it?' he asked.

'There's a dog in my granddad's field and it's attacking the sheep.'

Tom ran with the girl to find the flock frantically running around in circles chased by a small wire-haired terrier. The dog was racing and snapping and jumping up at the terrified sheep. It dived at a ewe and sank its teeth into the animal's ear. Tom ran into the field bellowing to drive the dog away, but the animal continued to savage the sheep.

'Give me your crook, Marjorie,' he told the girl.

She handed it to him.

Tom ran up to the dog and caught it a heavy blow across its head with the crook, laying the animal flat out on the grass. The animal struggled to its feet, snarled and showed a set of sharp teeth. Its muzzle was smeared in blood. The dog backed away when Tom moved forward brandishing the stick. A moment later a man ran across the field, yelling and waving his arms in the air.

'You hit my dog!' he cried as he approached. He was breathless and red in the face.

Tom did a very convincing impression of a furious farmer. 'Are you out of your bloody mind?' he shouted angrily. 'Look what your dog's done.' He pointed to the mauled sheep, which had run off to join the rest of the flock. 'What sort of idiot allows his dog loose into a field full of sheep?'

'He was only playing,' the man told him, his face still flushed in anger.

'Don't be so bloody stupid!' barked Tom. 'Didn't you see what it was doing to the sheep?'

'You hit my dog,' repeated the man, reaching down to pat the animal, which now lay panting at his feet.

'Yes, I hit your dog and if I had had a shotgun, I'd have shot it. Farmers have a legal right to protect their livestock and can shoot any animal that attacks their sheep or cattle.'

'I shall call the police,' blustered the man. 'You hit my dog.'

Tom gave a hollow laugh. 'Oh, the police will be informed, make no mistake about that, and it's likely you will be prosecuted and your dog put down.'

'Put down!' cried the man.

'That's the law,' Tom told him. 'I need your name and address so I can report this.'

'Eh?'

'The police need to be informed.'

'Well, I'm not giving it to you,' said the man belligerently. He put his dog on the lead. 'Come along, Basil.'

Tom was not going to let him get away so easily. He blocked his way. 'Just a minute, I haven't finished with you yet. Have you no sense of responsibility, letting your dog loose in the country? Thoughtless people like you come into the countryside and have no consideration for the people who live and work here. Now, take your dog and get off this land.'

When the man had departed, Marjorie, who had been watching the exchange with a fascinated look on her face, approached Tom. 'That was telling him, Mr Dwyer,' she said.

'Silly man,' said Tom, giving her back the crook.

'You used a swear word, Mr Dwyer,' said the girl, giving a mischievous little smile.

Tom looked a little shamefaced. 'Yes, I did,' he replied. 'I was angry.'

'Don't worry, Mr Dwyer,' she told him, 'my granddad uses a lot worse words than that when he's angry and I won't tell anyone that you used that word.' She had a broad smile on her small face.

Tom went back inside to get ready for his visit to Mrs Stanhope. He showered and shaved, put on a smart white open-necked shirt and pair of new jeans and splashed himself liberally with aftershave. The doorbell rang. Mr Olmeroyde stood on the doorstep.

'Nah then, Mester Dwyer,' he said. He was a big man, six foot six at the very least, broad as a barn door with arms the thickness of tree trunks. 'This is fer thee.' He held a most beautiful shepherd's crook with a polished beech shaft and curved horn handle. 'Our Marjorie told me what tha did. Best have thy own crook so next time some daft bugger lets 'is dog loose on my sheep, tha can fettle it wi' this.'

'Thank you, Mr Olmeroyde,' Tom replied, taking the crook from the farmer, 'that's very kind of you, however, I don't imagine I shall be repeating the episode. I'm afraid I've got a bit of a temper.'

'Aye, our Marjorie told me that tha lost tha rag. She'd never seen thee so angry. Put fear o' God into that chap, so I 'eard.'

'That's the Irish in me, I'm afraid,' replied Tom. 'As a race we are known for our hot tempers.'

'Aye, well,' said the farmer, 'that's summat thy 'as in common wi' us Yorkshire folk, an' it's nowt to be sorry abaat.'

Number 8 Rattan Row was a pretty, rose-coloured stone cottage with mullioned windows and blue-slate roof. The interior was warm and comfortable and tastefully decorated. A log fire burned in the hearth and on the mantelpiece were photographs of Leo and a handsome man standing before a light aircraft smiling for the camera. On one wall were several colourful watercolours and prints.

Tom placed Colin's picture on a small table. Mrs Stanhope examined it for a time. The picture was of a ruined castle;

huge corner towers and half-destroyed walls of grey stone enclosed a large grassy space on which a few sheep grazed. Above, in a pale blue sky, a lone kestrel hovered.

'Where is this?' she asked.

'It's Marston Castle, high up in the Dale,' Tom told her. 'It was once on the land owned by Colin's father, who had a smallholding there. The farm was sold a few months ago to Sir Hedley Maladroit.'

'It's astonishing to find this huge fortress so remote.'

'That's what I said when I first came across it. I said to Mr Greenwood that it was the last thing anyone would expect up here away from everywhere.'

'I must go and see it,' she said, examining the picture more closely.

Tom was keen to know what she thought of Colin's effort. 'So, what do you think of the painting?' he asked.

'How old is the boy?' she asked.

'Eleven.'

'You are right, he has a talent,' she declared. 'It's a very atmospheric piece. The combination of the frosted fields and the blue sky captures the scene well. He has a very good eye for detail, composition and perspective. There are bold hues and firm outlines and the brushwork is expressive. I should be happy to see him. Perhaps his father could bring him to see me one Saturday afternoon when I am in my studio.'

'That's excellent,' answered Tom, delighted with the comments. 'And if you would care to join me for a drink in the King's Head this evening, I should be delighted to introduce you to some of the locals, including Mr Croft, the farmer with the distinctive features.'

When Tom entered the public bar of the King's Head later that evening, accompanied by Mrs Stanhope, all conversation stopped and the weathered faces of a few old farmers turned in their direction. He approached the bar and was soon joined by Mrs Mossup. She smiled and patted her crisp, newly permed hair.

'Doris,' said Tom, 'let me introduce you to Mrs Stanhope, who has just moved into the village.'

'Pleased to meet you, I'm sure,' said the landlady. 'I hear you are renting the old Methodist chapel.'

'That's right.'

'It's about time the place was put to some good use. I hope that you are settling in. You'll find it's a quiet but friendly place up here.' She stopped speaking as she saw Toby Croft approaching. 'I thought it wouldn't be long before he pushed his nose in,' she said. 'After a free pint, I shouldn't wonder. You keep your wallet in your pocket, Tom. You're too ready to buy that old rascal a drink.'

'Evenin', Mester Dwyer,' said the farmer.

'Hello, Toby,' replied Tom.

'Are tha all reet?'

'I'm fine and how are you?'

'Oh, fair to middlin', tha knaas,' he answered, holding his empty beer glass meaningfully before him.

'Now, you are just the man I was hoping I'd bump into tonight,' Tom told him.

'Oh aye?'

'Yes. This is Mrs Stanhope, who is renting the old chapel, and she is very keen to speak to you.'

'Speak to me?' The farmer looked uncomfortable and shifted nervously.

'That's right,' Tom told him. 'I said I would point you out.'

'Good evening, Mr Croft,' said Mrs Stanhope. 'I was hoping I might have a word with you.'

'If it's about the cowpat,' said the farmer, 'it was only a manner of speaking, nothing personal, you understand.'

'Cowpat!' exclaimed Tom.

'I din't mean owt by it or to cause any hoffence. It 'ave 'ad been better if I'd said moths around a candle or butterflies flappin' round a fragrant flower.'

'I have no idea what you are talking about,' said Tom.

'It weren't what I said about t'cowpat and t'orseflies then?'

'Not at all. Mrs Stanhope is interested in painting your portrait.'

'She wants to paint his portrait?' interjected Mrs Mossup. She gave an empty laugh. 'What's it for, the Chamber of Horrors?'

'You have a very expressive face, Mr Croft,' Mrs Stanhope told him. 'I want to portray in my pictures some typical Dales folk, those with distinctive features. I should like to paint you.'

Toby placed his glass on the bar, raised his grand beak of a nose and scratched his neck. 'Well, I 'ave been telled I 'ave an uncommon happearance,' he said. He looked meaningfully at the glass.

'Let me get you another pint,' said Mrs Stanhope, 'and we can talk about it.'

Sir Hedley Maladroit, JP DL, baronet, squire, landowner, lord of the manor, owner of half the properties in Risingdale and the land surrounding, controller of many of the villagers' destinies, peered over the top of the Sunday newspaper he had been reading.

'What was that?' he asked, blinking distractedly.

His wife, a hawkish-looking woman with a hooked nose and bright eyes, the kind of face that makes you think that at any moment you are about to be pounced upon, sighed theatrically.

'I do wish you would pay attention when I am speaking to you,' she said in the hectoring tones of an angry schoolteacher. 'I was remarking that the Methodist chapel is being rented by some artist woman who is turning it into a studio or some such thing. I met the vicar in the village and he was telling me.

One wonders why anyone would want to set up a studio in such a godforsaken place as Risingdale. I hope she's not some sort of bohemian and establishing a squat with a horde of hippies. From what Mr Pendlebury told me, she's painted the walls a garish yellow and the beams a bright blue. It sounds frightful. I can imagine what Mr Cockburn will say when he sees it.'

'Actually, she's a very nice woman,' remarked her husband, 'and she's decorated the place very tastefully.'

'You've met her!' It was a high-pitched, clipped voice.

'She's one of my tenants,' her husband told her. 'She's renting one of the tied cottages on Rattan Row and, for your information, she is not a bohemian, but a very elegant and attractive woman and clearly very talented.'

'You've been to her studio?'

'Yes, I have.'

'When?'

'I called in yesterday.'

'You never said.'

'I imagined you would not be interested, Marcia. If I mention anything to do with the estate, you look bored.' He glanced down at his newspaper.

'Hedley!' she snapped. 'Would you please put that paper down? I am attempting to have a conversation with you.'

Her husband folded his newspaper carefully and rested it in his lap. He stroked his moustache.

'So, what is she like?' asked his wife.

'I've just told you. She's very elegant and attractive.'

Lady Maladroit sighed. 'I mean, what sort of person is she?'

'Very agreeable,' he replied.

'And?'

'And what?'

'Is that all you have to say? It's like getting blood out of a stone. What sort of woman is she?'

'She is gracious and sophisticated.' He gave a small smile. 'Not the hippy type at all. We had a most pleasant conversation.'

'Do you know why she is setting up here?' asked his wife.

'I imagine she's looking for some peace and quiet.' He might have added 'like me', but resisted the temptation.

'What is she called?' asked his wife.

'Mrs Stanhope.'

'What's her first name?'

'Amanda.'

Lady Maladroit thought for a moment. 'Amanda Stanhope,' she murmured. 'I know that name. If it is the same person I'm thinking of, she's a well-known artist. I read about an Amanda Stanhope in the Sunday colour supplement a while ago. She has an international reputation and her pictures sell for thousands. Whatever is she doing up here? Well, well, some culture and refinement in the village at long last. I must go and see her. I have a mind to ask her here for tea. It would be a change to have a civilised conversation for once.'

'What was that?' asked Sir Hedley, who was looking down at the crossword on the back of the newspaper.

His wife sighed theatrically again and left the room.

The following Saturday afternoon, two visitors arrived at the studio. The man, dressed in a smart tweed suit and wearing a collar and tie and mustard-coloured waistcoat, was a tall, handsome individual of indeterminate age with a ruddy, weathered face and abundant black hair. He looked as if he had stepped out of a hot bath. He was accompanied by a fat, moon-faced boy with lank black hair.

The man introduced himself. 'I'm Richard Greenwood.' He rested a hand on the boy's shoulder. 'Mester Dwyer said that tha might tek a look at some of mi son's paintin's an' give 'im a few pointers like.' He stared at Mrs Stanhope with eyes as large and as deeply brown and shining as a fox's and thought what a fine-looking woman she was.

'Ah yes, Mr Greenwood,' she said, holding out a slender hand for him to shake and giving him a gracious smile. 'I'm pleased to meet you.' She looked at the boy half hidden behind his father. What an unfortunate-looking child, she thought; so unlike his father. 'You must be Colin.'

'Yes, miss,' mumbled the boy shyly.

The man gazed around the room. 'By the 'eck, it's a bit different in 'ere.'

'That's what everyone who has been to see the changes has said,' she told him. 'Mr Cockburn, the Methodist minister, has been most accommodating.'

He glanced around the room again. 'Aye, it's a bit different from when I cum 'ere as a kid.'

'So you remember the chapel as it used to be, Mr Greenwood?' she asked.

'Oh aye,' he said. 'I came 'ere every Sabbath when I was a lad with mi Grandma Greenwood cum rain or shine for t'morning service an' Sunday school. She was very religious, was mi grandmother. Mi granddad used to say that she were so godly she'd 'ave been at t'crib but Virgin Mary got theer fust. Before we set off fer chapel she used to scrub mi neck wi' a rough flannel an' a bar o' carbolic soap to get rid o' t'tide mark, as she called it, an' then started scourin' behind mi ears. I used to sit next to a lad who was a reight young tearaway. Stewart Pepper, 'e were called. Nice enough lad but as awkward as a sow in reverse. There used to be an old 'armonium in that corner an' t'woman who banged out t'tune was Miss Percival an' she were a reight old tartar. I remember one time when t'minister announced t'ymn "All things bright an' bootiful, all creatures gret an' small", Miss Percival lifts t'lid on 'er 'armonium an' out jumps these frogs an' toads what Stewart 'ad purrin afore t'service.' He laughed at the memory.

'One gret warty toad jumped on her lap and she let out such a scream. I don't reckon she thowt t'creature was all that bright an' bootiful that mornin'.'

The boy listened intently. There was a fraction of a smile on his lips.

He loved to hear his father speak like this. Mr Greenwood had not always been as talkative and good-humoured as he was that afternoon. It had been a dark and miserable time after the death of his wife and he had gone into a decline: moody, unpredictable, rarely speaking, drinking too much and sometimes not even bothering to wash. His grief had been palpable. The farmhouse roof began to leak and the wind blew with a vengeance through the window frames and cracked glass. Fences and walls remained unrepaired, sheep began to die and the machinery was left out in the snow and rain and began to rust. Despite the efforts of neighbours, who tried to help, things had gone from bad to worse. The farmer had just given up. Colin had been deeply unhappy and desperately lonely, stuck on the farm high up on the Dale with an uncommunicative father. He hated doing the chores and then sitting in the gloomy, untidy kitchen, dishes piled unwashed in the sink, listening to the endless rain spattering against the window, with hardly a word passing between him and his father.

His usual mode of dress – the shapeless grey cardigan, the old waxed jacket and threadbare jeans patched at the knees – had been replaced with a smart tweed suit and tie. They had moved into a cosy cottage on the estate, a world away from the cheerless farmhouse. The best change for Colin was that his father was now like his old self.

'I never liked that 'ymn, "All things bright an' bootiful",' continued Mr Greenwood now. 'Every Sunday t'kids 'ad to sing it. Chap what wrote it glamourised country life. It's not all glowin' colours an' purple-'eaded mountains an' pleasant summer sunshine an' as fer playing in t'meadows, I can just see mi dad lettin' me do that when there was work on t'farm to do. Farming up 'ere is tough. There was this verse what really med me mad:

> T'rich man in 'is castle,
> T'poor man at 'is gate,
> God med 'em 'igh an' lowly,
> An' ordered their estate.

'I allus thowt it were unfair somehow that we should all know our place an' not 'ope for summat better. I suppose that sounds a bit daft, me being one o' Sir 'Edley's game-keepers. I'm sorry, Missis Stanhope, I din't mean to give thee a lecture.'

'It's very interesting,' she said. 'I am sure that many of the villagers have memories of how the chapel used to be.' She turned to the boy. 'Now, speaking of castles, Mr Dwyer showed me the picture you painted for him of Marston Castle, which I believe is on the farm where you once lived. I thought your painting was very good.'

'You did?' said the boy, sounding genuinely surprised.

'Yes, you have a good eye for detail and composition. It was very striking. If you want to, you can come along to my studio next Saturday afternoon and I'll show you how you can develop your work. I shall teach you a few techniques. Would you like that?'

'Yes, miss,' replied the boy. 'I'd like that.'

'But you must really apply yourself, work hard and not get upset if you receive criticism. Now, you have some talent and I shall show you how to develop it but, as I said to your teacher, I don't say things are very good if they are not. You will get an honest opinion.'

'Yes, miss, thank you, miss,' said the boy.

'That sounds very Yorkshire to me, Missis Stanhope,'

said his father, chuckling. 'You don't need to be in Yorkshire long afore tha gets an 'onest opinion. We're straight-talkin' folk.'

'I would like something in return,' she said. 'I believe there is an old Yorkshire saying that "if ivver tha does owt fer nowt, do it fer thi sen".'

Mr Greenwood laughed. 'Yer speakin' proper English now, Missis Stanhope. I don't mind payin' fer 'is lessons, if that's what tha means.'

'It's not money I want, Mr Greenwood,' she told him. 'I should like you to sit for me to paint your portrait.'

'I'm no oil painting, Missis Stanhope,' he told her.

She explained about the book she was producing and how she wanted to include some portraits of Dales people.

'Well, I suppose I could,' he said. 'It would only be the head, would it?'

Mrs Stanhope suppressed a smile. 'Oh yes, just the head, not au naturel.'

'What's that mean, Dad?' asked Colin.

Mr Greenwood coughed and turned red. 'Never thee mind.'

'So, will you?' she asked.

'Well . . . all right then,' replied Mr Greenwood, 'we'll see you on Saturday.'

On their way home, Colin slipped his hand into his father's. 'She was a nice lady, wasn't she, Dad?'

'Aye, she was.'

'You liked her, didn't you?'

'Aye, she were very . . . nice.'

'You never told me about when you went to the chapel as a kid,' said his son.

'Did I not?'

'I like hearing about when you were young,' Colin told his father. 'Was Stewart Pepper your best pal when you were a lad?'

'Aye, I suppose 'e was. 'E were only a little un, not t'height of a decent dog; not much to look at an' not much up top either, but 'e were a real tearaway an' cheeky wi' it. I remember once there was this other daft 'ymn we 'ad to sing.

> God whose name is love
> 'Appy children we,
> Listen to t'ymn
> That we sing to thee.

'We were at Sunday school an' Stewart puts up 'is 'and an' told Miss Percival, wi' an impudent smile on 'is face, that sad children wee as well as 'appy ones.'

'What did she do?' asked Colin.

'She boxed his cars.' He put his arm around his son's shoulders and they both laughed.

9

It was later that afternoon that Lady Maladroit made her appearance at the studio. Mrs Stanhope, coming in from the small garden at the back of the chapel, found an imperious-looking woman with unnaturally hard and angular features gazing closely at the half-finished painting on the easel, her head tilted to one side and her lips slightly pursed.

'May I help you?' she asked.

'I did knock,' replied the visitor defensively. 'The door was ajar. I hope you don't mind me having a look around. I am Marcia Maladroit, Lady Maladroit. My husband is Sir Hedley. I believe you rent a cottage from us.'

'Yes, that's right,' replied Mrs Stanhope. She took an instant dislike to the woman with the sharp features and equally sharp manner who had walked uninvited into her studio and was now inspecting her painting.

'I trust the cottage is satisfactory?'

'Perfectly. How may I be of help?'

'I was passing and thought I would call in and introduce myself.' She awaited an answer but when one was not forthcoming, she continued. 'I see that you have made a few changes in here. Most colourful. Of course, I don't remember this chapel as it was. I am not a nonconformist. My husband and I are of the established church.' Mrs Stanhope remained silent. 'You will find these changes will not be altogether approved of by the minister.'

'Actually, Mr Cockburn has been most helpful and is happy with the changes I have made,' Mrs Stanhope told her.

Lady Maladroit raised an eyebrow. 'You do surprise me. In my experience, Methodists prefer a plain-featured building, unlike those of the Roman persuasion who tend to go the other way.'

'It is no longer a chapel,' she was told.

'Quite. And how do you like it here in Risingdale?'

'I like it very much. The scenery is outstanding.'

'Oh yes, the scenery.' She made a dismissive noise. 'I can't say that I like it here. It's like living in a time capsule. It's a wonder that they ever allowed gas or electricity up here, it's so backward. Frankly, I'm surprised that you have decided to live in such a place.' Again she waited for some response but none was offered. She continued. 'Life up here is so insular and claustrophobic. I guess you have discovered that the inhabitants of Risingdale are not all that welcoming.'

'I have found the people in the village to be the very reverse,' replied Mrs Stanhope. 'Everyone has been most friendly.'

'Really?' Her lips stretched into a thin smile. Lady Maladroit had taken a dislike to this woman, who seemed to disagree with her at every turn. 'I gather you are from London?'

'Yes.'

'I should love to return to London. I do so miss all the theatres and the exhibitions, the restaurants, shops and the nightlife. The person who tires of London, tires of life.'

'Wasn't it Dr Johnson who said that?'

'I used to live in London,' said Lady Maladroit, ignoring the comment. She sighed. 'I do so miss it.'

'Well, I must get on, so if you will excuse me . . .'

'I see you are in the middle of a painting,' she said, making no effort to move. 'It's very skilful.' Mrs Stanhope found the comment patronising but said nothing. 'I do know something about art,' Lady Maladroit declared. 'I worked in one of the top art galleries in London before I was married.'

'Which one?' enquired Mrs Stanhope, whose pictures had been exhibited in many of the most prestigious London art galleries.

'Poskitt and Placket Fine Arts.'

'I can't say that I have heard of that gallery, but then I don't know every art gallery in London.'

Lady Maladroit flinched a little but retained her superior smile. She stared at the large watercolour on the easel.

'Mr Poskitt, the gallery owner, always preferred small paintings. He said subjects were often spoiled by being treated on too large a scale. He used to say that a lot of life can be conveyed in a small space.'

'And was this Mr Poskitt an artist himself?' asked Mrs Stanhope. She emphasised the 'this'.

'No, but he knew a great deal about art.'

That is questionable, thought the artist, but she didn't feel like responding. She did not wish to delay this woman any longer.

'Tell me, are you the same Amanda Stanhope whose work appeared in a feature in the *Sunday Times* colour supplement a couple of months ago?'

'Yes,' she replied simply.

'You won some sort of art prize, didn't you?'

'I did, yes.' Some sort of art prize, she said to herself. She had received one of the most celebrated art awards in the country but Lady Maladroit had made it sound like something won in a tombola.

'I imagined it was you,' said Lady Maladroit. 'I remarked to my husband that I thought you were the same person. Actually, I am minded to purchase a painting for the drawing room at Marston Hall.'

Mrs Stanhope could not resist. 'Something small,' she said.

Lady Maladroit ignored the pointed remark.

'Sadly, my husband and I do not share the same taste in art. He likes pictures of horses and dogs, I prefer landscapes. Perhaps you have some of your work to show me.'

'I'm afraid not,' replied Mrs Stanhope. 'I only exhibit in London. All my paintings are sent to my agent there and she arranges a retrospective in the Strand Gallery each year. They tend to be on the large side. I am sure she would be pleased to send you a catalogue.'

'Yes, I should like that,' said the Lady of the Manor, and, with a dry little smile, she took her leave.

That evening Lady Maladroit acquainted her husband with the exchange she had had with Mrs Stanhope.

Sir Hedley was concentrating on his crossword when his wife entered the drawing room carrying the colour supplement of the Sunday newspaper and sat, straight-backed, in an elegant mahogany chair by the window and scrutinised the magazine. She remained silent, reading for a moment, and then spoke. 'I met the artist woman today,' she announced.

'Did you?' replied her husband, not looking up from his paper.

'I found her to be very cold and stand-offish.'

'Really?' He gave a slight nod of acknowledgement.

'She was most unsociable.'

'I found her very amiable,' said Sir Hedley.

'Well, of course you would,' she retorted. 'You are a man and I guess when she fluttered her eyelashes, you were like clay in her hands.'

'She's not a potter, is she?' he asked.

'What?'

'Nothing.'

'For someone who purports to know something about colour coordination, the way she's decorated the chapel is unbelievably tasteless. Are you listening to me, Hedley?'

'Every word.'

'I saw one of her paintings.' She huffed. 'They certainly were not my cup of tea. How anyone could pay an inflated price for something like that mediocre work, I will never know. Mr Poskitt would not have entertained them in the London gallery where I worked. Of course, the art critics, who actually know very little about real art, get it into their heads that such pictures are wonderful and then everyone wants one.' She picked up the colour supplement and flicked through a few pages. 'This is how her work is described: "Amanda Stanhope is one of the country's most celebrated and sought-after artists. Her work is remarkable in its dexterity – technically adventurous and uniquely vibrant. Using bold and dense brush strokes, she achieves startling textual contrasts within the parameters of a nuanced palette." What nonsense.'

'So I take it you won't be buying one of her paintings then?' asked the baronet, casually.

'Certainly not. I can't for the life of me understand why someone, supposedly so celebrated and sought-after, should want to leave London and come and live up here in the back of beyond.'

'Yes, you have already told me,' remarked the baronet. He was concentrating on a particularly puzzling crossword clue.

'Speaking of London,' said his wife, 'I thought I might spend next weekend there. My sister asked me some time ago to visit but I have never got around to doing anything about it. You have no objection, do you?'

'What?'

'Really, Hedley,' she snapped. 'I am endeavouring to hold a conversation with you. I said I am thinking of spending next weekend with my sister in London.'

'Good idea,' replied Sir Hedley, thinking that this would be the perfect opportunity for taking Charlie and his mother to Scarborough and avoiding having to explain his weekend away from home to his wife.

Lady Maladroit stared out of the window over the parkland and thought how she might broach the next problematic topic. She adopted an uncharacteristically conciliatory tone.

'The new assistant gamekeeper seems to be getting on well,' she said.

'Yes,' replied her husband. 'I'm very satisfied with his work.'

'I was wondering if his wife might consider becoming the housekeeper here. Since Mrs Gosling saw fit to leave, it's been quite impossible for me to find a suitable replacement.'

'Saw fit to leave,' repeated her husband. 'You sacked the woman.'

'Oh, let us not go over that again, Hedley,' said his wife. 'I made a mistake. I admit it. Do you think Mrs Greenwood might be interested in the housekeeper's position?'

'She died a few years back,' Sir Hedley told her.

'I wasn't aware of that.'

Perhaps if you took a little more interest in the lives of the people in the village, he thought, you might have been aware. However, he said nothing and returned to his crossword.

'Hedley,' she said, 'would you please put down your paper? I wish to discuss something with you.'

Her husband sighed inwardly, placed the newspaper on his lap and looked in her direction. He predicted it would be another complaint about something or other. His wife spent most of her life grumbling. It was so very tiresome.

'What is it?' he asked.

'I have received a telephone call from our son.'

'Oh yes?'

'James is so very miserable up there in Scotland. It's so cold and wet and you know how he is plagued with his bad chest. He is not at all happy with the position you found for him at the distillery.'

'You surprise me, Marcia,' he said sarcastically.

'The job is not suitable for his capabilities.'

'And what are his capabilities, may I ask?' enquired Sir Hedley. 'I spent over sixty thousand pounds on his education at a top public school and he left passing just the one exam – woodwork. Perhaps he should train as a carpenter.'

'He wants to come home.'

'Does he, indeed?' A grimace crossed his face.

'He's very sorry for the misunderstanding about my necklace and—'

'Misunderstanding!' interrupted Sir Hedley angrily. 'Misunderstanding! He stole it. There was no "misunderstanding", as you put it.'

'That's water under the bridge now,' said his wife, springing, as she had always done, to her son's defence. 'James is very contrite about that and about the situation with the barmaid at the King's Head.'

'Situation!' exclaimed her husband. 'He got the girl pregnant.'

'These loose-living young women tend to lead the boys astray—' began his wife.

'Marcia, don't blame the young woman. James was more at fault than she and, by the way, the young woman does have a name. She's called Leanne and very soon James will be the child's father and we the grandparents.'

The thought of her being the grandmother of the illegitimate child of the barmaid at the King's Head filled Lady Maladroit with horror, but she held her sharp tongue and decided the best course of action to sway her husband was not to provoke him further.

'James is very unhappy, Hedley,' she said. 'I appreciate why you had to send him away, but he assures me he has turned over a new leaf and promises to keep out of trouble if you allow him to return.'

The baronet grunted.

'So can he come home?' she asked.

Sir Hedley opened his newspaper. 'Very well,' he said. 'He can come home – but let me tell you this, Marcia: it will not be the return of the Prodigal Son and there will be no fatted calf on the table. He comes back on the understanding that he will find a job, whether it suits his capabilities or not, and if in a month he is still acting the playboy, then he is out on his ear. I hope I have made myself perfectly clear.'

'I shall give him a ring,' said Lady Maladroit, pleased with the outcome. She rose from her chair and left the room with a feeling of triumph.

The following lunchtime, Sir Hedley called into the King's Head. He felt it only right and proper to inform the landlady that his errant son would soon be returning to Risingdale. When he entered the public bar, everything went quiet and all eyes turned his way. It was a rarity for the local squire to be seen in the King's Head and the regulars, most of whom were his employees or rented land from him, were curious why he should be visiting. Prior to the baronet's appearance Toby Croft was putting a rambler right about how hard it was to farm in the area. The rambler had commented that the farmer was lucky to live in such an idyllic place.

'Tha wun't say that if thy 'ad to farm it,' Toby had retorted. It was his usual riposte when anyone mentioned the pictur-esque countryside. 'All you visitors see is bootiful scenery but if thy 'ad to live an' work 'ere tha'd happreciate 'ow 'ard it is. We 'ave nine month o' rain up 'ere an' three month o' snow. It's bloody 'ard, farming up 'ere.' The reality was that the old farmer didn't have to farm it. He hardly raised a finger. His ill-used son did all the work on the farm with precious little thanks or reward. Toby continued to describe how he had to trudge through thick snow or up to the knees in muck and mud to feed his 'beeasts' (in fact it was his son, Dean, who was given the task) and for precious little recompense, the price of sheep being what it was. 'I can 'ardly afford to get miself a pint.' He looked down at his glass expectantly.

On seeing the baronet, Toby broke off his lecture and shot to his feet as if on a spring, clutching his empty glass. The rambler, who had listened patiently to his tale of woe, had not been forthcoming with an offer of a drink for Toby, but the wily old farmer was not one to give up.

'Afternoon, squire,' he said, approaching Sir Hedley and touching a forelock.

'Good day, Mr Croft,' replied the baronet.

'We don't offen see thee in 'ere.'

'No, it's been quite a while.'

'I 'ope you an' yer good lady are keeping well.' He placed his empty glass prominently on the counter.

'Yes, indeed,' replied Sir Hedley, who had now reached the bar, where he caught the eye of the landlady. Mrs Mossup scurried down to greet him.

'Good afternoon, Sir Hedley,' she said deferentially.

'Good day, Mrs Mossup. I wonder if I might have a quiet word with you.' He glanced towards Toby Croft. 'In private, if I may.'

'Yes, yes, of course,' she said. 'If you would care to come through and into the parlour, I'll just serve this customer and come and join you.'

'Get Mr Croft a drink before you do, will you, Mrs Mossup,' Sir Hedley told her, placing a note on the bar.

'That's very decent of you, squire,' said the old farmer.

In the parlour, away from the eavesdropping Toby Croft, Sir Hedley came straight to the point and informed the landlady of the imminent return of his son. Mrs Mossup shook her head and sighed.

'James coming back to Risingdale,' he informed her, 'could cause something of a problem, particularly for your daughter. Of course, so far, we have been able to conceal the identity of the baby's father, but knowing how gossip and speculation spreads in the village, I guess it will not be long before the cat is out of the bag.'

'I guess not,' murmured the landlady.

'Now, far be it from me to tell you what to advise your daughter, Mrs Mossup, but I am of the opinion that it might be best if she remains in Scarborough for the time being. I can envisage all sorts of difficulties should she return at this time.'

'Yes, I think you are right, Sir Hedley,' agreed the landlady.

'Well, I am glad we agree on that,' he said. 'So tell me, how is Leanne keeping?'

'She's doing very well and coping.'

'And the unborn child?'

'Doing very well, too.'

'When you came to see me to tell me about the baby, I said that I would give your daughter every support I could.' He reached into his pocket and produced an envelope. 'I hope Leanne will accept this to help cover any costs she might incur.'

'That's really not necessary, Sir Hedley,' replied Mrs Mossup.

'I insist. It is the least I can do.'

He pressed the envelope into her hand.

'This is an unfortunate situation, Mrs Mossup,' he said, 'but we will have to make the best of it. I can't promise that my son will rise to the challenge and be a good father, but I shall certainly make sure your daughter and her child are well provided for. Be assured of that.'

While Sir Hedley and Mrs Mossup were in deep discussion, Toby Croft was holding forth at the bar with his drinking pal, who had joined him, speculating on why the local squire had paid the landlady a visit.

'There's summat afoot, Percy,' he said to his companion, tapping his nose.

''Ow does tha mean?'

'Well, it stands to reason. T'squire 'asn't set 'is foot in 'ere fer months an' then when 'e does 'e wants a quiet word with Doris Mossup, an' we know what that's abaat.'

'Do we?'

'Course we do. T'squire's up fer buying t'place.'

'Gerron.'

'I'm tellin' thee, Percy. 'E's been buyin' up land fer 'is grouse shootin', then 'e gets 'is 'ands on Dick Greenwood's place an' I reckon 'e's med t'brewery an offer fer King's 'Ead.'

What Toby Croft reasoned was not beyond the bounds of possibility. The brewery, which owned the King's Head, had sent a representative the previous year to the hostelry, who had suggested the place could do with some refurbishment. The regulars had protested vociferously and threatened to veto the inn if any attempt was made to change things. Like the landlady, they liked it the way it was. The King's Head, they had told him, had 'olde-worlde' character and they were opposed to any alterations.

'Oh yes,' said Toby, before taking a great gulp of his beer, 't'squire's 'ere to tell t'landlady an' give 'er 'er marching orders.'

'What would 'e want wi' a pub?' asked Percy.

''E'll like as not turn it into one of these posh restaurants or bistros. I tell thee what, things in Risingdale are changing, an' not fer better neither. Farms goin' to t'wall, land sold off, Methody chapel turned into a fancy studio an' now t'King's 'Ead becomin' a wine bar. I can't be doin' wi' all these changes.'

'Well, speaking of changes,' said his drinking pal. 'Why don't you get yer wallet out an' get t'next round in fer a change?'

As Toby contemplated whether or not to reach into his pocket, he was approached by Mrs Gosling's son.

'Nah then, Toby,' said the young man.

'If yer after sending back that bitch yer selled me, yer can forget it. I've never seen a more useless, dozy mutt. Couldn't round 'ersen up, nivver mind a flock o' sheep.'

'I just come over to buy you a pint,' said the young man.

'Eh?'

'You did me a good turn.'

''Ow come?'

'I sold the dog you brought back to me to Albert Midgley,' said the young farmer. 'I got a really good price for her.' There was a great grin on his face.

'More fool Albert Midgley for buying it,' said Toby.

'Nay, he's trained her and he reckons she's one of the best bitches he's had. Has the making of a champion in her. Course, it's all about the training. He reckons he might be putting her in the Clayton Show next year for Best of Breed. I just thought you'd like to know. Let me get you that pint. You look as if you could do with it.'

As Mr Croft, grumbling to himself, made his way back home he came to the curve in the twisting road opposite the Fairborn farm where Tom had nearly collided with Janette and her horse. It was a particularly sharp and narrow dog-leg bend, notoriously dangerous for drivers unaccustomed to it. Out of the farm gate limped the Fairborn's ancient dog, a pathetic-looking old mongrel. Patches of fur were missing from its back as if someone had pulled out great handfuls. Half blind and largely toothless, it gave a sort of whimpering bark as the farmer approached. Toby looked at the wretched creature. If he had owned it, he thought, he would have had it put down years ago, but Janette, whose dog it was, was sentimental about the old mongrel they had rescued from an animal shelter as a pup.

As Toby crossed the road, the dog shuffled after him.

'Bugger off!' the farmer shouted at the animal.

The dog stopped at the command and stood in the middle of the road.

There was a screech of brakes, the smell of burning rubber and a loud thump. Toby turned to see that a car, coming around the bend, had hit the dog full on and knocked it into the ditch at the side of the road. The motorist, an elderly man in a loud tweed jacket, jumped from the car.

'Oh my God!' he cried. 'I didn't see it. It was standing in the middle of the road. I couldn't avoid hitting it.'

Toby crossed over and examined the animal.

'Is it dead?' asked the motorist, sounding flustered.

'Oh yes, it's dead all right.'

'I'm most terribly sorry,' said the man. 'I just didn't see your dog until the last moment.'

'It's a bad bend, is that,' said Toby. He did not enlighten the driver as to whose dog it was.

'Yes, it is,' said the man. 'I guess I should have been driving more slowly. I'm most terribly sorry.'

'I wouldn't lose any sleep over it,' the farmer told him nonchalantly. 'It never felt nowt. It were an owld dog, well past its sell-by date.'

'Yes, I can see that but nevertheless you must be heartbroken.'

'No, not really.'

'I say, you're taking this awfully well,' said the motorist.

''Appen so,' said Toby. 'Course it could 'ave been me what got knocked ovver an' ended up in t'ditch.'

'Yes, of course,' said the motorist. 'It could indeed.'

'Well, you'd best be on your way,' said Toby. 'I'll see to t'dog.'

'Now look,' said the man, reaching for his wallet. 'I would like you to accept this. It might go some way to make amends for what happened to your dog.' He pressed a twenty-pound note into the farmer's hand.

When the motorist had driven off at a snail's pace, Toby called at the Fairborn's farm and, fingering the twenty-pound note safely stowed in the bottom of a pocket, informed them that a speeding motorist had run over and killed Janette's dog.

Joyce Tranter was the first member of the teaching staff who Tom had met on his first day at Risingdale School at the beginning of the previous term. When he had seen where he was expected to teach – a dark, dingy classroom, the walls devoid of any displays or pictures and painted in a sickly green, he had had serious reservations about wanting the job. There were ranks of dark wooden desks of the old-fashioned lidded variety, a dusty old cupboard and a rickety bookshelf. Then Joyce Tranter entered the room. She was an extraordinary-looking woman: tall and slim with unnaturally shiny raven-black hair, startling glossy-red lips, perfectly plucked arched eyebrows and large, pale eyes. She wore an amazingly tight-fitting crimson turtleneck jumper, a thick black leather belt with a substantial shiny metal buckle and a black calf-length pencil skirt. She sported a pair of impressively pointed black patent-leather shoes with high heels. Silver earrings the size of onion rings dangled from her ears. There was the fragrance of expensive perfume in the air. Tom had immediately liked this unusual, bubbly character and after he had met the other teachers and the class he was to teach, he decided to stay. It was a decision that he did not regret.

The unfortunate incident of the stolen necklace had turned out well for Joyce. She had bought the jewellery at Smith, Skerrit and Sampson, the auction house in Clayton, and had been wearing it at a function in the church hall when Lady Maladroit, always eagle-eyed, had spotted it around Joyce's neck and demanded its return, unaware at the time that her son was the thief. Sir Hedley had prevailed upon the owner of the auction house, Mr Julian Sampson, to persuade Joyce to sell him back the necklace, which he returned to Lady

Maladroit. When Joyce saw the cheque on offer, she didn't hesitate and gave it back.

'To be honest,' Joyce had told the auctioneer, 'I don't really like it. As soon as I got it home, I thought it too flashy. Rather too ostentatious for my liking.'

'Yes, I agree,' Mr Sampson had said. 'I think you would suit a more delicate piece, perhaps a Belle Époque rose-cut diamond pendant.'

On meeting Joyce, Mr Sampson, a distinguished-looking widower with a head of carefully combed silver hair and the face of a Roman senator, was immediately taken, and she, for her part, found this wealthy and attractive man attentive and personable. He had invited her out for a meal in a swish restaurant and things had blossomed. Now most weekends she accompanied him to the opera in Leeds or the theatre in York and was in her element, able to enter the world of theatre again.

Over the weeks Joyce had seen a great deal of 'her gentleman friend', as Mrs Golightly termed Mr Sampson, and her colleagues at the school were frequently subjected to detailed and effusive descriptions of the meals she had been treated to and the trips she had been on with him. The teachers all agreed with Mr Cadwallader when he observed that it would not be long before they would hear the sound of wedding bells.

One lunchtime, Joyce was holding forth about a recent evening at the ballet.

'Julian had booked the best seats in the theatre and arranged for champagne at the interval, and then we went for a meal at Middleton Manor. He's so attentive and considerate. He's taking me to the coast this weekend. He won't tell me where. It's to be a surprise.'

'You seem to be getting on very well with him,' remarked Mr Cadwallader, before crunching on a biscuit.

'Yes, I am, Owen,' Joyce replied. 'He's real gentleman.'

'I'm very happy for you,' said Mrs Golightly. 'It must be nice to meet someone to share your life with.'

'Don't give up, Bertha,' said Mr Cadwallader. 'There's hope for you yet.'

Mrs Golightly gave a small smile. 'Yes, you may be right,' she chuckled.

As Joyce was regaling her colleagues with a description of her night out with Julian, Tom sat before the computer staring at the blank screen and shaking his head. Following the awareness course he had attended, he had returned to school fired with enthusiasm and soon had the computer working. He explained to the teachers that it was child's play using the new technology, that there was nothing to be afraid of in using the computer; it was so straightforward and simple.

'It's such a wonderful resource,' he had enthused.

His keenness and assurances, however, fell on deaf ears and the interest from his colleagues had been lukewarm, to say the least.

That morning Tom could have eaten his words, for things had not gone well. When he turned on the computer he was greeted with a blank screen and strange buzzing noise. He had telephoned Ms Babcock at the Education Office, who had been less than helpful. 'It might be a zip-drive malfunction or an error with the codepage on boot,' she told him, as if speaking a foreign language. 'I suggest you reghost. It's all explained in the manual. Must dash.'

'Having trouble, sir?' Charlie and Leo appeared at the classroom door.

'I'm afraid so,' said Tom. 'The computer has packed up.'

'Could I look?' asked Charlie, coming over and examining the keyboard.

'There's nothing you can do,' said the teacher. 'I shall have to get someone to look at it.'

The boy rubbed his chin. 'Have you tried this?' he asked. He pressed two keys together, then another and immediately the computer came to life.

'Good gracious!' exclaimed the teacher. 'However did you know how to do that?'

'I sometimes use the computer in the library in town,' said Charlie. 'I've seen people do that when it stops working. It's pretty straightforward, really.'

'Child's play,' muttered the teacher, recalling his earlier words.

That afternoon, Tom set his class the assignment to write an account entitled 'My Most Prized Possession'. He had discussed this topic with the children the previous week and asked them to share what they considered to be the one thing they owned that they valued the most.

The debate had been lively and wide-ranging. For George it was *The Complete Illustrated Handbook of Farm Tractors*; Marjorie decided it was the crook with the hawthorn shank and carved ram's horn grip that her grandfather had made for her. Carol said her sheepdog was the most precious thing, and for Simon it was his ferret. Vicky regarded her teddy bear with its one arm, which had been with her since she was a baby, to be her prized possession, and Colin valued a photograph of his mother more than anything. For Charlie, his guitar given to him by his father (although he didn't reveal the giver's name) was especially held dear, and for Leo it was the fountain pen that had once belonged to his father. Judith, the rosy-cheeked girl with the long plaits, told the class it would probably be her clarinet.

When the children went into the playground for their afternoon break, Judith stayed behind. She was the quietest child in the class but a model pupil: polite, hard-working and intelligent, and she always arrived at school immaculately dressed. She approached the teacher's desk shyly, holding a large brown envelope.

'Hello, Judith,' said Tom. 'Did you want to see me about something?'

'The clarinet is not my most prized possession, Mr Dwyer,' she said quietly, looking down. 'I said that because I didn't want all the others to know what the real one is.' She looked up. 'I'm not ashamed of it, but it's personal.' She held out the envelope. 'It's in here,' she said.

'You don't mind me looking?' asked Tom.

'No, Mr Dwyer, I don't mind. I would like you to know. It's very special, you see.'

Tom took an official-looking document out of the envelope and read what had been written. It was Judith's adoption papers.

The teacher smiled and nodded. 'Yes, I can see why this is a treasured possession,' he told the girl. 'It's the most precious thing anyone could have. It must mean the world to you.' She nodded. He returned the document and passed back the envelope. 'Thank you for showing me.'

'I was eight when I was adopted,' Judith told him, 'and it was the happiest day of my life.' She stroked the envelope fondly and smiled diffidently. 'I'm so lucky, aren't I, Mr Dwyer, to have a mum and dad who really wanted me and who love me?'

Tom was so moved by the child's words that he found it hard to speak. At last he found his voice.

'You *are* very lucky,' he replied, 'and your mum and dad are really lucky too, Judith, to have a daughter like you.'

The girl's face broke into a radiant smile.

10

Mrs Sloughthwaite, proprietor of the Barton-in-the Dale village store, was updating Mrs O'Connor with the latest gossip when a customer entered. He was a thin-featured individual with an untidy beard and shoulder-length hair tied back in a ponytail.

The shopkeeper raised herself from the counter on which she had been resting and greeted him with a cheery, 'Good morning.'

'Have you a local paper?' asked the man brusquely.

'Yes, I do,' she replied. Her good humour quickly evaporated, for Mrs Sloughthwaite took exception to any customer who lacked the common courtesy to reply in a friendly and civil manner.

'Could I have one?' asked the man.

'Please,' murmured the shopkeeper, pulling a face at the man's rudeness.

'What?'

She looked at Mrs O'Connor and frowned, then turned back to the man. 'Is that all?'

'Yes.'

'Newspapers are on the rack by the door.'

'I'm looking for a woman,' announced the man, not moving.

'This is a shop, not a dating agency,' replied Mrs Sloughthwaite, resuming her position leaning on the counter.

He gave a weak smile. 'It's someone I used to know. I'm trying to track her down.' He reached into the pocket of his leather jacket and produced a crumpled piece of newspaper, which he slid across the counter. 'It's the woman in the middle. Do you know her?'

Mrs Sloughthwaite, in no great hurry, glanced at the photograph.

'Look at this, Bridget,' she said suddenly and, ignoring the man, she passed her friend the cutting. 'There's a picture here of your Tom.'

Mrs O'Connor examined the paper. 'Oh yes,' she said, 'it was when he was in the Christmas pantomime at the Clayton theatre and played the part of the handsome prince. I never managed to go myself because there was a Union of Catholic Mothers meeting at St Bede's and Father Daly likes me to serve the tea.' She scrutinised the newspaper cutting. 'Yes, it's Tom, all right. It's a very good likeness of him, so it is. Mind you, his family have always taken a good picture.'

'So do you know the woman?' asked the man.

'He's very photogenital,' said the shopkeeper, again ignoring him. She chuckled. 'He certainly made a few girls' hearts a-flutter when he walked on to the stage in those tights. They left nothing to the imagination.'

'You should have seen the pair they wanted him to wear at first,' said Mrs O'Connor. 'Pale green, they were. He said his legs looked like two runner beans. That's why he changed them for black, so he did.'

'He made a lovely prince,' said the shopkeeper, 'and the young woman who played the princess was a picture. I thought to myself what a lovely couple they made. Does he see anything of her?'

'It's this woman here,' interrupted the man impatiently, snatching the cutting from Mrs O'Connor. He pointed to a smiling figure in the centre of the group of actors.

'I don't know her,' said the shopkeeper.

'It's the producer of the show,' said Mrs O'Connor. 'That's Miss Tranter.'

'Miss Tranter,' the man muttered. 'Do you know where she lives?'

'No,' said Mrs O'Connor, 'but she teaches with my nephew. He's the one in the photograph with her.'

'Where does she teach?'

'At Risingdale School.'

'Where's that?'

'If you go—' began Mrs O'Connor.

'It's at the top of the Dale,' interjected the shopkeeper, irritated by the man's continued rudeness. She was not inclined to give him any directions. Let him get lost in the twisting roads, she said to herself.

'How do I get there?' he asked.

'I suggest you follow the signs,' said Mrs Sloughthwaite.

The man stuffed the newspaper cutting in his pocket and headed for the door.

'Have you forgotten something?' she asked.

'What?'

'You wanted a newspaper.'

'I won't bother,' he told her and left the shop, banging the door behind him.

'What an ill-mannered lout,' said the shopkeeper. 'That sort is hard to ignore but well worth the effort. It doesn't cost anything to be congenital and say "please" and "thank you".'

'I didn't like the look of him at all,' said Mrs O'Connor. 'You couldn't like him even if you reared him, and all that hair. It looked as if his mother had knitted him.'

'I've always been septical of men with long hair and a beard,' said Mrs Sloughthwaite. 'They're not to be trusted in my experience. Never trust a man with a beard, it's a way of hiding something – like a hedge around a garden.'

'Jesus had long hair and a beard, so he did,' observed the customer.

'Yes, but Jesus didn't wear an old leather jacket, dirty jumper and baggy jeans, and he didn't ride on a motorbike and I reckon he had clean fingernails. That man looked as if he'd been scrabbling in the dirt. Oh, and speaking of Jesus . . .'

Joyce and Julian sat at a corner table in the elegant lounge of the Grand Hotel in Scarborough about to enjoy a pre-dinner drink. She was dressed in a stylish black cocktail dress and he in a smart dinner jacket.

'I must say, you look quite dazzling tonight, Joyce,' her gentleman friend told her.

'Just *quite* dazzling,' she said, playfully.

He smiled. 'Let me re-phrase that,' he said. 'My dear Miss Tranter, you are looking *unquestionably* dazzling this evening,' he said, resting a hand on hers.

She fingered the Belle Époque rose-cut diamond pendant draped around her neck.

'It was so kind of you to give me this,' she said. 'It's lovely.'

'It suits you,' he told her. 'I recall telling you when we first met and you returned Lady Maladroit's necklace, that you would suit an altogether more delicate piece like this.'

'It must have cost a great deal of money.'

He squeezed her hand. 'You are worth it.' He thought for a moment, considering what to say next. 'You know, Joyce, over the last few weeks it has been such a pleasure having your company.'

'It's been a pleasure for me, too,' she replied.

'I appreciate that we have only known each other for a relatively short time,' he continued, 'but I have come to think of you as someone very special in my life, very special indeed.'

'And you in mine,' she replied.

'Since my wife died, I have been very lonely,' he told her. 'We were not fortunate to have children, which would have in some way filled the gap she left in my life. I never imagined that anyone could take her place, but—'

Joyce suddenly snatched her hand away.

'I'm sorry,' he said. 'It was insensitive of me to mention my wife. I should have—'

'No, no,' she interrupted. 'It's not that. Look who has just walked into the room.' She tilted her head in the direction of the door.

'Why, it's Sir Hedley Maladroit,' he said.

The subject of their attention had entered the lounge, his arm around the waist of an attractive woman. They were accompanied by a small boy.

'But look who he's with.'

'I don't know who he's with,' admitted her companion.

'It's Mrs Lister. Her son is a pupil at the school where I teach. Whatever is she doing here with him?'

'Whoever it is, she seems to be on very good terms with him,' remarked Julian.

Joyce watched, riveted, as Sir Hedley put his hand on the boy's shoulder, bent down towards him and smiled. Then he turned and placed a kiss on the woman's cheek. They went to sit at a table by the bar.

Joyce sat open-mouthed and lost for words.

'Well, well,' said Julian. 'This is a turn-up for the book. He's a sly old dog and no mistake. She must be the other woman. Mind you, I can't blame him, married to that virago of a wife.'

'The other woman,' repeated Joyce. 'You think he's having an affair.'

'Did you not see him kiss her?'

'Yes, I saw.'

'Well, what do you think?'

'This is most embarrassing,' she said. 'It's a pity we are at a corner table. It's not easy for us to sneak away without them seeing us.' She began to move her chair so she had her back to Sir Hedley but was spotted by Charlie.

'It's Miss Tranter,' the boy told his mother. He smiled widely and waved at the teacher. Joyce gave a weak smile and managed a small wave back.

'Now what are we going to do?' she muttered to Julian through gritted teeth.

'I suggest we take the bull by the horns,' he announced, rising from his chair. 'We can't very well just ignore them since they must have seen us. Come along, Joyce, let us go and say hello.'

'I can't,' she told him.

'Yes, you can.' He took her arm and helped her to her feet. 'Come along.'

Reluctantly she joined him and they approached the table where Sir Hedley, on seeing them, became flushed and speechless, like someone caught in the act.

'My dear Sir Hedley,' said Julian amiably. 'We thought it was you.'

'I, er . . . er . . .' began the baronet.

'I think you know Miss Tranter,' said Julian.

'Yes, yes, indeed.' Sir Hedley stood and extended his hand. 'Good evening.'

'Good evening,' she replied. She could feel the colour flooding her face.

There was an embarrassed silence. Then Sir Hedley turned to his companion.

'May I introduce Mrs Lister,' said the baronet to Julian, 'and her son. I believe you are both acquainted with Miss Tranter.'

'Yes, indeed,' replied Joyce, feeling her face getting even hotter. Mrs Lister managed to mutter a 'good evening'.

'Hello, miss,' said the boy cheerfully. 'Fancy you being in Scarborough at the same time as us.'

'Yes, fancy,' said Joyce, trying not to meet the baronet's eyes.

'Would you care to join us, Sir Hedley?' asked Julian. There was not a trace of embarrassment on his face. 'We have just ordered our drinks.'

'Thank you, no, we are about to dine.' He looked at his watch. 'In fact, I think it is time we went in for dinner.'

'You said we were going to have a drink first, Dad,' piped up Charlie.

Sir Hedley froze. Miss Tranter's mouth dropped open, Mrs Lister sighed and Julian suppressed a smile.

It was getting on for eight o'clock when Tom entered the public bar at the King's Head. Being Saturday night, the inn was packed and noisy. Several of the locals, catching sight of him, nodded their heads, and some smiled and waved or wished him a good evening.

In the short time since he had lived in the village, Tom had quickly become accepted by the locals. This was an unusual occurrence for an 'off-comed-un', but Tom had made a real effort to fit in and had become popular not only with the children he taught and their parents, but with the local farmers and Mrs Mossup too.

Seeing Mr Greenwood standing at the bar, Tom went to join him. He was interested to hear how Colin was getting on with his art lessons at the studio. In quick time he was soon joined by Toby Croft, who was hopeful that a drink might be forthcoming from the young teacher. The old nosy farmer ('He would go down your throat for news', according to the landlady) was also interested in hearing the conversation between the two men. He scurried over and placed his empty glass on the counter ostentatiously.

'Evenin', Mester Dwyer,' he said, before Tom could speak to Colin's father.

'Good evening, Mr Croft,' Tom replied.

''Ow's tha keepin'?'

'I'm keeping pretty well, thank you. How about you?'

'Oh, tha knaas,' replied the old farmer, scratching his wrinkled neck, 'mustn't grumble.'

'Good evening,' Tom said to Mr Greenwood.

'Evenin', Mester Dwyer.'

'Let me get you a drink,' he said, 'and then you can tell me how your Colin is getting on with Mrs Stanhope. He says she is giving him some lessons in painting.'

'Put tha wallet back in tha pocket,' said the boy's father. 'This is on me.' He turned to Toby, who was tapping the top of his glass to gain the speaker's attention. 'An' if what tha doing is fer my benefit, Toby Croft, well, I wouldn't bother. Tha can get yer own drink. Yer as tight as a tick's arse, an' no mistake.'

'Now don't be like that, Dick,' said the old farmer. 'Tha can well afford to stand a pint fer an 'ard-up fella like me, trying to scratch a meagre livin' from t'land.'

'Scratch a meagre livin',' repeated Mr Greenwood. 'Tha's more brass than any farmer in t'Dale.'

'That's rich comin' from thee,' said the old farmer. 'I bet tha's med a pretty penny from sellin' yer farm an' all that land to t'squire an' now tha're gerrin' a nice little income from bein' 'is gamekeeper, an' all. Tha fell on tha feet. Then there's that windfall that tha's 'ad. I read in t'paper tha's come into a tidy sum when tha selled them owld coins what tha found near yon ruined castle. I reckon there's more of 'em buried up theer. I might go an' tek a look missen.'

'Tha'll do nowt o' sooart,' barked Mr Greenwood. 'It's Sir 'Edley's land now and if I find thee up theer, tha'll end up in front o' magistrate fer trespassin'.'

'By the 'eck, tha's changed, Dick Greenwood,' said the old farmer. 'Thy weren't above snarin' a few rabbits an' shootin' t'odd pheasant an' ticklin' one or two trout afore Sir 'Edley took thee on. Case o' poacher turned gamekeeper, if thy asks me.'

'Tha what?'

'Nowt.'

'Just thee watch what tha says an' keep away from t'castle or tha'll 'ave me to deal wi'. It's just been designated as an area o' special 'istorical interest and listed as an ancient monument. Sir 'Edley's asked folk from t'museum in Clayton to see if they can find owt else up theer. They're startin' some excavations when t'weather improves an' they don't want thee gerrin' under their feet an' stickin' yer oar in.'

'An excavation sounds interesting,' said Tom. 'Perhaps I could take some of the children up there. We could do a history project on the castle.'

'I'll 'ave a word wi' Sir 'Edley if tha likes, Mester Dwyer, but, as I said, they won't want people gerrin' in their way.'

'I 'ad a couple o' them 'istorical folk up to my farm,' said Toby. 'Nosy busybodies, they were, from some 'eritage group tellin' me that mi farm'ouse were listed as a building of special harchitectural an' 'istorical interest an' any changes I wanted to mek 'ad to be cleared wi' them. T'young lass nearly swooned when she saw one o' mi walls. "Oh, that's a perfect example of a medieval enclosure dating way back to t'fourteenth century an' in a wonderful state o' preservation." "Tha dun't say," I told her. "Well, it weren't medieval when I built it."' The old farmer chuckled to himself. 'Anyroad, if they need any 'elp wi' them hexcavations, me an' our Dean can give thee an 'and.'

'Aye, and keep what tha finds,' said Mr Greenwood. He then shouted down the bar to the landlady, who had just finished serving a customer. 'Can I 'ave a couple o' pints down 'ere, Doris, when tha's gor a minute an' yer berrer get one fer Mester Croft to shut 'im up.'

'Very decent of you, Dick,' said the old farmer, smiling.

'So how is Colin getting on with his painting?' Tom asked the boy's father.

'Champion. 'E's tekken a real shine to Missis Stanhope. She's quite a woman.'

'She is,' agreed Tom.

'I reckon tha's tekken a shine to 'er an' all, Dick,' remarked Toby. 'Tha're in an' out o' that studio of 'ers like a fiddler's elbow.'

'She's paintin' mi portrait, if tha must know,' Mr Greenwood told him.

'She were after paintin' mine,' said Toby, 'but I've 'eard nowt from 'er. 'Appen she's got bigger fish to fry.'

Mrs Mossup arrived with the drinks.

'I see Fagin here has wheedled a pint out of you,' she said to Mr Greenwood, nodding in Toby's direction. 'One of these days the old miser will surprise us all and get out his wallet.' Before Toby could respond, she turned to Tom. 'I had John Fairborn in here earlier,' she told him.

'Oh yes.'

'He was telling me that his Janette seems to be getting on very well in her new job in Nottingham and has really taken to the city life.'

'I'm glad to hear it,' said Tom half-heartedly.

'You know there were quite a few in the village who thought you and his daughter were very suited to each other. I thought myself that you made a lovely couple.'

'Really?' he replied coolly.

'It was quite a surprise to me, her up and going to Nottingham.'

Yes, thought Tom, it was for me, too.

'Mind you,' continued the landlady, 'her father was saying that she does miss some things.'

'Oh yes?' said Tom hopefully. 'What does she miss?'

'Her horse, for one,' replied the landlady. 'She misses her horse and that old dog of hers.'

'Her dog?'

'Some driver knocked it down and killed it. Didn't even stop. Left it at the side of the road in a ditch.' The landlady turned to Toby. 'You found it, didn't you?'

'Found what?'

'Janette Fairborn's dog.'

'Aye, I did,' he replied sheepishly.

'Mr Fairborn was telling me,' continued Mrs Mossup. 'He said it was good of you to let him know.'

'Well, you know me, Doris,' said the old farmer, 'if I can be of help to anyone . . .'

The landlady rolled her eyes.

When Miss Tranter arrived at school and made her way to the staffroom one morning later in the week, Mr Cadwallader poked his head out of his classroom door.

'In here!' he hissed.

Joyce jumped as if she had been doused in icy water.

'Owen!' she cried, placing a hand on her heart. 'For goodness' sake! You nearly scared me to death.'

'Quick,' he said, 'come into my classroom.'

'What for?'

'There is something I need to show you.'

'Show me in the staffroom,' she told him. 'I need a cup of coffee.'

'No, no, I can't show you in front of the others. It's too embarrassing. It's . . . well, it's a delicate matter.'

Joyce gave a heaving sigh. 'Oh, very well, but be quick. I can't start the day without my fix of caffeine.'

Once she was in the room, Mr Cadwallader closed the door behind her, then scurried over to his desk, pulled out the top drawer and took out a large brown envelope.

'It's in here,' he said.

'This is all very mysterious,' remarked his colleague.

'All will be revealed when you see the contents.' He passed her the envelope. 'Take a look at what's inside.'

Joyce peered into the envelope. 'Oh,' she said. 'It's a—'

'I know what it is,' the teacher told her. 'You don't need to spell it out.'

'Where did you get this from?'

'Young Jimmy Brogan in my class brought it to school. He told me his pen wasn't working. He said it lit up and buzzed a lot but it wouldn't write.'

'His pen!' exclaimed Joyce.

'That's what he thought it was. I asked him where he had got it from and he told me he found it in a drawer in his mother's bedside cabinet.'

'And what do you want me to do with it?' asked Joyce.

'You're a woman,' Mr Cadwallader told her.

'Yes, I won't argue with that.'

'I think it needs to be sent home in the envelope with a covering letter from you.'

'Why me? The child is in your class.'

'Because I would find it very embarrassing sending such an appliance home.'

'Appliance,' repeated Joyce.

'That piece of personal equipment.'

'The sex aid.'

'Yes, yes, if you wish to call it that.'

'Well, that's what it is.'

Mr Cadwallader sighed. 'Yes, Joyce, I do know what it is. I am not that unknowing about these things.'

'Really?' she said, raising an eyebrow.

'As I said, the letter and explanation would come far better from a woman. So will you do it?'

'Yes, I suppose so.' She put the envelope and its contents in her bag. Then she chuckled. 'You must tell me sometime, Owen, where you gained your knowledge of such pieces of – what did you call it – personal equipment?'

'Whatever is that dreadful smell?' asked Mrs Golightly at afternoon break as the teachers sat in the staffroom. She screwed up her face and sniffed the air.

'Is it you, Tom?' asked Miss Tranter, wrinkling her nose.

'Not guilty,' he replied.

'Is it you, Owen?' she asked.

Mr Cadwallader feigned not to have heard and pretended to be engrossed in his newspaper.

'Owen,' said Joyce, 'I'm talking to you. I was asking if that smell is coming from you.'

'Yes, I heard you,' he replied.

'Well, is it?'

'Yes, it is, if you must know.'

'Whatever is it?' she asked. 'It's most oppressive.'

'It's vomit,' he told her.

'Vomit,' repeated Mrs Golightly. 'Have you been sick?'

'No, I have not been sick,' he told her.

'Well, it's a wonder he isn't sick what with the amount of biscuits he consumes,' remarked Joyce. She began filing a long nail.

'For your information, Bertha,' Mr Cadwallader told her, ignoring his other colleague's comment, 'I have not been sick but I have been the recipient of it. Eddie Cooper threw up all over me. He has an irritating habit, that boy, of chewing in class and many has been the time I have asked him to put the offending sweet in the bin. On one occasion he meandered into the classroom masticating like a voracious cow and when I gestured to the said receptacle to deposit the sweet and asked, "Where's the bin?", he replied, "I've bin to t'lavatory."'

Tom, who was busy marking the morning's work of his pupils, smiled.

'I really didn't ask for a blow-by-blow account of your encounter with Eddie Cooper,' said Mrs Golightly. 'We merely wanted to know why you smell so obnoxious.'

'And I am endeavouring to explain,' answered Mr Cadwallader sharply, 'that is, if you would give me the chance.

Now as I was saying, I caught sight of Eddie Cooper at the rear of the classroom, where he always sits, with his mouth full of toffees or some such confection. It explains the size of the boy. It's no wonder that we have all these obese children when they are allowed to devour so much sweet stuff.'

'Such as biscuits,' Mrs Golightly interjected.

'Of course, I blame the parents for letting them eat such fattening foods,' complained Mr Cadwallader, ignoring the interruption. 'You should see the contents of the boy's lunchbox.'

'I wish I had never asked,' remarked Miss Tranter *sotto voce*.

'Anyway, I told him to spit out what he had in his mouth,' Mr Cadwallader carried on.

'I have an idea where this is going,' she observed, attacking a broken nail.

'I told him to spit out what he had in his mouth and at first the boy shook his head. Then when I told him to let me see what he had in his mouth, he did just that and the contents, which happened to be vomit, ended up all over me. And that is why I smell. I have endeavoured to clean myself up, but a smell like this lingers and—'

'Well, it's most unpleasant for us to endure,' said Mrs Golightly. 'It's making me distinctly queasy. Can't you change your clothes?'

'I don't happen to keep a spare outfit at school,' retorted the teacher, 'on the improbable likelihood of someone throwing up on me.'

'I always have a spare change of clothes,' said Mrs Golightly. 'I have learnt from experience that when it comes to children, it is best to be prepared for incidents like this.'

'Well, bully for you, Bertha,' said Mr Cadwallader.

'Perhaps you could change into one of Tom's PE kits, Owen,' suggested Joyce, who was now peering into a small mirror and stretching her mouth to apply some scarlet lipstick.

On hearing his name mentioned, Tom looked up. 'What was that?' he asked.

'I was telling Owen that you might have a spare PE kit for him to change into so he can get out of those smelly clothes he's wearing.'

'Or he might at a pinch squeeze into one of your tracksuits,' added Mrs Golightly.

'I have no intention of squeezing into any PE kit or track-suit,' answered the teacher.

'Suit yourself,' said Mrs Golightly, 'but sit over in the corner where we can't smell you.'

'I shall get some fresh air,' said Mr Cadwallader indignantly as he rose from his chair. Then he added sarcastically, 'And thank you, colleagues, for your sympathy and understanding.'

When the teacher had departed, Mrs Golightly turned to Joyce.

'So, how did your romantic weekend in Scarborough go?' she asked.

Joyce stopped her beautifying and smiled. 'Wonderful,' she said. 'Julian and I get on so well. We are like kindred spir-its. He's so considerate and kind and courteous. He's a real gentleman.'

And not short of a few bob, thought her colleague.

Joyce had agreed with Julian that nothing should be said about the sighting of Sir Hedley and 'the other woman' in the lounge of the Grand Hotel. Before they left on the Sunday afternoon, Sir Hedley had taken Julian aside.

'This is a rather delicate matter, Mr Sampson,' he had said, looking distinctly uneasy. 'The thing is, I should perhaps explain the . . . er . . . relationship between Mrs Lister and myself. You see—'

'There is really no need, Sir Hedley,' Julian had interrupted, holding up a hand. 'What other people do in their own time is of no consequence to me.'

'Mrs Lister and I have been friends now for some time,' the baronet had continued. 'She is—'

'Sir Hedley,' Mr Sampson had again stopped him mid-sentence, 'there is no need to explain yourself to me. As I have said, it is of no concern of mine.'

'You were most understanding over the matter of my wife's stolen necklace,' Sir Hedley had said, 'agreeing to keep my son's involvement in the sorry affair to yourself. I am most grateful for that. I hope that with regard to this situation I find myself in, you will show the same discretion.'

'Really, Sir Hedley—'

'No, no, do allow me finish. Should this . . . liaison become common knowledge, it would prove very difficult for Mrs Lister and Charlie and not least for myself. Therefore, I would ask that you and Miss Tranter—'

'Let me stop you there again, Sir Hedley, and save any further embarrassment on your part. I do not deal in tittle-tattle, and, as I have said, what people do in their own time is of no concern or interest of mine. Miss Tranter and I saw nothing in the lounge of this hotel. I hope I have made my position perfectly clear.'

Later, in the car driving back from Scarborough, Mr Sampson had acquainted Joyce with what had been discussed with Sir Hedley.

'It would certainly put the cat amongst the pigeons if this got out,' Joyce had remarked.

'But you will understand how difficult it would be for Sir Hedley if it did.'

'I'm not thinking of Sir Hedley. I'm thinking more of the boy and his mother. I have no sympathy for Sir Hedley. He thinks he owns everything and everybody around Risingdale. He's driven half the farmers out of their homes and acquired their land for his grouse shooting and for holiday lets. What Mrs Lister should see in such a man is beyond me.'

'There's no accounting for taste, Joyce,' Julian had told her. 'Actually, I find Sir Hedley a decent sort of chap and I certainly do not wish to get on the wrong side of him.'

'I count adultery as the greatest betrayal,' Joyce had said.

Julian had thought for a moment before replying. 'Actually, I feel sorry for the man, shackled to that woman at Marston Towers with that wastrel of a son. I can quite understand why he has sought some affection from another.'

'I still think it's wrong,' Joyce had said.

'Well, I hope we can keep things to ourselves.'

'Of course,' she had agreed. 'I won't say a word.'

As she looked at her colleagues now, Joyce imagined their reaction should she reveal the local squire's secret.

'I say, Joyce,' said Tom now, looking up from the exercise book he had been marking, 'did you see anything of Charlie Lister while you were in Scarborough?'

'What!' she cried.

'Charlie Lister – did you see anything of him while you were in Scarborough?'

'What makes you ask?'

'I always get the children to talk about what they have done over the weekend on Monday morning and then write about it. Charlie here says he stayed with his mother in a posh hotel on the seafront in Scarborough.'

Joyce was grateful for the intervention of Mrs Golightly.

'One wonders where the boy's mother finds the money to take him to a posh hotel in Scarborough,' she remarked. 'I mean, she doesn't work as far as I know. Of course, there's a bit of speculation in the village where she gets her money from to pay the rent and deal with bills.'

'So, did you see anything of Charlie?' Tom asked Joyce again.

'There are many hotels in Scarborough,' she replied evasively, 'and it was very busy.'

Before she could be quizzed further, Mr Gaunt came into

the staffroom. He sniffed the air. 'I say, there's a strange smell in here,' he said. 'I must get Mrs Gosling to get some air freshener. I just popped in to speak to Owen.'

'He's in the playground,' Joyce told him.

'Ah, right. Jimmy Brogan is looking for him. He says he has his pen.'

II

After lunchtime Tom gathered the class around him in a semicircle.

'Now, children,' he told them, 'last week Simon asked me which was my very favourite story when I was a boy. If you remember, I mentioned that it was a novel my father used to read to me.'

Tom often thought of the times his father had read to him as a child. His favourite story had been *Treasure Island*, the stirring adventure about the treacherous cut-throat mutineers, murderous pirates and a character who killed with a crutch. He would listen enthralled, snuggled up to his father and taken into another world. He was there with Jim Hawkins hiding in the barrel of apples from Long John Silver, overhearing the pirate's murderous plans. He was there with Jim in the sweet-smelling darkness trembling with fear in case he was discovered. He was there in the stockade shoulder-to-shoulder with Squire Trelawney fighting off the mutineers. For Tom, there was no other story so captivating as *Treasure Island*.

'This morning I am going to read you another favourite story of mine,' the teacher told the class now. 'This was one of my mother's favourites. It's by an Irish writer, Oscar Wilde, and called "The Happy Prince".'

'You were a prince in the Christmas pantomime, weren't you, Mr Dwyer?' said Vicky, smiling widely. 'My mum said you looked dead dishy and that you and Miss Fairborn made a lovely couple.'

Tom noticed a number of the children were grinning sheepishly. He wondered if he would ever live down his appearance as the handsome prince in Joyce's production of *The Sleeping Beauty*. Some of the locals, including Toby Croft, had had a field day following his appearance in the fancy costume, and there had been a raucous applause and mad hooting when he had kissed the sleeping princess to awaken her. There had been much speculation in the village that the love affair depicted on stage was blossoming off stage too. Tom thought of her now and pictured her enjoying her new life in the city. No doubt she had met someone by now and forgotten about him.

'Sir, are you listening?' asked Vicky. 'I was just saying—'

'Yes, I know what you were saying,' said Tom, 'but I've heard quite enough about the pantomime, thank you. Let us get back to the story.'

'It's very sad, "The Happy Prince",' said Holly. 'It was on the television.'

'There's not much that is happy in it,' added Hazel, her twin sister.

'In some ways, it is a sad story,' agreed the teacher, 'but I think it has a happy ending. Let us see what the rest of the class think after I have read it. "The Happy Prince" is a simply, told story that teaches us a lesson; there's a deeper message so I want you to listen carefully and see if you can grasp what it is.'

'So it has a moral,' said Charlie.

'Yes, it has a moral,' replied the teacher, smiling. 'That was the word I was searching for.'

'Like in the Parable of the Lost Sheep that Mr Pendlebury told us when he came into school,' said Holly.

'My dad lost three of his sheep in all this bad weather,' Vicky told the teacher.

'Yes, your grandmother told me,' said Tom.

'They were found frozen to death in the snow,' said the girl.

'That's very sad,' Tom told her. 'Now, about the story – it is rather like a parable, but more of a fable. Parables have human characters but fables have animals, plants and objects which are given human qualities, such as the ability to speak.'

'But animals and plants can't speak,' said David.

'It sounds babyish to me, Mr Dwyer,' added Christopher. 'Books with talking animals are for the infants. Sir, could we have a different story, something more exciting? Could you read *Treasure Island*? This story about a prince sounds as if it's a fairy tale for little kids and lasses.'

'Let me read it,' the teacher replied, 'and then you can decide whether or not it's a babyish story.' He ignored Christopher's dismissive grunt and opened the book and began.

'"High above the city, on a tall column, stood the statue of the Happy Prince. He was gilded all over with thin leaves of fine gold, for eyes he had two bright sapphires, and a large red ruby glowed on his sword-hilt."'

Tom continued with the story of how in the city the poor citizens suffered, enduring great hardship and misery, their sorry plight ignored by those in power. A lone swallow, which was left behind after the flock had flown off to Egypt for the winter, nestles in the statue of the late Happy Prince, who in life had never experienced true sorrow, for he lived in a great palace where sorrow was not allowed to enter. The Prince had been rich and powerful and had never witnessed the misery of his people. Looking down now upon all the suffering from his tall monument, his lead heart is touched. He asks the swallow to take the ruby from the hilt of his sword, the sapphires from his eyes and the gold leaf covering his body to give to the poor. As the winter comes and the Happy Prince is stripped of all his beauty, his lead heart breaks when the swallow dies in the severe cold as a result of his selfless deeds. The statue is then pulled down from the pillar and melted in a furnace, leaving behind the broken heart and the dead swallow and they are thrown in a dust heap.

Except for Christopher, who sat with a bored expression on his face, the children listened in rapt silence until Tom came to the end of the story.

"What a strange thing,' said the overseer of the workmen at the foundry. 'This broken lead heart will not melt in the furnace. We must throw it away.' So they threw it on a dust-heap where the dead Swallow was also lying.

'Bring me the two most precious things in the city,' said God to one of His Angels; and the Angel brought Him the leaden heart and the dead bird.

'You have rightly chosen,' said God, 'for in my garden of Paradise this little bird shall sing for evermore, and in my city of gold the Happy Prince shall praise me.'

'Now, this fable is packed with many themes and messages,' said Tom. 'I would like you to think for a moment and then suggest some of them.'

The children discussed with each other the meaning of the story until the teacher clapped his hands to get their attention. His pupils were keen to share their views about the story.

'I think it's about how unfair it is to have rich people who have everything and those who have nothing,' suggested Holly.

'That's what my dad says about Sir Hedley,' said Christopher. 'He's like the rich and powerful people in the story who are mean and cruel and don't help the poor.'

'But not all rich and powerful people are mean and cruel,' argued Charlie, thinking of his father. 'The Prince is rich and powerful with all his jewels and gold but he is kind to the poor and gives everything away.'

'But he didn't when he was alive,' said Christopher.

'But the Prince couldn't help being born into a rich and powerful family.'

'I know that,' said Christopher, 'but he could have given his fortune to the poor when he was alive.'

'So you enjoyed the story after all,' Tom told the boy, pleased that the pupil had been listening after all. 'Do you still think the story is babyish?'

'Yes, I do,' answered Christopher. 'There was no action or exciting characters. It was soppy.' He then repeated what he had heard at home so many times around the kitchen table when his father, a man of strong, uncompromising views, frequently held forth. 'My dad says that those who are rich like Sir Hedley don't know what it's like to be poor and have never worked hard for what they've got.'

'My dad reckons Sir 'Edley's a decent sooart,' said George.

'I think we can leave Sir Hedley out of this,' said the teacher.

'I really liked the story,' said Carol. 'It was really sad though at the end.'

There was a murmur of agreement from the rest of the class. Then Leo spoke.

'It's really more about being caring to those who have nothing,' he said. 'The Prince gives away all his jewels and gold when he sees so many starving people. He can't be blamed for not giving away his fortune when he was alive because, in his palace, he never saw all the poverty that was around him. The swallow too is kind-hearted by staying behind in the cold to take the precious stones and gold leaf to help the poor. I think "The Happy Prince" is a story about kindness.'

Tom looked at the boy, smiled and nodded. He had a pleasant feeling of inward satisfaction at the way the children had responded. 'And that is where we will leave it,' he said.

*   *   *

At morning break, Christopher approached Leo and Charlie who were sitting chatting on the small wall that surrounded the playground.

'You think you're dead clever, don't you?' he demanded of the new pupil. His eyes flashed. '"I think the story is about kindness."' He mimicked Leo's voice. 'Why don't you keep your stupid bloody comments to yourself?'

Leo looked at him blankly but said nothing. He brushed a strand of hair from his face.

Christopher's mouth pursed as if he had swallowed something unpleasant.

'I'm talking to you!' he cried. 'You think you're better than us, don't you? You think you're dead clever?'

Leo remained silent and straight-faced, as if unmoved by the words.

Christopher bristled with resentment. He curled a lip. His eyes flashed contempt. He disliked everything about the new pupil: his appearance, his way of speaking, his self-assurance and his obvious intelligence. He begrudged the way Mr Dwyer seemed to favour him and how the others in the class, for some reason, liked him.

'Are you deaf?' he demanded, now red in the face and angered by the boy's apparent indifference to his verbal attack.

'Leave him alone,' said Charlie, springing to his friend's defence. 'He's not done anything to you.'

'I can fight my own battles,' said Leo calmly, getting up from the wall. He had never shown any fear of bullies and had become accustomed to being laughed at and picked on at the schools that he had previously attended. Surprisingly, he didn't appear to be bothered. Maybe his stoicism was something to do with his illness. He had shown great courage and forbearance dealing with his condition. Nothing really could frighten him more than the treatments he had undergone at the hands of the doctors on his frequent visits to the hospital.

Of course, standing up to the bully often resulted in a punch, a cut lip or a bruised body.

'Fight me!' jeered Christopher. 'I could spit on you and drown you.' He poked the boy in the chest. 'Fight me! Fat chance.'

'Leave him be,' came a voice from behind him.

Christopher had been unaware of Colin, who had seen what was happening and wandered over. He spun around. 'What?'

'I said leave him be,' he repeated with redoubled emphasis. Colin's face was hard and set.

'What's it got to do with you, Greenwood? Clear off!'

Colin gripped the boy's arm fiercely and thrust his face forward. 'I said leave him be, unless you want another bloody nose.'

They glared at each other like a pair of angry cats.

The term before, Tom, summoned by Mr Cadwallader, had rushed into the playground at break to find Colin and Christopher rolling around in the dust with legs kicking and fists flying. They had been surrounded by a group of spectators. The teacher had dived in and separated the two boys, pulling each one up roughly by the collar of his shirt.

'Stop it at once!' he had shouted.

'He started it, calling me names!' Christopher had cried. The boy's nostril had been dribbling with blood. 'Then he hit me. He punched me on the nose.'

'What was this all about?' their teacher had asked.

'He said my dad was a crook and owed his dad money and wouldn't pay him back,' Colin had told Tom.

'Did you say this, Christopher?'

'I was only saying what my dad told my uncle last night,' the boy had replied, wiping a trickle of blood from his nose.

Since this incident Christopher had given Colin a wide berth. He now pulled his arm free and, spitting on the ground, stormed off.

'Let me know if he gives you any more trouble,' Colin told Leo. He left the two boys and headed for the school.

'Well, there's a thing,' said Charlie. 'Colin Greenwood used to bully me and now he's stopping others bullying.'

'"There's nowt as queer as folk,"' said Leo. 'Isn't that what they say in Yorkshire?'

The two friends laughed.

There was an element of self-interest in Colin's defence of Leo. He was keen to keep on the right side of the boy's mother. The Saturday after his visit to the studio with his father, he had spent the afternoon with Mrs Stanhope and listened intently as she suggested some ways in which he could improve his painting technique. He liked her from the start. She had a soft and quiet manner and didn't talk down to him as adults often do to children. She explained that her advice would be honest and that he shouldn't be upset or angry if she was direct and open with him about his paintings.

'It would be of no help to you,' she had explained, 'if I merely told you that all your work is wonderful. As I said when I agreed to take you on, I may be critical of it at times, but my comments will be constructive and helpful so you must be prepared for a straightforward evaluation.'

'Yes, miss,' the boy had replied.

'Now, I am sure you appreciate that I don't need to do this, Colin,' she had told him frankly. 'I am not your teacher paid to teach you. I am giving up some of my precious time to help you. I am happy to do this because I think you have a talent and a real interest in art, but I expect you to listen to what I tell you, do as I say and work hard. Are you prepared to do this?'

'Yes, miss,' he had replied.

She had smiled. 'Good. Then let us see how we get on.'

The following Saturday, Colin was accompanied by his father, who sat for his portrait. Anyone observing both father and son hanging on the artist's every word would be left in no doubt that they were both enamoured with this beautiful, colourful and unusual woman, something they had in common with most of the men in Risingdale.

Morning break found three of the teachers in the staffroom.

'So how did you get on with Mr Firkin at your WI meeting, Bertha?' asked Mr Cadwallader.

'Oh, very well,' replied Mrs Golightly. 'He was a big hit with the ladies. He was most agreeable and very kindly agreed to judge the cake competition. I made one of my mother's coffee and walnut cakes.'

'And I wonder who won,' said Joyce wryly.

'I got the first prize, as a matter of fact,' said Mrs Golightly.

'There's a surprise,' observed Joyce.

'Mr Firkin said my cake was as light as a nun's kiss.'

'And how would Mr Firkin know?' asked Mr Cadwallader, crunching on a Garibaldi. 'I don't imagine he's ever been kissed by a nun.'

'How did his talk go down?' asked Joyce.

'Not a barrel of laughs, I warrant,' said Mr Cadwallader.

'Actually, you're wrong, Owen,' she replied. 'It was most interesting. Mr Firkin is a very good speaker. I never realised how bizarre some funerals can be: vicars mixing up the deceased's names, people arguing over who should have the ashes, folks coming to blows, others staggering in worse for drink, mourners getting hysterical, ex-wives turning up unannounced, dropped coffins, hearses breaking down. You wouldn't believe the carryings-on. You could write a book. Mr Firkin's talk was a real eye-opener and very well-received. He told us that sometimes funerals can be quite comical affairs.'

'Comical!' cried Joyce. 'There's nothing comical about a funeral.'

'Oh, you should have heard Mr Firkin,' said Mrs Golightly, 'he was most entertaining and told us of some very funny incidents that had occurred at the crematorium.'

'Such as?' asked Mr Cadwallader.

'Well, there was one old lady in her nineties, not a very nice person by all accounts. She was very cantankerous, always complaining and didn't get on with any of her relations. Left everything to a donkey sanctuary, she did. Hardly anybody attended the service at the crematorium, which was just as well after what happened.'

'What did happen?' asked Mr Cadwallader.

'I'm about to tell you, if you give me a chance,' said Mrs Golightly. 'As I was saying, hardly anybody turned up at the crematorium – just a couple from the care home and some man from the donkey sanctuary. Anyway, the deceased wasn't particularly religious and wanted certain pieces of music to be played at her funeral. She had left instructions in her will for the executor to follow. When the coffin disappeared behind the velvet curtain, she had requested a recording of Judy Garland singing "Over the Rainbow" from *The Wizard of Oz*.'

'I love that song,' said Joyce. '"Somewhere over the rainbow, way up high, there's a land that I've heard of once in a lullaby." Beautiful lyrics. I'm thinking of staging it as a future production.'

'You could ask Mrs Gosling to be the Wicked Witch of the West,' said Mr Cadwallader. 'She's perfect for the part.'

'Unfortunately,' continued Mrs Golightly, 'the dear departed didn't get what she had asked for because the man who was in charge of playing the audio tape picked the wrong track. Instead of going out to "Over the Rainbow", the poor woman went to meet her Maker with "Ding-Dong! The Witch is Dead". You can imagine the look of horror on the vicar's face.'

'Oh my goodness,' exclaimed Joyce. 'How dreadful.'

'But that's not all,' Mrs Golightly carried on. 'You will never guess what happened next.'

'What?' asked Mr Cadwallader.

'The man in charge of the audio tape then played the next track: "We're Off to See the Wizard, the Wonderful Wizard of Oz".'

'That cannot be true,' said Joyce.

'Oh yes it was,' Mrs Golightly told her. 'Then there was the occasion when another elderly woman called Sally wanted a recording of Gracie Fields singing "Sally, Sally, Pride of Our Alley" when she passed on.'

'And?' asked Mr Cadwallader.

'It happened again. The person playing the audio tape put on the wrong track and the dear departed went up to heaven with, "Wish Me Luck as You Wave Me Goodbye". What made it even more diverting was that everyone in the congregation, including the vicar, waved her off.'

'I consider that's rather a nice way to go,' said Mr Cadwallader. 'I think I might like a send-off like that, to go out with people singing and waving and wishing me luck.'

'I don't wish to hear any more,' said Miss Tranter, holding up a hand. 'I think it is in rather bad taste to joke about funerals.'

'We all have to go, Joyce,' said Mrs Golightly, 'and there's no coming back. When you've gone, you've gone.'

'I am aware of that, Bertha, but I do not wish to talk about it.'

'I think funerals for old people who have had a good innings,' said Mr Cadwallader, 'should not be gloomy affairs, but more a celebration of their lives, for the loved ones to remember all the happy times they have had with the deceased, and share stories about them and relate some of their memories of them. I certainly don't want any doom and gloom when I die.'

'I'm having "We'll Meet Again" at my funeral,' said Mrs Golightly, 'and there'll be a fancy reception and everyone will—'

'Could we change the subject?' pleaded Joyce, interrupting. 'This conversation is very depressing.'

'It sounds to me, Bertha, as if Mr Firkin's talk went down very well,' said Mr Cadwallader.

'It was the best ever,' Mrs Golightly told him. 'He's coming back by popular demand to talk about embalming.'

'Look,' said Joyce. 'Could we please let the subject drop? I have heard quite enough about funerals and what goes on at the crematorium.'

The staffroom door opened and Mr Leadbeater made his entrance.

'Just to let you know, it's beginning to snow again,' he told the teachers, 'so I've put some ashes down on the path.'

James Maladroit sprawled on the bed, his hands interlaced behind his head. He had arrived that evening late and, after helping himself to a large whisky in the drawing room, crept up to his room, not wishing to see his father. He would face the inevitable confrontation the next morning. He had rung his mother to tell her of his expected time of arrival. She had not seen fit to tell her husband. She needed to see her son alone. There was something she had to say to him.

'So, what sort of mood is the old man in?' James asked his mother.

She sat at the head of the bed next to him.

'The mood he is always in,' she replied.

'God, how I hate the thought of listening to another of his tiresome rants,' said her son, yawning widely. 'I suppose I'm in for another bloody dressing-down.'

'Please don't swear, James,' she said.

'Don't you start scolding me, Ma,' he said, petulantly. 'I get enough of that from him. Why can't he get off my back for once? I knew I wouldn't take to that bloody job in Scotland. I did try but I know bugger-all about whisky, the place was in the middle of nowhere and they all had it in for me from the start. I couldn't understand a word they said.' He sighed with weary sufferance. 'I don't know how you put up with him.'

Lady Maladroit didn't respond.

'He's never had any time for me,' he continued. 'As far back as I can remember, he's always managed to find fault and made it perfectly clear that I was a dreadful disappointment, that I never came up to his expectations. I wish he wasn't my father.'

Lady Maladroit thought for a moment before replying. 'He isn't,' she said.

'What!' He shot up as if he had been stung. 'What did you just say?'

'I said he isn't your father,' she replied calmly.

'What do you mean?' He jolted upright.

'I mean, he isn't your father,' she told him, resting a hand on his arm. 'I can't be plainer than that.'

'Bloody hell!' He took a deep breath. The colour had drained from his face. 'Why didn't you tell me before?' he asked.

'I wanted to ... it's just ... well, I didn't think it the right time.'

'And he doesn't know?'

'Of course he doesn't know.'

'So, who is my father?'

'Really, James, I don't wish to go into all the details.'

'Come on, Ma,' he said, gripping her arm. 'You can't just drop this bombshell and then not tell me who my real father is.'

'Well, if you must know, it's Rupert Poskitt.' She pulled her arm away.

'The guy who owns the London gallery where you worked?'

'Yes.'

'Bloody hell!'

'I have asked you not to swear, James. You know I don't like it.'

'Well, how did that happen?'

'It doesn't matter how it happened,' she said. 'It just did.'

'Why haven't you told the old man?' he asked.

'You know, James, sometimes you surprise me with your naivety,' she said. 'Were I to tell him you are not his son, where do you think it would leave you? For a start, you would lose the title when he dies, and do you imagine that he would leave the house, his estate and his money to you?'

'Yes, you have a point.'

'Say nothing of this, because if you do you will throw away your inheritance. And when you speak to him tomorrow morning, don't provoke him, just listen and say nothing and tell him you will behave yourself.'

He shook his head. 'I can't take this in,' he said. 'It's incredible.'

Lady Maladroit thought for a moment. She put a hand on his shoulder. 'I know this has come as a shock,' she said. 'You're not too upset that he's not your father?'

'Come on, Ma,' he said, giving a snort of a laugh. 'What do you think?'

Rather shamefaced, James Maladroit arrived at his father's study at nine o'clock the following morning, having been summoned by Sir Hedley.

Lady Maladroit had told her husband that morning that their son had returned the previous evening, but after a long and arduous journey from Scotland he was tired and had gone straight to bed.

'And don't scold him, Hedley,' she had said. 'He has been reprimanded by you quite enough. James regrets what has happened and is determined to turn over a new leaf.'

Sir Hedley now stood by the window in his study looking out over the vast parkland, wondering what he should do about his wayward son, who currently sat stiff-backed with a suitably chastened look on his face. His words had had no effect in the past; he now determined to give an ultimatum.

James Maladroit bore no resemblance to Sir Hedley. Whereas the baronet was a large man with a ruddy complexion, a wide mouth, dark, hooded eyes and prominent ears, his son was of slight build with a long, bony face like a horse, papery skin as white as milk and the small, down-turned mouth of a peevish child.

'So, what happened in Scotland?' asked Sir Hedley in a calm voice.

'It just didn't work out, Pa,' replied his son.

'Why didn't it "just work out"?'

'For a start, I couldn't understand a bloody thing anyone said, and the manager of the distillery took a dislike to me from the very beginning.'

'I wonder why that was,' said his father, cynically.

'The work didn't suit me at all. I mean, I know nothing about whisky.'

'You do surprise me, James. You certainly have a taste for it, judging by the empty decanter in the drawing room and the amount of time you spent drinking it in the local pub. So, the work in Scotland didn't suit you. Tell me, what work do you think will suit you? Since you left school, you have done nothing and made no attempt to do anything. You have been reckless, extravagant and lazy.'

His son felt it politic not to respond, much as he would have liked to have done. He was weary of hearing his father's clamorous voice.

Sir Hedley stroked his moustache and thought for a moment about what he might say. 'Well,' he said at last, 'from now on, things will change. You will sort yourself out and get a job or you are out of that door. I have had enough of putting up with your excesses, James. You have done some deceitful things in your time but stealing from your mother was beyond the pale.'

'I said I was sorry, Pa,' replied James. He had hoped that the theft would not be raised again, but, true to form, his father had dredged it up. 'I know it was stupid and very wrong. I see that now.'

'And what about the young woman you got pregnant?'

'I'm sorry about that, too,' said his son feebly. 'It was a moment of madness and she did throw herself at me.'

'Don't you dare blame her!' snapped Sir Hedley. 'You took advantage of her. And don't you want to know how the mother of your child and the baby are getting on?'

'Of course I do. I was going to pop down to the King's Head later and see Leanne.'

'She's not there,' he was told. 'She's moved away and, from what I gather, wants nothing whatever to do with you – and who can blame her?'

'I do have rights as a father,' said James with a rare burst of displeasure.

'Oh, do you really?' said his father sardonically. 'And I suppose you are in a position to support her and her child, are you?'

'Well, not exactly.'

'So, it falls upon me yet again to cover your costs, does it?' asked the baronet, not expecting an answer.

James sighed. How he wished his father would shut up. He was weary of listening to the constant complaints and criticism. It was always the same old gripes: 'Why don't you get a job? When are you going to do something useful? Why don't you make something of yourself?' He went on and on like a repeated gramophone record. He looked at the angry red face that he despised. I'll be glad when the old man is dead and I become the baronet and inherit the estate, he said to himself. He gave a half smile thinking of the reaction of the old fool if he were to tell him he was not his father.

'Are you listening to me?' demanded Sir Hedley.

'Of course I am, Pa.'

'You can start tomorrow looking round for a job and you can get rid of that fancy sports car of yours, too. There will be no more gadding around the country and spending all day in the local pub or the betting shop. Is that clear?'

'Of course,' replied his son.

'Right. I have things to do so I suggest you get the local paper and start looking for a position.' James remained seated. 'Was there something else?' asked Sir Hedley.

'I was wondering if I could have my allowance back,' said James.

12

Before Tom started at Risingdale, there had been no provision for any sort of physical activity on the curriculum. When he suggested to Mr Gaunt and his colleagues that he would like to take the children for games and PE once a week, they were wholehearted in their support.

With the arrival of Leo, the teacher was faced with a dilemma. Tom had been made fully aware of the boy's illness and wondered whether it would be wise for the boy to exert himself on the games' field. The Risingdale children were fast and boisterous players and maybe too rough for such a delicate and ailing child. Tom's instinct was to let the boy miss Friday games, but he recalled the mother's words that she didn't want her son to be pitied or receive any special treatment, to be wrapped in cotton wool. He sought Mr Gaunt's advice.

'A tricky one, this,' pondered the headmaster, running a hand through his hair and tipping back in his chair. He stared at Tom for a moment as if trying to make up his mind what to say. 'I think you need to speak to the boy and see how he feels,' he said at last.

'Not contact Leo's mother and see what she thinks?' asked Tom.

'No, I don't imagine the lad would thank you for doing that. From what I've seen, he's a tough little character, despite his illness, and he does have a mind of his own. Let him decide and if he does feel able to take part, then you can keep a close eye on him.'

'I'm really not sure,' said Tom. 'I think it may be taking too big a risk.'

Mr Gaunt smiled, sat up, rested his hands on the desktop and locked his fingers. Tom could predict the headmaster was about to share with him one of his opinions. 'Well, you know, Tom, life is full of risks,' Mr Gaunt told him. 'There has never been any progress in the world without some element of risk. There would be no games of football, rugby, hockey, no mountain climbers or potholers, boxers or wrestlers, if we didn't accept there are risks involved. I am sure that you, as a former professional footballer, were well aware that there are certain dangers in playing any game. I used to referee rugby matches in my younger days. There was always the risk that someone would get injured. You yourself have suffered a few injuries in your time, I'd guess. Throughout history there have always been those who have done risky things that have paid off. Now take Nelson at Trafalgar, for example. Had he not risked his fleet and his reputation, he would not have won the Battle of Trafalgar.'

'With respect, Mr Gaunt,' replied the teacher, wearying of the monologue, 'we are not talking about Nelson. We are talking about a sick boy.' All he wanted was a straight answer.

'Look, Tom,' said the headmaster, leaning back again in his chair, 'I told you when you started at the school that I am not a head teacher who interferes with what my staff is doing. Provided the children get a good sound education and the teachers treat them with respect and relate well to them, I don't see any need to get involved. I'm not a dictator. My view is that if the lad wishes, you should let him play, but the decision is yours.'

'I am still uneasy about it,' said Tom.

'If you feel he should miss games to be on the safe side,' replied the headmaster, 'then that is up to you. You are his teacher.'

Leo had looked surprised when Tom asked him if he was well enough to play football.

'Of course I am, Mr Dwyer,' he replied. 'If I do get a bit tired, which sometimes happens, I'll sit things out, but I don't want to miss games. I enjoy football.'

'If you are sure,' said Tom. 'Though it might be safer to skip games on occasion.'

'I should like to play,' replied the boy. He then added, 'You have no need to worry.'

It was part way through the match when it happened. Vicky had just passed Leo the ball. He was a fast little runner, light on his feet, and he handled the ball well, skilfully dribbling around the players on the opposing team. As he headed for the goal, Christopher ran up behind him and tripped him up. It looked clear to everybody that it was a deliberate act. Leo fell heavily and banged his head on the hard ground.

'That was a foul!' shouted Vicky at Christopher. 'You did that on purpose.'

'No, I didn't!' he shouted back.

'Yes, you did,' she shouted, stabbing the air with a finger. 'We all saw you.'

Leo lay still.

Tom's worst fears had materialised.

'Oh my God,' Tom said under his breath as he ran to the boy, his heart thudding in his chest. He pushed his way through the group of children who had started to gather around Leo, standing in silence looking lost and bewildered. Tom knelt over the motionless figure, stroked the hair out of the boy's eyes and felt his forehead. When he had played professional football, Tom had been concussed a good few times and knew that after a while the body usually returned to normal. Leo, however, remained still, his face as white as milk and his breathing faint.

'Is he all right, sir?' asked Vicky.

Tom ignored her and spoke softly into Leo's ear. His voice quavered. 'Can you hear me, Leo?' There was no reply.

'Christopher did it deliberately,' she said angrily. 'We all saw it.'

There was a murmur of agreement from the others.

'I want you all to go back into school,' the teacher told the children, trying to keep his voice steady. 'Get changed quickly and without any noise and return to the classroom. Get a book and read quietly. Vicky, I would like you to run and tell Mr Gaunt what has happened.'

'Christopher tripped him up!' she cried. 'That's what happened.'

There was another murmur of agreement from the other pupils.

'I didn't mean to,' said the boy weakly. He looked shaken.

'Yes, you did!' retorted the girl. 'That was a nasty, horrible thing to do.'

'Do as you are told, Vicky,' Tom told her. 'Run and tell Mr Gaunt what has happened. Be quick about it.' He turned to the other children. 'Right, off you go, into school, all of you.'

Tom gently lifted the small body, surprised by its lightness, and carried him into school. The child cradled dejectedly in his arms like a broken puppet.

Mrs Leadbeater peered over the top of her unfashionable horn-rimmed spectacles when Tom entered her office, but when she saw the boy in the teacher's arms she shot up from her desk. There was an expression of horror on her face.

'Phone an ambulance, please, Beryl,' Tom told her. There was a tremble in his voice.

Tom travelled with Leo in the ambulance to Clayton Royal Infirmary, leaving Mr Gaunt in charge of his class and asking him to ring Leo's mother and let her know what had happened. The child, still unconscious, was rushed on a stretcher through the Accident and Emergency Department and disappeared down the corridor surrounded by nurses and a doctor. Tom was left standing by the reception desk and told to wait. He was soon joined by a young female doctor who asked about the accident. When Tom explained what had happened, she shook her head.

'He should not have been moved,' she reprimanded. 'He could have damaged his neck.'

Tom ran a hand through his hair and took a deep breath. He felt awful. 'Yes, I see that,' he said, 'but I couldn't leave him in the cold. It was freezing out there. The school is miles from anywhere and it would have taken an age for an ambulance to get there.'

When Tom, in a shaky voice, told the doctor about Leo's condition, she shook her head again and sighed.

'A brain tumour,' she said.

'Yes,' replied Tom.

'And he was playing football?'

Tom nodded.

'I see.'

'Will he be all right?' It sounded such a feeble thing to ask in the circumstances.

'That I can't say,' she replied. 'I'll see the young man's mother when she arrives.' With that she walked away.

As he sat anxiously in the crowded A&E Department surrounded by people with a variety of complaints, coughing and sneezing, nursing broken arms and bandaged hands, Tom thought about what had happened. At first, he partly blamed Mr Gaunt. Why had the headmaster not directed him to excuse Leo from games instead of telling him how important it was to take risks and rambling on about Nelson? Head teachers are appointed to make decisions. He should not have left it to him. This would never have happened, thought Tom, if he had followed his own instincts. But at the end of the day, it was he who had decided to let Leo play and it was he who must face the consequences. A great weight of guilt now pressed down on his shoulders. Whatever could he say to the boy's mother? The more he thought about it, the more irresponsible it seemed to have let a seriously ill boy play football. An accident was waiting to happen. Then there was Christopher Pickles. Everyone had seen that the reckless boy had purposely tripped Leo up. He would speak to that particular pupil later.

Back at school, another drama was about to unfold as Joyce walked across the playground on her way home with a spring in her step, looking forward to the weekend ahead. She was to meet Julian later that evening. He had booked a table at Le Bon Viveur, the smart restaurant in Clayton where they had dined on their first date. The choice, she felt, was significant. Julian had told her that he had something important to speak to her about and she had an inkling of what it was. At the weekend in Scarborough, he had said how lonely he had been since his wife had died.

'Margaret loved it here,' he had said. 'She loved the great stretch of beach, the fresh sea air, the walks along the cliffs and concerts at the Spa.' He had been thoughtful. 'I imagined that we would grow old together and one day maybe retire here. But sadly it wasn't to be. After she passed away, I didn't know what to do with myself. The house was dark and empty without her. My life was dark and empty without her. Then I threw myself into the business and had little time for much else, or for other people, for that matter. And then I met you and my life has changed. You've brought me back into the real world.' He had reached across the table and taken Joyce's hand in his.

So that afternoon when she walked across the playground to her car, thinking about the evening ahead and what was in store, Joyce was so preoccupied that at first she didn't notice the figure sitting on the wall, a cigarette between his lips. It was the thin-featured individual with an untidy beard and shoulder-length hair who had called into the Barton village store asking about her. On seeing Joyce, he stood, dropped the cigarette on the grass and ground it with the heel of his boot, walked through the school gate and approached her.

'Hello, Joycey,' he said.

She stopped in her tracks and turned. At first she was lost for words, stunned at seeing the very last person in the world she wished to see. Then she took a deep breath and found her voice. It was a strong, clear and determined voice.

'What are you doing here?' she demanded. The colour had drained from her face and she felt a sudden lump of misery as tight as a nut catch in her throat.

'I've come to see my wife,' he said with smirk on his face. 'I've missed you.'

'I'm not your wife!' she snapped. 'I am your ex-wife and I want nothing more to do with you. How did you find me, anyway?'

'By a stroke of luck,' he told her. 'I knew you moved away somewhere into the country. I saw your picture in the local paper. Bit of a comedown from being a professional actor, isn't it, Joycey, directing some miserable little amateurish pantomime?' He scoffed. 'Mind you, you were never much good as an actor though, were you?'

'You've not changed, have you, Stephen?' she retorted. 'You're still as nasty and patronising as ever.' She smiled coldly. 'And speaking of acting, I got a lot more theatre work than you ever did. Oh, and while we're on the subject, what West End production are you starring in at the moment?'

'You've changed, Joycey,' he said. There was a curl of his lip. 'Quite the feisty woman now, aren't you?'

'You're right,' she said. 'I have changed. I changed the day I left you. You treated me like a doormat, mocking me and saying all those hurtful things, controlling me. You let jealousy eat away at you like a canker. I'm ashamed I let you get away with it for so long. And now you think you can breeze back into my life and start intimidating me all over again. Well, think again. I don't want anything to do with you, so just go away and leave me alone.'

She pulled open the car door.

'You've not heard the last of me, Joycey,' he said.

As she drove away, she looked through the rear window and saw him waving.

The owner of Le Bon Viveur greeted Joyce and Julian in the foyer of his lavish restaurant that evening. He shook the hand warmly of one of his regular patrons, smiled to display a set of unnaturally brilliant white, even teeth and gave a slight bow. Then he took Joyce's hand in his own and planted a kiss on her hand. He smelled of expensive cologne.

'*Bonsoir, monsieur et madame. Enchanté de vous revoir,*' he said.

They were shown to a corner table covered in a stiff white cloth and set out with bone china plates, crystal glasses, starched napkins and heavy silver cutlery. In the centre was a slender vase containing one red rose.

'This is lovely, Julian,' said Joyce. She had been shaken at seeing her ex-husband again and her misery was etched on her face.

'Are you all right, my dear?' asked Julian. 'You're looking very pale.'

'Oh, I'm fine. Just a bit tired,' she said. She managed a small smile.

'You are overdoing it,' he told her. 'Working too hard.'

She smiled and nodded. 'Perhaps.'

'I thought it appropriate to come here tonight,' he said. 'You remember that we came to Le Bon Viveur after our first meeting.'

'And it was a lovely evening too,' she said.

'I thought so.'

During the meal Julian's conversation was largely inconsequential. Joyce listened patiently but said very little. He could see that her mind was on other things.

'You are very quiet tonight, Joyce,' he said suddenly. 'Is something bothering you?'

'We had a very upsetting time at school today,' she told him. 'I can't get it out of my mind. One of the pupils, a nice little boy, was rushed to hospital. He has a brain tumour, which we are told is not invasive, but it's still heartbreaking for one so young to have to cope with such an illness. He's a brave child and manages really well, but today he banged his head playing football and was taken to Clayton Royal Infirmary by his teacher. The headmaster rang the hospital and it doesn't sound good. As I said, it's very upsetting.' Of course this was not the main thing she could not get out of her mind. The image of her ex-husband sitting on the wall smirking suddenly filled her thoughts.

'Should the boy have been playing football with such a serious condition?' asked Julian.

'Pardon?'

'I asked if the boy should have been playing football with such a serious condition?'

'Possibly not.'

'It seems to me that the teacher was rather reckless to let the boy play such a sport.'

'Maybe so,' she said.

'Well, I hope the young man pulls through. It must be a dreadful time for his parents.'

'Are there any children in your family?' asked Joyce.

'I just have one nephew. Stanley works in London at the moment but is coming to work for me at the auction house later this year. It will be quite a change for him. At present he works for an investment firm in the city, but the hours—'

'There is something else on my mind,' interrupted Joyce. She took a breath. 'I should have told you before but never got around to it. The thing is . . . I was married. I got divorced after a little over a year.'

'I see.'

'I wanted to tell you about it, but . . .'

'But what?'

'I thought it might spoil things.'

He smiled. 'Why should it spoil things? People do split up, you know.'

'I'd like to tell you about it,' she said.

'If you like, but there is really no need.'

'There is,' she said. 'I met Stephen at drama college in London. He was funny and outgoing and seemed so good-natured and paid a lot of attention to me. I guess I fell in love with him. But he was putting on an act. After we were married, his true personality came out. I saw the real Stephen – moody, bad-tempered and petulant. He then started to be demanding and controlling, telling me what to do, what to wear, checking up on where I was going. It got worse when I started to get auditions and parts in plays and he didn't. He became obsessively jealous and began undermining my confidence and self-esteem. It was unbearable.'

'It sounds it,' said Julian.

'So I left him and trained to be teacher. But he kept turning up, watching and following me. I'd be at an art gallery and he would be there, or at the theatre, I'd see him in one of the seats in front. I'd come out of school and he'd be waiting for me. It was intimidating.'

'Did you not go to the police?'

'Yes, I did, but they told me there was nothing they could do. He didn't attack me or threaten me and most of the time he didn't speak to me, but it was menacing. I couldn't bear it. The police advised me to ignore him or move somewhere he couldn't find me. So, I got as far away as I could and came to Risingdale, the last place on Earth I thought that he would find me. I changed my life.'

'And you met me,' said Julian.

'Yes, I met you.'

'And you changed my life,' he said simply. 'I couldn't care less whether you were married or not. Just forget about the bully.'

If only I could, she thought.

Julian called the waiter over and whispered something in his ear. A moment later a bottle of champagne in a silver bucket and two crystal flutes were brought to the table. Julian reached into his pocket and produced a small red leather-bound box and opened it. Inside was an emerald and diamond ring.

'Will you marry me, Joyce?' he asked.

With his hands pressed between his knees and his head down, Tom sat in wretched silence in the hospital reception area in the A&E Department. He was oblivious to the sights and sounds around him and rehearsed what he might say to Leo's mother when she arrived. The words he repeated in his head sounded feeble.

'Hello.'

He looked up to find the person most on his mind looking down at him. It was Leo's mother.

'Oh.' He couldn't find the words. Tom stared up at her with quiet despair.

'How is he?' she asked, sitting next to him. Her voice was deliberately steady.

'I . . . er . . . don't know,' he said. 'When we arrived they took him off – a doctor and a nurse. That was about an hour ago. A doctor came and told me she would speak to you when you arrived. I've not been keeping track of time. No one's been to tell me anything.' His voice was tense and breathless.

'I see,' she said.

Tom was amazed at the woman's startling power of self-control.

'I had better go and see how he is,' she said.

'Mrs Stanhope,' said Tom, lightly taking her arm. There were bright spots of tears in the corners of his eyes. 'Before you go, I . . .'

'Yes?'

'I'm so sorry. I feel awful about what's happened. I should never have let Leo play football. It was irresponsible of me to let him . . .' His voice tailed off.

She gave him a small but kindly smile and rested a hand on his arm.

'You mustn't blame yourself,' she told him. 'I don't blame you.'

'I do blame myself,' he said miserably. 'I should not have allowed him to play.'

'Did my son want to play football?' she asked.

'Yes, he did, but—'

'You asked him?'

'Yes, I asked him if he felt well enough to play and I said that maybe to be on the safe side he should give games a miss, but he was keen on playing.'

'He wouldn't have wanted to miss the game, Mr Dwyer,' she said. 'I told you and Mr Gaunt that I wished Leo to live his life as fully as possible, to be treated no differently from any other boy of his age. That is what he wants. He doesn't wish to go through life being mollycoddled or protected or treated like some sort of delicate object to be watched over. He's a determined boy and he's brave too. You must have discovered that about him. And he's a fighter. This has happened before and he got through it.' Tears shone in her eyes but she regained control of herself quickly. 'You have nothing to reproach yourself for. Now, I must go and see him.'

'I'll wait,' said Tom.

'You might be waiting a long time,' she replied.

'Nevertheless, I would like to,' he said.

She gave a weak sort of smile and walked to the reception desk.

Sooner than expected, Mrs Stanhope arrived back in the A&E Department. She was accompanied by a tall man whose thin face was dominated by heavy, black-rimmed glasses.

'This is Mr Dwyer, my son's teacher,' she told the man.

'Good evening,' he said. 'I am Raymond Knight, Leo's oncologist.'

Tom jumped to his feet. 'How is he?' he asked.

'Not too bad,' replied the doctor. 'Not too bad at all.'

'He was unconscious when he came in,' said Tom.

'He's come around,' the specialist told him, 'and, as I was telling his mother, I don't think there is anything to be overly concerned about.'

'Thank God,' said Tom.

'It wasn't that bad a bang to the head,' said the consultant. 'He's a remarkable young man with a real determination not to let his condition get him down. To have such grit and will-power is important for someone with his illness, but I have to say it is unusual in one so young. We are keeping him in for a few days for observation and for further tests, but I am reasonably confident that he will be back at school next week.'

Tom sighed. 'Thank God,' he murmured again.

'Now, Mrs Stanhope was telling me you feel somewhat responsible for what happened,' said Dr Knight.

'I should never have allowed Leo to play football,' replied Tom. 'It was stupid of me.'

'Not really,' disagreed the specialist. 'It is unknown whether children with brain tumours have a higher risk of complications while participating in sports, but, interestingly, some doctors have sought to estimate the consequences of such sporting events by conducting research. I recently read a paper about it. They have discovered that sports-related complications are uncommon in children with brain tumours. Therefore, patients might not be at a significantly higher risk and should not need to be excluded from most sports activities. Of course, Leo needs to be careful and I wouldn't recommend that he play rugby.'

'Could I see him?' asked Tom.

The specialist looked at Mrs Stanhope.

'Yes,' she said, 'I'm sure he would like to see you.'

'But don't stay too long,' said Dr Knight. 'He needs the rest.'

Leo looked pale and drawn and his eyes had lost some of the brightness Tom had been used to seeing. The boy raised a small smile on seeing his teacher.

'Look who I've brought to see you,' said his mother.

'Hello, Mr Dwyer,' he said. He looked so small and frail, lying propped up in the bed with his thin white fingers resting on the cover of the sheet. He reminded Tom of some delicate china doll with his golden curls and pale, unblemished face.

'Hello, Leo. How are you feeling?' The question seemed feeble to Tom as soon as he had asked it, for it was clear that the child looked ill.

'Not too good at the moment,' replied the boy.

Tom rested a hand on the boy's shoulder. 'I'm so sorry about what happened,' he said.

'I'm sorry for all the trouble I caused,' said Leo.

'You've not caused any trouble,' Tom replied.

'These things happen,' said the boy, sounding like an adult talking to a child. 'It was an accident. I shall have to be more careful in future.'

Tom nodded, but kept his thoughts to himself. It was no

accident. He had seen the whole thing. Christopher had deliberately tripped the boy up.

It was as if Leo was reading what was in the teacher's head.

'It was an unlucky collision, Mr Dwyer,' he said, 'and I received a bit of a bump. I wouldn't want anyone to get into any trouble over what happened.'

That is all very well, thought Tom, but he determined to have a word with Christopher Pickles.

13

The following morning, Tom drove into Clayton. He was to meet his Auntie Bridget in the Ring o' Bells café before visiting the hospital to see if there had been any improvement in Leo's condition. Despite what Mrs Stanhope and the doctor had said, his decision to let the boy play football still preyed upon his mind. He needed to unburden himself and the best person to turn to was his Auntie Bridget. She had always been there for him, to support and help him. As an adolescent, Tom had gone through a bad patch – moody, short-tempered and angry at God for taking his mother from him. His father, before his own untimely death a few years later, had become withdrawn and uncommunicative after his wife had passed away, and found solace in the whisky bottle. It was said that he had died of a broken heart. His mother's elder sister had not been disposed to take care of this sulky, difficult teenager.

'I mean, I feel sorry for him, so I do,' she had told Bridget, 'but there's no question of him coming to live with us. I have a family of my own and he's such a contrary boy.'

So it was left to Tom's mother's younger sister, Bridget, to give the boy a home, and it was she who had helped her nephew through those dark days and encouraged him to follow his dream of becoming a professional footballer. She was still the closest person to him in his life.

The weather that morning reflected Tom's dismal mood. Watery sunshine struggled to make its way through the clouds in the gun-grey sky and a cold gusty wind blew litter down the high street and tugged fretfully at the window of the café. A thin rain began to patter on the glass.

They sat at their usual corner table and Tom told his aunt of the events of the previous week, of the frail little boy with the cruel illness, of how he had carried the child unconscious into school and gone with him to the hospital, of seeing him propped up in bed with his paper-white skin and flat, discoloured eyes half hidden below dark lids. He told her how wretched he felt about the whole business.

His auntie thought for a moment. 'You want my opinion?' she asked.

'Was I wrong?' he asked.

'Sure, who am I to say?' she replied.

'I just need . . .' Tom began.

'Reassurance that you did the right thing?'

'Yes, I suppose I do.'

'Is it helpful to cry over spilt milk?' she asked, avoiding giving him her opinion. It would have been no help to her nephew to tell him that, in her view, it might have been better to have erred on the side of caution.

'I just can't get it out of my mind.'

'To be honest with you, I don't know whether you did right or wrong,' said his auntie. 'I do know that it's not very helpful to keep going over things that you cannot change. It serves no purpose upsetting yourself over something that has happened. You can't alter the past, Tom. You have to live with it.'

'I know that.'

'If the occasion arose again, would you let the boy play football?' she asked.

'No, I don't think I would.'

'Well, there's your answer.'

When Tom went to pay the bill, there at the counter stood Janette Fairborn.

'Hello, Tom,' she said. She had not changed: still as he remembered her, the striking-looking woman with the flaming red hair and dazzling green eyes. His heart began to quicken. With all the recent upset, he had not given her a thought.

'Oh,' was all he managed to say. He locked eyes with her for a moment, blushed and looked away.

'How are you?' she asked.

'I'm fine,' he replied, turning to look into the green eyes. 'How about you?'

'I'm fine too.'

There was an embarrassed silence.

'What brings you back from the big city?' he asked.

'I'm spending the weekend at home,' she answered.

'And checking up on your horse.'

'Yes. I miss her.'

'I heard about your dog,' he said.

She gave a small smile. 'Yes, I miss him too. I got him from an animal shelter, you know – the runt of the litter and the ugliest dog you have ever seen – but I loved him.'

'I'm sorry,' he said. He changed the subject. 'And how are you liking your new job?' he asked.

'It's OK,' she answered.

'Just OK?'

'Well, there's lots to do.'

She could have told him the truth: that she hated the job and was lonely and unhappy and that things had not turned out as she had anticipated. She could have told him that the deputy manager at the bank, who expected to have been offered the position that she had been given, felt bitter at being passed over for a woman half his age and with half his experience. He was distant and devious and undermined her at every opportunity. Janette had been appointed to improve the efficiency at the branch but the necessary changes she effected had made the staff resentful and uncooperative. She could have told Tom the draw of the bright lights and the excitement of the big city had faded away. She could have told him too that she wanted to return to Risingdale and pick up with him where they had left off.

'I'm pleased for you,' he said.

'Actually, Tom, to tell you the truth—' she began.

She stopped mid-sentence as a handsome woman with a wave of bright blonde hair approached. She waved at Tom and smiled.

'Please excuse me for a moment, Jan,' he said, going to meet the woman, whom he greeted warmly. He took her arm, directed her to the table where his aunt was sitting and pulled out a chair for her to sit down. He introduced Mrs O'Connor, sat down himself and leaned closer to the woman, his face full of expectancy.

'I thought I might find you here,' said Mrs Stanhope. 'I recall you said you often call in this café for a coffee on Saturday mornings. I wanted to let you know how Leo is getting on.'

'How is he?' Tom asked.

'There's been little change, I'm afraid,' she replied. 'I think the bang to his head has proved more serious than the doctors thought at first. He seems pretty stable though, so I am optimistic. This setback has happened before. We are waiting for the results of the tests.'

Tom felt awful. His stomach tightened. 'I shouldn't have let him play,' he muttered, shaking his head.

Mrs Stanhope placed her hand on his. 'I've told you,' she said, 'you mustn't blame yourself. What's done is done. Nothing can be changed.'

'Exactly what I have told him, so I have,' said Mrs O'Connor. It was clear to her by the way the woman looked at Tom that she had taken a shine to her nephew. It was also clear to Janette, who was watching, that Tom had eyes for the handsome blonde.

'I was going to the hospital this morning to see how he is,' said Tom.

'I'd leave it for the time being,' Mrs Stanhope told him. 'I'll keep you informed.'

'I guess Leo won't be back at school next week.'

'No, I think not.'

'We will all be thinking of him,' Tom said.

'And saying a prayer,' added his aunt.

'And if there is anything I can do,' Tom told her, 'you need only ask.'

'I know that,' she replied. 'You've been very good.'

'Please excuse me for a moment,' he said, getting up. He had forgotten about Jan. He returned to the counter but found that she had gone.

Tom left his auntie to do her shopping and, with a heavy heart, set off back to Risingdale. As he left Clayton, the rain fell in earnest: cold, hard and relentless. It teemed down from a grey sky and fell slantways across the pavements. Cars and vans threw up waves of water, their bonnets steaming beneath the downpour. Gutters bubbled, rooftops glistened and trees bent and swayed in the squally wind. At the bus shelter, Tom caught sight of Mrs Sloughthwaite wrapped up in a shapeless coat, her head covered in a headscarf. He pulled over, wound down the car window and offered her a lift back to Barton-in-the-Dale.

'Thank you, Tom,' she said, climbing into the passenger seat. 'I've been stood standing here for over half an hour waiting for a bus and then when it does come, two others arrive with it. I tell you, you have to have the patience of a virgin to use public transport.'

'And how are you keeping, Mrs Sloughthwaite?' asked Tom, smiling for the first time that day.

'Mustn't grumble,' she answered before launching into a whole selection of grumbles.

'There's a lot worse off than me but I'm a martyr to my joints. Stiff as a coffin board they are and of course I suffer with my legs and have to wear these elastrificated stockings. Dr Stirling says my various veins are a result of all the standing behind the counter I do in the shop. He said that I should exercise more. I said to him that if walking is good for your health, ramblers would be immortal. Anyway, as I said to him, I can't walk far, what with my hips. It's a miracle that I can remain perpendicular. It'll not be long before they give way and I shall have to have a replacement like Mrs Fish. She's had hers done. I reckon that if they put all the metal hips that old people in Barton have in their bodies together, they could build a Spitfire.'

'You certainly seem to be suffering, Mrs Sloughthwaite,' said Tom.

'And my eyes are going.'

'I'm sorry?' he said. 'Your eyes are going?'

'Packing in,' explained the shopkeeper. 'It comes with age. I've had to close up the store this morning to come into town. I've been to the opticians to have my eyes tested and I've been told I have channel vision. And that receptionist, Mrs Crabb – and I have to say the name suits her – could curdle milk with that face on her. You remember, she played the wicked witch in the Christmas pantomime you were in and she was tailor-made for the part.' Then, true to form, she began her inquisition. 'And what have you been doing in Clayton?'

'I've just been for a coffee with my Auntie Bridget.'

'That's nice. You're a good lad, Tom, looking after your auntie as you do.'

'She looked after me when I was young,' he replied. 'She's been like a mother.'

'That's as may be, but a hundred aunties are not the same as one mother.'

'No,' said Tom, 'that's true enough.'

'She was telling me she's off to Ireland soon to see that sister of hers.'

'My Auntie Attracta.'

'I gather she doesn't get on with her all that well,' remarked Mrs Sloughthwaite, probing for information.

'No, she's not the easiest of women. When I was a lad, we didn't see eye to eye. Mind you, I was a bit of a mardy-arse, as they say in Yorkshire, when I was a youngster. I wasn't an easy boy to deal with. It was my Auntie Bridget who brought me up after my parents died.'

'Well, she did a good job. You've turned out well. Fancy being named after a piece of farm machinery. Attracta is not a name I would wish on my worst enemy.'

Tom smiled again. 'It's an Irish name. I was at school with twins called Concepta and Immaculata,' he said. 'Now there are names to be conjured with.'

'Your Auntie Bridget's flying to Dublin, she was telling me. I've only been on an aeroplane once and I shall never do it again. It was a nightmare. I was glad to get my feet back on terra cotta, I can tell you.'

'Some people do get frightened of flying,' said Tom. 'You are not alone in that. I think it's called aviophobia.'

'No, I'm not frightened of flying as such,' said Mrs Sloughthwaite. 'It didn't bother me being off of the ground. It was having to be crammed into a seat like a sardine next to a fat man who snored. And then there was the flatulence.'

'I think you mean turbulence, Mrs Sloughthwaite,' Tom told her, suppressing a laugh.

'No, I don't,' she replied. 'It was the flatulence. The man who sat next to me smelled awful.'

*   *   *

On the Sunday morning, Tom rang the Fairborn farm to speak to Janette. He felt she must have thought him rude to rush off and leave her standing at the counter of the café and wanted to explain why he needed to see the woman who had come in. He would explain about Leo in the hospital and why he had to speak to the boy's mother so urgently.

The telephone was answered by her father.

'John Fairborn,' came the gruff voice down the line.

'Good morning. This is Tom Dwyer. May I speak to Jan, please?'

'She's not here. She's gone back to Nottingham.'

'I don't know whether she mentioned that we met yesterday in a café in Clayton and—'

'No, she never mentioned it.'

'She said she was in Risingdale for the weekend and I thought—'

Mr Fairborn cut him off again. 'She was intending to stay but she decided to go back early. She has work to do.'

'I see. I wonder if I might have her Nottingham number.' There was a silence down the line. 'Hello, are you still there?'

'Yes, I'm still here. Now look, Mr Dwyer, Tom. I don't mean this unkindly, but I think you're wasting your time with my daughter.' He had heard rumours in the village that the young teacher at the school was keen on her and what a lovely couple they made. 'I know that she likes you, but that is as far as it goes. If it was anything more she wouldn't have gone off to Nottingham, now would she?'

'No, I guess not.'

Tom was of a mind to stop Mr Fairborn and explain he was not calling to ask the man's daughter out, but to apologise for his apparent rudeness in the café, but he let him continue.

'Jan's started a new life,' Janette's father was saying, 'and I think it's best if you got on with your own life and forgot about her. You're a young man, with a responsible job, and have made yourself very popular in the village. I'm sure that there is some lass out there for you but it's not our Jan.'

'I see,' said Tom. Of course he knew this well enough. Jan had made it clear to him back in January that there was no future in any relationship they might have had.

Mr Fairborn was still speaking. 'I'm sure that you've found out by now that Yorkshire folk are direct and say what they think. We don't beat about the bush. Sometimes the honest truth isn't always welcomed. As I said, I don't mean to be unkind but it's best that you know where you stand and don't get your hopes up.'

'Thank you for being so frank, Mr Fairborn,' said Tom. 'I appreciate your candour.' He placed down the receiver.

When Tom arrived at school on the Monday morning, he found the boy to whom he wished to speak waiting for him in the classroom, standing by the teacher's desk with his head down. Christopher, on hearing the door open, jerked his head around. He wore a dejected expression on his face.

'You're here early, Christopher,' said Tom.

'Yes, sir, I wanted to see you.'

'About the accident?'

'How's Leo, Mr Dwyer?' he asked the teacher.

Tom was minded telling him that Leo was very poorly but decided not to add to the boy's obvious misery and merely repeated the doctor's words. 'Not too bad.'

'Will he get better, sir?'

'I hope so. Would you like to tell me what happened, Christopher?'

The boy shifted from one foot to the other, staring at the floor morosely.

'I tripped him up, sir,' he admitted. 'It was my fault. I shouldn't have done it. I'm sorry.' His eyes were blurred with tears.

'I see,' said Tom gravely.

'I meant to do it. I told the others I didn't, but I meant to do it.'

At least the pupil wasn't trying to deny what he had done, thought the teacher.

'What made you do such a thing?' asked Tom. His voice was calm and steady.

'It's not been the same since he came to the school,' Christopher told him, rubbing his eyes. 'He gets all this attention from the other kids and from you. Everyone likes him. He knows all the answers and makes me feel stupid.'

It had been ever thus, thought the teacher. At the very root of bullying was envy. Christopher was jealous of the new boy.

'I don't like him,' Christopher continued, 'but I shouldn't have done what I did. I didn't think that it would . . .' His voice tailed off. Then he began to cry. He buried his face in his palms.

'Leo said it was an accident,' Tom told him. 'Now you and I know that it wasn't. What you did was very mean and dangerous.'

'I know,' sniffed the boy.

'So nothing like this will happen again, will it?'

'No, sir.'

'Leo said he didn't want anyone to get into trouble so I think we will leave it at that.'

'He said what, Mr Dwyer?'

'He doesn't want anyone to get into trouble,' the teacher told him. 'He didn't blame you. As I have said, I think we will draw a line under what happened.'

'Will you be telling my dad, Mr Dwyer?'

'I don't think there is any need for that,' Tom told him, 'but you must never do such a thing again. Is that clear?'

'Yes, sir,' answered the boy, wiping the tears from his cheeks. 'When will Leo be back at school?'

'I don't know,' replied the teacher.

*   *   *

There was an odd atmosphere in the classroom that morning. After Vicky had asked Tom how Leo was and was told that he was still poorly and in hospital and would not be back at school for the time being, the class fell into a strange sort of silence. The incident had clearly made a profound impact on the pupils. The first thing Tom did each Monday morning was ask the children to share with everyone what they had got up to over the weekend and then they would write a short account. This was usually a lively, good-humoured session, much enjoyed by both the teacher and his pupils, but that morning, try as he might to get the children to contribute to the lesson, Tom got no response; they remained tight-lipped. Even Charlie, who always had a great deal to say for himself, sat solemn-faced and silent.

'Look, I know you are all feeling sad and worried about Leo,' Tom told the class. 'I feel the same way, but all we can do is hope and pray he will get better. We do need to get on with our work. I bought a card on Saturday and want you all to sign it and I'll give it to Leo's mother to take when she next visits the hospital.' He decided not to persist in trying to get the children to talk and let them work in silence that morning.

'So how is the lad?' asked Mr Cadwallader at lunchtime.

'Not too good, I'm afraid,' Tom told him. 'He had a nasty bang to the head. He's remaining in hospital for a few days for some tests.'

'Poor child,' said Mrs Golightly.

'Should he have been playing football?' asked Joyce. 'I mean, with his condition it seemed rather rash to me.'

'I don't think that's a very helpful comment, Joyce,' said Mrs Golightly. 'I'm sure Tom's feeling bad about it as it is.'

'I'm merely asking the question,' said her colleague.

'You are probably right, Joyce,' conceded Tom. 'Leo shouldn't have been playing.'

'Hindsight is a wonderful thing,' remarked Mr Cadwallader pompously as he reached into the biscuit barrel. 'Don't feel too bad about it, Tom. We are all guilty of doing things that we later regret. You are new to the profession. When you have had a few more years under your belt like me, you will learn from your mistakes.'

'Listen to words of wisdom from the elder statesman of education,' remarked Joyce, sardonically. 'I don't forget when you took a school party to Whitby, Owen, and you lost a child near the harbour and the police found him later, soaking wet, holding a stick of rock and minus his shoes.'

'And then there was that time you threw a stick of chalk at Roger Allcock and nearly took the boy's eye out,' Mrs Golightly added. 'I remember Mr Allcock coming into school to punch your lights out.'

'And what about the occasion,' said Joyce, 'when George Lomax was in your class and you wouldn't let him go to the toilet and—'

'All right! All right!' snapped their colleague. 'We don't need to go over all that. I was merely pointing out to Tom that we all make mistakes.'

'Leo was keen on playing and his mother thought he should be allowed to take part in all the sporting activities,' said Tom, rather stung by his colleagues' criticism and defending himself. He could have added that Mr Gaunt had shared the view of the parent. 'Mrs Stanhope is quite insistent that her son should be treated like any other pupil and Leo feels the same and doesn't want any special treatment.'

'But he's not like any other pupil,' said Miss Tranter gently. 'He's a very sick little boy and he does need special treatment.'

'There's no need to tell me that, Joyce,' said Tom with a sharpness in his voice. 'I am well aware of Leo's condition.'

'Let's not go on about it,' said Mrs Golightly. She changed

the subject. 'Has anyone seen a strange-looking man loitering outside the school?'

'A man!' cried Joyce, fearing the worst. 'What sort of man?'

'Yes, I've seen him,' said Tom. 'He's a long-haired, scruffy individual with a beard. I've caught sight of him from my classroom window. I thought at first he might be a parent but none of the children in my class knows him. He was sitting on the wall watching the school.'

'Yes, I saw that chap when I was on yard duty at morning break,' Mr Cadwallader told him. 'Suspicious-looking character. I was about to ask him what he was doing but he jumped on his motorbike and scooted off before I could talk to him.'

'I think you should get Mr Gaunt to contact the police,' said Mrs Golightly. 'One can't be too careful these days. One reads terrible things in the newspapers about strange men trying to make off with children. It makes me shiver just to think of it. Yes, Mr Gaunt should get in touch with the police. Don't you think so, Joyce?'

'I'm sorry, I wasn't listening,' said Miss Tranter, whose mind was on other things. She thought, after the exchange at the school gate, that she had seen the last of her ex-husband, but it was now clear the past was repeating itself and he wasn't going to leave her alone.

'I was saying that the headmaster ought to get in touch with the police about this man who's been watching the children. I mean, he is clearly up to no good.'

'Well, who the devil is he, I wonder?' asked Mr Cadwallader of no one in particular.

Joyce took a breath. 'He's my ex-husband,' she said. 'You would all have got to know who he is soon enough. He's not making any secret of it. He's not been watching the children, he's been watching me.'

'Good God!' cried Mr Cadwallader.

'Your ex-husband,' said Mrs Golightly. 'I never knew you were married.'

'It isn't something I am proud of,' Joyce told her. 'The marriage was a dreadful mistake.'

'As I was saying to Tom,' said Mr Cadwallader, unhelpfully, 'we are all guilty of doing things that we later regret.'

'Well, I certainly regretted marrying him,' Joyce said. 'Soon after we were married and I started getting acting jobs and he didn't, he began criticising the way I dressed, comparing me unfavourably to former girlfriends, hiding things of mine and then saying I was irresponsible. He became a selfish and domineering man. I walked away from a difficult situation and came up here to Risingdale to get away from him. He's now found out where I work and has started pestering me.'

'Does Mr Gaunt know?' asked Mrs Golightly.

'He knows I was once married,' answered Joyce, 'and about the sort of man he is, but not about him coming to the school and watching me.'

'You should tell the police,' said Mr Cadwallader.

'There's nothing the police can do,' Joyce told him. 'When I first left him, he pursued me and I did go to the police. Since he hadn't threatened or hurt me, they said they could take no action. He'd not laid a finger on me or even raised his voice. The police advised me that I should just ignore him and he would eventually stop or move away. But he didn't stop. His presence was intimidating. My life became unbearable and bleak, that's why I had to get away. And now he's found me.' She became tearful.

'Well, something's got to be done,' said Mr Cadwallader.

'But what?' asked Joyce. 'I just wish he would go away and leave me alone.'

He will, after I have had a word with him, thought Tom.

★   ★   ★

It was near the end of the school day when Tom, glancing out of the classroom window, saw the figure sitting on the wall watching the school. He decided to take matters into his own hands. He set the children some work to do, left the room and strode across the playground. The man jumped from the wall and was about to mount his motorbike, but Tom pushed his way through the gate and barred his path.

'What is it you want?' he demanded.

'I don't want anything,' replied the man defensively.

'What are you doing here?'

'I'm admiring the view.'

'Facing the school?'

'Eh?'

'Is there something wrong with you?' asked Tom.

'Eh?' .

'Haven't you got it into your thick skull that Joyce wants nothing to do with you?'

'What?'

'What sort of person gets some sort of warped pleasure out of harassing women? You really need to get some help.'

'I don't know what you mean,' blustered the man.

'I don't like bullies,' Tom told him. 'They are sad, mixed-up, spiteful people. Joyce is a colleague and a good friend of mine and I don't like to see her upset. Now you get on your bike, don't come back and leave her alone.'

'Are you threatening me?'

'Yes, I am. And there are those who will do more than threaten.'

'Such as?'

'Such as this chap,' said Tom, pointing to a distant figure. Striding down the path to the school came a giant of a man. He was mountainous, six foot six at the very least, broad-chested with thick arms and heavy shoulders. He had a weathered face like creased cardboard, a bullet-shaped bald head and a neck as thick as a bulldog's.

'This is Mr Olmeroyde walking towards us,' Tom told the man. 'He's a local farmer and has something of a reputation for being a bit short-tempered, and at times he can be aggressive. It's not a good idea to get on the wrong side of Mr Olmeroyde.'

'Why would I get on the wrong side of him?' demanded the man.

'Mr Olmeroyde is a very possessive man when it comes to his granddaughter,' said Tom. 'She happens to be in my class. Were I to tell him that a strange-looking character has been coming up to the school each day watching the children, I guess he wouldn't take kindly to it. He might be just the man to persuade you not to return.' Tom turned to greet the Goliath. 'Now then, Mr Olmeroyde. Come to collect your granddaughter, have you?'

'I 'ave that, Mester Dwyer,' replied the farmer. 'Our Marjorie says she can mek 'er own way 'ome now she's in t'top class, but I likes to come an' walk back wi' 'er.'

'Very sensible,' said Tom. 'You have to be so careful these days what with all the stories you hear about strangers lurking around schools, giving children sweets and offering them lifts. I was just telling this man here that it's not a good idea for him to linger around watching the children. People might get the wrong idea.'

Mr Olmeroyde stared at the man and nodded. 'Aye, they might,' he grunted. He glowered at the man. 'Best get on yer bike.'

'So I think you will be on your way now,' said Tom to Joyce's ex-husband.

14

The following morning, Christopher was absent from school. When asked by Tom if any in the class knew why he was away, he was met with a muttered, 'No, sir', and shakes of the head.

It was at the end of the school day when the children were making their way home that Christopher's father arrived at the school. He threw open the door of Tom's classroom and marched in. Mr Pickles was a short, thick-necked individual with a nose as heavy as a turnip and great hooded eyes. Tom had encountered this belligerent parent before when he had come into school the previous term to complain about Colin Greenwood giving his son a bloody nose.

'What's going on?' he demanded, marching to the desk where Tom was sitting.

Tom had learnt from the head teacher of the school where he had trained, and from Mr Gaunt, that the best method for a teacher to deal with an antagonistic parent was to simply remain calm and agreeable and appear most attentive until the person had got things off his or her chest and become silent. It was a clever and disarming technique and a powerful way to overcome hostility.

'Good afternoon, Mr Pickles,' said the teacher pleasantly, remaining seated at his desk.

'I want to know what's going on,' said the farmer less aggressively.

'About what?'

'Our Christopher won't come to school. He wouldn't come out of his bedroom this morning and he's been roaring his eyes out. He won't tell me what's at the bottom of it, just that none of the other kids in his class is speaking to him.'

'I think I can tell you why, Mr Pickles,' said Tom.

The man folded his arms. 'Well, go on, I'm listening.'

'Do take a seat.'

'I'm all right standing,' said the parent.

'I should prefer it if you sat down,' said Tom.

The parent plonked himself down on a child's small wooden chair. It creaked ominously under his weight. He rested his hands on his knees and leaned forward. 'Well, go on,' he said, 'tell me why Christopher's in this state? I can't get a word out of him.'

'A new pupil has started at the school,' Tom explained, 'and for some reason your son has taken a dislike to him. During a game of football, he tripped the new boy up.'

'Aye, well, that happens a lot in football matches,' declared the parent. 'You must know that, having been a professional footballer yourself.'

'The boy banged his head and was taken to hospital and is in a serious condition.'

The wind was taken out of the man's sails. 'Oh, I didn't know,' he muttered. 'I'm sorry to hear that, but you have to expect accidents when you play sports.'

'It wasn't an accident, Mr Pickles. As I said, Christopher deliberately tripped the boy up.'

'Says who?' asked the parent.

'The children who witnessed it,' Tom told him, 'and I saw it myself. Christopher also admitted to it. The class has taken this badly and I guess that is why the pupils are not speaking to your son.'

Mr Pickles was silent. All the bluster had disappeared.

'And you say the lad's in a serious condition?'

'I'm afraid so,' said Tom.

'What can I do?' he asked, like a small child talking to a teacher.

'I shall speak to the class first thing tomorrow morning,' Tom told him. 'It is wrong of the children to treat Christopher like this. He knows he did wrong and feels badly about what happened. I have spoken to him and he has assured me nothing like this will happen again and I believe him.'

'Did you punish him?'

'No, I didn't think it necessary.'

'So you didn't cane him?'

'No, Mr Pickles,' responded Tom. 'I don't believe in giving children the cane. Hitting him would have served no purpose.'

Mr Pickles rubbed his chin. 'Well, I reckon he deserved it. A few strokes of the cane never did me any harm when I was at school. But what do I do about my son not wanting to come to school?'

'Would you like me to have a word with him?' asked Tom. 'I could call him later this afternoon. The school has your telephone number.'

'Well, yes, if you would,' said the parent. 'I'd appreciate that.'

When Tom called the number later, the boy refused to speak to him.

That afternoon, after school, Tom called at Mrs Stanhope's cottage on Rattan Row to deliver the get-well-soon card and see if there had been any improvement in her son's condition. Hearing the knocking on the door, the neighbour, Mrs Lister, came out of her cottage and told Tom that Leo's mother was at the hospital. She had been there all day.

'Charlie's not been the same since his friend has had the accident,' she said. 'It's affected him greatly. He's gone all quiet and taken to his room.'

'It's had a big effect on all of us,' he replied. 'It's

heartbreaking to see a child so young having to suffer like that. I can't imagine what his mother must be going through.'

'Yes,' agreed Mrs Lister, 'it's very distressing.'

'Mrs Stanhope seems to be coping remarkably well,' said Tom. 'She's an extraordinary woman.'

Charlie's mother had rather mixed feelings about her neighbour. To those in the village she appeared cheerful and friendly enough, but Mrs Lister had a feeling that the newcomer was not the person she appeared to be. Clearly she was a woman who was adept at getting exactly what she wanted.

Tom found Mrs Stanhope in a room to the side of the wards. Unlike the other areas in the hospital, with their plain pale walls and antiseptic smell, this room had a cosy appearance, with rose-coloured curtains, a small sofa and two matching armchairs. On a wall were three vividly painted seascapes below a large and noisily ticking clock, and on the windowsill a vase of large bright flowers made the room look cheerful and welcoming. A selection of magazines and leaflets, the latter warning of the dangers of smoking and drinking and advice on healthy eating, covered the top of a coffee table.

Leo's mother looked tired and tense as she sat stiffly on the sofa, her hands clasped together on her lap. She gave a slight smile when Tom came in and sat next to her.

'Hello, Tom,' she said. 'You don't mind me calling you Tom, do you?'

'Not at all,' he replied, touched that she had dispensed with the 'Mr Dwyer'.

'I've brought a card for Leo,' he told her. 'It's signed by all the children in the class.'

'How kind. I'll take it in to him when I visit him later. Dr Knight is with him at the moment and another specialist who has come from Leeds.' Her voice was strained with grief.

'How is he?' asked Tom.

'Not very good, I'm afraid.' She could feel the tears in her eyes but fought them back, biting her bottom lip. 'I thought from what they said he was getting better, but he seems to have taken a turn for the worse.' She reached out and held Tom's hand. 'Thank you for being here.' She looked at the pictures on the wall. 'They are rather good, those paintings, don't you think?'

'Yes,' said Tom. 'I like them. They remind me of the water-colours that Colin paints. He's really come on since you've been teaching him.'

'You were right,' she said, 'the boy has quite a talent.' She looked at the clock. Tom could see that her mind was on other things. She was quiet for a moment. 'I'm afraid I've not had much time to get on with my own painting, what with all that's been happening. I did manage to get Mr Croft to sit for his portrait, but I don't think he was very impressed. When he saw it, he told me I had done him no favours and made him look like a vagrant. I did point out to him that I am not in the business of beautifying my subjects. I paint what I see. I have to say he wasn't an easy sitter. He kept grinning at me despite the fact I kept telling him that he will not see a smiling face in the portraits in the art gallery. People don't smile when they are painted. You see, it's difficult for them to sustain a smile and . . .'

She broke off and her mouth suddenly began to tremble and her eyes filled with tears. 'Oh, Tom,' she said, 'tell me he's going to be all right.'

His arms went around her and he held her close and felt her body shake with crying.

Tom arrived at school early on the Wednesday morning just before the weather took a turn for the worse. The heavy rain of Saturday had abated but now returned with a vengeance. He sat at his desk and stared blankly at the pile of children's exercise books in front of him. He was unable to concentrate on anything other than what had happened in the hospital the previous afternoon. He couldn't remember how long he had held Amanda Stanhope in his arms, but it had seemed to him an age. When she had stopped crying and composed herself, sniffing and wiping away her tears, she had gently pulled away from him.

'Oh dear,' she had murmured.

Tom had felt acutely embarrassed. 'I'm sorry,' he had begun, 'I shouldn't have . . .' His voice had tailed off.

'I needed to be held,' she told him, looking into his eyes. 'Thank you.'

His thoughts were abruptly interrupted now. A jagged streak of lightning lit up the classroom, followed seconds later by a grumbling of thunder and a massive downpour that lashed fiercely at the windows and thundered on the roof. Water snaked down the window panes, gutters dripped madly and drains began to overflow. The steady deluge soon made the fields surrounding the school sodden, filled the paths with huge muddy puddles and turned the steep road leading up to the school into a foaming river. Never had Tom seen such rain and he immediately thought of the farmers. After the burning heat of summer and the thick snow of winter, now they had flooded fields to contend with. How they must yearn for the spring.

The door of the classroom suddenly burst open and in staggered Mr Gaunt, soaking wet and out of breath.

'I'm closing the school,' he announced. 'It's a torrent out there. Give me a hand, Tom, there's a good fellow. I need to blow the alpenhorn and let everyone know we're not open today.'

Tom helped the headmaster manoeuvre the heavy instrument into the entrance to the school. He then threw open the door and watched, fascinated, as Mr Gaunt thrust the horn through, licked his lips, took a deep breath, put the mouth-piece of the alpenhorn to his lips and produced the most amazing trumpeting sound, which echoed down the Dale. He gave the horn several more blows and then relaxed.

'There.' He sighed. 'Remarkable sound, isn't it?' He smiled and shook his head. 'Young Vicky Gosling once told me that when her grandfather heard the sound, he compared it to a dinosaur breaking wind.' He looked up at the oyster-grey sky and wrinkled his forehead. 'I think we are in for a lot more of this. It's coming down like umbrella spokes. Well, I'm going to leave you to it, Tom. I have my sheep to see to.' And, with that, the headmaster thrust the alpenhorn into the teacher's hands and departed with the words, 'Have a blow if you like.'

Tom smiled. 'Rain coming down like umbrella spokes,' he repeated. He thought of Mrs Sloughthwaite, the mistress of the malapropism, who informed him one wet day that the rain was coming down like steroids, meaning stair rods.

'Oh,' said the headmaster, turning back and tapping his head, 'I almost forgot, have you heard how young Leo is doing?'

'Not too good, I'm afraid,' Tom told him. 'I called in the hospital yesterday. He's still very poorly.'

'Damn shame,' said Mr Gaunt.

Tom was inclined to tell the headmaster that he wished he had followed his own instincts and not let the boy play foot-ball, but he considered it fruitless to do so. He determined, however, that should Leo recover he would not risk him play-ing a second time.

'By the way, how are you getting on with the new tech-nology?' asked Mr Gaunt.

'Oh, pretty well,' Tom fibbed. That morning the computer had failed to start.

'Well, I'll be off,' said the headmaster. 'You want to get off home yourself.'

Then he was gone.

Tom returned to his classroom and stared at the pile of unmarked exercise books on his desk.

A moment later the classroom door burst open. The cleaner (aka assistant caretaker), dressed in a shapeless gabardine and woolly hat like a tea cosy, made her entrance.

'It's not rained like this since Noah built his ark,' declared Mrs Gosling, dripping water on the floor and wiping her wet cheeks with the back of her hand. 'I've never seen the like. I must look like a drowned rat.' She removed her raincoat and pulled off the woolly hat.

'I'm sorry you've made a wasted journey, Mrs Gosling,' Tom told her. 'The school's closed.'

'I'm aware of that,' she said angrily. 'I wouldn't have made my way up here if Mr Gaunt had sounded that bloody horn of his – pardon my French – sooner. And I notice Mr Leadbeater isn't here. Mind you, he might as well not bother coming into the school at all, the amount of work he manages to avoid.'

'However did you manage to get here in this weather?' asked Tom. 'It looks as if the roads are flooded.'

'My son Clive dropped me off on his tractor. He's on his way to check on his cows. Anyway, now I'm here, it gives me the chance to have a word with you.'

'Yes, of course,' replied Tom. 'What can I do for you?'

'Our Vicky was telling me about that kiddie who's been rushed to hospital.'

'Leo.'

'Yes, that's him. How's he doing?'

'Not too good, I'm afraid,' Tom told her.

'Our Vicky told me it was that Christopher Pickles who did it. Tripped him up deliberate like, she said. I hope he's been given a damn good hiding.'

'I've had a word with him,' said Tom.

'Words don't butter no parsnips, Mr Dwyer. He wants six of the best across his backside. We had it when I was at school and it never did us any harm.'

Tom did not wish to discuss the rights and wrongs of corporal punishment so he returned to the books on his desk. 'Well, I must get on,' he said.

'I've had another do with Mr Cadwallader,' she told him.

'Oh dear,' sighed Tom.

'Do you know, one of the kiddies in his class was sick in his room, all over the desk, the floor, the books—'

'And the teacher,' added Tom.

'And it was left to me to clear the mess up,' grumbled the cleaner. 'He'd made a half-hearted attempt to clean the place with one of my hand brushes and two of my best dusters, but I had to deal with the brunt of it.'

'Well, I must get on,' Tom told her for the second time, staring down at the exercise books, a pen poised in his hand in an effort to give her the hint.

'There was something else,' said Mrs Gosling. He looked up. 'Them stuffed creatures.' She pointed up at the variety of birds and animals displayed along the windowsill. 'When I first started here, there were just a few. They've reproduced.'

'Reproduced,' repeated Tom.

'There's more of them.'

'Ah yes. I've borrowed a few more specimens from the museum,' he told her. In addition to the fierce-looking kestrel, wide-eyed owl, sharp-beaked raven and the magpie, a mole, a grey squirrel, a rabbit and a startled-looking pheasant had been added to the collection.

'I can't say I like them, Mr Dwyer. I can't say I like them at all. Sir Hedley has a collection of stuffed animals and birds up at Marston Towers. When I worked there, before that wife of his gave me the sack, they gave me the creeps.' She screwed up her face. 'Nasty, dusty creatures they were, with staring glass eyes and sharp beaks. Bit like his wife, they were. I can't for the life of me understand why anyone would want a lot of dead creatures on their shelves.'

'They're visual aids,' the teacher explained. 'I use them for creative writing and for the work we do in art. Rather than asking the children to use photographs, I encourage them to observe the creatures first hand, to look carefully at the shapes and colours and feel the texture of the feathers or fur and try to capture the—'

'Mr Dwyer,' interrupted the cleaner, 'I am not one of your pupils. I'm not really interested in what you use them for. I don't like them creatures staring at me when I'm doing your classroom. They make me feel very uncomfortable.'

'And you born and bred in the country, Mrs Gosling,' teased Tom. 'Fancy being afraid of a few stuffed animals. You do surprise me.'

'I don't mind them when they're alive,' she retorted. 'It's when they're dead that they put the wind up me.'

'I'll put them in the cupboard when I'm not using them,' said Tom.

'That's very accommodating of you, Mr Dwyer. Oh, I meant to ask you, what's that contraption in the corner?'

'It's a computer,' Tom told her.

'What's it for?'

'For children to learn how to use new technology,' Tom told her. 'Computers will change the face of education. They are things of the future, Mrs Gosling.' He resisted adding, *that's if they work, of course.*

'That's as may be, Mr Dwyer,' replied the cleaner, 'but as far as I'm concerned, it's just another thing to dust. Oh, and one more thing I wanted to have a word with you about.'

'Yes, what is it?' Tom sighed.

'The boys' toilets.'

'What about them?'

'They are disgusting, that's what. The floor was awash yesterday when I went to clean them and I don't mean with water. I reckon that some of the older boys are seeing who can get highest up the wall, and clearly the infants have been missing the toilet bowls and the urinals when they've gone for a wee. You men and boys are all the same. I was always telling my son to lift up the seat and the lid when he was a lad and not to splash. My husband was as guilty when he was alive. He used to flip it about like a fireman's hose and then—'

'Too much information, Mrs Gosling,' interrupted Tom. 'I shall have a word with the children.'

The cleaner would not leave it at that. 'I mean, it's not too much to ask, is it, for them to point it in the right direction. The girls' toilets aren't at all dirty and smelly like the boys'. Going in the girls' lavatory is like a breath of fresh air. I'll put the kettle on.'

Tom had just settled down to marking the children's work when the telephone in Mr Gaunt's office rang. It continued to ring incessantly for most of the morning and he was backwards and forwards to answer it and getting increasingly annoyed at being disturbed. There were parents checking that the school was closed; a tutor from the Teacher Training College in Clayton; Mr Nettles, the education officer at County Hall, and book reps and school suppliers all wishing to speak to the headmaster. Tom had just returned to his classroom having explained to a parent for the umpteenth time that he didn't know whether the school would be open the following day, when the telephone rang again. Back he trooped to Mr Gaunt's study and snatched up the receiver.

'I'm afraid the school is closed,' he said rather sharply, 'and I can't tell you if it will be open tomorrow. The headmaster is not available. I suggest—'

'Tom. It's me. Amanda Stanhope.'

'Oh, I'm sorry, I thought it was someone else.'

'I'm calling from the hospital. I want you to be the first to know.'

Tom held his breath. He couldn't speak.

'Are you still there?' she asked.

'Yes, I'm still here,' he said.

Mrs Gosling found Tom standing by the window staring at the rain-soaked landscape that stretched beyond the school. She placed a mug of tea on his desk and went to join him.

'The rain's stopped, thank goodness,' she said.

'Yes, the rain's stopped,' he muttered.

'It's like a swamp out there. Do you think the school will be open tomorrow?'

Tom didn't answer but continued to gaze through the window.

'Mr Dwyer,' she said, 'I was asking if you think the school will be open tomorrow. I mean, I don't want another wasted journey.'

'I'm sorry, Mrs Gosling, what did you say?'

She sighed. 'The school, will it be open tomorrow, do you think?'

'Yes, I imagine it will.'

'You were miles away.'

Tom blinked away the tears. 'Miles away,' he repeated.

'Are you all right, Mr Dwyer?' she asked. She saw the tears in his eyes and thought it strange, for he was smiling.

'Yes, Mrs Gosling,' he told her, 'I'm more than all right. I have just received some most wonderful news. I must go,' he said, and leaving the cleaner open-mouthed, he rushed from the room.

'What about your tea?' she called after him.

After a slow and laborious drive out of the village along rain-soaked roads, Tom finally arrived at his destination: a square, solid, run-down Victorian farmhouse with crumbling outbuildings. He had found the address in the grey metal filing cabinet in Mr Gaunt's study. The journey from the village had been long and arduous, for the narrow, twisting roads were dangerously wet and muddy. He had lost his way several times and then he caught sight of Toby Croft supervising his son, Dean, who was rounding up a flock of saturated, dishevelled sheep. Tom stopped to ask directions.

'Fellside Farm!' the old farmer spat out. 'Tha'd be barmy to go theer in this weather,' the old farmer told him. He peered up at the iron-grey sky and scudding clouds. 'I knew we were in for a spot o' bad weather. Cows lie down when it's goin' to rain. We're in fer another downpour by t'looks on it. 'Tis bleak and treacherous up theer. Tha'll no doubt end up in a ditch ageean like tha did when tha nearly knocked John Fairborn's lass off of 'er 'orse.'

When will I hear the last of it, thought Tom. The story, suitably embellished by Toby Croft, was now something of a legend in Risingdale.

'If you could just point me in the right direction, I should be very grateful,' Tom told him, keen to be away.

The old farmer wasn't going to let him escape so easily.

'I'll not be theer this time to pull thee out, if tha ends up in a ditch ageean,' he warned, grimacing.

'It weren't you what pulled 'im out. It were me,' shouted Dean, who had overheard his father.

'Shurrup, thee,' the farmer shouted back, 'and gerron wi' fettlin' them sheep.'

'Do this, do that,' the boy mumbled. 'All tha does, is give orders.'

'Gerra move on an' stop thee mitherin'.'

'So could you direct me to Fellside Farm, please?' asked Tom.

''Appen I could,' replied Mr Croft, 'but as I've telled thee, tha best not go up theer today.'

'I'll take it really easy,' said Tom.

'Anyroad, what's tha want to go up to Fellside Farm fer?'

'Business,' he replied evasively.

'Well, tha'll not get a warm welcome from 'im what lives theer, I'll tell thee that. 'E's a miserable old beggar, is Dennis Pickles.'

'Aye, an' 'e's not t'only one,' muttered his son.

'Thee stop earwigging an' gerron sooarting them sheep out an' then tha can shift some o' this muck off t'road.'

Having at last extracted the information from Toby Croft, Tom set off again and arrived at the journey's end. The building, with its sagging slate roof, greened over with moss, stood alone at the end of a mud-covered track full of tyre-gouged ruts and potholes full of water. The neglected garden to the front was choked with rough, spiky grass, dead weeds and briars. In a field full of thistles, a forlorn-looking donkey stared as Tom climbed from his car. The front door of the farmhouse, partially covered by dense holly and laurel bushes, was colourless, the paint having peeled away many months ago. The guttering, choked with weeds, dripped. Tom rattled the tarnished-brass door knocker in the shape of a ram's head.

The door was opened by a thin-faced woman with a melancholy countenance. She wiped her hands on her apron, screwed up her eyes and then recognised her son's teacher.

'Mrs Pickles?' asked Tom.

'Oh, it's you, Mr Dwyer.'

'I hope you don't mind me calling unexpectedly?' he asked.

'My husband's not in,' she said. 'He's in one of the outbuildings. They were flooded in all this rain.'

'It's Christopher I've come to see,' Tom told her.

'Christopher?'

'Yes, that's right.'

'Well, you had better come in,' she said. 'You'll have to excuse the mess.'

The interior of the farmhouse was indeed messy: cluttered and untidy and smelling of damp. A shabby, colourless carpet covered part of the flagstone floor and a solid kitchen table overlaid with a patterned oilcloth was piled with crockery, boxes, tins and bottles. There were four hard wooden ladder-back chairs that had seen better days, a threadbare armchair, a pine dresser and on the far wall a black-leaded kitchen range. Despite the blazing fire, the room was cold and draughty. A brown stain from the leaking roof covered a corner of the ceiling. It was obvious little money was coming into this home. Observing the impoverished scene before him, Tom could understand rather more why Christopher was so impassioned after he had heard the story of "The Happy Prince". 'My dad says that those who are rich like Sir Hedley don't know what it's like to be poor,' he had said, 'and have never worked hard for what they've got.'

Mrs Pickles stroked back a strand of greying hair that had fallen over an eye and frowned.

'I don't think Christopher will see you, Mr Dwyer,' she said. 'He wouldn't speak to you when you phoned and I don't think he'll speak to you now. Poor lad's been in a terrible frame of mind since that poor boy was knocked over and taken to hospital. My husband told me why he's got himself into such a state. After speaking to you, Dennis came home in such a bad mood and I'm afraid he hit him.'

'I wish he hadn't have done that, Mrs Pickles,' said Tom. 'I really don't think that was helpful.'

The woman had a haunted look. 'No, you're right, but my husband has quite a temper. I've tried talking to Christopher but he won't come out of his bedroom. I appreciate you coming out, Mr Dwyer, but I don't think seeing him will do any good.'

'Is he in his room now, Mrs Pickles?' interrupted Tom.

'Yes, he is, but—'

'Top of the stairs, is it?'

'First room on the right,' she said, 'but, again, I don't think he'll talk to you.'

Tom climbed up the stairs two steps at a time and stood outside the door of the boy's bedroom. He knocked loudly.

'Christopher,' he said, 'it's me, Mr Dwyer. Will you open the door, please?'

'I don't want to talk to you,' came a voice from inside. 'I want you to go away.'

'I've come a long way to see you,' said Tom. 'The least you can do is give me five minutes.'

'No.'

'You will want to hear what I have to say. Now come on, open the door. I'm not moving until I've spoken to you.'

After a moment, the door opened and the boy let the teacher in. Christopher looked shamefaced and had clearly been crying. He slumped on the bed and stared at the floor.

'I don't want to talk about it, Mr Dwyer,' he told the teacher, rubbing his eyes.

'I've just heard from Leo's mother. She's with him at the hospital,' Tom told him.

Christopher looked up quickly.

'Leo's getting better. He should be back in school next week.'

The boy broke down. Suddenly the tears came welling up, spilling over. He began to sob, great, heaving sobs. Tom put a hand on the boy's shoulder. Christopher wiped the tears away with his fists and sniffed.

'So, I want you back at school tomorrow,' said Tom. 'All right?'

'Yes, sir,' replied the boy.

The driver of the sports car travelled at speed along the narrow grey ribbon of road, without seeing a soul – just the tumbling acres of dark green, the rolling, empty tracts of rusty brown bracken to either side of the car and the grim, silent moor stretching ahead of him to the purple hills in the far distance.

The road unexpectedly took a sharp turn, almost at a complete right angle – a blind bend that would be impossible to negotiate without slowing down almost to a halt. Any car coming around the corner at speed would be a hazard to hikers, animals and other vehicles. There were no road signs, just a homemade square of plywood nailed to a tree, on which was written in faded red letters, 'Tek care! Lambs on t'road!' It was half-concealed by the spreading branches of an ancient oak. Further on was another plywood square warning 'Tek care! Tractors turning!' The usual chevrons indicating there was a bend ahead were missing. Presumably Highways England expected anyone driving along this narrow, out-of-the-way stretch of road would take the necessary care and slow down.

After the heavy downpour, the road was even more treacherous. The sports car sped up the steep hill, its engine roaring loudly. This driver was well aware of the curve in the road, having hurtled around the bend many times before. They thought they could take it at speed as they had done so in the past. That day, however, they took no account of the dreadful weather conditions. The car suddenly hit some mud and skewed across the road. The driver slammed their foot on the brakes and the car skidded as if on a patch of black ice. Wheels locked and tyres screeched as the car slid out of control on the slippery surface. It happened in seconds. The motorbike travelling in the opposite direction hit the car head on; the rider was thrown over the bonnet and dead before they reached the ground. The impact threw the driver of the sports car forward on to the steering wheel. The vehicle hit the tree. Glass shattered in glittering fragments. A few wet and bedraggled sheep looked up from eating their fodder and stared blankly at the scene. All was still and silent.

15

The following morning, thankfully, there was no sign of rain. A weak sun shone faintly, high in a cloudless sky, and the air was fresh and clear. When Tom told the class that Leo was getting better there were loud cheers. Christopher sat sheepishly at the back of the class. It was clear to the teacher that the children were still angry with the boy about what had happened, but he decided not to say anything and started the day's lesson. Following Mr Pickles's visit, he had told the class he wanted no more cold-shouldering of Christopher, who, he said, felt very badly about what had happened.

At morning break Tom informed his colleagues that Mrs Stanhope had telephoned him the day before to say that her son was getting better and would be back at school the following week.

'Evidently, he's been responding well to the medication,' he said. 'It has been a worrying time for his mother but she is putting on a brave face.'

'Wonderful news,' said Mrs Golightly.

'Hear, hear,' echoed Mr Cadwallader.

'I think in future, Tom,' advised Miss Tranter, 'it might be best to be on the safe side and let Leo give football a miss.'

'You're right, Joyce,' he agreed.

'All's well that ends well,' remarked Mr Cadwallader, looking around.

'And if you're looking for the Garibaldis,' Mrs Golightly told him, 'there aren't any. You finished the last one.'

'So what's this meeting about after school?' asked Joyce.

'I don't know,' said Mrs Golightly, 'but it bodes ill. Mr Gaunt's had this official-looking letter in a brown envelope with a fancy crest on the front,' she told her colleagues. 'Mrs Leadbeater told me. You mark my words, it'll be from the Education Office informing him they are going to close the school. I knew they'd get around to us. It's a dreadful shame. So many of the lovely little Dales village schools are disappearing; it's so depressing. Well, I don't intend to be redeployed to the other side of the county. I shall take early retirement if it's offered.'

'It was to be expected,' pronounced Mr Cadwallader gloomily. 'We are in for the chop, make no bones about it. We had that stay of execution when Mr Gaunt went to talk to the councillors but clearly it did no good. As I said at the time, most of these politicians are only in it for what they can get. I wouldn't trust them as far as I could throw them. They are like bananas: they start off green, become bent, turn yellow and end up rotten. There is no doubt in my mind that they'd already decided to shut down the school when they saw Mr Gaunt and were pretending they were prepared to listen. Two-faced, the lot of them. I'm with you, Bertha. I don't intend to be shunted off to some other school in the back of beyond or in the city and start all over again. I'm too long in the tooth for that.'

'You'll be all right, Tom,' said Mrs Golightly. 'You could return to the school where you trained. I'm sure they would jump at the chance of having you back and I guess Joyce won't have a problem finding another job either.'

Miss Tranter was thoughtful. A move to another school well away from her ex-husband might well be the answer to her problem but then there was Julian to think of. She had told him that she needed a little time to think over his offer of marriage. He had been so understanding, realising it was a big

step for her to take, and the fact that he was older than she
might be a barrier. After a deal of thought, she had decided to
accept the proposal. After all, why should her ex-husband,
who had appeared like the villain in a pantomime, spoil her
chances of happiness?

'You seem to be jumping the gun,' Tom told his colleagues.
'The letter may not be from the Education Office.'

'That's true,' agreed Mr Cadwallader. 'It might be to tell us
that Miss Tudor-Williams HMI is coming back to do another
inspection.'

'God forbid,' cried Mrs Golightly.

'We can do without that,' said Miss Tranter.

After school the teachers gathered in the staffroom. Mr
Gaunt entered, holding the brown envelope.

'Thank you for staying,' he said. 'I won't keep you long.
There are just a few things I need to acquaint you with. First,
I've had a call from Mrs Stanhope telling me that her son is
doing very well in the hospital and will hopefully be back at
school next week.'

'Yes, Tom told us,' Joyce said.

'Poor child,' murmured Mrs Golightly, 'having to go
through all that.'

'I have passed on our best wishes and told her how pleased
we are to hear that he is on the mend.' He held up the
envelope.

'Here comes the bombshell,' muttered Mr Cadwallader.

'I have had a communication,' the headmaster told the
teachers.

'From the Education Office,' interrupted Mrs Golightly.

'No, Bertha, not from the Education Office.'

'From the HMI,' said Mr Cadwallader.

'If I might be allowed to finish,' said the headmaster. 'It is
from St John's Teacher Training College in Clayton asking if
we might have a student with us for the day to observe some

lessons. She is particularly keen to teach the early years, so I guess she will spend most of the time with you, Bertha. Her name is Miss Balfour-Smith.'

'I say, that name rings a bell,' said Mr Cadwallader. 'I wonder if she's any relation to our esteemed Member of Parliament.'

'I shouldn't think there are many people called Balfour-Smith,' remarked Miss Tranter.

'She's probably the daughter of that pal of yours, Tom,' said Mr Cadwallader.

'Mr Balfour-Smith is not a pal of mine,' said Tom. 'I've only met him a couple of times.'

The first occasion Tom had encountered the local Member of Parliament was on the road to Clayton one Saturday night. He had been driving to see his Auntie Bridget when he came across a large black car at the side of the narrow road just beyond the bend where he had had the skirmish with Janette Fairborn and her horse. An urbane-looking middle-aged man with a wide, tanned, Roman-nosed face and short, carefully combed white hair and a neat moustache was staring at the bonnet, his hands on his hips. Tom had pulled over on to the grassy verge behind, opened the side window of his car and stuck his head out.

'Having a spot of bother?' he had called.

The driver turned out to be the Member of Parliament for Clayton and Urebank on his way to address a public meeting concerning the proposal to build a supermarket in the area, but his car had run out of petrol. Tom had come to his aid and driven him to the meeting. On the journey they had had a lively conversation about the state of education. Mr Balfour-Smith, recently appointed as a Minister of State for Education, had shown a great deal of interest in what Tom had had to say about small rural schools and had been impressed by the young man's enthusiasm. Some weeks later he had arranged for Miss Tudor-Williams, a senior member of Her Majesty's Inspectorate, to visit Risingdale School to examine the education of children in a typical small village school. The inspection report had been positive. Despite this, Tom's colleagues had not been best pleased to discover the HMI's visit had been occasioned by the newest addition to the teaching staff.

'I have written to St John's College,' Mr Gaunt informed the teachers now, 'to say we should be very happy to accommodate Miss Balfour-Smith.'

As the teachers made ready to go home, Tom took Joyce aside and described the exchange he had had with her ex-husband outside the school.

'What did you say?' she asked.

'I warned him off,' he told her. 'I don't think you will have any more trouble from him from now on.'

Sir Hedley's study was a large room dominated by a heavy mahogany desk, on which was an impressive brass inkwell in the shape of an eagle with outstretched wings, a stationery holder and a pile of papers. Displayed on the walls were oil paintings showing different animals: grazing cattle, fat black pigs on stumpy legs, bored-looking sheep, leaping horses and packs of hounds. In a glass dome on a side table were a variety of stuffed hummingbirds hovering around a branch. Other stuffed creatures included the head of a snarling fox mounted on a wooden plaque on the wall, a stoat with a rabbit in its jaws and a falcon, the latter two displayed in a glass-fronted cabinet. The baronet, when at home, spent a great deal of time in his sanctum, away from his wife.

After the acrimonious departure of Mrs Gosling, his study, like the rest of the house, needed a thorough clean. The oak floor and furniture were dusty, the windows grimy and the carpet unpswept.

Lady Maladroit had appointed Mrs Gosling's replacement – the only applicant who had answered the advertisement in the *Clayton Gazette*. Mrs Moody was a stout woman with a hennish bosom, severely permed chestnut hair and an over-emphatic voice. She had proved unsuitable and was quickly given her marching orders. Mrs Gosling had cleaned and dusted, wiped and polished with a vengeance. Her successor had merely flicked a feather duster and occasionally, when she felt inclined, washed a few dishes. Sir Hedley and his wife, who rarely agreed on anything, were in accord that Mrs Moody should go. Finding a suitable replacement was prov-ing extremely difficult, for the people in the village had rallied to support Mrs Gosling, whom they felt had been shabbily treated by the lady of the manor.

'I must apologise for the state of the room, we are at present without a housekeeper,' Sir Hedley told the two police officers who stood before him.

The smaller of the visitors was a tubby individual with a round, pinkish face, large blue, bulging eyes and a thatch of black hair. He was dressed in a police sergeant's uniform. The other man, wearing a shiny black suit, was a tall, angular individual with a long nose, flared nostrils and a drooping Stalin-like moustache. He held a rather crumpled hat, the brim of which he stroked uneasily.

'It's so difficult to get the staff these days,' continued the baronet. 'I'm afraid I can't offer you gentlemen a cup of tea. Do sit down.'

'Thank you, no, Sir Hedley,' said the plain-clothed officer, 'we should prefer to remain standing.'

'I guess you are here about the poachers,' said the baronet. 'Greenwood, one of my gamekeepers, tells me there has been a spate of thieving going on. I don't mind the odd pheasant or a trout or two being taken, but I draw the line at—'

The inspector held up his hand as if stopping traffic.

'No, no, Sir Hedley, do forgive my interjection.' (The inspector was fond of peppering his sentences with the more obscure terminology.) 'It does not appertain to the poaching. It is with regard to another more significant and pressing matter.'

'I sincerely hope that this significant and pressing matter has nothing to do with my son,' said the baronet.

'I'm afraid that it does, sir,' the uniformed officer told him, nodding gravely.

'Sergeant Pollock!' snapped the inspector, irritated by his colleague's intervention. 'Please leave this to me.' After all, he thought, he was in charge of the interview and it was he who wished to acquaint Sir Hedley with the news.

'So, what has James been up to now?' asked the baronet.

The inspector cleared his throat. 'There has been an accident, Sir Hedley,' he said.

'A motoring accident,' added the sergeant.

The inspector sighed and glared at his colleague. 'Yes, indeed, a motoring accident. A serious collision involving your son. He was proceeding along one of the narrow, twisting lanes and came to a sharp bend.'

'By the Fairborn farm,' said the police sergeant. 'It's a very dangerous stretch of road.'

'Sergeant Pollock, may I be allowed to finish?' said the inspector. He coughed again. 'As I was explaining, Sir Hedley, your son came to this hazardous section of road, which was wet and muddy after the recent substantial rains. From what we conjecture, he swerved to avoid an oncoming motorcyclist and struck a tree. The ambulance was called—'

'Inspector Hollis,' interrupted Sir Hedley, 'could you please come to the point? Has my son been injured?'

'No, Sir Hedley, sadly he didn't make it.'

'Didn't make it,' repeated the baronet.

'He was killed,' said the police sergeant who, unlike his superior, was a blunt-speaking man of few words.

The inspector, who had hoped to have broken the tragic news rather more sensitively, glared again at his colleague.

'He's dead?' asked the baronet, almost inaudibly.

'I'm afraid so, Sir Hedley,' said the inspector. 'May I offer my sincere commiserations?'

News of James Maladroit's death spread like wildfire through the village. It was the main topic of conversation in the King's Head on Saturday night.

'I don't wish to speak ill o' t'dead—' started Toby Croft, who was propping up the bar with his pal Percy and, as usual, holding forth.

'Then don't,' said Mrs Mossup before he could complete the sentence.

'I am hallowed to hexpress a view,' said the old farmer peevishly. 'When t'day comes, Doris, when I can't venture an hopinion, then I shall tek mi custom elseweer.'

The landlady gave a snort. 'Take your custom elsewhere? You are very welcome,' she told him. 'I shall not get rich on the amount you spend on beer and a respite from your blathering will come as a blessed relief.'

'What I were sayin', Percy,' said Toby, 'afore I were rudely hinterrupted, was that I don't wish to speak ill o' t'dead but that Jamie Maladroit was a reprobate. He was allus up to some mischief or other and led them parents of 'is a merry old dance. Course they spoiled t'lad rotten. Parents what don't put their foot down allus end up wi' kids what tread on their toes. It's a fact. An' I'll tell thee summat else an' all, he used to drive through t'village like a maniac. 'E nearly flattened two ducks and knocked Mrs Partington off of her bike. I'm not surprised 'e come a cropper.'

'I wonder what'll 'appen to t'estate now t'lad's dead,' observed his wrinkled companion.

'Aye, that's a point, Percy,' said Toby. 'Whoever comes into it will be left a tidy sum an' all that property and land, not to mention t'big 'ouse an' a title what gus wi' it.'

Mrs Mossup was thoughtful. It had not occurred to her when she had heard the news of the death of James Maladroit that her future grandchild, being the nearest blood relative to Sir Hedley, might be the one to inherit. He or she would undoubtedly have a strong claim. There would be no denying that the child was the baronet's grandchild. Why, hadn't Sir Hedley recognised that very fact himself?

'Are tha serving 'ere, Doris, or what?' called Toby, tapping his empty pint glass on the counter.

'What?'

'Tha were miles away,' said the old farmer. 'We're gagging fer a drink 'ere.'

'An' I reckon it's thy round,' Percy said before draining the contents of his glass.

As the landlady pulled the pints, Toby leaned over the bar. 'I were just sayin' to Percy 'ere, that when t'Squire Maladroit's pushin' up t'daisies, someone's in for a nice little windfall. Tha knows what they say, "Weer's there's a will, theer's a relative sniffin' abaat". I reckon there'll be distant relations settlin' like vultures, all these third cousins once removed seein' what they can get their claws on.'

'Don't you think about anything else but money?' Mrs Mossup asked him, tired of hearing his voice.

'Couse, Sir 'Edley might 'ave a love child 'idden away someweer who'll come in fer t'lot. That'd put t'fox in t''en coop. I shouldn't imagine there's much connubial bliss up at Marston Towers, knowing what Lady M is like. Nobody'd blame t'squire for 'avin' a bit on t'side. And young Jamie, for that matter, might 'ave been purrin it abaat a bit. 'E might 'ave a kiddie.' He looked knowingly at the landlady. 'I mean, there might be some young lass out there—'

Mrs Mossup banged down the two pints of bitter on the bar, spilling some of the contents.

'Will you give it a rest,' she said. 'I'm sick of hearing your voice. And I'll say this, Toby Croft, if you want to take your custom elsewhere, as you have threatened, I shall be more than happy to show you off the premises. Now, who's paying for these drinks?'

'Let me get these,' said an elderly man dressed in a loud tweed jacket who had approached the bar. 'It's the least I can do.'

'Very decent of you,' said Toby.

'You don't remember me, do you?' asked the man.

The old farmer looked at him suspiciously. 'Should I?'

'I was the driver who knocked down your poor old dog. It was at that bad bend where the young man you were talking about was killed.'

'Eh?'

'Don't you recall? I was coming around that bend and I ran over your old dog.'

'What old dog would this be then, Toby?' asked Mrs Mossup, her ears pricking up. 'As far as I know, you've only got the collie.'

'Oh, it wasn't a collie,' the man in tweeds told her. 'It was a very old mongrel, a sad creature that had lost most of its hair and was half blind.'

'Sounds like John Fairborn's dog to me,' said the landlady. 'His dog was run over outside his farm gate, wasn't it, Toby?' There was a smile playing on her lips.

'I wouldn't know,' grunted the old farmer, his embarrassment showing in the redness of his face.

'Tha must remember,' said Percy. 'It were thee what found it. As I recall, 'e bought thee a pint fer finding it and lerrin 'im know.'

'I felt very bad about knocking this gentleman's dog down,' said the man, 'but I was told the animal was well past its sell-by date.' He turned to Toby, who was looking decidedly ill at ease. 'I must say you took it very well. Most understanding, you were.'

'Oh, he's like that,' said Mrs Mossup sardonically. 'Very understanding, aren't you, Toby?'

'I hope you managed to buy another dog,' said the man. 'Do let me know if you paid more than the twenty pounds I gave you. I'd be happy to pay any extra.'

'You gave him twenty pounds!' exclaimed the landlady.

'I've just remembered, I've got to be someweer else,' said Toby and made a hasty retreat.

'Well, will tha look at that?' remarked Percy. 'That's t'fust time in livin' memory that Toby Croft 'as turned daan a free pint.'

Lady Maladroit sat stony-faced and straight-backed in a dusky pink upholstered chair. She stared out of the window in the drawing room. Her husband, when he told her of their son's death, expected her to break down in a paroxysm of shrieking and tears but there had been no outpouring of grief. Her face had turned the colour of the white marble mantelpiece where Sir Hedley now stood. The shock had rendered her speechless.

'Would you care for a drink?' her husband asked. 'A brandy, perhaps?'

His face was pale, his manner grave.

'Nothing,' she replied, continuing to stare out of the window.

There was a long silence, broken only by the steady ticking of the longcase clock.

'Parents imagine that they will die before their children,' said Sir Hedley at last. 'They think that they will outlive them. That is the way it should be.' He shook his head sadly. 'They are never prepared to hear that their child has died. It's a parent's worst nightmare.'

His wife turned her head a fraction and stared at him. 'Is that supposed to make me feel any better?' she asked coldly. Her mouth tightened with disapproval.

'No, Marcia,' he replied. 'I guess nothing I say will make you feel better.'

'You must be weighed down by guilt, Hedley,' she said spitefully.

'Guilt?' he repeated. 'Why should I feel guilty?'

Then came the outpouring, a torrent of accusations. 'The way you treated him,' she said icily. 'You never really loved James as I did. You were never a proper father.'

'That's unkind, Marcia,' he said sadly.

'It's true. Everything he did was wrong in your eyes. He knew, oh yes, he knew how disappointed you were in him. He told me so often enough. At every turn you made him feel worthless. You never took his part when he got into a few scrapes, as a proper father would have done. You were always there to find fault with him. And now you stand there telling me it's a parent's worst nightmare to lose a child. You lost James years ago. What a hypocrite you are, Hedley.'

Her husband was too weary and downhearted to respond. His jaw was fixed as if he was biting down on something. This was not the time to argue with her, he thought. Perhaps when his wife had later thought about what she had said, she might regret it. But he doubted that and he left the room without a word.

In his study the baronet buried his head in his hands and wept.

At the start of the following week Leo returned to school. He arrived after morning break accompanied by his mother. They were shown into Mr Gaunt's untidy study by a fussy Mrs Leadbeater, who smiled at the boy, patted his head as one might pet a dog and told him he was a brave little soldier and it was good to have him back.

'Well, young man,' said Mr Gaunt, 'you've been through the mill, haven't you?'

'Yes, sir,' replied the boy.

'We were very worried and all of us here at school missed you,' the headmaster told him. 'It's good to see you looking so well.' He leaned back in his chair and thought for a moment. 'I think perhaps in future you should give the football a miss, Leo. I know you would like to play, but it might be better not to tempt providence, as they say. We don't want a repetition of what happened, do we? There are many other sporting activities in which you can take part. What do you think?'

'I would still like to play football,' said Leo, 'and I'll be more careful next time.'

Mr Gaunt looked at the boy's mother as if to enlist her help, but she just smiled and shrugged.

'Just like his father,' she said. 'Stubborn as a mule.'

'Welcome back,' said Tom when Leo entered the classroom. There were cheers and clapping from the children.

'Thank you, Mr Dwyer,' replied the boy. 'It's good to be back.'

'There's quite a lot of work for you to do,' said the teacher, tongue-in-cheek. 'Charlie will tell you what you've missed. You will have to spend all your breaks catching up.'

The boy looked worried.

'It's all right, Leo,' said Tom. 'I'm only joking.'

Leo smiled. 'Could I say something, please, sir?' he asked.

'Go ahead,' said Tom.

'I want to thank everybody for the card and what you said.' He stopped and looked down, trying to compose himself. He was close to tears. 'Everybody has been really kind.'

'Ah, bless,' murmured Vicky.

Leo then walked to the back of the classroom to where Christopher was sitting. The children turned in their seats.

Not a sound could be heard. Tom feared what the boy would do and was minded to say something but held back. Leo held out his hand.

'It was an accident,' he said. 'No hard feelings.'

Christopher thought for a moment and then shook Leo's hand. 'No hard feelings,' he replied.

At lunchtime Tom asked Joyce if she would step into his classroom. He wanted to have a word with her but didn't want their colleagues in the staffroom to hear what he had to say.

'This sounds intriguing,' she said, perching on the corner of his desk as she had done when he had first met her. Tom smiled. He recalled that occasion when this extraordinary-looking character, tall and slim with shiny black hair, scarlet lips and large, pale eyes, had introduced herself.

'So what is it that's so secretive?' she asked.

'Could I ask you what your ex-husband's name is?'

'That's a strange thing to ask. Why do you want to know?'

'I'll explain in a minute,' said Tom.

'It's Stephen. His name's Stephen Harrison, but since you had a word with him – and I don't know what you said – I've not seen anything of him.'

Tom passed her a newspaper.

'My Auntie Bridget gets the *Clayton Gazette*,' he told her. 'Sometimes she passes the old copies on to me.'

'And?'

'I think you should look at the front page.'

Joyce read the headline: 'LOCAL SQUIRE'S SON KILLED IN TRAGIC CAR CRASH.'

'Well, I know about that. It's no mystery,' said Joyce. 'It's the talk of Risingdale.'

'Read on,' said Tom.

Joyce looked back at the newspaper. Her face soon began to drain of colour.

The article described the collision of the driver of the car and the motorcyclist, both of whom had been killed. The name of the latter was Stephen Harrison.

'Oh my God!' gasped Joyce, sliding off the desk. 'He's dead.'

At the end of school Tom was on bus duty. The coach driver, catching sight of him, clambered from his cab and approached, straightening his tie and smoothing down his hair. There was a look of expectation on the cheery red face.

'Hello, Mr Firkin,' said Tom.

'Did you have a quiet word with Mrs Golightly?' the coach driver asked, in a confidential tone of voice.

'Yes, I did,' replied Tom.

'What did she say?'

'She is aware.'

'Aware,' repeated the bus driver.

'Aware of your, of your . . . your interest,' Tom told him.

'Anything else?'

'Well, no, not really. Just that.'

'I see,' he said, scratching his head. 'I spoke at the Women's Institute meeting and my talk went down well, even if I do say so myself.'

'Yes, I heard it was most entertaining,' said Tom.

'She's a member of the WI, is Mrs Golightly. I judged her cake to be the best. She's a very good cook. She'd make a man a fine wife. So, you think she might be disposed to give me the nod then?'

'I'm not sure,' Tom told him, 'but I wouldn't give up hope. "Faint heart never won fair lady" and all that. Perhaps you might approach her yourself.'

'Oh, I'm not sure about that,' he said. 'I wouldn't know what to say.'

'You could ask her out.'

'Yes, I suppose I could,' said Mr Firkin. 'I'm not such a bad catch, you know. There's the funeral directors' annual dinner and dance at the Station Hotel in Clayton. Do you think she might like to accompany me? I'm into coffins and burials now, and I've just done a course on embalming. Bus driving's not my main job.'

'Yes, so I believe.'

'It's a tidy business and it's thriving. I mean, people have to die, don't they?'

'They do, indeed,' replied Tom, looking at his watch.

'I provide a bespoke service. "Firkin's Friendly First-Class Funerals". Quite catchy that, isn't it? I have a nice new hearse, a chapel of rest with adequate parking and office premises in Clayton. As I said, trade is brisk at the moment.'

'That's good to hear,' said Tom.

'I've been asked to do a funeral for Sir Hedley and Lady Maladroit. You'll have heard about their son, of course.'

'Yes, it's very sad.'

'You could maybe drop me into the conversation when you're talking to Mrs Golightly. You might say that I am comfortably off and if she's disposed to give me the nod . . .'

'Yes, I'll certainly do that,' said Tom, keen to be away.

'Can you get a move on, Mr Firkin?' Vicky called from the bus. 'Some of us have homes to go to.'

Back in his classroom, Tom found a card on his desk. It was from Amanda Stanhope inviting him for a meal on the Saturday next to thank him for his support during their trying time. He telephoned her straight away to accept.

16

Tom made a real effort with his appearance for his dinner date. On the Saturday morning he drove into Clayton and bought a new set of clothes at the expensive gentlemen's outfitters: a dyed linen shirt, tailored grey trousers and a black herringbone woollen jacket. Amanda Stanhope had also made an effort with her appearance for the evening, dressed in a silver embroidered Chinese jacket. Her hair was immaculately coiffed, her make-up flawless. Tom expected that Leo would be joining them for the meal, but the boy, having chatted to him for a while, was despatched to his room.

'I'm afraid I'm not a very good cook,' admitted his host. 'The best I can do is a lasagne and salad and I have to admit that the apple pie is a gift from my neighbour.'

'Mrs Lister,' said Tom.

'That right. She's been so kind and her son has become a good friend to Leo. They are like kindred spirits.'

'Ah, young Charlie,' said Tom. 'He's a really nice lad and very clever. He won a scholarship to the grammar school last term and starts there in September if he passes the county eleven-plus examination, which I think he will take in his stride. I should like to put Leo in for the exam. I don't think he will have a problem in passing. It would be a good thing if the two of them could stay together.'

'I would like that,' she said. How good-looking he is, she thought, with his tanned face, shiny black curls, long-lashed, dark blue eyes and winning smile. It was a classically hand-some face, with high cheekbones and a strong jaw.

It was after the dinner, as they sat before the flickering fire in the grate, that their conversation turned to something of a more personal nature.

'Tell me about yourself,' said Amanda.

'It's not that exciting,' he said.

'I should like to know.'

'I was born in Ireland,' Tom told her, 'an only child and, I suppose, indulged. I had a happy childhood until I became a teenager, when things got difficult. My mother died when I was fourteen; my father passed away a couple of years later. I became a bit of a rebel, moody and unapproachable, but my mother's younger sister in Barton-in-the-Dale took me in. It was then I moved to England. It was my Auntie Bridget who helped me through some pretty dark times. I always said as I grew up that she was the mother I lost. "A hundred aunties are not the same as one mother," someone said to me recently, but I couldn't have wished for a better person to raise me. When I got into a bit of trouble at school with the Christian Brothers, she took my side. "Ah well," she said, "they say the wildest colts make the finest horses."' He smiled. 'She has a wealth of old Irish sayings – one for every occasion. But she was like a mother to me and encouraged me all the way. I became a professional footballer, but too many injuries on the pitch ended my career.'

Amanda nodded. And it nearly ended Leo's, she thought.

'I wasn't much of a scholar at school,' Tom continued. 'When I gave up the football, Auntie Bridget persuaded me to get some qualifications, so I went to evening classes and then took a part-time degree. After that I trained as a teacher. That's about it, really.'

'And you clearly love your job,' she said.

'Yes, I do. I don't think there is any other profession like it.'

They sat there for a moment in contented silence, both staring at the fire in the grate.

'What about you?' Tom asked.

'I had a typical middle-class upbringing,' she told him. 'I attended a convent high school, went on to study art in London and married early. I believe I told you my husband was killed flying a light aircraft. They think his plane came down over the English Channel; he never arrived in France. He was never found. Of course, the year of his death was hard for me. I had a pretty dark time, too. It was made even harder when I discovered Leo was ill. My son never settled in any of the schools he attended. He was lonely and bullied. Risingdale is the first school in which he has been truly happy and a lot of that is down to you. He loves having you as his teacher.'

The evening passed quickly. When Amanda said goodbye to Tom on the doorstep, she reached up and kissed him lightly on the cheek.

Tom stopped at the gate of the cottage. The trunks of the silver birches shone luminously in the darkness. He stared up at a vast sky as black as jet and studded with tiny stars. It had been an evening to remember. He breathed in deeply. There was the smell of cigar smoke in the air. He sensed that someone was in the shadows watching him.

'Who's there?' he asked.

Sir Hedley appeared out of the darkness.

'Good evening,' he said, before drawing on his cigar and blowing out a cloud of smoke. 'Mrs Lister doesn't like me smoking in the cottage. Stale smell lingers.' He didn't look in the least troubled or embarrassed to be discovered lurking in the darkness. Tom didn't know what to say at first and then found his voice.

'I was sorry to hear about your son,' he said.

'Ah yes, James,' sighed the baronet. 'Very sad.' He drew

again on his cigar. 'I see you have been visiting Mrs Stanhope. She's a remarkable woman, don't you think?'

'Er . . . yes, she is,' replied Tom.

'Quite a wonderful artist. Member of the Royal Academy, you know.' He looked up at the stars. 'Beautiful night, isn't it?' Cigar smoke was suspended in the air.

'Yes.'

'One never gets nights like this, so clear with a vast sky full of stars, in the towns.' He looked up at the sky. 'You seem to have settled in well in Risingdale.'

'I like it very much,' Tom told him.

'So you think you will stay here?'

'Yes, I will,' he replied.

'I noticed the other day that some of the children were playing football on one of Mr Sheepshanks' fields. Not the most suitable of pitches, I should have thought.'

'No, but it's the only one we have. I'm afraid it's a question of beggars can't be choosers.'

'I gather you were a professional player.'

'I was, yes,' replied Tom.

'Do you miss it?'

'Some aspects, perhaps, but I am very happy teaching and, as I said, I like the life here in Risingdale.'

'The people are friendly,' said Sir Hedley, 'but I guess you will have discovered they like to know your business. Gossip travels like wildfire in the village. I am sure you are aware of that.'

Tom took the hint. 'I don't deal in gossip, Sir Hedley,' he replied. 'I am not really interested in other people's business.'

The baronet took another pull on his cigar and blew out the smoke before dropping the remains, which he crushed with his shoe.

'Well, I shall bid you goodnight, Mr Dwyer,' he said, before he returned to the cottage.

'Did I hear you speaking to someone in the garden?' Mrs Lister asked Sir Hedley when he walked through the cottage door.

'Yes, I was chatting to the young schoolmaster,' replied Sir Hedley. 'He was visiting your neighbour.'

'Mr Dwyer?'

'Yes.'

'He was visiting Mrs Stanhope?'

'Yes.'

'A strange hour to be visiting,' she said. 'What were you talking about?'

'Oh, we were just passing the time of day,' replied Sir Hedley. He stood by the fire and warmed himself. 'It's become quite chilly out there tonight.'

'What was he saying?' she asked.

'Just that he is very settled in Risingdale. Nothing of any consequence. He seems like a pleasant young man.'

'So do you think he knows about us?' she asked, sounding anxious.

'Yes, my dear, I have no doubt that he does now. I don't think it requires a deal of intelligence to guess what I was doing visiting you at this time of night.'

'I suppose one might imagine the same thing of Mr Dwyer visiting Mrs Stanhope at this time of night.'

'You think that there may be something going on?'

'I really don't know, Hedley.'

'Anyway, I'm sure Mr Dwyer is aware of our relationship, but I imagine he will not say anything.'

'No, I don't think he will,' Mrs Lister agreed. 'He's a very discreet young man, not the sort of person to indulge in idle gossip.'

'Yes, he said as much.'

'I just hope that his colleague up at the school is as circumspect,' she said. 'It was an unfortunate coincidence meeting her as we did in Scarborough.'

'I don't think Miss Tranter will be spreading anything around the village,' Sir Hedley told her. 'Mr Sampson assured me that they would keep things under their hats.'

'Let's hope so,' she said, looking worried. 'I'm not that bothered what people might think about me. It's the effect it will have on you and Charlie. People can be very unkind.'

Sir Hedley put his arm around her and kissed her cheek. 'You worry too much,' he said. He changed the subject. 'So what do you make of Mrs Stanhope?' he asked.

'She seems friendly enough.'

'But?'

'There is something about her that concerns me a little,' she replied. 'It's probably a silly notion, but she seems rather too nice and sociable to be true.'

'I find her charming and witty,' said Sir Hedley.

'Yes, everyone does,' agreed Mrs Lister. 'She's certainly managed to make herself very popular with all she meets, particularly the men, and everyone seems to bend over backwards to please her. She is one of those women who is fully aware of her attraction and knows how to use it to her best advantage.'

'That's a little uncharitable of you, my dear,' said Sir Hedley.

'You are doubtless right,' she replied, 'but I've seen how the men in her presence flutter around her like moths around a candle, fascinated by the bright light. I just hope that Mr Dwyer doesn't get his wings burned.'

'I have something to say,' Joyce told her colleagues as they gathered in the staffroom before school.

Mrs Golightly put down her knitting, Mr Cadwallader stopped crunching his biscuit and Tom looked up from the books he had been marking.

Joyce gave a small cough. 'You all know that things have been very difficult for me of late. The unexpected appearance of my ex-husband was most distressing. You are also aware, I am sure, that he was killed in the road accident. I take no satisfaction from this. It is not something I would wish on anyone, but I have to say that it is a great relief that I will not be bothered by him ever again. Perhaps that sounds rather heartless, but it is the honest truth. It's difficult for people who have not been in the position that I have to appreciate how very stressful it is to know there is someone watching you, following you and harassing you.'

'I must say, Joyce—' began Mr Cadwallader.

'Please let me finish, Owen,' she cut him off. 'As I said, I would not wish what happened to Stephen on anyone, but knowing that he will not be there to bully and pester me any more is like having a great weight taken off my shoulders. I just want to say to you how I appreciate your support and understanding, particularly yours, Tom.' Tears pricked the corners of her eyes. 'I could not wish for kinder and more considerate colleagues.'

'Well,' said Mr Cadwallader, 'I don't wish to be unkind, but if he hadn't taken it into his head to pursue you in the way he did, he would still be alive today.'

'Anyway, Joyce,' said Mrs Golightly, 'you can put all that behind you now and get on with your life.'

'That is what I intend to do, Bertha,' replied Joyce. 'And with that in mind, I want you to know that I am to be married.'

'Good God!' exclaimed Mr Cadwallader.

'Getting married!' cried Mrs Golightly.

'That's right. I know it might sound rather callous so soon after Stephen's death, but I am determined to move forward. I have had a proposal and have accepted it.'

'Oh, Joyce, I'm really happy for you,' said Mrs Golightly. 'I take it the lucky man is Mr Sampson?'

'It is.'

'Congratulations,' said Tom. He stood up, went to her and kissed her on the cheek. 'This is wonderful news.'

'You deserve to be happy, Joyce, after all you have been through,' said Mr Cadwallader.

'We are to be married at Easter. Of course you are all invited. I would like you, Owen, to give me away and Julian has agreed that Tom should be asked to be the best man, if you are both prepared to do that. Bertha, I hope you will be my matron of honour.'

'Of course,' her colleagues replied in unison.

'Mr Pendlebury is coming into school this morning,' Joyce continued, 'and I intend to ask him if we can get married at St Mary's. It might not be possible because I am divorced, but at least he might be prepared to give us a blessing.'

Mr Gaunt entered the staffroom. 'Now, I don't know what is so important that is keeping you all in here at this time chattering away,' he said, 'but the bell has gone and the children are coming into school.'

'This morning, children,' said Tom, surveying the sea of expectant faces before him, 'Mr Pendlebury has come into school to speak to you. I want you all to sit up smartly and listen very carefully to what he has to say.'

'Good morning, children,' said the vicar, rubbing his hands together and looking around the classroom. 'I must say that your teacher has done wonders in here. It is so bright and cheerful with all the colourful displays and shelves full of books.'

'Mr Dwyer used to have a load of dirty books on the shelves,' Vicky shouted out, 'but he got rid of them.'

'I beg your pardon,' said the vicar, taken aback.

'Dirty books,' repeated the girl. 'They were dead mucky.'

Tom laughed nervously and his face went pink. 'Vicky means some very old, out-of-date and dusty books,' Tom explained. 'I guess they were rather grubby to handle. I inherited them from Miss Cathcart.'

'Ah, I see,' said the vicar, giving a faint smile.

The teacher turned to the children.

'Now, I shall be taking Miss Tranter's class for games this morning while the vicar speaks to you,' Tom told his pupils, 'so best behaviour, please.' He turned to the visitor. 'I'll leave you to it, Mr Pendlebury.'

When Tom had gone, the vicar smiled, placed a plastic bag he was carrying on the teacher's desk and again rubbed his hands together vigorously. 'Good morning, children,' he said brightly.

'Good morning, vicar,' chorused the children.

'What have you got in the bag, Mr Pendlebury?' asked Vicky.

'All will be revealed in a moment,' the cleric replied. 'Before anything else, I want to thank you all for coming to tidy up the churchyard last term. You did a wonderful job and I am very, very grateful.'

'We liked doin' it,' George shouted out.

'Can we do it again?' asked Carol.

'Perhaps. I will have a word with your teacher,' the vicar told her.

'We could do it next week,' said Holly.

'Maybe later in the year.' Before there were any more interruptions, he continued quickly. 'Now, it was very kind of you all to help me out and that is what I wish to talk to you about this morning, about being kind and helpful to others.'

'Like Jesus,' Vicky shouted out.

'Yes. Like Jesus.'

'He was really kind to people,' Vicky continued, 'and they killed him.'

'Well, let us not go into that for the moment,' Mr Pendlebury told her. He picked up the plastic bag, reached inside and produced a banana and a stick of rock. He placed the banana on Marjorie's desk and the stick of rock on Charlie's.

'Now, young lady,' said the vicar to the girl, 'could you read for me what is written on the little label on the skin of the banana?'

'"Best Bananas. Produce of Costa Rica",' Marjorie read out.

'And you, young man,' the clergyman asked Charlie, 'could you read out what it says on the label on the stick of rock?'

'"Whitby Rock, a present from the seaside",' the boy told him.

'Thank you,' said Mr Pendlebury. 'Now both these items, the banana and the stick of rock, have labels on the outside telling us what we will find on the inside. If I peel the banana like this, get rid of the skin and break it in half, what do you see?'

'Half a banana,' replied Marjorie, looking puzzled.

'But it doesn't say what it is on the inside, does it?' said the vicar.

'But I know what it is,' replied Marjorie. 'It's half a banana. Everyone knows that it's a banana.'

'That's right,' said the vicar, 'but it doesn't say that.'

'I don't like bananas,' remarked Simon. 'They bring me out in spots.'

'I like bananas,' said Judith. 'They are my favourite fruit.'

'My gran makes banana bread and it's lovely,' said Carol.

'Yes, yes, that's very interesting,' said the cleric, moving swiftly on before he received any further interruptions. He returned to Charlie. 'Now, young man, if I unwrap the stick of rock and break it in half like this, what does it say that runs right the way through it?'

'"Whitby Rock",' replied Charlie.

'So you see,' said the vicar, 'on the outside of the banana, on the label, it tells you what is on the inside, but when you peel it, the inside doesn't tell you what it is. But on the stick of rock, it tells you what is on the outside and when you undo the wrapping and break the rock in two, you see what it says on the label running right through it. So what you read is what you get.'

Mr Pendlebury's analogy was lost on the children, who stared at him, completely baffled.

'You see, children,' said the vicar, 'it is the same with people.'

'That they are like bananas?' asked Vicky.

'No, not actually like bananas,' replied the vicar. 'What I mean is, it is about labels. What people claim to be like on the outside is sometimes not what they are like on the inside. They say that they are good and kind on the outside but on the inside they are not. Their label is false. Others say they are good and kind on the outside and on the inside they are. Their label is genuine. They are like the stick of rock. Does that make sense?'

'So is it better to be like a stick of rock rather than a banana?' asked Marjorie.

'In a sense, yes,' replied the clergyman.

'But a stick of rock is full of sugar and will rot your teeth,' she said. 'A banana is healthier.'

'The banana and the stick of rock are examples,' the vicar told her. He was getting hot under his clerical collar. 'Does anyone understand what I am trying to say?' He looked at Leo. 'What about you, young man?'

'Yes,' replied the boy, 'I know what you mean. You are saying that some people go around saying they are good and kind but they are not. They are hypocrites and pretend to be something they aren't.'

Mr Pendlebury sighed. 'Exactly.'

'It's like the Parable of the Good Samaritan,' continued Leo. 'When the man is attacked by thieves and left for dead, he cries for help. The priest who is passing doesn't stop and he crosses the road. The next person, a teacher, does the same. These are the two people who tell us how to be kind but are not kind themselves. So what you see on the outside is not what is on the inside. They are hypocrites.'

'Yes, indeed,' said Mr Pendlebury, wishing he had used the parable to illustrate his point in the first place rather than a banana and a stick of rock.

'So what's this got to do with bananas?' asked Vicky.

'How did the lesson go?' asked Tom when his visitor sat with him in the staffroom at morning break.

'Oh, not too bad,' replied the vicar, staring out of the window where he caught sight of George sitting on the playground wall sucking half a stick of rock and Vicky eating half a banana.

Tom had not been teaching at the school for very long when he had gone to see Mr Gaunt about the possibility of entering some of his pupils for the grammar-school eleven-plus examination. He thought that for bright youngsters, like Charlie Lister, a grammar-school education would suit them better than that of a comprehensive. He had been surprised by the headmaster's reaction to the idea. Mr Gaunt had explained that he did not put the pupils in for the eleven-plus examination. With one or two exceptions, whose parents had pressed for their children to sit the paper, the pupils at the school had all moved on to Clayton Comprehensive, where, on the whole, they had done well. The headmaster had explained that he was not really in favour of putting the children through the stresses of the exam and felt cramming them for the test would affect the breadth and balance of the curriculum and cause undue stress.

When he had seen the disappointment on the teacher's face, he had continued: 'I have taught for many years, Tom, and I think you will allow that I know rather more than you, who have just started in the profession, what is the most appropriate education for my pupils. I feel it would be more fitting if young Charlie, and indeed all the Risingdale pupils, went to the comprehensive. The school offers a good all-round education and the students achieve very commendable results.'

Tom had argued the point and Mr Gaunt had finally conceded with a proviso.

'Look, Tom,' the headmaster had told him, leaning back in his chair, 'if you wish to look into the question of a scholarship for Charlie and enter him and some of the children for the eleven-plus, then go ahead, but before you do, I suggest you have a word with the children themselves and explain what it involves, and write to their parents and see what they think.'

Tom had done just this and eight of the children, with the encouragement of their parents, were keen to sit the examination. Tom had explained that it involved a lunchtime a week for extra tuition and quite a bit of homework, but this put no one off. The group included those Tom felt would have a strong chance of passing: Charlie, of course, Marjorie, Judith, Carol, Holly and Hazel and Simon. Leo had been added later to the list. The one exception in the group was Colin. Although he had made real progress and was working hard, Tom didn't feel he would have much chance of passing. He was concerned that the boy, who had had a number of setbacks in his young life, might be greatly upset and become disillusioned should he fail, particularly if all the others passed. However, when he explained to the pupil how hard the exam was and asked if he really wanted to sit the test, Colin was adamant.

'I want to have a shot at it, Mr Dwyer,' he had said vehemently.

The teacher had nodded. 'OK, Colin,' he had said, 'but you need to put a lot of work in.'

Tom had entered all nine pupils for the exam.

*   *   *

Mr Pendlebury had been asked to call at Marston Towers to discuss the arrangements for the funeral of James Maladroit. Sir Hedley and his wife were awaiting his arrival in the drawing room. The baronet, with a forlorn expression fixed on his face, stood by the white marble mantelpiece. He was so utterly motionless he might have been a figure carved out of stone. Lady Maladroit sat in a hard-backed chair by the window with an impassive expression on her face.

The vicar found the room stuffy and oppressive. A large crystal vase of wilting white lilies exuded a sickly smell. He looked around, taking in the lavish decoration not at all to his simple tastes. The walls, lined with fixed mahogany bookcases, were set between tall sash windows overlooking a vast parkland. Everything conveyed comfortable opulence, from the heavy, plum-coloured velvet curtains to the thick carpet, from the delicately moulded ceiling to the deep armchairs and magazine-laden tables. The room smelled of dust and lilies.

'Good morning, Mr Pendlebury,' said Sir Hedley. His face was pale and drawn. The vicar caught a whiff of whisky and cigars as he came to shake the baronet's hand. 'Please do take a seat.'

The vicar perched himself on the end of a huge plum-red, overstuffed armchair beneath a large portrait in oils of a self-important-looking man. The figure, posing with his hand on his hip and two German pointers at his feet, had the same dark eyes, large ears and wide mouth as Sir Hedley's.

'I am conscious that this is a most difficult and melancholy time for you both,' sympathised the cleric, 'a time of great sadness and grief, but perhaps also a time for us to remember the life God gave James, to share memories and to encourage us to lean on each other.'

Lady Maladroit stared fixedly at her husband. Her face was a dead white mask of misery. Her voice was cold, hard and precise when she spoke.

'A terrible time,' she said. 'Unbearable.'

'To lose a child is the most devastating blow, one that no parent should have to face,' continued the clergyman, pressing his long hands together as if in prayer. 'The Bible tells us in Ecclesiastes that "It is better to go to a house of mourning than to go to a house of feasting, for death is the destiny of every person; the living should take this to heart." There are no clear and simple answers when a child we love has died, but God has promised that no matter how deep the pain we feel—'

'Mr Pendlebury,' interrupted Lady Maladroit, the irritation clearly sounding in her voice, 'I know that you mean well and I don't wish to appear discourteous, but you have not been invited here to give us a sermon, however well-meaning; you are here to discuss the arrangements for James's funeral.'

'Marcia,' said the baronet, embarrassed by his wife's sharp remarks, 'Mr Pendlebury was only trying to offer some comfort.'

'Yes, yes, I know that,' she replied, not looking at her husband, 'but nothing said will alleviate the sorrow I feel. I just need things to be organised as quickly as possible.' Her eyes held the vicar's, unblinking. Her unwavering gaze unnerved the clergyman.

'Of course, of course, Lady Maladroit,' said the vicar. 'I appreciate that.' He leaned forward in his chair.

'The funeral will be a simple affair,' she said. 'There will only be my husband and I attending. We have few relatives. I only have a sister who lives in the south and she will not be present. My husband has no family save for some distant cousin, whom we haven't seen for years.'

'I am sure the villagers would like to pay their respects,' suggested Mr Pendlebury. He looked at Sir Hedley but the baronet remained silent. On this occasion he was content to leave the arrangements to his wife, wishing to avoid any further disagreements. Since the death of their son they had exchanged few words.

'Pay their respects,' repeated Lady Maladroit, her mouth twisting into an awful smile. The hawk's-beak nose tilted up in defiance. 'The people in Risingdale hated James. Oh, don't look at me like that, Mr Pendlebury. They hated him. They resented him because he had money and position. They are a nosy, selfish and unfriendly people and I don't want a church full of them, gawping and gossiping and smirking behind their hands.'

'I feel that is unfair, Lady Maladroit,' responded the clergyman, stung by the comments. 'The people in Risingdale have a great deal of respect for the Maladroits. They are a generous people and not without compassion and—'

'Please, Mr Pendlebury,' she interjected. Her tone was dismissive. 'Let us not argue the point. I am too weary.' Her narrow eyes were bright with resolve. 'The funeral will be a quiet affair, with the service conducted at Clayton Crematorium.'

'Not at St Mary's?' gasped the vicar.

'No,' she replied.

'So James will not be buried in the family tomb in the churchyard at St Mary's?' The vicar looked again at Sir Hedley. The baronet did not meet his eye. He seemed self-possessed, grave, remote.

Lady Maladroit sighed a long theatrical exhalation.

'James will be cremated,' she said decisively.

'I see,' said the vicar faintly. He rubbed his forehead and frowned. He looked again at her husband. 'Is this your wish, Sir Hedley?' he asked.

'It is my wife's wish,' said the baronet. His long face was anguished. 'It is what she wants.'

'Mr Firkin, the funeral director, has things in hand,' said Lady Maladroit. 'He has booked the crematorium for eleven o'clock next Friday. I should be grateful if you would conduct a short service. There will be no readings, no hymns and no homily.'

'This is most unusual, Lady Maladroit,' protested the vicar.

'It is my wish,' she told him again, fixing him with a gaze of fanatical intensity. Her voice was metallic. 'And now, if there is nothing else?'

The vicar shook his head. 'No, nothing else,' he murmured.

'Thank you for coming, Mr Pendlebury,' and with that she rose from her chair and swept from the room.

17

On his way back to the vicarage, the clergyman, head bowed in meditation, mulled over what Lady Maladroit had said about the villagers. They would be gawping and gossiping and smirking behind their hands were they to attend the funeral, she had told him. He knew this would not be the case. Risingdale was a close-knit community and the people, though a little too straight-talking at times, were warm and affable when you got to know them. When one of their number was ill or in need of help, or when tragedy struck, they proved to be sympathetic and ready to lend a hand. It was true that James Maladroit had not been popular in Risingdale, but at a time like this they would be understanding and supportive of the bereaved parents.

The clergyman recalled the occasion when Richard Greenwood's wife had died. Her grieving husband suddenly changed from being a gregarious and hardworking man into a bad-tempered malcontent and a frequenter of the King's Head, from where he staggered home at closing time worse for drink. Overwhelmed with grief, he didn't bother with the farm, had little time for his broken-hearted son and was snappish with his neighbours. The villagers had tried to help. His fellow farmers offered to feed his animals, mend his walls and repair the roof of his farmhouse but he refused their help. Their wives had brought him cooked meals but they were often left uneaten. These were not the actions of selfish and unfriendly people.

Mr Pendlebury genuinely liked the inhabitants of Risingdale and his conversation with Lady Maladroit had disturbed him profoundly. He also loved his church and his parishioners. He had been the priest there since his ordination, first as the young curate, then as the vicar when the old canon, Dr Bentley, retired. He had no ambitions for preferment in the Church, to climb up the ecclesiastical ladder with all the trappings and responsibilities of a dean or an archdeacon. He even declined when asked to become a canon at the cathedral. When it had been suggested by the bishop that he might move to a larger and more prosperous parish, he had refused. He was a country parson and wished to remain so. His vocation was to serve the small community and to hopefully make some difference to people's lives.

Mr Pendlebury had never really got on with the Lady of the Manor. Sir Hedley had always been most courteous and generous, but his wife he found stand-offish and patronising. Furthermore, she was an out-and-out snob who rarely had a good word to say about anybody or anything. He felt very sorry for people like that. They were to be pitied. As he walked up the high street, he thought of the lesson he had given in the school about labels, those people who profess to be one thing and are in reality quite another. Each Sunday, Lady Maladroit had dutifully attended his Sunday morning service. She had sat upright and stern-faced in the reserved front pew of the church, singing the hymns, hearing the gospels, listening to his sermons. Did she consider herself a Christian, he wondered? Did the words in the Bible about kindness and compassion, of loving one's neighbour, mean anything to her? He shook his head. 'A very sad and uncharitable lady,' he said out loud.

'I hope you are not talking about me, Mr Pendlebury.'

The vicar jumped and looked up suddenly.

Mrs Stanhope stood outside her studio smiling at him.

'G ... good gracious, no,' he spluttered. 'It was ... er ... someone quite different.'

'You were in a world of your own,' she told him.

'I was about to call to see you,' said the vicar, 'to enquire about your son. I believe he has been in hospital. I saw him in a recent lesson I gave at the school and he seemed well; I pray that he is all right.'

'That's most kind of you,' she replied. 'Leo is doing very well. In fact, he's back to his usual self, lively as ever and with a lot to say, and as you noted he's returned to school. He was keen to get back.'

'It must have been quite a harrowing time for you,' said the vicar. 'I hear he was quite ill.'

'Yes, he was, but he's fine now. Do you know, I have been so touched by all the people who have asked after him and offered help. I have been quite overwhelmed by their kindness and concern.'

Mr Pendlebury thought of Lady Maladroit for a moment.

'Yes, indeed,' he said, 'people are very kind, particularly when they see others in need of support.'

'I am just about to make a cup of tea,' said Mrs Stanhope. 'Would you care to join me?'

'I should like that very much,' he replied. 'I take it with milk but no sugar.'

In the studio, while Mrs Stanhope filled the kettle, the vicar looked at the painting of Sir Hedley's assistant gamekeeper, which was resting on the easel. He leaned closer, scrutinising the portrait.

'This is magnificent,' he said. 'You have captured Mr Greenwood's likeness exactly. It's unnervingly good.'

'He was a very good sitter,' she replied, reaching into the cupboard for a teapot, 'and a very interesting man. He's had quite a difficult time by the sound of it.'

'Yes, indeed,' said Mr Pendlebury. 'He went through a dark period when his wife died, you know. She was a lovely woman and he greatly relied upon her. It was such a shock to all of us in the village when she passed away. Richard took her death very badly and got into a terrible state but, thank God, he has come through it and is doing very well working up at Marston Towers.'

'I was sorry to hear about Sir Hedley's son,' she said. 'His parents must be devastated. I can't imagine what it must be like to lose a child.'

'Yes, indeed, a sad time for them both,' replied Mr Pendlebury.

Mrs Stanhope pointed to a small collection of landscapes displayed on a wall.

'These are by Mr Greenwood's son,' she said. 'Colin comes down here on Saturdays and I teach him a few techniques. He has quite a talent.'

'My word, he does, indeed,' agreed the vicar. 'These are very good. Why, this is of St Mary's, and if I am not mistaken, the figure in the painting is me. Of course, his mother was an artist, you know. Not in your league, of course, but she enjoyed painting. When she died, Colin went through such a difficult time, like his father. I gather he was quite a handful at school. In my experience, people deal with grief in different ways. I hope I am not speaking out of turn but, from what I have been told, the boy was disruptive and took to bullying the other children. Colin's teacher at the time, Miss Cathcart, was at her wits' end trying to deal with him.'

'What happened to Miss Cathcart?' asked Mrs Stanhope. 'Did she retire?'

'Sadly not,' Mr Pendlebury informed her, shaking his head. 'She had a dreadful accident, discovered by a rambler in the river. Drowned. It was assumed that she was walking along the towpath on a blustery day, lost her balance and fell in the water. It was tragic. I guess that people outside the village imagine that life in Risingdale is forever peaceful and uneventful, but we have had our share of incidents.'

'So it seems,' said Mrs Stanhope.

'But Colin's is a good-news story,' continued the vicar. 'With the arrival of his new teacher, his behaviour changed dramatically. It was quite a transformation. He became well-behaved and, from what I have been told, started working hard at school. Then his talent for art was discovered. Of course, this was down to Mr Dwyer. That young man has really brought the boy on, taking an interest in him and encouraging him. Everyone in Risingdale speaks well of Mr Dwyer. He has great personal charm, and a warmth and a kindliness and tolerance, which are so important in a teacher. You know, Mrs Stanhope, he is quite a remarkable young man.'

'Yes, he is,' agreed Mrs Stanhope, 'quite a remarkable young man.' She thought for a moment. 'I'll make the tea.'

The morning of the cremation of James Maladroit was bitterly cold and drizzly, the sort of weather that suited well this kind of occasion. Clayton Crematorium was a featureless block of a building with an equally featureless interior of plain oatmeal-painted walls devoid of any religious imagery, functional, insipid pine furniture and long windows containing a hint of coloured glass. Bunches of garish plastic flowers in large vases were positioned strategically on the windowsills and a spray of three lilies had been placed on the simple coffin, which rested on a bier before a carpeted stage.

Sir Hedley and his wife stood in the front pew during the brief service, both stony-faced, neither speaking. There had been no hymns, no readings, no homily, precious few prayers and the only flowers were the lilies. Soon after the coffin had disappeared behind the red velvet curtain, accompanied by some soft, unidentifiable recorded music, Lady Maladroit made a speedy exit from the building, leaving her husband to thank the vicar.

'Well, that was a rum do and no mistake,' remarked the funeral director, scratching his head. He was walking out of the crematorium with Mr Pendlebury. 'You would have thought that being the big-wig around here, and with a title to boot, that Sir Hedley would have had something a bit fancier. I mean, he's not short of a bob or two, is he? Mind you, as they say in Yorkshire, "There's nowt as queer as folk". Since I've started with my funeral business, I've seen the lot. Last time I was here, it was for an army veteran who had passed on and they played "Keep the Home Fires Burning". In a crematorium, I ask you! You wouldn't credit it. I could write a book.'

'Sir Hedley and his wife preferred a quiet funeral, Mr Firkin,' replied the vicar tactfully. 'Some people like it that way, without a deal of fuss.'

As he said this, he thought about the arrangements for the funeral of the present baronet's father. He was a man who did like a fuss. His polished-ebony coffin with elaborate, burnished brass fixtures had arrived at St Mary's in a shiny black carriage pulled by four white horses sporting black feathers on their heads. There had been a full choir, organ music, Bible readings, a sermon from the Bishop of Clayton and testimonies from the High Sheriff and the Lord Lieutenant. The church had been bursting with flowers. The old baronet had been interred in the family tomb in the churchyard and a grand reception had taken place at Marston Towers, to which all the villagers had been invited.

'Yes,' said Mr Firkin, who had stopped scratching his scalp and now proceeded to rub his chin, 'the stories I could tell. At one funeral there was a punch-up between the deceased's former wife and his new partner over who should have the ashes.'

'Look, I must be off,' the vicar told him. 'I have another appointment.'

Mr Pendlebury shook his head sorrowfully as he walked to his car. He could not understand why Lady Maladroit had insisted on such a minimalist funeral and why Sir Hedley, a man of strong views and robust determination, had conceded. The vicar had reluctantly carried out their wishes and conducted the short service with no mourners present, save for them. He had endeavoured to persuade them to change their minds but Lady Maladroit had been adamant.

When the bereaved parents arrived back at Marston Towers, Lady Maladroit went straight to her bedroom and Sir Hedley retired to his study. They had exchanged few words on the way back from the crematorium. Sir Hedley splashed a couple of inches of whisky in a heavy crystal glass and downed it in one great gulp. He poured another, then lit a fat cigar. He had never felt quite as low. He sat at his desk, nursing the glass and smoking, and thought of his son. Their relationship had never been a good one. They had always seemed to be at loggerheads. James had been a difficult and demanding child, sly and disobedient and indulged by his mother. He grew to be arrogant and deceitful. Expelled from his public school, caught driving worse for drink, a liar, a thief and a seducer. The baronet wondered why his son had turned out as he had done. He had had every advantage. Perhaps that was why. He had never had to work for anything in his life. His forebears had been industrious, shrewd, ambitious, determined people, who had over the years accumulated a considerable portfolio of property, land and investments. They had been fair-minded, honest and considerate employers who had gained the respect of those in the neighbourhood. Had he lived, thought Sir Hedley, James would have been a poor employer and would have probably squandered away his inheritance. Hadn't he heard somewhere the axiom, 'Clogs to clogs in three generations'? Marcia was right, people in Risingdale had hated their son, but not because they resented him having money and position; it was because he treated them with contempt. James would, had he lived, have lost all Sir Hedley and his forebears had worked for. The estate would have been sold.

Lady Maladroit entered the study and stood before the desk. Her thin hands were clasped before her. Her face was rigid.

'I'm leaving you,' she informed her husband.

'I beg your pardon,' replied the baronet, looking up and setting down his glass. He stubbed out his cigar.

'I said that I am leaving you, Hedley.'

'Oh.'

'Is that all you have to say – "Oh"?' she asked.

'Well, what do you want me to say? I am sure that whatever I say will make not the slightest iota of difference, will it?'

'There is nothing for me here now,' she told him. 'Nothing. The only reason I stayed in this godforsaken place and put up with you all these years was because of James. He was the only thing we had in common. I blame you for his death. I blame you because you made him feel worthless and reviled. I shouldn't wonder if he took his own life. I can't bear to look at you any more.'

Sir Hedley was too weary to argue. He picked up his glass and took a sip of his drink. 'I see,' he murmured.

'I am to live with my sister. I spoke to her before the funeral. It is all arranged. I shall take what I need for now and send for the rest later. Of course, you will be hearing from my solicitor.'

Her husband's silence angered her.

'So, are you just going to sit there? Have you nothing to say?'

'As I have said, Marcia, nothing I say will change your mind, I am certain of that.'

She gave a twisted smile. 'No, you are perfectly right, nothing you could possibly say will prevent me from walking out of the door.'

Her husband remained resolutely silent.

'Of course, I should never have married you,' she carried on relentlessly. 'My sister warned me against it. She thought you were odd. "Stuffy and tedious," she said and that I would be bored to tears living up here in the back of beyond, after a life in London. She was right.'

Sir Hedley was minded to inform his wife that her sister was the last person to advise anyone on marriage and family life after two acrimonious divorces of her own and children who didn't speak to her, but he resisted the temptation.

'And don't think I was oblivious of your carryings-on,' his wife persisted. 'Did you suppose I was so blinkered, so simple-minded, that I didn't know about your philandering? All those pathetic lies about going to your club. Then you came back smelling of drink and cheap perfume. And do you imagine I minded you having some adulterous relationship with some tart in Clayton? I was glad it got you out of the house.' She scoffed. 'I wonder what sort of woman would look twice at you.'

'I think you have said quite enough, Marcia,' said Sir Hedley.

His wife could have said a whole lot more. She could have told him that James was not, in fact, his son, but the result of a short affair she had conducted soon after they were married with the owner of the art gallery where she worked. She could imagine the distress that would cause him, his great sense of shock and betrayal. Of course she would not tell him, for to do so would be to admit to an adulterous affair of her own.

'I never loved you, you know,' she said. 'I freely admit I married you for the title and for the lifestyle. There was never any real affection. Our marriage was a sham, an empty shell, nothing more.' There was a look of pure loathing on her face.

Sir Hedley rose to his feet. His eyes were blazing.

'If you intend to go, then I suggest you do that,' he said.

'I hope I never see you again,' she hissed.

With that final riposte, she left the room.

Tom was getting ready to go out. He had telephoned Amanda the week before and asked if she would like to join him for a meal the following Friday night and she had accepted. He had felt as excited as a teenager going on his first date as he combed his hair and then splashed himself liberally with aftershave. He had booked the Le Bon Viveur where he had planned to take Janette. Joyce had recommended the restaurant but warned Tom to be prepared for the hefty bill.

'So who is the lucky girl, then?' she had asked.

'Never you mind,' he had told her, tapping the side of his nose.

'Oh, come along, Tom,' she had persisted. 'I've known you long enough for you to confide in me. I won't broadcast it, if that's what you're worried about. Is it that curator at the museum? She is a starry-eyed admirer of yours, from what I've heard.'

'If you must know, it's Amanda Stanhope,' Tom had told her.

'Well, well,' Joyce had said. 'You are a dark horse. You've kept pretty quiet about that. So how long has this tryst been going on?'

'It's not a tryst,' Tom had answered. 'I'm just taking her out for a meal, nothing more. I thought after all the worry she has had recently with Leo it would do her good.'

'That's very thoughtful of you.' She had smiled. 'But you do like her, don't you?'

'Yes, I do. Actually, Joyce, I like her a lot. She's clever and funny and full of life.'

'And very attractive,' his colleague had added.

'Well, yes, she's a lovely woman.'

'And everyone thought that you and Janette Fairborn were something of an item.'

'Well, we aren't,' Tom had told her. 'I was keen on her but she's very career-minded and clearly she didn't feel the same about me.'

'She was foolish to let you go,' Joyce had said. 'You're a real catch. Most young women would be over the moon to have a tall, fit, good-looking boyfriend like you. If I were a few years younger and not engaged to be married—'

He had laughed. 'Let me stop you there, Joyce, you're making me blush.'

She had smiled. 'Well, be careful with the femme fatale on Friday.'

'Who?'

'Mrs Stanhope. She strikes me as the sort of woman who has men for breakfast.'

Tom had not thought much about Janette since Leo's mother had come into his life. Amanda was not only beautiful, with an appealing grace and elegance, but she was also a strong-minded, courageous, determined woman. He had seen these qualities in her when dealing with her son's illness. He had never met anyone quite like her before. He loved being with her and was flattered and pleased that she seemed to think something of him.

The doorbell rang. On the doorstep stood Janette Fairborn.

'Hello, Tom,' she said. 'May I come in?'

'Yes, of course.'

'You're going out?'

'Yes.'

'Well, I won't keep you.'

'Come in for a minute,' he told her. 'Would you like a drink?'

'No, I'm fine.' She perched on the end of a chair.

'I did try and get in touch after I met you in the café in Clayton,' he explained.

'You did?'

'I called the farm and spoke to your father.'

'He never mentioned it.'

'He said you had gone back to Nottingham. He wouldn't give me your telephone number,' said Tom, 'otherwise I would have called you to tell you the reason why I appeared rude and left you standing at the counter when we met in the café.'

'Why would he not give you my number?' Janette asked.

'I think you should ask him yourself,' answered Tom. 'I get the impression that he's not all that keen on me.'

'Oh, that's just his manner. He's like that with everyone. He's never approved of any of my boyfriends.' Then, realising what she had said, she added quickly, 'Not that you are a boyfriend.'

'No,' said Tom.

'I'm afraid he sometimes tries to live my life for me. He's been so overprotective since my mother died. I shall have a word with him when I get home.'

'Anyway,' said Tom, 'I just wanted to apologise for my apparent bad manners. You see, the person who came in—'

'The very attractive woman.'

'Yes,' said Tom. 'She is a parent. Her son, who is in my class at school, was very ill in hospital. I had to know how he was.'

'And how is he?' she asked.

'He recovered, thank God.'

Tom glanced at the clock on the mantelpiece. He was running late.

'I wanted to see you,' Janette told him, 'to tell you that I'm thinking of coming back to Risingdale. I've not really settled at the bank in Nottingham. The assistant manager was passed over for the manager's position that I got and has been difficult, and the staff, who have taken his side, have been unfriendly and less than cooperative. I've not finally decided to come back, but I am seriously considering it. Dad thinks I should not be hasty and it would be foolish to throw away a plum senior position.'

'I suppose he has a point,' said Tom.

It was not the response Janette was expecting. She thought perhaps that he might be keen for her to return, and would jump up and say how wonderful it would be if she came home.

'I miss things here in Risingdale,' she said. 'I didn't think that I would but I do.'

'Your horse, for one,' said Tom.

She gave a weak smile. 'No, not just my horse. I miss other things.' She looked at him intently. She wanted to say, 'I miss you, and I would love for you to take me out for that meal you suggested, and we could take things up from where we left off.' She had been desperately unhappy and lonely in Nottingham. She had made no friends, had no social life and hated the crowds and the traffic. Her flat above the high street was dark and the view from the window was over the rear of a warehouse. She had thought more and more about Tom. It was clear to her now that he had thought little about her.

'Well, I'll not hold you up any more,' she said, getting up. There were tears in her eyes.

The following day Tom went in to Barton-in-the-Dale to see his Auntie Bridget. He was in sore need of some of her homespun advice. Having called at her house and found her out, he visited the village store and discovered her listening to the proprietor.

Mrs Sloughthwaite, as was her wont, was leaning on her counter holding forth when Tom entered. She broke off abruptly at seeing him.

'Well, well, look what the rat's brought in,' she said amiably.

'Good morning, Mrs Sloughthwaite,' said Tom. When would the woman get the words right? he thought. He gave his aunt a kiss. 'I thought I might find you in here, Auntie Bridget.'

'You never said you were coming to see me today,' said Mrs O'Connor. 'There's nothing wrong, is there?'

The shopkeeper's ears pricked up.

'Nothing's wrong,' he told her, 'but I am here to take you for morning coffee and get a bit of advice.' He turned to Mrs Sloughthwaite. 'I'm sorry to drag her away.'

The shopkeeper was not going to let him escape so easily.

'We've just been talking about that terrible accident in your neck of the woods,' she said. 'I was telling your auntie that I read in the *Clayton Gazette* that some young man – James Maladroit was his name, if my memory serves me right, only in his twenties and from an affluential background – came off of the road in his sports car to avoid hitting a motorbike rider and struck a tree. Evidently when the paramedics arrived on the scene they found both men were dead.'

Tom had to hand it to the shopkeeper. Not only was she adept at extracting information from her customers, she possessed the most amazingly retentive memory and a gift for remembering the finest details. It was a wonder, he thought, that she didn't know the make of sports car and the variety of tree.

'Travelling too fast around one of them sharp bends, I shouldn't wonder,' she added. 'Did you know the young man?'

'We had met,' replied Tom. He did not intend to go into any details of his rancorous relationship with James Maladroit.

'Came from some aristocratical family, it said in the paper.'

'Yes. His father is the local squire.'

'The police want to nip it in the butt,' stated the shopkeeper.

'Nip squires in the butt?' asked Mrs O'Connor.

'No, these boy racers in sports cars and on motorbikes, driving like maniacs along twisting country roads.

I remember once, young Clarence Massey came through the village on that old tractor of his at such a speed, shedding silage and I don't know what all over the high street like there was no tomorrow. Mrs Fish nearly went full length and ended up prostate in all that muck and nearly discollating her hip. I said to Clarence's Uncle Fred when he came in my store, I said . . .'

After ten minutes of listening to the shopkeeper's monologue, Tom managed to wrest his aunt away and they retired to the Ring o' Bells café.

'So what's on your mind?' asked Mrs O'Connor.

Tom explained his dilemma, that he had started to fall for the parent of one of his pupils but he still had strong feelings for another woman.

'I'm just so confused,' he told her. 'I didn't think it possible that I could have feelings like this for two women.'

'I'm sure you are not the first in the world to fall in love with more than one person, but two loves don't make a right, Tom. Are you drawn by a stronger pull to one of these women?'

'That's my problem,' he said. 'I don't think I am. I really don't know what to do.'

'Well, time will tell, but when you do decide who the one for you is, you must be kind and honest with the other.' She patted his hand. 'And I don't need to tell you that either.'

On the evening of the day when his wife left him, Sir Hedley sat at his desk in his darkened study alone with his thoughts. There was a large measure of untouched whisky in the glass before him. His face betrayed neither anger nor relief, his features as immobile as the marble bust of his grandfather that sat on a small table in the corner of the room. He contemplated the wreckage of his marriage with equanimity. He knew in his heart that after the first few months of matrimony the union had been doomed to fail. They had stayed together with a mutual dislike. He often wondered why. The death of his son had acted as a catalyst. The baronet remained motionless like that until he heard the striking of the longcase clock in the hall, which roused him out of his reverie. He closed his eyes and massaged his eyelids with his thumb and forefinger. Then he picked up the receiver and telephoned Marcia's sister.

'Hello,' came the strident voice down the line. 'May I help you?'

'It's me,' he said.

There was a short silence. 'Oh.'

'I'm calling to see if Marcia has arrived safely.'

'Huh,' she scoffed. 'It's a little late in the day for you to show any concern for your wife, isn't it?'

'She was in rather an agitated state when she left,' he said, tightening his grip on the receiver. 'I just wanted to make sure she has got there.'

'Yes, she is here with me now and, as you say, she was in an agitated state when she arrived and she still is. And can you blame her? You should be ashamed of the way you have treated my sister. I told Marcia when she said she was to marry you it was a mistake and I was right. I have always thought you odd but you have proved to be callous and unfeeling. All you think about is your wretched estate and your shooting.'

Sir Hedley decided not to respond; he knew it would be fruitless.

'She doesn't want to speak to you,' Marcia's sister told him.

'I guessed she wouldn't,' he replied.

'I shall arrange for her possessions to be collected at a later date. She does not wish to see you or Marston Towers ever again.'

Sir Hedley sighed and shook his head. He was inclined to say something back but really couldn't be bothered.

'Are you still there?' she shouted down the telephone.

'Yes, I am still here.'

'And she told me about your unfaithfulness, your adultery, seeing another woman all those years and poor Marcia having to put up with it, stuck alone in that rambling great house all by herself. Well, she doesn't want anything more to do with you. You will be hearing in due course from her solicitor and don't think you will be getting away without giving her the financial settlement that is her due. Don't call here again.' She thumped down the receiver.

18

Mrs Pocock called into the village store in Barton-in-the-Dale to find the proprietor in her usual leaning posture. She was in earnest conversation with a bony, colourless woman with eyes as leaden as the ocean on a dull day. The woman's grey plaited hair circled around her head like a coil of old rope.

'Oh, hello, love,' said Mrs Sloughthwaite, straightening herself and rising from the counter.

'Good morning,' replied Mrs Pocock, her thin lips pursed . She glanced at the other customer. 'And how are you keeping, Mrs Fish?' she asked.

'Mustn't grumble,' replied the woman with a pained expression.

'I was just telling Mrs Fish,' said the shopkeeper, 'that I was stood standing for over half an hour in the bus shelter waiting for a bus in Clayton. I would have been there a lot longer had not Mr Dwyer caught sight of me and gave me a lift. Went out of his way, he did, to drop me off.'

'I reckon that young man will be out of a job soon,' Mrs Pocock told her. 'I just called in to tell you the news. Skillington School is to close. I told you I'd heard it was up for the chop.' She had a smug look on her face. 'All the children there at present are to move to the school at Bloxton after Easter. Mind you, I knew it would happen. The head-master there is waste of space and has managed to upset most of the parents and all the governors. Children were leaving in droves. It was only a matter of time before they closed the school. Didn't I say so when Mr Dwyer was in here? I said the County Council are shutting the small village schools right, left and centre and I reckoned the one at Risingdale will be the next on the list.'

'And I said he wouldn't find it difficult to get another job,' replied the shopkeeper. 'He's a very fine teacher.'

'That's as may be, but him finding another position is a moot point,' said the customer. 'They'll be all these teachers looking for jobs. He missed out getting a job at the village school here in Barton when they appointed a redeployed teacher. I reckon the writing's on the wall for that young man.'

'I wouldn't like to teach,' remarked Mrs Fish. 'Teachers deserve medals dealing with youngsters these days.'

'I won't disagree with you there,' said Mrs Pocock. 'I was on the Clayton bus last weekend and do you know I could have been standing all the way back to Barton? Not one person offered to let me sit down. All these schoolkids were taking up the seats. I had to tell this long-haired youth to shift. Where has common courtesy gone, I ask you? There's no discipline in school, that's the trouble. It's at the root of the problem.' She now held forth on her perennial theme: the poor behaviour of modern youth. 'A lot of kids today are rude, misbehaved and spoiled. They get away with murder. When I was a governor at the village school, I was the only one in favour of the teachers using the cane. When my husband was a lad, he was always bending over the head-master's desk to get "six of the best" on his backside and at the school I went to, Miss Pratt was a dab hand with a ruler across your knuckles, and it didn't do us any harm.'

That's questionable, mused Mrs Sloughthwaite, thinking of the lazy great lump of a man her customer had married. He hadn't done a day's work in his life and spent most of his time propping up the bar at the Blacksmith's Arms. And as for the son – that sullen-faced, surly boy of hers, who was light-fingered to boot – she wants to put her own house in order before she starts commenting on the behaviour of other children.

'Actually,' said the shopkeeper, 'I find adults ruder and more inconsiderable than some of the youngsters. I have grown customers in here with not a "please" or a "thank you". It does make me mad.'

'I tell you what makes me mad,' said Mrs Fish, managing at last to get a word in. 'It's what a man was doing on the Clayton bus yesterday. It was very disconcerting.'

'What was that?' asked Mrs Sloughthwaite.

'My husband used to do it,' continued the customer, 'my next-door neighbour is always doing it. My son-in-law does it. I'm sick of seeing men doing it. They don't seem to be able to stop themselves.'

'Doing what?' asked Mrs Pocock.

'Genital adjustments in public, that's what,' said the customer, leaving the other two women mute and open-mouthed.

When Tom arrived at school on the Monday morning, he was met at the entrance by Mr Leadbeater. He was wearing his usual cheerless expression and jangling a great bunch of keys.

'There's a young lass in the staffroom,' he said. 'She says she's expected.'

'That must be the student-teacher,' Tom told him. 'She said she was coming today.'

'I didn't know anything about a student-teacher,' grumbled Mr Leadbeater, 'but then why bother to tell me? I'm just the caretaker, cleaner, handyman, gardener and general factotum. Nobody tells me nothing.'

Having got that off his chest, Mr Leadbeater departed, jangling his bunch of keys again and mumbling to himself.

Tom found a pretty young woman sitting in the corner of the staffroom. She could have been featured in a fashion magazine.

'Hello,' he said cheerfully, going to meet her. 'I'm Tom Dwyer. You must be Miss Balfour-Smith?'

She jumped up from the chair looking as guilty as a child caught with her hand in the sweet jar.

'Oh, good morning,' she said, breathlessly. 'I'm sorry I arrived early. I hope you don't mind my waiting in the staffroom?'

Tom laughed. 'Why ever should I mind?'

'Well, some schools I've visited don't like student-teachers in the staffroom.'

'Sounds a stupid idea to me,' said Tom. 'Anyway, just so you know, the headmaster and the teachers usually arrive here at about a quarter to the hour and the children turn up for nine o'clock or thereabouts – well, most of them. It depends on the weather how many we get. I'll put the kettle on. I guess you would enjoy a cup of tea?'

'That would be lovely,' she said. 'I just have milk. I'm not sitting in anyone's chair, am I?'

'No, we don't have special chairs here,' Tom told her. He put on the kettle.

'It's just that, at my last school, the teachers had their own chairs and student-teachers weren't allowed to sit in them. They also had their own mugs. We had to bring our own tea and coffee and we had to eat our sandwiches in the classroom.'

'What utter nonsense,' said Tom. 'You will find things different here. We are a happy, if somewhat eccentric team. You will find us friendly and you will like the headmaster and the children.'

'I have been so looking forward to visiting Risingdale School,' she said. 'My father says it is one of the best in the county and you are one of its finest teachers.'

Tom coloured a little. 'I am assuming that your father is the Member of Parliament,' he said.

'That's right,' she said. 'I believe you met him when his car ran out of petrol. He tends to be absent-minded at times but he wouldn't thank me for telling you that. He suggested I visit here and the college was happy for me to do so. I want to teach the little ones. Small children are so endearing and captivated by all that is around them, aren't they?'

'But they have their moments,' said Tom.

The door suddenly burst open and Mr Cadwallader stormed into the room, red in the face and breathing like a carthorse.

'That bloody woman will be the death of me!' he cried. 'I would wring her wretched neck if I could find the damn thing. She has to go.'

'Owen, this is Miss Balfour-Smith,' Tom told him, indicating the young woman sitting in the corner of the room. He bit his lip to hide his smile and made the pot of tea.

Mr Cadwallader, who had not noticed her, swung around.

'Oh,' he said. 'I didn't see you there. I'm pleased to meet you. Do pardon my outburst, but it is Mrs Gosling, the cleaner. She is driving me to distraction.'

'Assistant caretaker,' prompted Tom.

'Whatever she wants to call herself,' said the teacher. 'There are quite a few things I could call her. The woman is a walking nightmare. She moves things, hides things, tidies things, throws things out and is forever reorganising my classroom. She gives me advice on how to teach and tells me off as if I were an infant in Mrs Golightly's class. I've had it out with her time after time and she never listens. The woman has a hide as thick as that of a rhinoceros. Now she has polished the floor in my classroom to such an extent that it's like an ice rink and when I told her I nearly went full length, she had the brass neck to tell me that I should take more care at my age.'

Tom passed a mug of tea to the visitor. He looked accusingly at his colleague. 'We did have some biscuits but they have mysteriously disappeared.'

The door opened again and in walked Joyce, immaculately dressed in an elegant cream-coloured jacket and tailored slacks.

'I could hear you down the corridor, Owen,' she said. 'I don't know what's got you in such a state but you must get a grip. The children can hear you bellowing away.'

'Joyce, this is Miss Balfour-Smith,' Tom told her, again indicating the young woman sitting in the corner of the room.

'Oh, hello,' said Joyce. She smiled and shook her head. 'Welcome to the madhouse.'

When Mrs Golightly bustled into the staffroom and was introduced to the visitor, she took Miss Balfour-Smith under her wing.

'Now come along with me, dear,' she said. 'You can bring your tea with you and I'll show you the infant classroom and we can have a little talk about teaching in the early years.'

'We were not allowed to take hot drinks into the classroom at the last school I visited,' said Miss Balfour-Smith. 'It was to do with health and safety.'

'Gracious me, dear,' replied Mrs Golightly, 'we don't bother with that sort of nonsense here. You're not likely to throw it over the children, are you?'

En route they came across a small plump woman with purple hair and a scowl on her face. She was wearing a pink nylon overall and standing at the end of the corridor holding a mop like a spear.

'I've done your classroom, Mrs G,' Mrs Gosling informed the teacher, 'but it would help if you got the kiddies to tidy up a bit after themselves. I mean, it's not too much to ask them to put things back where they should go. It makes my task that much easier.'

'I shall endeavour to do that, Mrs Gosling,' replied Mrs Golightly. She gave a patient, tolerant smile. 'Now, if you would excuse me.'

'There's another thing I wanted to have a word with you about, Mrs G.'

The infant teacher sighed. 'Yes, what is it now?' she asked.

'The boys' toilets.'

'What about them?'

'I've already raised it with Mr Dwyer and he's going to talk to the children in his class about keeping them clean and not dribbling or splashing. The floor was awash last week and I don't mean with water. I would like you to speak to the infants, who I reckon are the culprits by missing the urinals when they have gone for a wee. I also have an idea that the juniors are competing to see who can get highest up the wall.'

'I shall have a word,' replied Mrs Golightly. 'Now, if you will excuse me . . .'

'It might be an idea to get one of the men teachers to show the little ones what to do.'

'I really don't think that will be necessary,' replied the infant teacher, with mounting impatience. 'Now, I must get on.'

The cleaner looked at the visitor. 'And I would appreciate it if you would take that mug back to the staffroom where it belongs when you are done with it.'

As Mrs Gosling waddled off down the corridor, grumbling to herself about the state of the toilets, Mrs Golightly turned to her visitor, who had observed the exchange with an open mouth. 'If you become an infant teacher, Miss Balfour-Smith,' she said, 'you will soon learn that working in a school involves a great deal more than just teaching children.'

The infant classroom was bright and colourful. Plastic-topped tables and small red melamine chairs were arranged around the centre. There was a small carpeted area in one corner with cushions and an easy chair, and in another a Wendy House. On a low shelf was a collection of picture books and simple dictionaries. Along one wall were the children's paintings: bold, round figures with smiling faces, huge eyes and stick-like fingers. On another wall were glossy post-ers of animals and birds alongside a list of key words and the rules of the classroom. On a large table were painting materi-als, coloured crayons and pencils, a sand tray and boxes containing a variety of building blocks and educational toys.

Mrs Golightly stood with her visitor at the door proudly surveying the room.

'It is very important, Miss Balfour-Smith,' she said, 'to provide for the early years' children a rich, cheerful, interest-ing and stimulating environment.'

Mrs Golightly sat at her desk and gestured to a small chair used by one of her pupils.

'Do take a seat, Miss Balfour-Smith,' she said, 'and we can have a little chat.'

The visitor sat down, placed the mug on the desk, and crossed her long legs.

The 'chat' turned out to be more of a lecture.

'Now, people think handling the little ones is an easy matter,' said Mrs Golightly. 'Well, let me tell you, it is not. Of course infants are a delight most of the time, and it is a pleasure – and indeed a privilege – to teach them, but young children are very unpredictable. They are easily moved to laughter and just as easily moved to tears. I remember when I was at college donkey's years ago, one lecturer, a Miss Billings, said that when working with young children, one should always expect the unexpected. She was right.'

And so, Miss Balfour-Smith listened patiently to further advice and opinions from the infant teacher, who carried on with her views on number work, art, reading, writing and suit-able resources.

Mrs Golightly held up a large picture book with cartoon depictions of three goats and a troll on the cover. 'I believe that at this age the children should hear the traditional stories. You would be surprised by how many of them have never heard of "The Little Red Hen", "The Gingerbread Man", "The Three Little Pigs" or "Little Red Riding Hood". They can tell you all about the television programmes they watch but they know little of these long-established tales. These time-honoured stories with their morals teach them about the qualities of kindness, selflessness and patience. I'm going to read "The Three Billy Goats Gruff" this morning. If you would like to join us in the reading corner, Miss Balfour-Smith, when the children come in, we'll make a start.'

At the sound of a bell the children hurried into school, removed their coats and hung them on hooks in the corridor. They then filed quietly into the classroom, took their seats, folded their hands and faced the teacher with expectant looks on their small faces. After the register had been marked, the children, without being instructed, gathered around the teacher's chair on the small square of carpet with the visitor sitting at the back. Some of the infants yawned widely, one large girl with bunches of hair like giant earmuffs stuck a thumb in her mouth, another began energetically poking his nose with his index finger, and several of the children rubbed the sleep out of their eyes. One little shuffler, right at the front, looked as if he were polishing the floor with his bottom.

The teacher clapped her hands to gain the attention of the class.

'Quietly, please. Look this way, children,' she instructed. 'Stop shuffling, Freddie, you'll wear away the carpet. Bethany, please take your thumb out of your mouth and, Jason, stop doing that with your nose. Noses are for smelling with and not for poking at. This morning we have a special visitor joining us. This is Miss Balfour-Smith.' All heads swivelled around and the children looked at the visitor. 'Shall we all say a nice good morning?'

'Good morning, Mrs Golightly, good morning, Miss Balfour-Smith, good morning, everybody,' chorused the children.

'Good morning, children,' said the visitor cheerfully.

'Miss, that lady at the back looks just like Rapunzel,' announced a small boy with a thatch of straw-coloured hair and a missing front tooth. He sported a small green candle of mucus, which appeared from a crusty nostril. He sniffed it away noisily but it re-appeared immediately. 'Rapunzel was beautiful with long hair just like the lady at the back.'

Miss Balfour-Smith smiled weakly and her cheeks flushed pink.

Mrs Golightly made a mental note to tell Miss Balfour-Smith later that it was advisable that teachers of the little ones tied their long hair back or had it cut short otherwise they would have the devil's own job getting rid of the nits. Infestation with head lice was par for the course in an infant teacher's life.

'This morning's story,' the teacher told the children, 'is a very exciting tale of "The Three Billy Goats Gruff".'

'I've heard it, miss,' a child shouted out.

'Yes, well, you are going to hear it again, Freddie,' she replied. There was a slight sharpness in her voice.

'But I know what happens,' persisted the child. 'There's a horrible troll who lives under a bridge and—'

Mrs Golightly clapped her hands. 'Thank you, Freddie. That will do. Just sit up smartly and pay attention. Now, as I have said, this morning's story is a very exciting tale of "The Three Billy Goats Gruff".'

'Miss, our Christopher's got a goat,' announced a frizzy-headed boy with large ears and a healthy-looking brown face.

'Yes, I know, Andrew,' replied the teacher, recalling the unfortunate incident in the village church. Mr Pendlebury had conducted a service in which the children had been encouraged to bring along their pets for a blessing. Andrew's brother had arrived after the hymns had been said and blessings given with a very lively goat. The animal had caused mayhem and ended up butting the poor vicar.

'Miss, I don't like goats,' announced a mousy little girl with large glasses and a pale face. 'They're smelly and they have horns and they butt you.'

'Yes, I know that, Melanie,' replied Mrs Golightly, recalling the image of poor Mr Pendlebury rubbing his bruised legs. 'But the goats in this story are nice goats.'

'But they butt the troll in the river,' said Freddie.

'Freddie, what are ears for?' asked the teacher.

'To wash behind, miss,' replied the child.

'They are used to listen and that is what I have asked you to do. At this rate we will not know what happens in the story.'

'But I know what happens in the story, miss,' the boy told her. 'The troll gets butted in the river.'

The teacher sighed. 'Let's not get ahead of ourselves. As I said, these are very nice goats. They're called the Billy Goats Gruff.'

'Miss, they don't sound like nice goats,' said Melanie. 'Freddie said they butt the troll in the river.'

'My goodness,' said Mrs Golightly, 'we will never get on with the story with all these interruptions. Now, no more calling out, sit up smartly and pay attention. And, Marigold, don't do that.' The teacher glanced at her visitor and shook her head. 'This is the tale of "The Three Billy Goats Gruff", as I have told you,' she said to the children and she began to read. 'Once upon a time there were three Billy Goats Gruff. There was the father, Big Billy Goat Gruff, the mother, Medium-Sized Billy Goat Gruff, and—'

'Little Billy Goat Gruff,' added Freddie.

'They call little goats kids,' said Bethany, smartly.

'And Little Billy Goat Gruff,' the teacher repeated, not wishing for any further disruption. She fixed Freddie with an eagle eye. 'They lived in a valley in the cold winter to keep warm, but when spring came, they climbed up to the rich green meadow on the hillside to eat the sweet grass.'

'And crossed a bridge,' interrupted Freddie, before wiping his nose on the sleeve of his cardigan. 'They have to cross a bridge.'

'We've not got to the bridge yet,' he was told curtly. 'Now I shall not tell you again, Freddie. Stop interrupting or you will sit on the naughty seat.' The teacher looked at Miss Balfour-Smith. 'One has to have clear classroom rules,' she told her. 'When a child does not do as he has been told, a good technique is to give him a chance to calm down and give him the opportunity to think over what he has done wrong.'

The threat of the dreaded 'naughty seat' had the desired effect, for Freddie remained silent as the teacher continued with the story without further interruption. It wasn't long, however, before the little boy began shuffling again.

'Freddie,' snapped the teacher, 'are you listening?'

'Yes, miss,' replied the boy.

'Well, since you have heard the story before, you can tell us what you think the troll said to the little Billy Goat Gruff when it trip-trapped noisily across the bridge.'

The child thought for a moment and his small brow furrowed.

'Can you remember?' prompted Mrs Golightly. 'What do you think the troll might say to the goat that made such a loud noise?'

'Bugger off! I'm trying to have a kip down here,' said the boy.

'I'll have a word with you, young man, at playtime,' she said, with a face as hard as a diamond.

As the day progressed, Miss Balfour-Smith came to appreciate what an exacting, enervating and challenging job the infant teacher took on. The children, though they could be delightful and amusing, were also self-centred, persistent and constantly demanding attention, she discovered. Mrs Golightly never sat down and was continuously on the go. She also appreciated what the teacher had told her about expecting the unexpected. In the course of the lessons, one child trapped a finger, another had a tantrum and a third was sick. There had also been frequent nose-wiping and visits to the toilets. The teacher had taken all this in her stride and still managed to be patient and cheerful – for most of the time, at any rate. Miss Balfour-Smith's decision that this phase of education was not the one for her was strengthened with the arrival of Freddie's mother at home time. A large woman with dyed blonde hair, a menacing bosom and huge hips appeared at the door of the classroom.

'Could I have a word, Mrs Golightly?' asked the parent.

'Yes, of course,' said the teacher. 'Come in.'

'It's about my Freddie.'

'I guessed it might be.'

The woman waddled into the room. Mrs Golightly thought it inadvisable to ask the parent to take a seat, for the only chairs available were those used by the children and were too small to bear the weight.

'It's bit embarrassing,' said the parent. She glanced in Miss Balfour-Smith's direction. When Mrs Golightly didn't respond, the parent continued in a lowered voice. 'He gets his winkle caught.'

'I beg your pardon?'

'Freddie, he gets his winkle caught.' She pointed downwards. 'You know, his whatsit.'

'I'm sorry, Mrs Bowman, I don't follow,' said Mrs Golightly, knowing perfectly well what the parent meant but wanting the woman to explain in plain English.

'Could you make sure that when my Freddie goes for a wee, that he doesn't get his little nipper caught in his zipper?'

The student-teacher's mouth dropped open. Mrs Golightly's face was expressionless.

'He got it caught yesterday and I had to put an Elastoplast on it,' explained the parent, 'so I was wondering if, when he goes for a wee in future, you could keep an eye on it and make sure he doesn't get his little nipper caught in his zipper again.'

'I take it you mean that Freddie gets his penis caught in his zip,' said the teacher.

The parent coloured up. 'Well, yes,' she mumbled.

'Mrs Bowman,' the teacher told her, 'first of all, we do not use baby language in my classroom. We use the correct English. We call things by their proper names. We don't have moo-cows and chuff-chuffs and we don't have winkles, whatsits and little nippers. Secondly, I have asked parents not to send their children to school with pants that have zips. Little boys with zips in their pants have an unfortunate habit of doing what your Freddie has done. Thirdly, I am not in a position with fifteen little boys in my class to oversee each one when he goes to the lavatory. Do I make myself clear?'

'Well, my husband did say that it was a bit much to ask you, but as I said to him, Mrs Golightly's been teaching at Risingdale for as long as I can remember and she's had lots of kiddies through her hands in her time.'

Mr Pendlebury walked down the aisle at St Mary's running a hand along the old, polished oak-panelled pews, his heels echoing on the ancient glazed-tile floor. He stood in the Norman chancel looking up at the pale stone pillars and then knelt before the massive altar slab, which was enclosed by an ornate, carved wooden rood screen that somehow had escaped destruction at the time of Cromwell. An afternoon sun shone through the perpendicular west window, which was filled with glass of subtle colours, singularly beautiful in the amount of light it allowed to flood through to illuminate the whole church. He put his hands together and bowed his head in prayer. He thanked God for the recovery of Mrs Stanhope's son, prayed for Sir Hedley and Lady Maladroit and their loss, and for the poor and neglected in the world, the lonely and the distressed.

On his way out, he discovered a boy watching him. He was sitting in a pew at the back of the church.

'Hello,' said the vicar, approaching. 'It's Colin, isn't it?'

'Yes, sir.'

'How long have you been sitting there?'

'Not long,' replied Colin. 'I didn't want to disturb you.'

Mr Pendlebury came and sat next to him.

'I often come in here towards the end of the afternoon to pray. It's so peaceful. I think of all the people who used to come here to pray. Hundreds of them have sat in these pews over the centuries, you know.' The vicar sighed. 'Now, young man, what can I do for you?' he asked.

'I've brought you this,' said Colin. He reached under the pew and passed the clergyman his painting of the church. It was in a simple frame. 'Mrs Stanhope said you liked it. She says I've not quite got the shadows right and the figure is a bit out of proportion but she's showing me how to do shadows and figures.'

'Well, for what it's worth, I think it's perfect.'

'My dad made the frame. If you want to change it, he said—'

'I don't want to change it,' interrupted the vicar. 'It's very kind of you, Colin, to give me this. You must let me give you something in return.'

'No, it's a gift,' said Colin.

Mr Pendlebury was touched by the kindness. 'Thank you very much. I shall treasure it.'

It was true what he said to Lady Maladroit: the people of the village *were* generous.

19

The day after Lady Maladroit had departed, Sir Hedley decided to make three visits. On his way down the drive to the front of Marston Towers, he came across Dick Greenwood washing the Range Rover. The assistant gamekeeper touched his forelock. 'Good afternoon, Sir Hedley,' he said.

'Good afternoon, Richard,' replied the baronet.

'I was sorry to 'ear about tha son.'

'Thank you. James and I didn't always see eye to eye, but it's not easy losing a child.' He took a breath and changed the subject. 'By the way, how is that son of yours getting along?'

''E's doin' well, thank you, Sir 'Edley. I did 'ave a few problems wi' t'lad after 'is mam passed on, but 'e seems to 'ave turned a corner, pulled 'issen together an' is now doin' well. Mester Dwyer's put t'lad in for t'eleven-plus.'

If only my son had turned a corner and pulled himself together, thought the baronet, but it wasn't to be.

'Colin 'as quite a flair for paintin',' continued Mr Greenwood. ''E 'as lessons from t'lady who bought t'Methodist chapel. 'E's reight tekken wi' 'er.'

'Yes, Mrs Stanhope is most personable,' said Sir Hedley. 'I think there are quite a few in Risingdale who are very taken with her. Now, Richard, I was wanting to have a word with you. Silas, who has been my gamekeeper here for over twenty years, is due to retire soon.'

'Aye, 'e did mention it to me.'

'He's been a loyal and hardworking keeper,' said the baronet, 'and I shall be sorry to see him go, but as he says himself, he is getting rather too long in the tooth. He intends to go and live with his sister in Whitby. The thing is, I have been most satisfied with your work and would like you to step into his shoes.'

'To become 'ead gamekeeper?' asked Mr Greenwood.

'If you would like the position, it's yours.'

'Well, aye, I would, Sir 'Edley, I'd like that very much, but to be 'onest, I've not been a gret success in catching them poachers.'

'They are a clever lot and no mistake,' said Sir Hedley. 'I have never worked out how they manage to catch the birds in the dark.'

'It's quite simple, really,' Mr Greenwood told him. 'Tha sees at night t'pheasant flies up into t'lower branches of t'trees to escape t'prowling fox. T'poacher creeps up an' shines 'is torch into t'eyes of t'sleepy bird. Then 'is mate sneaks up behind t'bird an' grabs it by its legs an' 'e's gorra nice fat pheasant for t'pot or to flog to t'butcher. Wi' t'rabbitin' they usually 'ave a ferret which runs along t'warrens an' flushes t'animals out.'

'It sounds to me, Richard,' said the baronet smiling, 'that you speak from some experience.'

'Nay, nay, Sir 'Edley,' replied his assistant gamekeeper, colouring a little. 'It's just summat I've bin telled. But don't thee worry, I'll catch t'rascals.'

'Well, I have other things on my mind at the moment without worrying about losing a few pheasants or rabbits. I'm going into the village now but we can settle matters about you becoming the new head gamekeeper when I return. Of course, you will be wanting an assistant, so if you know of anyone reliable, keep your eye out and let me know.'

'I'll do that, Sir 'Edley,' replied Mr Greenwood.

'Silas will be moving out of his cottage very soon. The place is bigger than the one you're in at present, so if you wish, you may move into it.'

'That'd be champion.'

'That's settled then,' said Sir Hedley.

'Would tha like me to drive thee into Risingdale?' asked Mr Greenwood. 'I'm just abaat to gu theer missen.'

'Thank you, no, I could do with the exercise.'

It had been quite a while since Sir Hedley had walked the narrow path through the forest surrounding his estate. As a child he had loved the shadowy, mysterious woods, where he would build hiding places and hidden dens in the thickets, climb trees, collect conkers, watch the birds and squirrels and set traps. He had liked to wander the twisting hidden paths with the sun on his face in summer, soft rain in his hair in autumn and snow crunching under his feet in winter. His had been a happy childhood. As he approached the village, the path dropped steeply and took a sharp turn by an old stone farmhouse drenched in a great mass of twisting ivy. In the adjoining field, an old horse ambled towards the gate, hopeful that there might be some food in the offing.

'Nothing for you, I'm afraid, old chap,' he said.

His first port of call was to see his former housekeeper.

'Oh, Sir Hedley,' she said when she opened the door to find him standing on the doorstep.

'Good afternoon, Mrs Gosling,' said the baronet. 'I trust I am not calling at an inconvenient time.'

'No, no,' she said. 'Come along in.'

She ushered him into her small and cluttered sitting room, snatched up a half-knitted and garish pink cardigan from a chair and gestured for her visitor to take a seat.

She shook her head solemnly. 'You don't look at all well, Sir Hedley, if you don't mind me saying,' she told him.

'I am a little low at the moment,' he admitted.

'It's not surprising. Anyone would be feeling low if they'd lost a son like you. I was sorry to hear of the accident.'

'Yes, as you might imagine, it came as quite a shock. It's not sunk in yet that James won't be around.'

Mrs Gosling went to a cupboard and took out a bottle of whisky. 'For emergencies,' she said. She then poured Sir Hedley a very generous amount in a china teacup and passed it to him.

'You drink this, Sir Hedley,' she said. 'It'll do you good. I knew you liked a drop of the hard stuff when I worked at Marston Towers.'

He looked down at the cup half-full of whisky. 'It's a little early,' he said.

'You get it down you, Sir Hedley. You'll feel the benefit.'

He took a drink. 'I'll come straight to the point, Mrs Gosling. I should like you to return to Marston Towers as the housekeeper.'

'Oh, I don't think so, Sir Hedley,' she replied. 'As I told you when you called after the unfortunate incident with the necklace, when I was falsely accused of stealing it by Lady Maladroit and given the sack, I couldn't come back. I said at the time I have always found you to be a decent and approachable person who appreciated my work, a real gentleman, but I didn't get on with your wife and that's a fact, and if I was to return, we'd be at loggerheads.'

'Well, I think that particular problem has been solved,' he told her.

'In what way?' she asked.

'Lady Maladroit has left me.' He took a drink of the whisky.

'Left you!' Mrs Gosling exclaimed.

'The death of our son has had a dire effect upon her, I'm afraid. She felt she couldn't go on living at Marston Towers with all the memories and with me. She needed to get away and has gone to live with her sister down south.'

'I see.' Good riddance, Mrs Gosling thought to herself. She certainly was not going to express any sympathy. The woman made the poor man's life a misery, always complaining about one thing or the other, nagging and needling. He is well shot of her. 'When will she be back?' she asked.

Sir Hedley took another gulp of the whisky. 'She will not be coming back. From now on I shall live alone, and that is why I am in need of a housekeeper. After you had left, we did employ a replacement, but the woman turned out to be unsatisfactory. To be honest with you, Mrs Gosling, I think you are irreplaceable.'

'That's very kind of you to say so, Sir Hedley,' she said.

'Were you to come back, you would have carte blanche.'

'Cart what?'

'You would have complete charge of the day-to-day running of the house with no interference. You could employ a cleaner and a cook, and I would provide you with a parlour where you would have your own private space to relax when you are off duty. I would, of course, increase your salary.' He took another gulp of his drink.

'That's very generous of you, I'm sure,' said Mrs Gosling, 'but as you know, I'm the assistant caretaker at the school, and the headmaster and teachers and the caretaker would be very upset if I was to leave. Devastated, they'd be. You see, they are so dependent on me.'

'I can well appreciate that,' said the baronet, 'but I could have a word with Mr Gaunt, if you wish. He is a reasonable man and I am sure he will understand how much I am in need of your services.' He finished the whisky.

'Oh, I wouldn't do that, Sir Hedley,' she said. 'I'll have a word with him myself. He needs careful handling, does Mr Gaunt.'

'Well, I hope you will give the offer your serious consideration, Mrs Gosling, and let me know.'

'When do you want me to start?' she asked.

Sir Hedley's next port of call was to Rattan Row to see Mrs Lister.

'I wasn't expecting you,' she said when she opened the door of the cottage.

'Not a good time?' he asked.

'You know you are welcome here any time, Hedley. Come in. Charlie's upstairs in his room with his friend. I'll call him down.'

'Not for the moment. I should like a word with you first.'

She noticed how tired and drawn he looked. The death of James had clearly placed a heavy weight on him. Sir Hedley had called her soon after the accident and explained that he couldn't see her for the time being.

She took a bottle of whisky from the sideboard and poured a liberal quantity into a glass, which she placed in his hand.

'I think you look as if you could do with a drink.'

'It's a little early,' he said, repeating what he had told Mrs Gosling earlier.

'You're not driving, are you?'

'No, I walked. I wanted to clear my head.'

'Have a drink, Hedley,' she said. 'It will do you good.'

As he took a sip of the whisky, she put her arm around him and gently kissed his cheek. He rested his head on her shoulder. 'So, how are you?' she asked.

'Pretty low at the moment. I don't know what I would do without you. You never complain, you always make the best of things, you never ask me for anything.' He took another mouthful of whisky. They sat in companionable silence for a while. 'Marcia's left me,' he said suddenly.

'She's left you?'

'Yes, packed her bags and gone. I gather she wants a divorce.'

'My goodness,' she said. 'I really don't know what to say.'

'Perhaps you might say what I am thinking, that the break-up of the marriage is long overdue?' he asked.

Later that evening, Sir Hedley made his way to the King's Head to see the third person on his list. Eagle-eyed as ever, Toby Croft spotted him coming into the public house. The old farmer jumped to his feet and, leaving his three drinking pals and clutching his empty pint glass, approached.

'Evenin', squire,' he said.

'Good evening, Mr Croft,' replied the baronet.

'I were sorry to 'ear about yer lad.'

'Thank you.' Sir Hedley headed for the bar, not wishing to engage in conversation with the farmer.

'Terrible tragedy, it were,' said Toby, following him like a dog at heel. 'Mind you, folk 'ave been complainin' abaat that theer bad bend fer donkey's years an' nowt's been done. They might do summat abaat it now and purrup some proper signs. I were only sayin' to Percy—'

'Excuse me,' said Sir Hedley, dismissively. 'Mrs Mossup, might I have a word?' he called down the bar to where the landlady was chatting to a customer.

At the sight of the baronet, she broke off the conversation abruptly and hurried down to join him.

'Come through into the parlour, Sir Hedley,' she said, eyeing Toby Croft, who was standing close by eavesdropping. 'It's more private in there.'

Sir Hedley was shown into the back room of the inn. Toby went back to join his drinking companions, still clutching his empty glass. He sat and turned to his tooth-less, wrinkled friend.

'I told thee that there's summat afoot, Percy,' he said. 'Yon squire's been in an' out of 'ere like a fiddler's elbow lately. I reckon there's summat goin' on between them two closeted in t'back room.'

'Like what?' asked Percy.

'Hanky panky, that's what.'

'Gerron.'

'Oh yes, t'squire's playin' fast an' loose wi' t'landlady. Thee mark my words.'

'You have a wicked mind, Toby Croft,' one of the other farmers told him.

'Nay, she's a good-looking woman for her age and 'e cuts a fine figure.'

'They're well past it, them two,' ventured another farmer.

'Aye, well, I don't reckon t'squire's gerrin' much up at Marston Towers,' said Toby. 'It'd be like goin' to bed wi' a Rottweiler sleepin' next to Lady M.'

'All men and all women look t'same in t'dark,' said Percy, giving his pals the benefit of his homespun wisdom, 'an' when tha's pokin' t'fire, tha dun't bother lookin' at t'mantelpiece, does tha?'

In the parlour, Mrs Mossup gestured to a chair.

'You sit down, Sir Hedley,' she said. 'I'm sure you would welcome a scotch.'

'Really, no, Mrs Mossup,' he replied, 'I've had a good sufficiency today, thank you.'

'Are you driving?' she asked.

'No, no, I've walked, but I really have had enough.'

'Nonsense, a small dram will take the chill out of your bones,' she told him. Taking a bottle of whisky from a cupboard, she poured half a glassful in a tumbler and placed it on the small table before him. She sat opposite and adopted a sympathetic expression. 'I was sorry to hear about your son,' she said.

'James, as you know, was something of a thorn in my side,' said the baronet. 'I'm afraid we never seemed to hit it off. I thought perhaps that when he got older he would settle down, give up his errant ways and make something of himself. I find it very sad that this never happened. However, the one thing he did that has pleased me more than anything is to give me a grandchild. I hope your daughter is keeping well?'

'Very well, thank you, Sir Hedley, and the baby's fine.'

'My son's death has, in a way, simplified matters for Leanne,' he said.

'In what way?'

'Returning to Risingdale with the baby and seeing James might have proved embarrassing and distressing for her. She will now not have to contend with that.'

'It depends whether or not she is going to come back and if she intends to keep the child,' Mrs Mossup told him.

'Oh, she must do that!' he exclaimed.

'She's not really made up her mind yet,' said the landlady. 'Leanne's worried what people might say and how they will treat her if she comes back, an unmarried mother, with the baby. There'll be all that speculation as to who the father is. As you well know, Sir Hedley, gossip in Risingdale spreads like wildfire. She thought she might have the baby adopted and start a new life where she's not known.'

'I sincerely hope she will not take that course of action,' he said. 'We could make it clear that James is the father, should she return, and put a stop to any tittle-tattle. I could make it patently clear that I am the proud grandfather of the child, and if I hear any disparaging comments about Leanne or the child, they will have me to deal with.'

'And how would Lady Maladroit feel about that?' asked the landlady.

'My wife has left me, Mrs Mossup, so that doesn't pertain.'

'She's left you?' She sat up in her chair.

'Gone off to live with her sister and unlikely to return. Our son's death has taken its toll on her. She felt she needed to get away.'

'Dear me,' the landlady muttered. 'So, she will not be coming back?'

'No, she is gone for good. So, might I urge you to encourage your daughter to keep the baby and to return home?'

entreated Sir Hedley. 'With her agreement, of course, I wish to be part of the child's life. She and her baby will want for nothing.'

'You've not touched your drink,' said Mrs Mossup, thinking over what she had heard.

Sir Hedley took a swallow. 'If she is intent on having the child adopted, I shall be more than willing to take on his or her care, well-being and education. I would employ a nanny and the child could stay at Marston Towers and Leanne could visit whenever she pleases.'

'We're getting ahead of ourselves here,' said Mrs Mossup.

'And the child is in line to inherit a great deal—' began the baronet.

'Money has never been a consideration, Sir Hedley,' Mrs Mossup told him.

'Of course not,' he said. 'I apologise for sounding condescending. I merely mention this because money will be no problem.' He reached for the whisky and took a great mouthful.

'I agree with you that I hope she keeps the child,' said Mrs Mossup, 'and comes back to live with me, although a pub is perhaps not the best place in which to bring up a child. However, I would like to have a little kiddie around the place, but it has to be her decision.'

'Yes, of course, I appreciate that,' he said, slightly slurring his words. He finished his drink in one great gulp. 'You will speak to Leanne?'

'Of course,' replied Mrs Mossup. 'I'll ring her tonight.'

The landlady saw her visitor, who was now unsteady on his feet, to the door. 'Will you be all right getting back, Sir Hedley?' she asked.

'I shall be fine,' he said. 'Goodnight.' He turned to the locals, who were watching with interest, and waved. 'Goodnight to you all.'

'Will you look at that,' observed Toby Croft. 'Drunk as a lord.'

'It's a terrible thing to lose a son,' remarked one of his companions. 'It's no wonder the poor man is drowning his sorrows.'

'Don't be daft,' said Toby, 'it stands to reason what them two were getting up to in the back room. Carousin', that's what.'

Sir Hedley headed for home rather the worse for drink. He walked slowly and unsteadily past the Norman church with its spire spearing the sky, past the adjacent Victorian vicarage, the squat grey-stone former Primitive Methodist chapel and past the row of pretty rose-coloured stone cottages, until he arrived at the imposing wrought-iron gates of Marston Towers. Rather than returning via the long drive, he decided to take a shortcut through the woods, the way he had come. As he walked up the path of damp, trodden earth, he was aware of the stillness around him. The wind had dropped and the clouds moved across the sky, leaving a constellation of glittering stars and a pale moon. He sat on the stump of an ancient tree, lit a cigar and thought about the events of the day. He was pleased that Mrs Gosling would be returning as his housekeeper and was optimistic that Mrs Mossup would prevail upon her daughter to come back to the village with her child. He thought of Mrs Lister. When the inevitable divorce with Marcia had been settled and she was out of his life forever, he would marry the woman he had loved for many years. She would move into Marston Towers with their son. She would become the new Lady Maladroit. There would be gossip, of course, but that would neither deter him nor bother him. His thoughts were interrupted by the flashing of a torch and by hushed voices. Sir Hedley remained still and waited until two figures appeared.

'Good evening,' he said loudly.

'Bloody hell!' cried one of the men, jumping up in the air as if he had been poked with a cattle prod. He shone the torch directly into Sir Hedley's eyes.

'Please lower your torch,' ordered the baronet. 'You're blinding me.'

'Bloody hell,' repeated the man under his breath, 'it's Sir Hedley.' He lowered the torch and stepped back.

'And, if I am not mistaken, from the sound of your voice I believe it is one of my tenants to whom I am speaking? It's Mr Pickles, isn't it?'

'Y . . . yes,' replied the man.

'And your companion is?' enquired the baronet.

'M . . . my brother, Sir Hedley.'

The owner of Marston Towers and all the surrounding land and woodland drew on his cigar and blew out a cloud of smoke into the night air. He had caught the poachers red-handed but was feeling in a generous mood that evening. His visits had been very satisfying.

'Just taking a walk, are you?' he asked. He noticed that Mr Pickles's brother was trying to conceal a sack he had been holding by placing it gently on the ground behind a bush.

'Y . . . yes, we were just on our way to the village,' replied the poacher, 'and thought we'd take a shortcut across the woods.'

'My woods,' said the baronet. He paused for a moment to suck in his cigar.

'Yes, indeed,' said the man weakly.

'You are no doubt aware, Mr Pickles, that you are on private land?'

'Yes, Sir Hedley, I'm sorry.' Then, sounding like a naughty schoolboy in front of the head teacher, he added, 'I won't do it again.'

'Very wise, Mr Pickles,' said the baronet. He puffed on his cigar. 'I wouldn't want you to end up in hospital.'

'Hospital?'

'It is not advisable to wander around my woods in the darkness,' said Sir Hedley, enjoying the man's discomfiture. 'I have a new head gamekeeper, Mr Greenwood, who is very keen, very keen indeed. I wouldn't want him to set his dogs on anyone trespassing on my land.'

'Dogs?' repeated the other man nervously.

'Mr Greenwood has persuaded me to get two dogs to help him in his search for poachers. Nasty great brutes, they are. Dobermanns. I wouldn't want anyone to come across them on a dark night while they were strolling through my woods and taking the night air.' Of course, there were no dogs but what the baronet had told the men was clearly having the desired effect.

'N . . . no, Sir Hedley,' muttered Mr Pickles.

'Well, I will bid you gentlemen a good night. I don't think I'll be seeing you in my woods again.'

'Certainly not, Sir Hedley,' said Mr Pickles. When his brother turned to retrieve the sack, he hissed, 'Leave it!'

The baronet blew a cloud of cigar smoke in the air and smiled as he saw the two figures scuttling down the path, leaving their booty behind.

Toby Croft's son, Dean, was a fair, thick-set young man with a weathered face and tight, wiry hair. In summer he invariably dressed in a loose-fitting grey jumper with holes at the elbows, pair of baggy shorts and large, heavy, military-style boots. His legs were wind-burned to the colour of copper. In winter the only concessions he made to his appearance were to wear old corduroy trousers in place of the shorts, tied up at the knee with baling wire, and a shapeless waxed jacket that had seen better days. Dean did most of the work on the farm where he lived with his parents. Toby Croft's meanness was legendary and so was his aversion to labour. As one local observed, he is 'as lazy as Ludlum's dog, which has to lean against the barn door to bark, it's so idle'. He would watch the boy, giving him orders, commenting and criticising at every turn, but rarely stirring himself to lend a hand.

Dean was sweet on Leanne and had asked her out on numerous occasions, but the girl would have nothing to do with him. She had found his talk about sheep and farming tedious and he always seemed to smell of the farm. She had been flattered by the attentions of James Maladroit, who drove a sports car and smelled of expensive cologne. After the Young Farmers' barn dance, to which he had taken her, they had consumed a lot of drink and then one thing had led to another. Pregnant with his child, Leanne had been packed off by her mother to Scarborough to live with her aunt. With her departure, Dean had become miserable and uncommunicative and his mind had not been on his work, which had given his father further cause to complain.

The afternoon that Sir Hedley made his visits in the village, Toby had watched his son trying to sink some fence posts.

'Tha wants to frame thissen,' he barked at his son. 'Tha mekkin a reight pig's ear o' that. Put thee back into it. Tha's about as much use as a chamber pot wi' an 'ole in t'bottom.'

'Why don't thee frame thissen fer a change?' retorted his son in a rare flash of temper. 'Tha does nowt around t'farm 'cept go on at me. My mam an' me do all t'work while thee sits suppin' in t'King's 'Ead.'

People in the village wondered why Mrs Croft and the son put up with such a mean, lazy and curmudgeonly old man.

'I'm sick and tired o' thee goin' on at me all t'time,' shouted Dean, kicking a fence post in frustration. 'I'm not thy bloody slave, tha knaas.'

'Oi, less of thy lip!' shouted his father. 'Who does tha think thy're talkin' to? Tha wants to think thyself lucky that I employ thee. There's plenty o' blokes lookin' fer a job an' who'd do a better job o' work than thee, an' all. Anyroad, if tha dun't like it, then tha can find another job and I'll set somebody else on. An' I'll tell thee this, there's nob'dy in their reight minds'd tek thee on, mooching abaat t'place wi' a face like a smacked arse.'

'Well, we'll see abaat that,' his son shouted back. He threw down his hammer. 'An' thee can repair thy own bloody fence.'

That evening, as his father joined his drinking pals in the King's Head and complained about ungrateful children, Dean sat on the bench by the duck pond. He watched the coots and moorhens paddling at the water's edge, wondering what he would do now.

''Ey up,' came a voice from behind him.

The young man turned to find Dick Greenwood striding towards him.

''Ello, Mester Greenwood,' he replied, getting up from the bench to face him.

'Not wi' tha dad suppin' in t'King's 'Ead?'

'I don't drink much an' 'e's t'last person I wants to be wi'.'

'I'm not gunna disagree wi' that. I've never enjoyed yer dad's company missen.'

''E's allus goin' on at me. Do this, do that, an' I get no thanks an' 'e pays me near to nowt. I'm sick of it, slavin' fer 'im all 'ours o' day an' night. I wish I could get reight away. Anyroad, I've telled 'im to stick 'is job.'

'So tha lookin' fer another job then, are tha?' asked the newly appointed head gamekeeper.

'I shall be, but t'old man reckons n'body'd set me on.'

'Tha's a fit young fella an' not afraid of 'ard work. I've seen 'ow tha slogs away fer tha father up at t'farm. Place'd be in ruins if it weren't fer thee an' thi mam.'

'I telled 'im that.'

'Well, if tha's lookin' fer another job, I might be able to 'elp thee. I've just 'ad a word this afternoon wi' Sir 'Edley up at t'big 'ouse. I've been promoted to t"ead gamekeeper an' am on t'lookout fer someone to give me an 'and. Wor abaat it?'

'Tha means as a sooart o' hassistant gamekeeper like?' asked Dean.

'Aye, that's what I were thinkin'. I'll give thee a trial an' if tha's up to it, job'll be thine. Are thy interested?'

'I . . . I don't know what to say, Mester Greenwood,' cried the young man. 'I'd love a job like that. It'd suit me down to t'ground I won't let thee down.'

'I shall 'ave to 'ave a word an' clear it wi' Sir 'Edley but I reckon 'e won't object. But thy 'as to prove thissen.'

'Hassistant gamekeeper,' muttered Dean. He laughed. 'That'd be a turn-up fer t'book, wun't it, catching mi dad poachin'?'

20

Mr Cadwallader was in an angry frame of mind. His colleagues sat in the staffroom listening to his diatribe in silence.

'That Gosling woman will have to go!' he exclaimed. 'I shall bring it up at the staff meeting this lunchtime and I expect your support in getting rid of her. It's gone beyond a joke. The woman is a tyrant. She pursues me like a hound after a fox. She appears from out of nowhere whinging and moaning and complaining. This morning she collared me as soon as I arrived at school, grumbling about some piece of chewing gum she had discovered under a desk. She presented it to me on a piece of paper like some offering and then told me that I shouldn't allow the children to eat in class. What the devil is it to do with her and what was she doing looking under the desks anyway? Yesterday, she complained about the children trailing mud into school. "I'm not here to clean all that up," she tells me. But she is! The woman's a cleaner, for goodness' sake! I cannot number the times she has brought up the vomit. And this morning she berated me about the state of the boys' toilets, saying that the floor—'

'Was awash,' interrupted Mrs Golightly, finishing his sentence. 'We have all been given the lecture on the state of the boys' lavatories.'

'And do you know what she asked me to do?' continued her colleague.

'No, do tell.' Joyce sighed indifferently, continuing to file a long nail.

'She only asked me to supervise the boys when they went to the toilet. I told her that I could get twenty years in prison for watching little boys doing such a thing.'

He caught sight of Tom shaking his head and grinning from ear to ear.

'I can't see there is anything to smile about,' Mr Cadwallader told him crossly.

'Owen is quite right,' said Mrs Golightly, 'the woman is insufferable.'

'I'm smiling,' Tom told the teachers, 'because I'm thinking about what I overheard in the corridor today.'

'Well, come along,' said Joyce, 'share it with us.'

'Mrs Gosling has had a word with me about the boys' toilets as well,' he said, 'and I spoke to the boys in my class about leaving them clean and not to go wetting the floor. George informed me that it was probably his little brother Gareth, who is in your class, Bertha, who was responsible for the wet floor. He said his mother often complained about him not being careful when he went to the toilet and that his willy seemed to have a life of its own, which, I admit, did make me smile. Anyway, I suggested to George that he might show his little brother the right way to go. Later I was in the corridor and overheard the conversation between the two brothers. That's what made me smile.' Tom then entertained his colleagues with the full account.

He had been pinning a display of the children's work on the wall in the corridor just outside the boys' toilets, when he eavesdropped on the exchange between the two brothers.

'Look what I do, Gareth,' George had said in a loud voice, 'then tha won't go wettin' t'floor. Tha gets reight up to that big white bowl on t'wall like this an' not stand 'alf a mile away. Then tha stands on tiptoe and points yer willy at it, not up but down, like this. Then when tha's done, tha wiggles it abaat a bit to stop it drippin'. Naw then, thee 'ave a go.' There had been a pause and then George had spoken again. 'Nay, nay, Gareth, not wi' my willy, wi' yer own.'

Tom had dropped the stapler and smacked his hand over his mouth to stop himself bursting into laughter.

'That's all very amusing,' said Mr Cadwallader, not looking in the least amused, 'but as I said, I shall raise the matter of Mrs Gosling's conduct at the staff meeting and I expect everyone to support me.'

At this point Mr Gaunt entered the staffroom.

'I am sorry to interrupt your lunchtime,' he said, 'but there are one or two important things with which I think you should be acquainted.'

'And may I say, headmaster,' piped up Mr Cadwallader, 'there is something important we would like to raise with you.'

'We will deal with that under "Any Other Business",' replied the headmaster. 'Now, I have received a number of letters and, as the old chestnut will have it, there is good news and bad news.'

'Let's hear the bad news first,' announced Mr Cadwallader, 'and get it over with.'

'They're going to close the school!' announced Mrs Golightly. 'I knew it. They're closing Skillington and now it's our turn.'

'Nobody is going to close the school, Bertha,' the headmaster told her, shaking his head and sighing. 'I really don't know how many times I have to tell you this. It's not come to that. Just bear with me.'

'Let's have the good news first,' said Joyce. 'I could do with cheering up.'

'Yes,' agreed Mrs Golightly. 'It will put us in a happy frame of mind before we hear the bad news.'

'Very well,' said the headmaster. 'The good news, it is. One piece of correspondence, which I have received this morning, is from the Department of Education and Science, which should reassure you, Bertha, that the school is not closing. It is a letter from HMI Miss Tudor-Williams, informing me that she is to use some of her findings from her visit to our school last term in a major national report concerning the education of children in small rural primaries. It describes good practice. A copy of this report has gone to the Education Office at County Hall. As you are aware, Miss Tudor-Williams was most impressed with what she saw. Related to this, I have received a most complimentary letter from the Director of Education for the county, Ms Tricklebank, who congratulates us on achieving such a commendation and wishes me to pass on to you her congratulations.'

'That's quite a feather in our cap,' said Mrs Golightly.

'Indeed it is,' agreed the headmaster. 'So you see, Bertha, with such an endorsement, it is unlikely that the school will close. I have received another letter from Sir Hedley Maladroit. Poor man is going through a very difficult time at the moment, what with losing a son in that tragic car accident and then his wife leaving him.'

'I am sure he misses his son, although he was a dissolute young man and must have been a great disappointment to him,' remarked Miss Tranter, 'but I should think he opened a bottle of champagne to celebrate when that dreadful wife of his cleared off.'

'Yes, I have to say Lady Maladroit was not the easiest person to deal with,' agreed the headmaster, 'but it must have come as a second shock for Sir Hedley. Anyway, that is by the by. He has written offering the school a parcel of land for a football pitch. He has become aware that we are at present using one of Mr Sheepshanks' fields, which he appreciates is quite unsuitable. He suggests he could make available a small field of his to be turned into a pitch and that Tom should get in touch to discuss this with him and his estate manager. I feel this is very decent of Sir Hedley.'

'That's splendid,' said Tom.

'Large, wealthy landowners like Sir Hedley Maladroit,' said
Joyce, 'have a moral obligation to support local initiatives. It's
the least he can do. I can't say that he has been very proactive
in that area in the past. I don't have very much sympathy for
the man, to be honest. He thinks he owns everything and
everybody. Having driven half the farmers out of their homes,
he has acquired their land. He prefers grouse to sheep farming and that is why the population is declining. He should
know that feudalism and the manorial system have died out.
They are a walking mass of outdated values, the Maladroits.
Anyone would think we're living in the eighteenth century
and not in the 1980s. Country squires ruling the roost are a
dying breed and the sooner they are extinct, the better.'

'Oh, dear,' sighed Mr Gaunt again, wishing he had not
raised the matter. It was always the case at staff meetings that
the teachers felt almost obliged to air their views and depart on
tangents. 'Anyway, I feel it is very generous of him and I have
accepted his offer.' Before Joyce could respond, he moved on
quickly. 'Now the next letter is from Miss Balfour-Smith,
thanking us for welcoming her so warmly when she spent a
day with us in school. She has singled out Bertha for special
mention and thanks. She says the experience was most enlight-
ening, but she does, however, conclude that she is perhaps
better suited to teaching the older children. Having observed
the infants, she has come to realise how very demanding,
draining and unpredictable the small child can be.'

'She was a delightful young woman,' said Mrs Golightly. 'It
was a pleasure to have her visit. I thought she would make a
very good infant teacher. Of course, she is quite right, young
children can be capricious and very tiring. I mean, take the
lesson she observed—'

'Another letter I received yesterday morning concerns you,
Tom,' said Mr Gaunt, cutting her off and moving on swiftly.

'Is this the bad news?' asked the teacher, pulling a pained face.

'No, no, it's another piece of good news, actually. Dr Merryweather, the curator of the Clayton Museum, has asked if you might like to take your class up to the remains of Marston Castle where they have started the excavation of the site. She thinks it might be of interest and she could tell the children about the history of the stronghold and let them watch and maybe help with the dig. I believe Mr Greenwood asked her on your behalf. She mentions that our pupils were very well-behaved when they visited the museum last term. Perhaps you might get in touch with her.'

'Yes, I certainly will,' said Tom.

'Now to the bad news,' announced the headmaster solemnly. He held up a square of paper. 'I have had another memorandum from Mr Nettles.'

The teachers groaned in chorus.

Mr Nettles, a tubby man of unfortunate appearance with thick blond hair sticking up from his head like tufts of dry grass and pale protuberant eyes behind small steel-rimmed spectacles, was the education officer based at County Hall. Mr Gaunt considered him to be a useless individual, elusive and ineffectual, someone who was intoxicated with the sound of his own voice and obsessed with burying schools beneath a snowstorm of paper. Each week the headmaster would receive questionnaires, memoranda, guidelines, policies, directives, programmes of study, schemes of work and other documents from Mr Nettles, most of which he ignored. On the few occasions that he had tried to contact the education officer, he had been informed by a snappish clerical assistant that 'he's tied up'. Such was the ineffectiveness of the man that he had been moved from department to department in the education service and in each position he had proved to be inept.

'That man,' complained Mr Cadwallader, 'is responsible for the deforestation of half the Amazon rainforest with all the paper he uses. He has the brains of a melting ice cube.'

'If I may continue,' said Mr Gaunt. 'You will remember one of his earlier missives was about playground hazards. We were advised, if you recall, not to let the children play potentially dangerous games. He provided us with a detailed list of those we should discourage: skipping, conkers, jacks, hopscotch, touch and tag, British bulldog, leapfrog and marbles.'

'How the devil is playing marbles hazardous?' asked Mr Cadwallader. 'The man's a poltroon.'

'A marble could shoot up and hit a child in the eye,' suggested Mrs Golightly, tongue-in-cheek.

'Playground games teach children team-building skills and cooperation quite apart from giving them healthy exercise,' said Tom, sounding like a lecturer addressing students.

'Look, you don't need to justify it to us,' interrupted Joyce. 'As I recall, we discussed his silly memorandum and agreed to ignore it.'

'We did, indeed,' responded Mr Gaunt, 'and we shall do the same with his latest communication. However, I am obliged to inform you of the contents. This update from Mr Nettles concerns winter playground hazards, which I have been asked to display prominently on the staffroom notice-board. I shall not do this, but will read it instead.' Mr Gaunt coughed theatrically.

'"As a result of the inclement weather, teachers are advised to be extra vigilant in their supervision of the children in their care in order to ensure they do not suffer accidents in the snow and on the ice. They should be deterred from throwing snowballs and sliding, skating and skidding on slippery surfaces."'

'You have to hand it to him,' commented Joyce. 'He certainly has a way with alliteration.'

Mr Gaunt carried on. 'I have done what is required of me by reading this mindless memo and shall now consign it to the file in the cabinet in my study marked FIFI.'

'FIFI,' repeated a puzzled Mr Cadwallader.

'File It and Forget It,' Mr Gaunt told him. 'Now I shall give you the bad news, which will affect us all. This indeed will come as an unwelcome development. Mrs Gosling has tendered her resignation.'

'What!' shouted Mr Cadwallader. 'She's leaving?'

'Sadly, yes,' replied Mr Gaunt. 'I know this must come as a great disappointment to you all, but Sir Hedley has prevailed upon her to return as his housekeeper. She says in her letter of resignation that she feels conscience-bound to take up her previous position at Marston Towers now that Sir Hedley is all alone and has no one to cook and clean for him. Mrs Gosling has given me two weeks' notice, which is good of her, in order that I can find a replacement.'

'She will be greatly missed,' said Mr Cadwallader disingenuously.

'Whatever will we do without her?' added Joyce sardonically. She exchanged a look of amused complicity with her colleague.

'The school will not be the same,' added Mrs Golightly, not able to conceal her smile.

'I must say I was surprised by Mr Leadbeater's reaction when I told him,' the headmaster told his colleagues. 'He didn't seem unduly upset. Indeed, I detected a trace of a grin on his lips. Most strange. Now, Owen, what was the important matter you wished to raise?'

'Oh, it is of no consequence, headmaster,' replied Mr Cadwallader, leaning back in his chair and folding his arms.

As Mr Gaunt made his way back to his study, he stopped for a moment in the corridor. Was that a cheer he heard coming from the staffroom? he asked himself.

On his way home, Tom came across Mr Leadbeater scraping the snow from the path.

'Mr Gaunt was telling us at the staff meeting that Mrs Gosling is to leave,' he said.

'Thank the Lord,' replied the caretaker.

'Won't you miss her, Bob?' Tom asked, impishly.

'Miss her!' repeated the caretaker. 'I'll miss that woman as much as I'd miss a rotten wisdom tooth or a burst blood vessel. Mr Gaunt says I can get another cleaner but I'd sooner play blind man's bluff with a stampeding elephant than have another Mrs Gosling on the premises. I'm better off without. She makes my life a misery, charging down the corridor every morning like Boadicea herself clutching that wretched mop of hers like a weapon.' He continued to scrape at the snow. 'Huh, miss her, indeed!' he muttered.

The following week Tom took his class up to the archaeological dig at Marston Castle. They were met by the curator of the Clayton Museum, who was in charge of the excavations.

Dr Merryweather looked very pleased to see Tom again that morning and welcomed him warmly. She allowed her hand to linger a fraction when Tom shook it and smiled, displaying a set of perfect white teeth.

'It's really good of you to let us come,' he told her. 'I promise we will try not to get in the way.'

'Not at all,' she said. 'You will all be a great help. You can lend a hand with the dig.'

Tom gathered his class around Dr Merryweather and explained that she was going to talk to them about the history of the castle and then about the excavations and that she would be pleased to answer any questions.

'Marston Castle,' the curator told the children, 'has long been a mystery to those who live in the Dale. So little remains that you must use your imagination and try to picture what it must have looked like when it was built all those centuries ago.'

The children stared at the ruin.

'Just think what it was like in its heyday,' said Tom, 'with knights in shining armour, battles and sieges, banquets and jousting. It excites me just to think about it.'

'It was once a great majestic fortress of solid stone that towered over the surrounding area,' Dr Merryweather told the children.

'When was it built, miss?' asked Charlie.

'We think the castle dates back to the twelfth century and was originally built of timber,' he was informed.

'How do you know that it was built then?' persisted the boy.

'We have discovered that the castle was defended by a large rectangular gate tower, which helps us to date it around that time.'

'Who built it, miss?' asked Simon.

'A Norman nobleman called William de Burgh,' she answered. 'The castle probably had four towers, each four storeys high. Two of them would have been close together to form a gatehouse. We have already discovered that the east tower contained a well, which we estimate was over a hundred and twenty feet deep. The double-walled keep would have had guardrooms, storerooms and servants' quarters on the ground floor. The main hall and private apartments would have been on the second floor. The tower rooms had garderobes. Does anyone know what a garderobe was?'

'Was it where they used to put their clothes, miss?' asked Holly.

'No, that's a wardrobe,' said Dr Merryweather, 'but it was a good guess. The word does sound similar.'

'It was a lavatory,' said Leo.

'It was,' she said, 'and this garderobe discharged – well, I think you all know what – on to the outer walls of the keep.

They didn't have flushing toilets in those days, I'm afraid. Marston Castle eventually passed to another rich and powerful family called the D'Arbours, who were loyal supporters of the king. If you visit the church in the village, you will see the tomb of Sir Marmaduke D'Arbour, who was a great man, considered one of the most eminent persons in the county in the reign of Henry VIII. Now, I am sure you have all heard of Henry VIII, haven't you?'

'Yes, miss,' chorused the children.

'So who can tell me something about him?'

'He had six wives,' volunteered Vicky. 'One was called Catherine of Harrogate and another was called Ann of Leeds.'

Dr Merryweather smiled. 'Nearly right,' she said. 'It was Catherine of Aragon, a Spanish princess, and Anne of Cleves, a German princess.'

'He chopped off people's heads,' volunteered one of the twins.

'You are right: he had executed those who didn't agree with him. I'm afraid he wasn't a very nice man.'

'Not a very nice man,' repeated Simon, turning to George and pulling a face. He lowered his voice. 'He was a bastard.'

'That will do,' said Tom, who had overheard.

'Well, he was, sir, wasn't he?'

'When Henry VIII died, he was put in a lead coffin and he blew up,' said Leo.

'What?' cried Vicky.

'He was really fat and all the gases inside him built up and he exploded. It's called internal combustion. Pieces of him were scattered all over and dogs ran off with bits of him.'

'Uuuurgh!' groaned the children.

'Is that true?' Tom asked Dr Merryweather.

'It is, yes,' she replied. 'Let us move on. Over the centuries, the castle remained in the hands of the same aristocratic family. After a short and bloody siege during the English

Civil War, the Royalists surrendered to the Parliamentarian forces.'

'Did the dogs eat him then?' asked Simon.

'I think we will leave Henry VIII for the time being,' Tom told him. He turned to Dr Merryweather. 'Were all the Royalists put to death when they surrendered?' he asked.

'No, they were promised that if they laid down their arms and opened the gates, they would be allowed to leave the castle without being harmed. The Royalist general Sir Richard Leslie marched out with his officers and men.'

'How do you know, miss?' asked Charlie.

'The siege was recorded; you can read about it if you visit the museum,' he was told.

'What happened to the castle after the siege, miss?' asked Hazel.

'It was largely demolished,' answered Dr Merryweather, 'and its lead, glass and contents were sold off. Most of the stonework was stolen and its walls became as you now see them, crumbling and overgrown with heather, ivy and peat. Now, today, we are excavating one of the outside walls and you can all help. The students from the university will show you what to do.'

'This is fascinating,' Tom told Dr Merryweather as he watched the children set to work with trowels. 'It brings history to life. I have to admit when I was at school I found the subject boring. It's so good of you to let us take part in this. I hope we find something.'

'For me, it is more about discovering what the castle actually looked like when it was built than finding things, although it would be good if we could uncover some artefacts.'

'You have a very good manner with the children,' Tom told her.

'Thank you, kind sir,' she said, giving him a coquettish smile.

That morning something indeed was discovered, but not what those who were busy digging expected to find.

'Could you tell me who that old man is?' asked Dr Merryweather, pointing to a figure dressed in a grubby collarless shirt and waistcoat and wellington boots turned down at the top, with a smouldering cigarette between his lips. He was digging a small distance from the ruins.

'It's Mr Croft, a local farmer,' Tom told her.

'When we arrived this morning, he was digging a hole right under the remaining castle wall. He wasn't too pleased when I asked him to move, and when I enquired if he had permission to be here, he said Sir Hedley said it would be all right. Then he started to dig over there.'

'He's heard about the coins discovered here,' said Tom, 'and no doubt is looking for a cache of buried treasure.'

'Well, if he finds anything, he must surrender it to us,' she said.

'I'll see if I can get him to leave,' said Tom. 'He doesn't have permission to be here.'

He approached the old farmer, who was standing knee-deep in a hole enthusiastically shovelling spadefuls of soil into a heap.

'You shouldn't be here, Toby,' said Tom.

The farmer dropped the cigarette and ground it with the toe of his boot. 'I wasn't aware that thee owned this land,' he replied. He rested on his spade and squinted up at the teacher. 'I've as much right as that lot ovver theer.'

'They have permission,' Tom told him. 'This is private property. It belongs to Sir Hedley Maladroit.'

'Thy dun't need to tell me who owns it. I've lived 'ere a sight longer than thee.'

'You shouldn't be here,' repeated Tom.

'Well, you and all them kids are 'ere.'

'We've been invited.'

'I'm not doin' any 'arm.'

'How would you like someone digging on your property without your permission?'

'I'd welcome someone digging on my property,' retorted the old farmer. 'It needs diggin' ovver. I asked our Dean to do it but e's buggered off.' He lifted up his spade and dug in the ground. There was a metallic clang.

''Old up,' he cried, 'I've found summat.' He bent down and cleared away some soil with his hands. 'I might 'ave struck gold 'ere. Give us an 'and, will tha.'

Tom jumped into the hole and helped him move away the earth from the find.

Toby jabbed with his spade at a round and rusting metal object. There was another clang as metal hit metal.

'I reckon it could be a chest or summat or mebbe a suit of harmour.'

'I'll tell the person in charge of the dig,' said Tom, climbing out of the hole.

''Ang on! 'Ang on!' cried the old farmer. 'Don't thee be so 'asty.' I wants to see what I've found fust. I found it, an' by rights I should keep it.' He dug around the object, revealing more rusty metal, and jabbed at it with his spade.

Tom bent down to examine what had been unearthed and then stood back. Then he began to slowly back away.

'Oh dear,' he said. 'I don't think it's a very good idea to keep banging it with your spade,' he told Toby, 'and I wouldn't move if I were you.'

'What's up wi' thee?' He then tapped the metal again before digging around the object.

'I think you should stop what you are doing,' said Tom. 'It's not a suit of armour. I have an idea that it's something very different.'

'Oh aye,' said the old farmer, leaning again on his spade. 'What does tha reckon it is, then?'

'I may be wrong,' replied Tom, 'and I hope I am, but I think you are standing in front of an unexploded bomb.'

'Bloody hell!' shouted the old farmer, about to leap out of the hole he had dug.

'I shouldn't move if I were you, Toby,' warned the teacher. 'Any vibrations might set it off. Stay perfectly still. Any slight movement and you might be blown to smithereens.' Tom was much enjoying the old farmer's distress. He knew that the bomb, if indeed it was a bomb, was very unlikely to explode after so many years buried and having been banged with a spade. He adopted a particularly nervous-sounding tone of voice. 'I think you should remain as still as possible. You might have set it off, hitting it with your spade. I'll get some help.'

'Don't thee leave me 'ere with a bloody gret bomb!' cried the farmer.

Tom jogged off smiling and told his pupils to stop what they were doing and stand behind one of the castle walls. He then informed Dr Merryweather what he thought the old farmer had dug up.

'I don't think it is anything to worry about,' Tom told her, 'but it might be best to stop the excavations to be on the safe side.'

'Could everyone stop what they are doing,' shouted Dr Merryweather, 'and move right away from the site? I think we might have an unexploded bomb on our hands.'

As everyone vacated the site, there came a plaintive cry from the man in the hole. 'Can somebody 'elp me?'

21

On the way back to school, Tom joined George. He noticed the boy had become uncharacteristically quiet and now walked behind the rest of the children, who were chattering excitedly about the discovery of the bomb, with his hands dug deeply in his pockets. He had a thoughtful expression on his face.

George was not the best in the class when it came to reading and writing, and notwithstanding the teacher's efforts, his heart was not in the work he undertook in school. He was a country lad through and through. Being stuck in a stuffy classroom behind a desk he felt confined, like a captive animal desperate to be running free. Despite his lack of interest in school, Tom liked the boy. George was biddable and good-humoured and invariably had a smile on his face. He had been honest with his teacher, admitting that he didn't really 'tek to book learnin'' and longed for the day when he could leave school and work on his father's farm, a farm that one day would be his.

From the start of his teaching career, Tom had shown a genuine interest in the children's lives and what they had to say, and he encouraged them to speak about their interests outside school. He soon found that many of his pupils were authorities when it came to farming. With George, once he had started talking about sheep or cows there was no stopping him. Tom discovered that the boy could chain harrow a field as well as any adult, dig a dyke, help build a drystone wall, repair a fence, milk a cow and lamb a ewe. He could identify a bird by a faded feather and had an encyclopaedic knowledge of tractors. He had once enlightened a dazed Mr Pendlebury, who had come into school to read a story, on how to deal with a breeched calf.

'Tha sees, if t'vet can't turn t'calf, t'cow 'as a caesarean section,' he had told the vicar. 'Mi dad let me watch when t'calf was pulled out.'

'Now this is all very fascinating,' the vicar had replied feebly, wishing to quickly change the subject.

That morning as they walked back to school, Tom approached the boy.

'Are you all right, George?' the teacher asked him. 'You look a bit down in the mouth.'

The lad pushed back the black curls from his face and shook his head like a wise old man.

'I'm not champion, Mester Dwyer, if truth be telled,' he replied.

'Do you want to tell me about it?'

'Nay, Mester Dwyer, tha wun't be hinterested.'

'"A trouble shared is a trouble halved", as an aunt of mine would say,' Tom told him. 'Come along, you tell me what's on your mind.'

The boy sucked in his bottom lip. 'Well, we've 'ad a bit of a do up at t'farm. Mi dad bought this Belgian Blue bull at Clayton t'auction mart an' paid a pretty penny fer it. Mi granddad thowt 'e shelled out too much. It's a gret big beast this bull, wi' solid legs, box-shaped body and massive muscles, an' 'e were well hung an' all. We called 'im Samson. Mi dad reckoned 'e thowt 'e were t'bee's knees stomping abaat t'field an' bellowin' like there were no tomorra. He were put to cows, which were comin' ovver again after three weeks.'

'Coming over?' Tom was puzzled.

'Comin' in season ageean. Anyroad, Samson sets abaat doin' what 'e were bought fer an' 'e fettles all t'cows 'e could gerra grip on. Went round t'field like a dose o' salts, 'e did. Mi dad were dead chuffed seein' 'im get crackin'. Sex mad, 'e were. Anyroad, two or three months pass an' there's nowt 'appenin'.'

'In what way?' asked Tom.

'Well, none o' t'cows are in calf. Mi granddad reckoned Samson'd been firin' blanks and mi dad would 'ave been better off gerrin' in t'bull wi' t'bowler 'at.'

'Bull with a bowler hat,' repeated Tom.

The boy gave the teacher the sort of look an expert might give to an ignoramus, a sort of patient, pitying look. 'Tha knows, Mester Dwyer – t'AI man, artificial inseminator. 'E does it to t'cows instead o' t'bull.'

'I see,' said Tom.

'Like I said, mi granddad reckoned that Samson was firin' blanks – that means 'is wrigglers was infertile.' The boy looked up at the teacher. 'Wrigglers are t'bull's sperm, Mester Dwyer.'

'Yes, I understood that,' said Tom.

'It sometimes 'appens and not just wi' bulls.' The boy wrinkled his nose.

'Well, that's very interesting, George,' said the teacher, wishing he had never enquired why the boy was looking so gloomy. 'I think perhaps we might—'

'So mi dad sent fer t'vet,' continued George, undeterred, 'an' she said we'd 'ave to gerra sample o' Samson's sperm an' examine it to see if t'bull 'ad what it teks, so mi dad gorra cow what was bullin' an'—'

'Bulling,' repeated the teacher.

'In season,' explained the boy. 'A cow 'as to be in season to get pregnant.'

'Yes, of course.'

'Mi dad borrowed a cow from Mester Sheepshanks,' continued the boy. ''E 'as an 'erd of Charolais.'

'Oh dear,' muttered Tom, wondering where this was going.

'So t'vet used a bovine sheath to fit on t'back o' t'cow to collect some o' Samson's wrigglers,' said the boy. 'Do you know what a bovine sheath is, Mester Dwyer, or shall I hexplain?'

'I've not seen one,' replied the teacher, 'but I have a good idea what it is.'

'So, t'vet attaches this bovine sheath at t'back of t'cow an' she brings over t'bull an'—'

'I think perhaps we'll leave it at that, George,' interrupted the teacher.

'An' she puts Samson up to t'cow,' continued the boy, undeterred, 'but when t'bull gets crackin' she falls down – t'cow that is, not t'vet. She were only used to t'bull wi' t'bowler 'at, tha sees, not this gret big beast climbin' on top o' 'er. Mi granddad gives t'cow a kick an' tells 'er that it's t'only chance she'll ever likely get to do it properly. By this time Samson needs a break, but hafter 'alf an 'our, 'e gets frisky ageean.'

'I think we'll leave it there, George,' the teacher told him.

'What's up, Mester Dwyer?' asked the boy innocently. 'Dun't tha want to know what t'result were?'

'If I must.'

George shook his head. 'Poor owld Samson, 'e were as barren as a brick in a desert.' He shook his head sagaciously. 'Ended up as dog food.'

Tom, after nearly two terms as a teacher at Risingdale School, still found the farming children refreshingly honest when it came to describing the sexual reproduction of the animals on their farms. There was no embarrassment on their part; they were accustomed to seeing birth, and many helped with the lambing and the calving and their parents made no bones about discussing the natural biological process. Tom's first encounter with this candour was early in his career, when he had sat with one of his pupils on the playground wall one lunchtime. Carol had demonstrated a comprehensive knowledge of sheep rearing. She had given him a lesson about tups and gimmers, hoggets and shearlings, stots and stirks, wethers and tegs. The girl had become animated as she had realised the extent of her teacher's ignorance, surprised that there were people in the world who couldn't tell a Bluefaced Leicester sheep from a Texel, or a Masham from a Swaledale. When Tom had asked her what the characteristics of a prize-winning sheep were, she had told him without gloss.

'You have to check that the tups and yows are ready for breeding,' the girl had said. 'Make sure that they are in tip-top condition with no diseases or viruses. Good breeding yows are fit and healthy with a solid body, straight legs, a good set of teeth and two working teats.'

Back at school that afternoon, Tom set the class a writing task of describing their visit to Marston Castle that morning. He had hoped that their compositions would be full of historical information, which drew on what Dr Merryweather had told them about the stronghold and about what they had discovered while taking part in the excavation. However, most of the accounts were about the discovery of the unexploded bomb and the exploding monarch. As his pupils scribbled away, Tom opened a note given to him by Dr Merryweather before they left the site. She said that she had been delighted to see him again and hoped that they might meet up for a drink sometime. She had written down her telephone number and looked forward to hearing from him.

The two teachers were on yard duty enjoying the warmth of the unseasonal sunshine as they wandered around the playground.

'Are plans going well for the big day?' Tom asked Joyce.

'Oh yes,' she replied, excitedly. 'Julian's arranging everything. He won't let me do a thing apart from choose the dress, and then he told me what he thinks would suit me and the style of shoes I should wear and the bouquet I should hold. There's not that many bridegrooms who would do that.'

'No,' thought Tom. He wondered if his colleague was getting involved with another controlling man, but he merely smiled and nodded.

'He's so well organised,' she continued. 'He could put a wedding planner to shame. By the way, he wants to speak to you, just to go over the best man's duties. He's very keen that nothing risqué should be included in the speech. I told him, of course, that you are the very last person to say anything taste-less or improper, but he just wants to go over what you intend to say.'

'Does he,' muttered Tom, rather peeved that Joyce's future husband felt the need to vet his speech.

'He's booked the reception at Marfleet Manor,' Joyce carried on, 'and our honeymoon is to be a two-week Caribbean cruise – Bermuda, Nassau, the Bahamas, Antigua – which came as a lovely surprise.' She gripped Tom's arm and sighed. 'Being so happy sometimes frightens me.'

'You deserve every happiness, Joyce, after what you have been through,' Tom told her. 'I'm delighted for you.'

'Julian thinks I should give up teaching after we're married,' she said.

'Does he?'

'He says I could be a real help in the auction house.'

'And will you give up teaching?' asked Tom.

'I don't know, but Julian thinks it's a good idea. After all, we don't need the money.'

'It's not just about money, though, is it, Joyce? Teaching is your vocation. It's your career. It's what you love and you're good at it.'

'I'll have to think about it,' she replied.

Their conversation was interrupted by a small ginger-headed boy of about seven with a runny nose. He ran up to the teachers, frantically waving his hand in the air.

'Miss! Miss! Miss!' he cried. 'Mark's just kneed me in the nuts.'

'Just calm down,' Joyce ordered, 'and stop jumping up and down like a kangaroo.'

'Mark's just kneed me in the nuts, miss,' repeated the boy.

'I think you might use a better word than that, Nicholas,' she told the boy, sharply.

'What word, miss?' the child asked.

'The word beginning with "n",' the teacher told him.

'Kneed?' asked the boy, looking puzzled.

'Nuts,' she snapped. 'There is a better word you should use. "Nuts" is a rude word when it refers to . . . well, to that part of the body.'

'But I thought I'd get into trouble for saying he kneed me in the bollocks, miss.'

Joyce rolled her eyes. Tom stifled a laugh.

'Go and tell Mark I wish to see him,' Joyce told the boy, 'and stop wriggling about. The pain will soon go away.'

The boy rubbed his nostrils on his coat sleeve, sniffed noisily and hobbled off with a smug expression on his freckled face. He returned a moment later with the reprobate, another small, freckled individual with a runny nose.

'Did you knee Nicholas Wilkinson in the downstairs department?' Joyce asked the boy. She put on her stern expression.

'I never kicked his ankle, miss,' replied the child.

'Miss means just here,' Nicholas told him, pointing between his legs.

'In your nuts?' asked the boy.

'Miss says you're not supposed to say "nuts" because it's rude,' said the other boy.

'What do I say?' asked young Mark, looking perplexed.

'You could say "goolies",' suggested Nicholas.

'No, you could not!' exclaimed Joyce, pulling a horrified face. 'Just say you were kicked in the private parts.'

'I wasn't kicked, miss,' the boy told her. 'I was kneed.'

Joyce turned to Tom. 'I think you had better deal with this, Mr Dwyer,' she said. 'Man to man.' With that, she hurried off towards the school entrance.

Two little innocent faces looked at Tom expectantly. The teacher decided not to prolong the discussion concerning the various alternative words for 'nuts'.

'So why did you knee him, Mark?' Tom asked the young assailant.

'Because when I bent over to pick up my football, sir,' replied the boy, 'he pinched my arse.'

Tom shook his head and decided to leave any further discussion on the most appropriate words to describe parts of the human anatomy.

'Well, no more pinching or kneeing,' he said. 'Is that clear?'

'Yes, sir,' chorused the duo.

'Now off you go, both of you,' Tom told them.

When he arrived at the staffroom, a lively debate was taking place between his colleagues concerning Joyce's conversation with the two little boys.

'Well, you do surprise me, Bertha,' Joyce was saying. 'Are you advocating that we allow children to use such terms?'

'I am not suggesting we accept the colloquial terms like "nuts" or "goolies",' replied her colleague. 'Of course not. What I am saying is that children should be taught the proper names for those parts of the body, not encouraged to use silly euphemisms. It's just prudery. There is nothing crude or vulgar about referring to the correct medical terminology. I would have told the child the appropriate word is "testicles". I mean, I had Mrs Bowman telling me her son "got his little nipper caught in his zipper". Now, what sort of term is that? I told her that we do not use baby language in my classroom. We use the correct English. We call things by their proper names.'

'So what did you tell her?' asked Mr Cadwallader.

'I said I take it you mean that Freddie gets his penis caught in his zip,' said the teacher.

'You said what!' exclaimed Miss Tranter.

'Well, what would you have said?' she asked.

'I wouldn't have been quite as blunt.'

'There was no place for euphemisms when I was in the army,' Mr Cadwallader said. 'We called a spade a shovel. I have to say it came as quite a shock when I joined up to hear all these new terms. I was very innocent in those days, having had a strict upbringing and a stern Welsh grandmother who was very strait-laced.'

'But these children are not in the army, are they, Owen?' retorted Joyce. 'And it is unacceptable in my book for a child to say that he was "kneed in the nuts". We have to educate them as to what is appropriate and what is not.'

'That is exactly what I have been saying,' said Mrs Golightly.

'But I don't agree with Bertha,' continued Joyce, ignoring the interruption. 'I think there is an age when children should be taught the medical terminology and it isn't at the age of seven. There's a time and a place for that sort of thing. Words like "penis" and "testicle" should be introduced when they are in the top juniors and not before.' She turned to Tom. 'So what did you tell those two boys?'

'I didn't tell them anything,' he replied. 'I felt it better to leave the matter alone.'

'Well, that's a bit of a cop-out,' she said.

'The two boys are in your class, Joyce,' he told her, 'so it seems to me that the balls are in your court.' Then, realising what he had just said, he tried to hide his amusement.

'My Welsh grandmother was the mistress of the euphemism,' said Mr Cadwallader. 'Anything to do with certain parts of the human anatomy, sex or bodily functions was taboo in our house. She never referred to the breast of chicken – it was always the white meat – and she would ask for the dark meat rather than a leg. She would never say "lavatory" or "toilet". If she felt the call of nature and she wanted to go, she would say, "I'm just going to turn the vicar's bike around" and we all knew what she meant.'

His three colleagues were lost for words.

Mrs Gosling was spraying the window panes in the classroom liberally with sickly lavender-smelling insecticide when Tom arrived at school the following morning. The smell was oppressive.

'I don't know where all these wretched flies have come from, Mr Dwyer,' she said. 'They're all round the school, buzzing and crawling in every room. I opened all the windows but it doesn't shift them. Too cold out there for bluebottles, I shouldn't wonder. We don't usually get flies at this time of year.'

'It's very strange,' said Tom, sitting at his desk and taking out the children's exercise books from his briefcase, which he placed in a pile before him. He was keen to get on with his marking but Mrs Gosling was showing no sign of leaving him in peace.

The cleaner (aka assistant caretaker) continued to spray vigorously.

'Mr Gaunt tells me you're leaving,' said Tom.

'Yes, I'll be going back to Marston Towers. I don't like to leave you all here at the school in the lurch, but Sir Hedley is in need of me. Begged me to go back, he did. "I'm lost without you, Mrs Gosling," he said. Poor man must feel very lonely up there in the big house all by himself, rattling about like a dried pea in a tin kettle. Mind you, his wife was no company. She could freeze soup in pans with that face of hers.

Good riddance, I say. I mean, I wouldn't have gone back if she had still been in situ.'

'Well, you will be greatly missed by all of us, Mrs Gosling,' Tom told her. The lie came easily. His colleagues could not have been more delighted when they were given the news of her imminent departure.

'Yes, I guess I will be missed,' she said smugly. 'This school was in a right state until I came, even if I do say so myself. Mr Leadbeater will have to pull his finger out when I've gone, otherwise the teachers, present company excepted, will have to put up with the dust, dirt and untidiness.'

'And when do you leave?'

'At the end of the week,' she replied. 'Course, I have to thank you for getting me the job here in the first place, recommending me to Mr Gaunt after Lady Hoity-Toity up at the big house accused me of stealing her necklace and then sacked me, so I do feel a bit awkward about letting you down.'

'Don't worry yourself about that,' said Tom.

'Mind you, I won't miss that computer in the corner. It gathers dust like nobody's business and I'll be glad to see the back of them stuffed creatures you have on your windowsill. I thought you were going to put them in a cupboard, anyway.'

'When I heard you were leaving, I thought there was no point,' he replied.

'Sir Hedley has some stuffed animals and birds up at Marston Towers, but I shan't be dusting them, I can tell you.'

'Well, I had better get on,' Tom told her, opening the first exercise book.

'Our Vicky was telling me they found an unexploded bomb up at the ruined castle,' said Mrs Gosling, not taking the hint for her to make herself scarce.

'That's right,' said Tom.

'I remember planes flying over during the war but I don't recall any bombs dropping up here. In fact—' She stopped mid-sentence when she caught sight of a small boy standing at the classroom door.

'I'm sorry to disturb you, Mrs Gosling,' said Leo, 'but may I have a quiet word with Mr Dwyer, please?'

'Yes, love, come in,' said the cleaner, 'I've finished in here.' She patted the boy on his head. 'You're a polite young man,' she told him. 'I wish all the kiddies were as well-mannered as you. I was very glad to hear that you're feeling better.' Then, with a final flourish with the fly spray, she waddled off.

'You're early,' Tom told Leo. 'Don't you usually get the school bus from Risingdale?'

'Yes, I do,' he replied, 'but I've walked up this morning. It's a nice day and the fresh air is quite bracing.'

Tom smiled to hear such an old-fashioned phrase coming from the mouth of one so young. 'So, what can I do for you, Leo?' he asked.

The boy sat in a chair before the teacher's desk, crossed his legs and rested his hands on his lap. He waved away a fly, which had settled on his hand. 'It's a personal matter, Mr Dwyer,' he said. 'I wanted to see you before everyone arrives so we are not disturbed. I have been thinking for a while about something I would like to ask you.'

'I have always believed that if someone has something on their mind, it is best to get it off their chest,' Tom told him.

'Yes, that's what my mother says,' said the boy. He thought for a moment before continuing. 'My mother doesn't know I am talking to you about this, by the way, and I hope you won't tell her.'

'Not if you don't want me to.'

'I should prefer it if you didn't mention our conversation.' He brushed another fly from his hand. 'Before we came to Risingdale, Mr Dwyer,' the boy continued, 'my mother was unhappy. After my father died, she went very quiet. I was told by my grandfather that she didn't laugh and hardly ever smiled and spent most of her time painting. I suppose her art helped her take her mind off things. I was unhappy too, not only because I was worried about her and because of my illness but also because I was having a bad time at school. I was called names and was bullied. The teachers told me to ignore it and the bullies would get tired and stop. They never did. Anyway, we decided to move, to get away to somewhere different, and when my mother was asked to illustrate a book about the Yorkshire Dales, we came up here to the top of the Dale. Shall I go on?'

'Please do,' said Tom.

'I don't think my mother intended us to stay here for very long but she seems very taken with the place.'

'And what about you?' asked the teacher.

'I really love it here. I've not been bullied at this school and I like the children in our class and have made a best friend. I've never had a best friend before.' The boy fidgeted in his chair, crossing and uncrossing his legs. 'I never liked the other schools I attended, but I really like Risingdale and I like having you as my teacher. You are the best teacher I have ever had, Mr Dwyer.'

'I'm pleased to hear it,' said Tom. 'Now, what is this question you wish to ask me?'

'I will tell you in a moment,' said the boy. 'My mother really likes it in Risingdale. I have never seen her look so happy. She smiles a lot and laughs. She's like her old self. Now I get to the bit that is a little tricky.'

'Go on.'

'It's the question I want to ask you.'

'Which is?'

'Do you like my mother, Mr Dwyer?'

Tom was taken aback by the question. 'Well ... er ... yes, I do.'

'She likes you. She likes you a lot and talks about you quite often. She says you're a really good man. I was thinking that if you like my mother and she likes you, that you might get married.'

Tom, as they say in Yorkshire, was gobsmacked. 'Marry? Marry your mother?'

'I would be very happy to have you as my father. I think you would make a very good father. I wanted to tell you that.'

Tom was lost for words.

'You've gone very quiet, Mr Dwyer,' said the boy.

'To be honest, Leo,' Tom told him, 'I wasn't expecting that.'

'If two grown-ups like each other, isn't that what they do, get married?' asked the boy.

'It's a bit more complicated than that,' Tom told him, wafting away a fly that had settled on his cheek.

'It seems pretty simple to me,' said Leo.

'When you are older, you will understand what I mean,' said the teacher. 'Getting married is a big step for anyone to take. It means sharing your life with that person. It involves rather more than just liking someone's company, of being fond of another person. It's something much more.'

'I'm afraid I don't understand grown-ups,' said Leo. He stood up. 'Well, I can hear the children arriving, so I had better go. I hope you didn't mind me mentioning it.'

'No, I didn't mind, Leo,' Tom replied. 'Now you run along.'

'I have enjoyed our chat, Mr Dwyer,' said the boy. When he reached the door of the classroom on his way out, he turned. 'You might think about it.'

Tom found it difficult to concentrate on anything that day, other than what Leo had told him that morning. It was undeniable that he liked Amanda Stanhope – more than liked; he realised that he was falling for her in a big way. He thought of the evening they had spent at Le Bon Viveur. He had waited anxiously at the table, rehearsing in his head what he would say when she arrived, and then he had seen her reflection in the tall gilt mirror in the entrance to the restaurant. People at the tables had turned their heads to observe the tall, elegant woman with the soft mass of golden hair. She had spotted Tom, smiled, waved and approached him. He had felt a sudden rush of physical excitement when he saw her, his breath lightening and his stomach churning. He had gone over in his head what he would say when she arrived, to tell her that she looked lovely, but like a besotted, nervous teen-ager on his first date, he stuttered out a 'Good evening' as he rose from his chair, spilling a glass of water in the process and knocking over the table centrepiece – a slender silver vase containing a single red rose. As Tom had clumsily tried to mop up the mess, the restaurant owner, a lean, olive-skinned individual with glossy boot-black hair scraped back over his scalp, had glided to the table, clicked a finger and a waiter had hurried over.

'Allow me, sir,' he had said in a rather patronising voice.

Amanda had sat down and smiled.

'Not a good start,' he had told her, red with embarrassment.

That evening he had watched her, infatuated, as she had chattered and laughed, her blue eyes shining and her beautiful face flushed with pleasure.

Tom had dropped Amanda off later at her cottage. She had thanked him for a lovely evening, shook his hand and wished him a good night. It wasn't what he had hoped for. As he had driven off, he had regretted his diffidence and determined he would be more confident in his advances the next time they met.

Now in the staffroom at morning break, Tom stared out of the window thinking of her.

'And for goodness' sake, don't tell her,' said Mr Cadwallader.

Tom was jolted out of his reverie by the sound of his colleague's clamorous voice.

'I'm sorry, Owen,' he said. 'Did you say something?'

'I was talking to Joyce,' he replied. 'I was telling her to keep it to herself. It's most embarrassing as it is, without Hitler in the pink overall finding out and giving me an ear-bashing.'

'I'm sorry. I don't know what you are talking about,' said Tom.

'The flies,' Mrs Golightly told him. 'I am assuming that your classroom is like ours, teeming with the irritating insects. It was a nightmare getting the infants to settle down this morning. I was going to read the poem about the old lady who swallowed a fly but thought better of it.'

'Now you mention it,' Tom said, 'I have had a lot of flies in my room. I don't know where they've come from.'

'They have come from Owen's classroom,' Joyce told him. 'He is responsible for them and he doesn't want Mrs Gosling to find out.'

'How is Owen to blame?' asked Tom.

'As part of a biology project I was undertaking with my class,' Mr Cadwallader explained, 'we were studying the life cycle of insects. I thought as a practical example I would use the common housefly. I bought a box of maggots from the fishing shop in Clayton, put them in what I thought was a sealed tank in the classroom and we watched as they turned into larvae. Unfortunately, overnight the larvae hatched out as flies and they escaped from the tank.'

'And now we have a plague of bluebottles,' said Joyce, 'and Mrs Gosling is rushing around the school like a dervish spraying everything with insecticide.'

'So please don't mention it to her that I am the culprit,' said Mr Cadwallader to Tom, 'or I'll not hear the last of it.'

At that very moment the person under discussion entered the staffroom brandishing the fly spray and a fly swat.

'Are there any flies in here?' asked Mrs Gosling.

*　　*　　*

At lunchtime Tom sat at the computer cursing under his breath. Now, after he had turned on the machine and began to type, all the text moved at high speed down the screen and disappeared.

'Now what?' he said out loud.

'Having some more trouble, Mr Dwyer?'

Charlie, who had been observing from the classroom door, came over to join him.

'Everything I type vanishes off the screen,' the teacher told him.

'I see why,' said the boy.

'You do?'

'The cursor key at the bottom is stuck,' said Charlie. He tapped one of the keys several times and the problem was solved. 'There,' he said, giving a broad smile, 'all sorted.'

22

At lunchtime Tom was summoned to see Mr Gaunt.

He knocked on the headmaster's study door and when he heard the shout 'Come in', he entered. Mr Gaunt was staring down at an unopened brown envelope as if wondering whether to open it or not.

'You wanted to see me?' asked Tom.

'Yes, do sit down a moment, please.' He tapped the envelope, then sat back in his chair. 'Here are the results of the eleven-plus. I was telephoned last week and told that they would be arriving today. I've not opened the envelope yet. I was minded to share the information with you before the children, but have decided not to – for the time being, at any rate.'

'May I ask why?' Tom was desperate to know how his pupils had got on. He was surprised that the headmaster wasn't as anxious as he to see how the pupils had fared.

'I am going to see each child who sat the test individually at afternoon break, rather than come into your class and read out the results for all to hear,' Mr Gaunt told him. 'I recall when I got the result of my own eleven-plus, the headmaster read out the results in assembly. He called out the names of those of us who had passed and invited us into his room to congratulate us. Nothing was said to those who had been unsuccessful. I imagine those who failed must have felt pretty miserable.'

Tom could understand that, but not why Mr Gaunt was unwilling to open the envelope and tell him the results there and then. After all, it was his pupils they were talking about and he had spent a good few lunchtimes tutoring them. He thought for a moment, assessing whether or not to say anything. In the end he merely said, 'I see.'

'I do not wish to make a great thing of this,' the headmaster carried on. 'There will doubtlessly be children who will be delighted and others who will be disappointed. I wish to explain to those who have failed the eleven-plus that it is not the end of the world and that many who have not done all that well at school have gone on to great things.'

'I appreciate that,' replied Tom, suddenly prompted to respond, 'but as the children's teacher, don't you feel it might be better coming from me?'

'No, I don't,' said Mr Gaunt. 'I am sure, however, that you will take the opportunity to speak to the children later to congratulate or to commiserate.' He sat up in his chair. 'That's all, thank you.'

Tom was on tenterhooks at afternoon break waiting in the corridor as his pupils went to see Mr Gaunt to hear if they had passed or failed. One by one the children went into the headmaster's study and one by one they emerged with great smiles on their faces. Then they were congratulating each other and crowding around their teacher, chattering excitedly. The exception was Colin, who stood apart from the rest, hands dug deeply in his pockets, looking pensive. Tom felt for the boy. He should never have entered him for the exam. It was too hard for him. Now he had been judged a failure, something that might stay with him for the rest of his life. He chivvied the successful children to go into the playground and get some fresh air, but asked Colin to see him in his class-room. The boy stood by the teacher's desk, a tall, fat, moon-faced boy with lank black hair.

'Are you all right, Colin?' asked Tom.

'Yea, I'm fine, sir,' replied the boy.

'You know, Colin, you might not have got through the eleven-plus, but you are a talented young man with a lot going for you. There is nobody in the class as good as you at art. I can see you one day exhibiting your paintings in London like Mrs Stanhope and becoming a famous artist. I've been really pleased with the way you have behaved and you have made massive progress this year with your work, so try not to be too disappointed.'

The boy looked at his teacher with a puzzled expression on his face.

'But I passed, Mr Dwyer,' he said.

'You passed!' exclaimed Tom.

'Yes, I got through, but I'm not going to the grammar school. I want to go to Clayton Comprehensive. I always have. It's got a much better art department there.'

Tom shook his head. 'Then why did you sit the exam?' he asked.

'To prove to you and my dad that I could do it,' he said.

That evening, Toby Croft was regaling two of his drinking companions about his experiences up at the castle the day before. His account was rambling and suitably embellished.

'So I was left sittin' on a bloody gret unexploded bomb an' everyone else 'ad buggered off an' left me theer,' grumbled the old farmer. 'I could 'ave been blown to kingdom come fer all they cared. I was sat theer on two ton of hexplosive fer a good 'alf 'our afore our Dean shows up, puffed up like a Christmas turkey in a new tweed suit an' bloody deerstalker 'at. 'E comes ovver an' looks down at me wi' 'is 'ands on 'is 'ips. Does 'e 'elp 'is owld dad out o' t''ole? Does 'e 'ell as like! "Tha shall 'ave to gerrup' out o'theer," 'e tells me. "This is private property an' tha's trespassin'."'

'Aye, well,' said Percy, 't'lad were only doin' 'is job. After hall, 'e's hemployed by Sir 'Edley now, in't 'e?'

'Doin' 'is job,' spluttered Toby. 'I'll give 'im' doin' 'is job! Yon gamekeeper's job 'as gone to 'is 'ead. "Come along," 'e says to me, "or I shall 'ave to report thee." Report 'is own father! I'm stood standin' theer lookin' up at 'im—'

'I thowt tha said tha were sittin',' said Arnold Olmeroyde.

'Eh?'

'Tha said tha were sittin' on t'bomb.'

'Sittin' or standin', it meks no odds. So I gets out o' t''ole—'

'Why din't tha gerrout o' t''ole in t'fust place?' asked Percy.

'I'll tell thee why,' Toby retorted, 'because that theer know-it-all teacher up at t'school told me not to move 'cos I might set t'buggcr off.'

Toby's two drinking companions laughed.

''E were 'avin' yer on,' said Arnold. 'It's been theer fer years. It's not likely to explode when tha were sittin' on it.'

'I know that now,' snapped Toby. 'Tha wun't be laughin' if I'd been blown to kingdom come, would tha?'

'Oh, I don't know about that,' said Mrs Mossup, who had been listening. 'We might get a rest from listening to you blathering on.'

'An' I'll tell thee this,' continued Toby, 'when I next see that clever dick, Mester Dwyer, I shall give that young man a piece o' my mind.'

'Well, now's tha chance,' said Percy, tilting his wrinkled head in the direction of the door, 't'lad's just walked in.'

'I'd gu careful if I were thee, Toby,' remarked Arnold. ''E's got quite a temper on 'im, has Mester Dwyer. Tha'll no doubt remember 'ow 'e floored young Jamie Maladroit in 'ere.'

Before Toby could give the teacher the promised piece of his mind (something he was not inclined to do anyway), Tom was collared by John Fairborn.

'Could I have a word?' asked Janette's father.

'Yes, of course,' replied Tom.

He looked over to the bar, where Toby Croft and his

drinking pals were watching. 'Let's sit at the corner table out of earshot,' he said.

They sat down.

'Now, Mr Fairborn,' said Tom. 'What can I do for you?'

'Look, Mr Dwyer ... Tom,' said Janette's father, laying two hands as flat as spades on the table top, 'I owe you an apology. When you telephoned the farm and asked for Jan's number, you will remember, I wouldn't give it to you.'

'That's right,' Tom said. 'You see, I only wanted to tell her that—'

'Let me finish,' interrupted the farmer. 'I said I wouldn't give you her number because I thought she wouldn't thank me for doing so. You see, I assumed she wasn't interested in you and didn't want to get involved and I didn't want you getting your hopes up. I knew you were keen on her. Well, it seems I got the wrong end of the stick. I did that before when I had a go at you, thinking you were the driver of that sports car and nearly knocked Mrs Partington off her bike. Anyway, I was wrong then and I'm wrong now.'

'Look, Mr Fairborn—' began Tom.

'Please, let me finish. When she got back from visiting your cottage and learnt I had withheld her number, she was not best pleased with me, not pleased at all. I'm afraid my daughter has a bit of a temper. You've probably noticed that. She told me I was trying to control her life and I had no business interfering. I thought I was only doing what was for the best. Anyway, as I've said, I got it wrong. I thought Jan wasn't that keen on you; I thought that you were a decent-enough chap, but not her sort – not exactly dull, but a bit too safe and conventional for someone like her. You see, she's a feisty lass and has always gone for men in the past who had a spark about them, a touch of danger, the adventurous sort. I don't think I'm putting this very well, am I?'

'I think you are,' replied Tom. 'I've never thought of

myself as being dangerous or very adventurous.' He had thought the very same thing as Mr Fairborn had concluded. When Janette had told him there was no future in their relationship, maybe she had thought him good-natured and dependable but unexciting. Hadn't she told him how insular and predictable life was in Risingdale, that there was nothing to keep her there and how she longed for more challenge and excitement?

'When Jan had calmed down,' Mr Fairborn continued, 'I discovered that she is keen on you; in fact, she's fallen for you in a big way. She only realised it when she was in Nottingham.' He looked into Tom's eyes. 'She misses you.'

Tom sighed. 'She misses me?'

'An' what are you two plotting, tucked away in t'corner?'

Mr Croft had ambled over.

'Bugger off!' Mr Fairborn told him. 'This is a private conversation.'

'Charming,' muttered the farmer, before returning to the bar.

'Anyway,' said the farmer to Tom, 'I've put my cards on the table. I don't want Jan to know that I've seen you and told you all this. I'd be in trouble again for interfering. Let's keep this conversation to ourselves.'

'Yes, of course,' said Tom.

'I want the best for my daughter, Tom,' said Mr Fairborn. 'Maybe I've been a bit overprotective but I always did what I thought was for the best.' He reached in his pocket and produced a scrap of paper that he placed on the table in front of him. 'This is Jan's number. I imagine you will want to give her a ring.'

Later that evening in his cottage, Tom stared at the telephone, thinking what he might say to Janette. He felt confused. Of course he still had feelings for her, but there was someone else in his life now. He picked up the handset and dialled.

'Hello, Jan, it's me.'

'Oh, hi, Tom,' she said.

'I was wondering, are you coming home next weekend?'

'Yes, I am.'

'Could we meet?'

'That would be lovely,' she said. 'We could go to that smart restaurant that you mentioned, if you like. Le Bon Viveur, wasn't it?'

'Yes, it was, but could it be the Ring o' Bells café in Clayton? What about eleven o'clock on Saturday morning?' This was to be a meeting, thought Tom, and not a date.

'Oh . . . yes. If you prefer that.' She sounded disappointed. 'I'll see you there, then.'

Janette was already in the café when Tom arrived the following Saturday morning. She was sitting at a corner table looking as pretty as ever and smiled when she caught sight of him.

Tom ordered coffees and sat down opposite her.

'It's good to see you,' she said, rather nervously, he thought.

'Likewise,' he replied. There was an embarrassed silence. 'So, how's the high-powered job going in Nottingham?'

'A bit too high-powered,' she admitted. 'I expected a change but not quite as exacting or as exciting. As I mentioned to you, I think I might give it up and return to Risingdale. It really depends.'

'It's a big decision,' said Tom. 'You might feel differently after you've been a bit longer in the job. If you give it time—'

'Look, Tom,' she said suddenly. 'I wanted to see you . . .' She broke off when the coffee arrived.

'It's the princess,' said the waitress. 'You were in the pantomime at Christmas.'

'That's right,' said Janette.

'And you're here with the prince. You were both dead good,' the young woman told them. 'It was really romantic.

Everyone said you were dead perfect for the parts, the perfect couple.'

'That's nice of you to say,' said Tom. The waitress made no effort to move, but smiled and stared. 'Thank you for the coffee,' he said, hinting that the waitress should be about her business.

'No problem,' said the young woman, returning to the counter, where she pointed out the stars of *The Sleeping Beauty* to a colleague.

'I was about to say,' continued Janette, 'that when we spoke in the King's Head that evening before I left for Nottingham, I said things I now realise I shouldn't have. I have a bit of a disposition of sometimes opening my mouth and later regretting what I said. I think you know that from past experience. Anyway, I told you I didn't think there was any future for us, that things might have been different if I were staying in Risingdale, but . . .' She took a deep breath. 'I've been thinking about things lately – actually, I've been thinking about you – and if I come home, I hope we might pick up where we left off. I hope you might forget what I said.'

'Oh dear.' Tom sighed, thinking of the kindest way of saying what he needed to tell her. 'I remember that evening in the King's Head as if it were yesterday. I really thought that there was a future for us. I'd not met a girl like you: spirited, strong-minded, clever, amusing and very pretty, but—'

'But?' she interrupted.

'I don't know what to say, Jan,' he told her. He looked down at his coffee cup, not wishing to meet her eyes. 'You see, I've met somebody and—'

'Is it the very attractive woman I saw you with the last time we were in this café, the parent with the poorly child?'

'It is,' he replied. 'I've grown to really like her. I don't know whether or not she feels the same way about me, but . . .'

'Oh, I think she does,' said Janette. 'I'm not blind, Tom. I saw the way she looked at you. I seem to have made a bit of a fool of myself, haven't I?' She got up to go. 'I hope things work out for you. She's a lucky woman.' Then she was gone before he could say anything.

Tom sat, still staring at his coffee cup. He felt so confused. He still had feelings for Jan, but now he had a strong affection for Amanda, too. He sighed as he recalled his aunt's words that 'two loves don't make a right'.

The teachers were in a buoyant mood when Tom arrived at the staffroom before school on Friday morning.

'I know it's uncharitable of me,' Mrs Golightly was saying, with a giggle in her voice, 'but I have to admit I had a small touch of satisfaction when Mrs Leadbeater told us the news.'

'*Schadenfreude*,' remarked Mr Cadwallader.

'What?'

'To take delight in another person's misfortune, Bertha,' he explained.

'I wouldn't go so far as to say that I take delight in what happened to him, just that I can't feel a whole lot of sympathy for the man.'

'Hung by his own petard,' said Mr Cadwallader.

'The phrase is "hoist with his own petard",' corrected Joyce.

'I thought it was "hung",' replied her colleague.

'It is what Hamlet says of Polonius,' Joyce told him. 'I did study drama and theatre arts, so I think you will allow that I know what I am talking about.'

'Will you stop speaking in riddles, you two,' Mrs Golightly told them.

'What I mean is—' Mr Cadwallader began.

'Well, I, for one, am delighted,' interrupted Joyce. 'He's finally got his comeuppance. He should have practised what he preached.'

'I was about to say that,' said Mr Cadwallader.

'Will somebody tell me what you are all talking about?' asked Tom.

'It's about Mr Nettles,' he was told. 'Mrs Leadbeater telephoned the Education Office.'

'To speak to Mr Nettles,' added Joyce, 'and that sharp-tongued clerk said he was unavailable.'

'That's not surprising,' said Tom. 'He's always tied up.'

'Well, this time he's strapped up.'

'What?'

'Our least favourite education officer has had a fall,' she said. 'From what Mrs Leadbeater was telling us, he was coming out of County Hall "in the inclement weather", as he termed it, when, failing to be vigilant, he began sliding, skating and skidding on the slippery surface, fell down the steps and succeeded in breaking both wrists.'

'Ouch,' said Tom, pulling a face.

'He is, of course, now unable to write,' declared Joyce.

'Which means,' said Mr Cadwallader, 'that we will not be subjected to any more of his meaningless memorandums for some time to come.'

'Memoranda,' said Joyce.

'Do you mind not correcting me,' he responded.

'Actually, I think both are acceptable,' said Tom. 'We were studying plurals in class and—'

The discussion ended when Mr Gaunt entered the staffroom accompanied by Mrs Gosling and a morose-looking Mr Leadbeater. He was carrying a box wrapped in coloured paper with a red ribbon around it. The cleaner had changed out of her usual electric-pink nylon overall over a thick knitted cardigan and red and white gingham frock and was wearing a heavy woollen coat of blue and green check as shapeless as a sack of potatoes, topped with a wide-brimmed red hat sporting two pheasant feathers. She held an old canvas bag and an ancient umbrella with a fox-head handle.

'Whatever is the woman wearing?' Joyce muttered to Mrs Golightly.

'I imagine she thinks she's the Lady of the Manor now she's back at Marston Towers,' whispered Bertha.

'If I might have your attention for a moment,' said the headmaster. 'You will all be aware that today Mrs Gosling is leaving us to take up her position as Sir Hedley's housekeeper. I am sure you would all not wish this occasion to pass without joining with me in thanking her for the sterling work she has undertaken while she has been with us. The school has never looked as spotless and I am sure I can speak for all of us when I say that she will be greatly missed.'

'Thank you very much, I'm sure,' said the cleaner (aka assistant caretaker). 'I can't say that it's been a total pleasure cleaning up after the kiddies.' She looked in Mr Cadwallader's direction. He had secreted the biscuit he had been eating down the side of his chair when Mr Gaunt and his antagonist entered the room. 'And some of the teachers,' Mrs Gosling added, 'but I have to say that I have enjoyed my time here. Well, most of it, anyway. In many ways, I shall miss being with you but, as I have said to Mr Gaunt, Sir Hedley needs me.'

'Would you care to say a few words, Mr Leadbeater?' asked the headmaster.

'No, not really,' replied the caretaker, thinking the sooner the woman was off the premises, the better.

'Then, without more ado,' said Mr Gaunt, passing Mrs Gosling the brightly wrapped box, 'I should like to present you with a small token of our appreciation. It is a cut-glass vase with an inscription.'

'Thank you very much,' said the cleaner, taking the box and placing it on the table before her. She reached into her bag and produced a large, multicoloured tea cosy. 'This is a little present for the teachers,' she said. 'I've knitted it myself.'

Mrs Golightly exchanged a glance with her colleagues. It

was an identical article to the monstrosity her mother had purchased at the WI 'bring and buy' sale, which had ended up on the head of Mr Sheepshanks' scarecrow and did a magnificent job scaring away the rooks.

'We shall treasure it,' said Joyce, with a wry smile.

Mr Gaunt accompanied Mrs Gosling to the gate of the school. Parked on a small square of land just off the road was a battered white van. The driver wound down the window.

'How do, Gerry,' he shouted.

'Oh, hello, Clive.'

'Here to pick my mam up. She's done up like a dog's dinner today,' replied the young farmer, 'because I'm taking her to that posh restaurant in Clayton for her lunch and then up to Marston Towers.'

'Stop rabbiting on,' Mrs Gosling told her son, climbing into the passenger seat. 'And you could have opened the door for me and given me a hand with this box.'

Her son pulled a face. 'Sorry, Mam,' he said.

'I was sorry to hear about you losing the three ewes,' said Mr Gaunt to her son.

'Aye, well, these things happen,' replied the young farmer philosophically. 'I've now got a cow down with something. I had the vet out this morning.'

'Do you know,' said the headmaster, 'I haven't seen Jack Eddleston since he came out to see my sheep scab. How's he doing?'

'Oh, he's gone,' replied Clive. 'Sold the practice and took off to live in Spain. The new vet is very good and up on all the modern methods. Sorted my sick cow out in no time.'

'He's a decent chap, then?'

'Are we moving or what?' came a strident voice from inside the van.

'Just hold your horses, will you a minute, Mam,' her son told her. He resumed his conversation with Mr Gaunt. 'The new vet's not a man. It's a woman. She's Scottish but I won't hold that against her. She's only been down here for a couple of weeks and is making a very good impression from what I've heard. She was up at the Lomax farm and Neil Lomax said she knew what she was doing. Actually, she was asking after you. I gather she used to work for Jack Eddleston some years back and you know her.'

'What's her name?' asked Mr Gaunt. His heart suddenly began to hammer in his chest.

Clive scratched his head. 'Now, then, I did know it,' he said. 'It's a Scottish name – MacTavish, MacGregor—'

'It wouldn't be Macdonald, would it?' asked the headmaster.

'Aye, it is Macdonald, although she's not at all stand-offish. "Call me Moira," she said.'

The assignment Tom set his class that day was to ask the children to write about what they might like to do when they left school. Their accounts contained some unlikely ambitions. Vicky wanted to be a film star, Judith an astronaut and Christopher a racing-car driver. Others were predictable. Colin, of course, dreamed of being a famous artist and George and Carol of running their own farms. The most surprising aspiration was Simon's. He wanted to work in an abattoir. At morning break, Tom, intrigued by the boy's desire to work in such a place, approached Simon, who was sitting on the play-ground wall.

'Hello, Mr Dwyer,' said the boy. He was halfway through eating a chocolate bar.

'Hello, Simon,' replied Tom, sitting down next to him. 'So you want to work in an abattoir when you leave school?'

'Yes, I do.' The boy popped a square of chocolate into his mouth and chomped noisily.

'It strikes me as a rather unusual ambition,' said the teacher.

'Why's that, sir?'

'Well, I don't suppose many people would think of wanting to work in such a place.'

'It's a good job and someone's got to do it, Mr Dwyer, otherwise we'd all be vegetarians.'

'I thought you would want to work on your parents' farm,' said Tom.

'No chance. That'd be like too much hard work.'

'So what attracts you about working in an abattoir?' asked Tom, genuinely interested.

The boy placed the chocolate bar on the wall beside him. He then counted the reasons on his fingers. 'First, it's good money. It's much better paid than working on a farm. Second, it's mostly indoor work and the place is at a constant temperature. With farming, it's freezing cold in winter, red hot in summer and chucking it down with rain for the rest of the time. Third, you get good holidays. A farmer can't take a holiday because the animals have to be fed. Fourth, you get prime cuts of meat. My Uncle Terry, who works at the Clayton abattoir, only eats fillet steak and the best cuts of pork. Five, it's an interesting job. Does that answer your question, Mr Dwyer?'

'Yes,' Tom told him, 'you've explained yourself very well.'

'When I say interesting,' the boy continued, 'I mean there can be a fair bit of excitement at the abattoir. Last week one of the cows – I think it must have sensed something unpleasant was going to happen to it – bolted. A lot of people think cows are meek and mild animals and that it's the bulls you have to watch out for. Well, a herd of cows in a field, especially if there are calves about, can be very dangerous, and a frightened cow can be a killer if you get in its way.' He picked up the chocolate bar and broke off another square and popped it in his mouth.

'So what happened?' asked Tom.

'My Uncle Terry sent for the police and they cornered it in that posh school in Clayton, but not before it caused bloody mayhem. That's what my Uncle Terry told my dad.' The boy gave Tom the most innocent of looks. 'I don't use words like that, Mr Dwyer.'

'Did they manage to catch it?' asked Tom, smiling.

'Oh no, Mr Dwyer,' said the boy, 'a police sniper shot it.'

'I can't help feeling sorry for the animal,' said Tom.

'That what my dad says about people who don't come from the country. They feel sorry for animals. He says they're too sentimental. "Oh, the poor fox being hunted," they say. They might change their minds if they saw what a fox does if it gets in a hen coop. It bites the heads off all the chickens. My dad shoots them. Then there's "the cute little squirrels". Tree rats, they are, and can strip a sapling and destroy a forest. My dad shoots them as well.' The boy was getting into his stride. Tom didn't stop him but listened, fascinated. 'Then there's "the furry little rabbits". They can clean a vegetable patch and a garden in a day; the only thing they don't eat is the rhubarb. Those are other pests my dad shoots. Then there's your "cute little moles". They shovel soil up at lightning speed and ruin a field. My dad doesn't shoot them, though. He puts traps down. So you see, Mr Dwyer, sometimes animals have to be killed.'

'I see that, Simon,' said Tom, 'but these animals you describe are pests. Wouldn't you be upset seeing cows and pigs and sheep killed day after day?'

'I don't suppose I'd enjoy it,' replied the boy, sucking on his bottom lip, 'but the animals in an abattoir are killed in a humane way and I suppose you'd get used to it after a bit.'

'I wouldn't like to see those animals killed,' said Tom.

'Then you should stop eating meat, Mr Dwyer,' the boy told him.

'I think you have made your point, Simon,' the teacher told him, getting up from the wall.

'Did you know that pigs can have brown eyes?' asked the boy.

'No, that's something I didn't know,' replied the teacher. 'The only pigs I've seen have pink eyes.'

'Do you know why some pigs have brown eyes?' asked the boy.

'Is it the breed of pig?'

'No, you see, to fatten the pigs up, they give them chocolate.' He held up the half-eaten chocolate bar. 'They get it from one of the big chocolate factories – off-cuts and misshapes and bits they don't want. Chocolate is the best food for fattening pigs and they eat so much their eyes turn brown. That's a fact. Interesting, isn't it?'

'It is,' said Tom.

'There is one thing I wouldn't like about working in an abattoir,' said Simon.

'What's that?'

'Rats, Mr Dwyer, rats. Where there's lots of meat about, you'll always get plenty of rats. My Uncle Terry says they can grow to the size of a rabbit – more than a foot long, and weigh over a pound – but you can get them much bigger. They can't put poison down because it's an abattoir and traps aren't much good.'

'So what do they do?'

'Cats, Mr Dwyer, cats. That's the best and quickest way to get rid of vermin. That's what my Uncle Terry says.'

Tom thought of Mrs Golightly's cat that he had seen on his first visit to her cottage. He could not see that fat, lazy purring feline, which stretched out in front of the fire, stirring itself to tackle a rat the size of a rabbit.

'Now, when a cat gets hold of a rat—' the boy was still explaining.

'That's really interesting, Simon,' cut in the teacher, having heard quite enough, 'but I think it's nearly the end of break.'

'No, there's plenty of time yet, sir,' said the boy. 'I haven't told you yet what they do with the carcasses.'

'Perhaps later,' Tom told him.

'Would you like my last piece of chocolate, Mr Dwyer?' asked Simon.

'No, thank you.'

'You know you've been arranging these trips for our class,' said the boy.

'Yes.'

'Going to the museum in town last term, and up to the castle – well, I could ask my Uncle Terry if he could arrange a visit to the abattoir. What do you think, Mr Dwyer?'

'I'll give it some serious thought,' the teacher told him, thinking to himself that it would be the last place on Earth he would take a party of schoolchildren.

23

In the parlour of the King's Head, mother and daughter were having a heart-to-heart.

'I'm dead nervous, Mam,' said Leanne Mossup.

She was a large healthy-looking and heavily pregnant young woman with curly brown shoulder-length hair, big, watery grey eyes and prominent front teeth. She was wearing an extremely tight-fitting dress that emphasised the considerable pre-natal bump, on which she rested her hands.

'Well, there's nothing to be nervous about,' her mother told her. 'Sir Hedley is a real gentleman and he's been very kind and considerate, sending you money and asking after your health. He could have reacted very differently when he was told you were having his son's baby. He could have denied it and told us he wanted nothing to do with it. I bet that wife of his reacted very differently when she heard the news. You want to be thankful that Sir Hedley has been so understanding.'

'I know that,' replied Leanne, petulantly, 'but I'm still dead nervous.'

'You were not that nervous, my girl, when you walked through the public bar this lunchtime as bold as brass, turning people's heads and getting them gossiping.'

'That were different,' pouted her daughter. 'They were just the locals and I couldn't care less what they think. I've got nothing to be ashamed of. There are lots of women these days that have kids with no father on the scene, and people don't think any worse of them.'

But these people don't live in Risingdale, thought Mrs Mossup. She could name a good few residents who would be very disapproving of an unmarried mother. She smiled. Mind you, they'll keep their critical comments to themselves when they learn who the grandfather of the child is.

'It's just that Sir Hedley's, well, he's really posh and important,' said Leanne. 'That's why I'm nervous.'

When the landlady's daughter had informed her mother that she was pregnant and refused to reveal the identity of the father, Mrs Mossup had been less than sympathetic. After a few well-chosen words, she had packed Leanne off to Scarborough to stay with her Auntie Rita, who ran a boarding house. It was decided that the girl should remain there and have the baby and then Leanne would either keep the child or put it up for adoption. Auntie Rita had managed to wheedle out of her niece the name of the father. It came as a shock to Mrs Mossup that the father turned out to be James Maladroit, the baby the result of a roll in the hay after the Young Farmers' barn dance.

Things, however, had not gone to plan in Scarborough. Mrs Mossup's sister, not the most sensitive and kind-hearted of women, found in her niece an unpaid worker and made the girl cook the residents' breakfasts, wait at table, do the washing, make the beds and take on numerous other domestic tasks. Leanne had finally had enough of being a skivvy and told her aunt, in no uncertain terms, what she could do. She had arrived home unannounced that lunchtime and told her mother she would not be returning to Scarborough. Mrs Mossup had lost no time in telephoning Sir Hedley, acquainting him of her daughter's return. He had asked to call in at the King's Head that evening.

'So what does he want?' asked Leanne now.

'You'll find out when he comes,' her mother told her, 'and take that mardy look off your face.'

'Well, I'm dead nervous,' said the girl for the umpteenth time.

Sir Hedley's arrival at the King's Head did not go unnoticed by the regulars. Toby Croft turned to his pal Percy when he saw the baronet striding for the bar and he nodded knowingly and winked.

''Ere ageean,' he remarked. 'Yon squire's in an' out of 'ere like there's no tomorra an' we know why, don't we? Can't keep away from 'er.'

Wayne, the young barman, had been told by the landlady to expect the important visitor and to show Sir Hedley into the parlour as soon as he arrived and, before Toby could make himself known to the squire in the hope of getting a free pint, the baronet disappeared through the door behind the bar. The old farmer stared at his empty glass. Moments later his son came into the inn. He was dressed in a smart sports jacket and tie.

'Look what t'cat's dragged in,' he grunted.

'Evenin', Dad,' said Dean brightly. He ordered himself a pint.

'Don't thee "Evenin', Dad" me,' growled Toby. 'Layin' daan t'law up at t'castle, hevictin' me what was doin' no 'arm an' me hofferin' to 'elp.'

'Tha were only up theer to see what tha might find,' said his son.

'An' then 'avin' not an 'a'peth o' sympathy for yer owld dad when I were nearly blown to kingdom come by a bloody gret bomb,' grumbled his father.

'Fat chance o' that,' his son told him. 'T'bomb's been theer fer years. Tha were in no danger o' being blown to kingdom come.'

'There's your pint, Mr Croft,' said the barman to Dean.

'Thanks, Wayne. 'Ave one yer sen.'

'Oh, ta very much, Mr Croft.'

'What's wi' t'Mester Croft?' cried Toby. 'Since when 'ave thee been Mester Croft?'

'That lad o' yourn's gone up in t'world now,' said Percy. 'Tha should show 'im a bit more respect.'

'Respect! I'll show 'im t'toe o' my boot, that's what I'll show 'im.'

'So what 'appened abaat that bomb then, Dean?' asked Percy. 'I don't recall 'earin' any hexplosion. Did they not blow it up then?'

'Army come out an' defused it,' he was told. 'Then they took it away. From what they said, it were a dud bomb anyroad an' were no risk, so there were no chance of mi dad bein' blown up.' Then he added under his breath, 'More's t'pity.'

'Aye, well, I din't know that it weren't dangerous!' cried Toby. 'An' nob'dy else did.' He turned to his pal. 'I'll tell thee this, Percy, there's nowt as cruel as an hungrateful child.'

'I were only doin' mi job,' his son told him. 'Tha were trespassin'. Tha shun't 'ave been theer.'

'Aye, well, don't thee come runnin' back to me when that fancy job o' yourn dun't work out,' grumbled the young man's father, 'because I shan't 'ave thee back.'

'An' 'ow's it goin' on t'farm then?' asked Dean, grinning. He had heard that the farm workers his father had employed after his son had left had downed tools after a couple of days, unprepared to work for such a cantankerous and constantly complaining employer.

'Never thee mind,' barked Toby. 'It's nowt to do wi' thee.'

'Your lad's lookin' in fine fettle,' said Percy. 'Quite a difference from when 'e worked fer thee up at t'farm. 'E scrubs up well, does thy Dean, an' from what I've 'eard, lad's med a real good himpression at Marston Towers.'

Toby scowled.

'Let me get thee a drink, Percy,' said Dean. 'Mi dad can gerris own fer once in 'is life.'

In the parlour of the King's Head, Sir Hedley nursed a glass of malt whisky that Mrs Mossup had thrust into his hand before he could refuse. He sat opposite a tense-looking Leanne, who nervously twisted a strand of stray hair. She eyed him uneasily.

'And how are you, my dear?' the squire asked, smiling warmly.

'I'm fine, thank you, Sir Hedley.'

'And the baby?'

'The baby's fine, as well.'

'That's very good to hear,' he said. He took a sip of his drink. 'You must be wondering why I am here?' he asked.

'Mam said you'd tell me,' Leanne replied.

'And indeed I will.' He placed his glass down on the table, sat back in the chair and fingered the silver watch chain dangling from his waistcoat. 'Now, while you have been in Scarborough, your mother and I have been having a conversation about your future and that of your baby's. We are agreed that we feel you should keep the child.'

'I want to,' replied the girl mulishly.

'That is good to hear,' said the baronet. 'We also feel that a public house is not the best environment in which to raise a child and—'

Leanne shot up in her chair. 'You're not taking my baby away, are you?' she cried.

'No, no, nothing of the sort,' he reassured her. 'Nobody has the power to take away your baby.'

'Just listen to what Sir Hedley has to say, Leanne,' said the girl's mother.

'As I have said,' continued the baronet, 'we feel a public house is not the most beneficial place to bring up a child and I am suggesting, and your mother is in agreement with me, that I make available one of my cottages in Rattan Row for you. Number 8 will be coming vacant very soon. I . . . we feel were you to live there, you would have your own home near your mother – who will be on hand to give you any help you might need – but you wouldn't be under her feet. The cottage is warm and cosy with a fully equipped kitchen and has recently been furnished.'

'You mean I could have my own little cottage?' asked Leanne.

'That is what we are proposing.'

'I'd love that,' she said, suddenly becoming animated. 'I really would, but what about the rent?'

'There would be no rent to pay and all your bills will be taken care of. You don't need to worry at all about money. I shall see to all that. My only condition is that you let me be a part of your child's life.'

'What do you think, Mam?' asked the girl.

'Did you not hear what Sir Hedley said?' replied her mother impatiently. 'He said I was in agreement. I think anyone who turns down such a generous offer wants her head examining. I think it's a wonderful idea.'

'So what do you think?' Sir Hedley asked Leanne.

'I'd love it,' she said. 'I'd really love it.'

Before returning to Risingdale, she had anticipated with dread having to live with her mother and bring up the baby under her watchful eye. She visualised a life being ordered about and criticised and made to work for her keep. Her mother was not unlike Auntie Rita in this. Now she had been offered freedom and independence, a chance of escaping to a place of her own. It was perfect.

Sir Hedley picked up his glass and took a drink. 'That seems to be settled then,' he said. He placed down his glass and looked at Leanne. 'Now, something else I have discussed with your mother is whether you would feel comfortable with me making it clear to everyone that my son is . . . was, the father of your child.'

'I was sorry to hear what happened to James,' said Leanne. 'I know a lot of people didn't get on with him, but I liked him. He could be really nice when he wanted to be.'

'I'm pleased to hear that,' said Sir Hedley, who had never seen this side of his son's nature. He reached for his glass again and took a gulp of his drink. 'So how do you feel about making it known that James was the father?'

'I thought you and Mam wanted it to be kept a secret,' said Leanne.

'No, I think the time has come to be up front about it,' said Sir Hedley. 'I feel we need to be open and honest about the child's paternity, for it will stifle all the speculation and stop any gossip.'

'Well, I'd like that,' said Leanne, 'because if we don't, people would be asking me questions and making comments.' She was still angry with her Auntie Rita, who had never missed an opportunity of quizzing her about the father until, sick of being interrogated, she had blurted it out.

'That's another thing settled then,' said Mrs Mossup, looking very pleased that things had turned out so amicably. People would not be so quick to judge her daughter when they discovered who the grandfather of her baby was. She visualised being a regular visitor to Marston Towers, mixing with the great and the good. Yes, she thought, her daughter had landed on her feet.

'When shall we tell people?' asked Leanne.

'There's no time like the present,' said Sir Hedley. 'The public bar must be about full of the locals by now. I suggest I go out there and tell them. If you don't feel you can face everyone, Leanne, then you can stay here.'

'No, I'm not stopping here,' she said bullishly, getting up from her chair and looking, like her mother, very pleased with herself. All her previous nervousness had evaporated. 'I'd like to come with you.' I shall enjoy seeing the astonished faces, she thought to herself, when they hear I am carrying the grandchild of the richest and most influential man in the Dale.

The three of them went into the public bar and Mrs Mossup rang a large brass bell behind the counter, used to indicate orders for the last drinks, to gain the customers' attention.

'Could I have you all listen for a moment, please!' she shouted. 'Sir Hedley would like to say a few words.' She then joined her daughter behind the counter and, in a rare show of affection, put her arm around Leanne's shoulder.

The squire stood in a prominent position in the middle of the room, legs apart, one hand in his pocket, the other fingering his silver watch chain. He surveyed the faces before him and recognised many of his tenants and some of his estate workers.

'I am sorry to disturb your evening,' he said, 'but there is something I need to say. I will not keep you long.' He coughed. 'I am telling you this to stifle any gossip and stem any speculation. You will, no doubt, have noticed that Mrs Mossup's daughter has returned to the village.' All eyes turned to look at Leanne. She gave a small, self-satisfied smile. 'You will also be aware that she is having a baby soon. Well, with her permission, I should like to tell you who the father of her child is.'

'Good God,' muttered Toby. 'T'babby's t'squire's love child.'

'The father is . . . or rather, was, my son,' said Sir Hedley. 'You all know that James was killed in a tragic accident. Well, I have lost a son, but am to gain a grandchild, and I am delighted at the prospect.'

There was not a sound in the room, but many amazed expressions on the faces of the villagers.

'Now, those who know me will be aware that I am not a man who makes threats, but I will say this. I hope that Leanne is treated with kindness, understanding and respect as the mother of my grandchild. Should she not receive this consideration, then I shall not be best pleased. Now, I would like to invite you all to have a drink – on me, of course – and toast the baby.'

Sir Hedley's speech was greeted with applause and then by a rush to the bar. Toby was the first in the queue.

When Mrs Mossup went to help Wayne serve the customers who were crowding around the bar to order their drinks, Dean approached her daughter.

''Ello, Leanne,' he said shyly.

'Hi, Dean,' she replied, giving him one of her sweetest smiles and putting on her sweetest voice.

'Tha're looking well.'

'So are you,' she replied. 'You look different.'

Leanne remembered Dean as an awkward, gawky, unsophisticated youth whose only conversation seemed to be about sheep and tractors. His usual mode of dress, when not working on his father's farm, looked as if he had trawled the remnants of a jumble sale: white shirt, a size too big, a shapeless, woolly grey jumper, baggy jeans and old trainers. He gave off a smell of silage and earth. That evening he did indeed look different, dressed in a smart herringbone jacket, cream shirt, stylish corduroy trousers and brown brogues. He also smelled of aftershave.

'I don't work fer mi dad any more,' he told her. 'I'm hassistant gamekeeper up at Marston Towers. I work fer Sir 'Edley.'

'You've gone up in the world,' she said.

So have you, he thought.

'So how's t'babby?'

'Fine.'

'I'm pleased that things 'ave worked for thee, Leanne.'

The girl was touched by his comment and bit her bottom lip. 'Thanks, Dean,' she said.

'I were wonderin' like,' he said, brushing back a tuft of hair, 'I was wonderin' if yer not doin' owt tomorra neet, if tha wants to come to t'cinema wi' me. There's a new picture on at t'Gala. You wun't 'ave to gu on t'bus. I can borra Mester Greenwood's pick-up.'

Leanne looked at him for a moment and then smiled.

'Course, if yer busy, then—'

'I'm not busy,' she cut him off, 'and I'd like to go.'

Dean gave a great grin. 'Really?'

'That's what I said.'

'I'll pick thee up at seven then.'

At the end of the bar, the couple's tête-à-tête had not gone unnoticed.

'I see yer lad were quick off of t'mark,' observed Percy.

'Aye, I can see that,' replied Toby thoughtfully, rubbing his bristly chin. 'If our Dean plays 'is cards reight, 'e's quids in. Thee mark my words, that lass waint gu short o' money, not after what t'squires just said, an' 'er kid'll in'erit t'squire's estate an' big 'ouse an' all.'

Tom was missing all the drama that was unfolding at the King's Head, for on his way back from a visit to his Auntie Bridget's, he noticed the lights were on in the studio. He parked his car and decided to call on Amanda. He had thought about her a great deal lately, picturing her smile, her bright eyes, the soft golden hair and flawless complexion. But it wasn't just the physical attraction that drew him to her like a moth around a flame. She was clever and confident, with a tender heart and a captivating personality. She was also brave, dealing with her son's illness with great courage and fortitude. Tom was smitten, that was for sure. He sat for a moment in the car, wondering if this might be the right moment to tell her his feelings. He thought of what Leo had said: 'She likes you. She likes you a lot and talks about you quite often. She says you're a really good man.'

He found Amanda standing with hands on hips examining her pictures, which had been laid out on the floor before her. She was dressed simply in a loose-fitting blouse, cherry-coloured cardigan and black slacks, and looked beautiful. Tom stood at the door for a moment and watched. Then he coughed.

'Oh, hello,' she said, looking around. 'Come in.' She went to meet him and kissed him lightly on the cheek. 'You are just the man I'm looking for.'

'Really?' replied Tom. 'That's good to hear.'

'I need a fit young man to help me mount my pictures on the wall. I am trying to arrange an exhibition before the first batch goes to the publisher in London next week and want to show those in the village the fruits of my labours. There is still much more to do, but I have the sketches and photographs and can complete the rest later. Next Saturday I'm going to host a bit of a do – just drinks and nibbles – to thank everyone for being so cooperative and for making me feel so welcome.'

'I thought you might like to join me for a drink this evening,' he said.

'Not tonight, Tom, I have so much to do. Perhaps another time.' She looked down at the pictures and frowned. 'I think I'll put the two landscapes of the castle together. They make a nice pair. Did Colin tell you he has given his picture of the church to Mr Pendlebury? That was kind of him, wasn't it?'

'What about tomorrow?' asked Tom.

'Pardon?' She had a faraway look in her eyes.

'To go out for a drink.'

'I'd love to, but there is so much to do,' she said. 'It's really hectic for me at the moment, trying to get things organised and finish a couple of landscapes. I've not stopped.'

'Then you need a break,' persisted Tom. 'I'll give you a hand with all this tomorrow. Leave it tonight and come for a drink with me.'

'Another time,' she said. 'Now what about the portraits? Who do I put with whom?'

Tom stood beside her and studied the pictures. She smelled of expensive perfume. There were some stunning landscapes and detailed studies of buildings, including the ruined castle, the duck pond and the school, but what interested him the most was the collection of portraits. These included likenesses of several locals, including Toby Croft scowling, Percy with a startled expression, a solemn Dick Greenwood, Mrs Gosling staring like a fish on a slab, Mrs Mossup looking queenly and Mr Gaunt gazing thoughtfully. Sir Hedley, red-cheeked, sporting the impressive walrus moustache above a wide mouth and with the dark hooded eyes, looked every inch the squire. The artist had captured the likenesses perfectly, but all her subjects looked so serious. There wasn't a smile between them. He recalled what Amanda had told him, that those sitting for their portraits are unable to sustain a smile. Nevertheless, he thought, the collection will certainly give the impression to those who view them that Dales folk are a miserable lot.

'What do you think?' she asked.

'They're brilliant,' Tom replied. 'You're brilliant.' He took a breath. 'Amanda,' he began. 'I need to say something—'

She was clearly not listening. 'I thought I would put Sir Hedley in the centre of the portraits. I was minded to ask to paint his wife, but I found her a frightful woman. She called into the studio, you know.'

'I've been wanting to speak to you,' Tom started again. 'I've been thinking about you a lot lately, about us, and—'

'Could it wait?' she said, resting a hand on Tom's arm. 'It's just that I can't concentrate on anything until I've sorted out the exhibition.'

'Yes, of course,' he said sadly. 'It can wait.'

It had been an unusually quiet morning at the general store and post office in Barton-in-the-Dale. The proprietor, Mrs Sloughthwaite – she of the impressive memory and sharp observation, the very eyes and ears of the village and surrounding area – had had only the one customer that day, an unforthcoming youth with long hair and spots who had hardly exchanged a word and who had pushed the packet of cigarettes he had bought into his pocket without so much as a 'Thank you'.

Things, however, looked as if they might pick up when the door of the shop opened to the tinkling of the bell, and a small plump woman with a broad face and darting eyes entered.

This was the sort of customer the shopkeeper liked: someone from whom she might extract a great deal of gossip and interesting information.

'My, but it's back-endish out there this morning,' said the customer, shivering. 'I thought spring was around the corner, but it's cold enough to freeze the flippers off of an Arctic penguin.' The woman wore a thick multicoloured woollen scarf, matching gloves and a yellow and pink knitted hat shaped like a tea cosy. She carried a shapeless canvas shopping bag and an impressive umbrella with a fox-head handle.

'Hello, love,' the shopkeeper greeted her cheerfully, raising herself from the counter on which she had been resting her bay window of a bust. 'It is unfeasible weather for this time of year, I'll give you that, but I can see you are well-instalated against the cold. It's a very fetching outfit you're wearing, very colourful.'

'I knitted it myself,' said the customer. 'I'm a dab hand with the needles, even if I do say so myself.'

She could stand on a cliff and stop shipping in that get-up, thought Mrs Sloughthwaite.

'What can I get you?' asked the shopkeeper.

'I'd like to place this card in the window,' said the customer. 'I'm looking for a part-time cleaner.'

Mrs Sloughthwaite examined the card that had been slid to her across the counter.

'Marston Towers,' she said.

'That's right. I'm Mrs Gosling, the housekeeper there. I do for Sir Hedley Maladroit, the local squire and big-wig. You've no doubt heard of him. He's very important and influential. I just need somebody who isn't afraid of hard work for the mornings to help with the cleaning.'

'You're a bit out of the way, up there at the top of the Dale,' remarked Mrs Sloughthwaite. 'Can't you find somebody in Risingdale who could do it?'

'It's not through want of trying,' she was told. 'Nobody seems interested. It's the devil's own job getting staff these days.'

'I'll pop the card in the window and I'll mention it to those who call into my store.'

'Thank you,' said Mrs Gosling, taking out her purse.

'Oh, don't bother with that, love,' said the shopkeeper.

'That's very kind of you. Well, I'll wish you a good morning.'

She wasn't going to get away so easily.

'So you live up in Risingdale yourself then, do you?' asked Mrs Sloughthwaite.

'I've lived there all my life, as have my family, who have been there for generations,' said Mrs Gosling. 'My grandfather was the mole catcher and chimney sweep at the big house and my grandmother was Martha Gosling, known as "the demon knitter of Risingdale". She started knitting at four years old. Happen you've heard of her?'

'The name rings a bell,' Mrs Sloughthwaite fibbed. 'You'll no doubt have come across the new teacher at the village school, then?'

'Mr Dwyer? Oh yes, I know him very well. He's a very nice young man and, unlike the other teachers, keeps his classroom neat and tidy. I'm a stickler for neatness. He's a very good teacher, too. My granddaughter Vicky is in his class and she thinks he's the bee's knees. I used to do the caretaking at the school before I moved to Marston Towers.'

'I was saying to one of my regulars,' said Mrs Sloughthwaite, 'that I guess there's not much going on for a young man like him up there in such an insulated place. He must find it to be a bit of a change from what he used to do. He was a professional footballer, you know.'

'Yes, I was aware of that,' said Mrs Gosling.

'He used to teach at the village school here in Barton.'

'I knew that,' said Mrs Gosling.

'Comes originally from Ireland.'

'Yes, I know. There's not much I don't know about Mr Dwyer.'

Here was a woman who could give Mrs Sloughthwaite a run for her money when it came to extracting information and dealing in gossip.

'Actually, it's been very eventful in Risingdale lately,' said Mrs Gosling.

'Really,' said the shopkeeper, resting her bosom on the counter again and leaning forward to glean all the gen.

'A very famous London artist has settled in the village. She's renting the old Primitive Methodist chapel and causing quite a stir.'

'How come?'

'All the men in the village have eyes like chapel hat pegs when she makes an appearance. She's illustrating one of these fancy coffee-table books of the Dales and picked Risingdale as being the most typical around here.'

'Well, I think Barton-in-the-Dale has more to offer,' said Mrs Sloughthwaite, feeling piqued.

'I feature in it,' continued Mrs Gosling, not rising to challenge the comment. 'She's done a portrait of me for her book. Told me I have very distinctive features, she did.'

She's not wrong there, thought Mrs Sloughthwaite. The woman was probably inbred.

'She's throwing a party this weekend and invited all the villagers. She's very well in with Sir Hedley and rents one of his cottages. He's going through a rough patch at the moment, poor man. You might have heard that his son was in a road accident. He was in his sports car and hit a motorcyclist head on, skidded off of the road, hit a tree and both of them were killed outright.'

'I read about that in the paper,' said Mrs Sloughthwaite. 'Mind you, some of these young men drive like rats out of hell.'

'Then, just after the boy's funeral, his mother ups and leaves. Body not cold in the grave – actually, he was cremated, but that's neither here nor there – and she absconds.'

'She what?'

'Ups and leaves Sir Hedley and goes to live with her sister. Nobody in the village was sorry to see her go, and I reckon her husband was glad to see the back of her as well. Stuck-up and full of airs and graces was Lady Maladroit, and she was only some jumped-up assistant in a London art gallery before she married the squire. Then she hadn't been gone long and Sir Hedley announces in the village inn that his son, the one what got killed, was the father of the baby that the barmaid is expecting.'

'Good gracious,' gasped the shopkeeper. 'I've never heard the like.'

'Then they found the bomb.'

'The bomb,' repeated Mrs Sloughthwaite.

'Up at the ruined castle when they were doing these excavations. They dug up an unexploded World War Two bomb and they had to get the army out to defuse it.'

'Well, I never,' murmured the shopkeeper.

'How it got there is a mystery,' said Mrs Gosling. 'I mean, there was nothing to bomb up there at the top of the Dale unless they were after the sheep. That's why we had all these evacuees from the towns and cities.'

'The plane could have been heading for the airfield at Clayton Bank,' suggested the shopkeeper. 'My parents lived near there and bombers used to fly over their house regular. They lived in a terraced house next to a very odd couple, did my parents. Mr and Mrs Evans, they were called. She worked in the munitions factory and her old man had a reserved occupation. My father was away fighting. He was in the East Anglican Regiment. The only time Mr Evans spoke to my mother was to complain about the Anderson Shelter that they put in our garden. He was miffed it wasn't in his. One day when the siren sounded, Mrs Evans shot out of the shelter.' She stopped suddenly. 'Am I boring you?'

'Not at all,' said Mrs Gosling, 'it's very interesting.'

'Well, as I was saying,' Mrs Sloughthwaite carried on, 'Mrs Evans shot out of the Anderson Shelter like a rabbit with its tail on fire, heading back for her house. The Air Raid Warden shouts at her to get back in the shelter because German bombers would soon be over. "I've left my teeth on the kitchen table," says she, "and I'm going back for them." The Air Raid Warden shouts back at her, "Germans are dropping bombs, not bloody sandwiches." We did laugh.'

'You ought to write a book,' Mrs Gosling told her.

'I've often thought about it,' replied Mrs Sloughthwaite. 'I do have a way with words, even if I do say so myself.'

24

The studio was crowded and noisy when Tom arrived for Amanda's party. He stood at the door, unnoticed by the assembled guests, and looked around the room. It seemed that the whole of the village had turned out. He smiled as he caught sight of Leanne and Dean in a corner, laughing and chattering away. It was clear the young woman had changed her view of the boy. A little distance away, Mrs Mossup watched the young couple with a self-satisfied expression on her face. She could no doubt envisage a bright future for her daughter and future grandchild. Tom saw an animated Mrs Golightly speaking to Mr Firkin, who was hanging on her every word. Perhaps Bertha was disposed to 'give him the nod' after all. Staring intently at one of the pictures with her father was Janette, looking beautiful and elegant as ever. Mr Gaunt, dressed in a smart grey suit, was in animated conversation with a tall, red-headed woman Tom didn't recognise. She had a homely face and an engaging smile and it was clear that the headmaster was very attentive and in high spirits. There was a lugubrious-looking Mr Cadwallader, trapped in a corner by Mrs Gosling, who was no doubt hectoring him about something. She was wearing the most outrageously multicoloured cardigan and resembled some huge, exotic tropical bird. Would the poor man never escape the woman's haranguing? Joyce looked ecstatically happy as she clinked glasses with Julian, probably discussing their forthcoming nuptials. Tom chuckled to see the incorrigible Toby Croft, unsurprisingly standing by the drinks table, pint glass in hand, as vociferous as ever and probably giving his farming companions the benefit of his strongly held opinions.

Tom had a real affection for these people – even Toby Croft – and found pleasure in their company. They were a shrewd, good-natured, blunt-speaking folk with genuine warmth and he felt as settled and happy to live in Risingdale as any of them. He could understand why Mr Gaunt, who could have become the headmaster of a much bigger and more prestigious school, had decided to stay in the village. He could also understand why Mr Pendlebury had declined the offer of the bishop to move to a larger and more prosperous parish and refused to become a canon at the cathedral. He could even understand why Owen, Bertha and Joyce had no ambition to move. There was something very special about the quality of life in Risingdale, the village at the top of the Dale. He recalled Mr Gaunt's words in one of their earlier conversations: 'As a child, I didn't really go very far out of the Dale,' he had said. 'There was too much to do on the farm. There were occasional day trips to Scarborough and Whitby, but that was about it. Of course, over the years I have done a bit of travelling but, do you know, I can't wait to get back home.' That evening as he observed his friends, colleagues and neighbours, Tom had never felt as contented. This was about to change.

He walked in amongst the throng. Amanda, surrounded by a circle of admiring men, which included Sir Hedley, Richard Greenwood, Mr Cockburn and Mr Pendlebury, was laughing at something that had been said. She looked magnificent. Tom stared at her, enchanted.

'She's very beautiful, isn't she?'

Mrs Lister had come to join him.

'Yes, she is,' agreed Tom.

'Mrs Stanhope has that effect on people,' she said, 'particularly the men. I am sure it hasn't escaped your notice, Mr

Dwyer.' She gave a knowing smile. 'She is one of those rare creatures whom men find fascinating and, of course, one can see why.'

Tom didn't respond but continued to stare at Amanda.

'I'm pleased to have this opportunity of speaking to you,' she said.

'I'm sorry, I was miles away,' he answered. 'What was it you said?'

'I am glad to have this chance to speak to you. I want to thank you for all you have done for my son,' she told him.

'He passed his eleven-plus with flying colours,' answered Tom, 'but of course I knew he would. You must be very proud of him. He's done really well.'

'And you have done really well too,' she replied. 'How lucky we are in the village to have you teaching at the school. His former teacher, Miss Cathcart, took little interest in the children. She was rather a sad character. Charlie could not have achieved what he has done without you, I'm certain of that.'

'Oh yes, he could,' Tom disagreed. 'He is a gifted young man. He'd have sailed through the examination without any help from me.'

'It's not just about helping him with his studies,' she said. 'It's the way you have treated him, listened to him and encouraged him. You have inspired him. I once read that education is not about the filling of a pot, but about the lighting of a fire.'

'My favourite poet, W.B. Yeats, wrote that,' Tom told her.

'Well, you lit that fire in my son, Mr Dwyer. Charlie likes and respects you, and if there is one person whom he can trust and be open and honest with, it's you. I know that. I told you as much the time I came to see you before Christmas.'

'And you brought me an apple pie.'

'I did.'

'It didn't last long. It was like the apple pies my mother used to make.'

'You remember, I said that Charlie didn't know who his father was and I had never told him, but that lately he had kept asking me about him. Well, I felt he was of an age when he should know, so I told him and he has met his father.'

Tom could have told her that he already was aware of this, that her son had confided in him.

Mrs Lister looked Tom in the eyes. 'I think you have met his father too, one evening in the garden of my cottage.'

'I did,' said Tom, 'and I can assure you, as I assured him at the time, Mrs Lister, that the information will go no further. I don't deal in gossip.'

'Yes, he told me he had met you,' she replied. 'I never doubted what you said. You are a good man, Mr Dwyer.' She looked over to where Sir Hedley was standing. Their eyes met for a moment. 'One day it will become common knowledge, I guess, but for the moment we are to let sleeping dogs lie.'

Their conversation was interrupted by Sir Hedley, who banged sharply on a table with a spoon.

'May I have your attention, please,' he shouted. 'Mrs Stanhope would like to say a few words.'

'Thank you, Sir Hedley,' she said, before walking to the middle of the room like an actor taking centre stage. She had the look on her face of a woman who knew she was being admired, and gave a dazzling smile. She gently brushed a strand of blonde hair from her forehead. Her blue eyes sparkled. 'I am so pleased that so many have come along this evening. This social event is my small way of thanking you all for your warmth, hospitality, understanding and friendship during the time my son and I have been with you. I should like to thank Mr Cockburn for allowing me to use this lovely old chapel as my studio. I hope he doesn't disapprove of the changes I have made.'

'Not at all,' called out the minister, good-humouredly.

'I should like to thank Sir Hedley for renting me one of

his delightful cottages on Rattan Row and for his generous offers of help. A great thank you must go to Mr Gaunt and the teachers at the village school, in particular Mr Dwyer, who has been most supportive during my son's illness. Leo, my son, has been so very happy at the village school. Finally, my gratitude is to those of you who have allowed me to paint their portraits. You have given up your time selflessly and sat for me with great patience. I hope that you feel that my efforts capture the very essence of the Dale and the people within it. On Monday, I shall be returning to London to finish the final portraits and landscapes for the exhibition, which will take place at the Garret Gallery in a couple of months' time. I still have a few more paintings to do. Then they will be sent to the publisher to be included in a book called *The Living Dale*. It only remains for me to thank you again for your kindness. I have loved being with you and I hope to visit Risingdale again in the not too distant future.'

This was followed by loud applause.

Tom was stunned.

'Did she say she is leaving?' he asked Mrs Lister.

'Yes,' she said, 'she is going back to London.'

Sir Hedley came to join Amanda.

'May I thank you, Mrs Stanhope,' he said, 'for spending time with us in our small community and bringing with you such colour, vibrancy and sunshine. I know I speak for all here in saying that you will be greatly missed.'

There were shouts of 'Hear! Hear!' and more clapping.

Tom did not hear a word Sir Hedley had said for his mind was in a whirl.

'Would you excuse me,' he said to Mrs Lister and hurried across the room.

He took Amanda's arm gently and guided her to a quiet part of the studio.

'You're leaving?' He was breathless. His stomach churned and his throat felt dry.

'That's right,' she said. 'Back to the bright lights of London.'

'When did you decide to go?'

'Well, I never intended to stay here for good, Tom. After I had completed most of the paintings and made sketches for others, there was nothing to keep me here.'

'Nothing to keep you here,' he repeated. 'But I thought you liked it in Risingdale.'

'I do like it in Risingdale, but I don't wish to spend the rest of my life here.'

'But I thought . . .' He struggled to find the right words. 'I thought that you and I . . . that we might . . .'

'Might what?' She looked puzzled.

'I thought you had some feelings for me,' he said in a voice barely sounding like his own.

'Of course I have feelings for you,' she told him. 'I'm very fond of you. You have become a dear, dear friend and you were wonderful during that dreadful patch when Leo was ill. You were so caring and sympathetic and helped me to get through it. I shall be forever grateful for that.'

'I'm just a friend, then?' asked Tom. 'Nothing more?' He gave a small, sad smile.

'If you are telling me you thought there was something more than friendship, Tom, then I must tell you, you were mistaken.'

'I see,' he said sadly. He looked at her with wounded eyes, wanting more than she was able to give.

'As I said, I'm very fond of you, but you must know I could never settle in a little, rather parochial village high up away from everything. I'm a city animal. I have loved my stay here and the scenery and the people, but it is not the way of life I want. I miss the theatres and galleries, the museums and the buzz of London. I am sorry that you thought there was something more between us.'

'I did think that,' said Tom quietly.

'And now you're upset.' She rested a hand on his arm. 'Oh dear. Look, Tom, if I stayed in Risingdale, I should be like a caged bird beating its wings against the bars, yearning to be free. I am not the sort of woman for you. I could never make you happy.'

'And what about Leo? He's got a place at the grammar school. He's really looking forward to starting there next September.'

'Well, of course he doesn't want to leave, but he's become accustomed to moving around. I've managed to get him a place at the English International College in Marbella, which has a superb reputation. I have been offered a commission to illustrate a book on Spain and we fly out next month. It's an assignment I couldn't refuse.'

'Well, I hope things work out for you and for Leo,' said Tom. His voice was barely audible.

'You will come to the launch of my London exhibition, won't you? Sir Hedley has kindly agreed to open it. I'll take you to Simpson's in the Strand for lunch if you come.'

'No, Amanda,' said Tom. 'I don't think I'll come.'

'You're angry with me,' she said. 'I can tell.' She rested a hand on his. 'Oh, Tom, I'm so sorry you thought that—'

She was interrupted by Toby Croft, who clearly was worse for drink.

'Now then, young Mester Dwyer,' he said, 'stop monopolisin' our 'ostess. Some others want to speak to 'er, tha knaas.'

Amanda turned to the old farmer. 'Just give us a moment, please, Mr Croft,' she told him. 'I do need to speak to Mr Dwyer.'

When she turned back, she found he had gone.

Tom walked slowly through the village with a sinking heart. He had obviously misread the signals and felt a fool. He had been certain that Amanda had had deeper feelings for him and he had been wrong. She was fond of him, nothing more. He thought of what his Auntie Bridget's counsel might be at this moment. She would tell him he was not the first person in the world to be disappointed in love and would certainly not be the last. She would tell him that self-pity wasn't the answer, but to resign himself to the fact that the woman he had fallen head over heels for had no more feelings for him above that of a fond friendship. Get on with your life, Tom, she would say, put it behind you, there will one day be someone who will return your love. But it was hard to think that way. His feet had been knocked from under him. His hopes and dreams had been shattered.

He arrived at the duck pond and sat on the bench facing the oily black water, beyond which the white limestone walls stretched upwards to the great whalcback hills and a lowering sky massed with gloomy grey clouds. The scene had a cold and eerie beauty about it.

'Do you remember the last time we met here at the duck pond?' Janette came and sat down beside him. She had seen him leave the studio and followed him.

'Hello, Jan,' he said. 'Yes, I remember. You gave me a good telling-off for feeding bread to the ducks.'

'And you were sarcastic and called me the resident duck expert.'

'And you said I was a know-all and put on airs and graces.'

'And you said that was rich coming from me.'

They both laughed.

They sat for a moment without speaking.

'You didn't know she was leaving, did you?' she said.

'No, I had no idea,' he replied.

'I guessed as much. I saw you talking to her. You looked shell-shocked.'

'She told me she couldn't settle in Risingdale. I suppose I should have realised that. I should have guessed that London has too much draw and that she would miss the bright lights.'

'The bright lights are not all they are cracked up to be,' she said. 'They certainly weren't for me.'

'Sometimes things don't turn out the way you hope they will,' he said.

'That's true. I hoped the job in Nottingham would work out. It didn't.'

'So you are returning to Risingdale?' he asked.

'Yes,' she said. 'I'm coming home. I've got my job back at the bank in Clayton. The powers that be have been very good about it. I imagine that my messing up the manager's position in Nottingham has put paid to any further promotion but, you know, I'm not that bothered. There are more things in life than status and money.' She got up to go. 'Goodnight, Tom. Don't stay out here too long or you'll catch cold.'

'Goodnight, Jan,' he replied and rested his head on the back of the bench and closed his eyes.

Tom had a fitful night, and lying awake in the early hours his mind kept dwelling on the events of the evening before in the studio and what Amanda had said to him. He should have realised that she could never have settled in Risingdale, away from the excitement of London, for a life with a village school-master. He had been deluded to think she could. Was it infatuation on his part, he asked himself during those sleepless hours, was it a fascination with her loveliness and vivacious personality – a sort of schoolboy crush? Whatever it had been, it was over and she would vanish from his life.

He rose late on Sunday. His routine each morning, when he got out of bed, was to pull back the bedroom curtains and look out at the panorama that stretched beyond the cottage. The landscape, whatever the season, always filled him with awe, whether the fresh bursting life of spring, the bright summer when the sunlight danced on the fells, the mellow golds of autumn or the vast white world of winter. The scene before him that morning was spectacular: emerald-green undulating fields studded with outcrops of rock and criss-crossed with bone-white limestone walls, thick bracken slopes and dark and distant soaring fells flecked in white. In a vast and dove-grey sky, a heron flew lazily overhead, its long legs trailing behind. Tom knew he could never trade all this for a life in the city. He smiled to think of another of his Auntie Bridget's aphorisms: 'Each day is wonderful when the sun rises and there isn't a flood.'

'Come on, Tom,' he said out loud, 'pull yourself together. Get over it.'

All week for school, he wore a white shirt, college tie and smart suit or sports jacket, but at the weekend, if not going out, he dressed down. As was his custom, that Sunday he had not bothered to shave and wore his old pair of jeans, the shirt with a frayed collar and a baggy jumper. He didn't even bother with a comb and just ran his fingers through his hair. That afternoon he decided to spend tidying up the garden to try and take his mind off other things. He was busy digging in the overgrown border to the front of the cottage when he heard the click of the gate catch. He looked up to see Leo coming down the path. The boy's small face was decorated with misery.

'Hello,' said Tom, resting on the spade.

'Hello, Mr Dwyer,' replied the boy.

'As you see, I'm trying to get the garden in shape.'

'I had to see you,' Leo told him.

'I'm pleased you called. I was hoping to see you before you left.' Tom had at first been minded to visit Amanda at her cottage before she set off for London, but decided against it. It was best, he thought finally, to have a clean break and not go through again the embarrassing encounter of the evening before.

Leo stood before the teacher. Tom had never seen the boy look so downcast. Even in the hospital bed, he had managed to smile.

'We're going away tomorrow, Mr Dwyer.'

'Yes, your mother told me you are going back to London.'

'I don't want to go,' said the boy. There was a tremble in his voice. He rubbed his eyes. 'I want to stay here in Risingdale. I've been really happy here, the happiest I've ever been. I was looking forward to going to the grammar school with Charlie. I've never had a best friend and I will really miss him. I will miss the rest of the class at school and the lessons.' He looked up at the teacher. 'I will miss you, Mr Dwyer.'

'Well, I shall miss you too, Leo,' Tom told him.

'I don't want to go,' said the boy again. His eyes were brimming with tears and his bottom lip was beginning to tremble. 'I want to stay here.'

Tom put down his spade and approached the boy. He rested a hand on Leo's shoulder.

'But you know that you have to go, don't you,' Tom said.

'Yes, I know that,' replied Leo, rubbing his eyes again. 'I do love my mother, you know, but sometimes she doesn't think of me. She thinks of her career, her artwork, her exhibitions. I know that sounds unfair, particularly when you think how she's looked after me all through my illness, and I know how important her painting is to her, but just when I am truly happy, we have to leave and I have to start another school in another country, where I won't know anyone. Do you think I'm being selfish, Mr Dwyer?'

'No, I don't think you are being selfish, Leo,' Tom told him. He might have said that it was the boy's mother who was probably the selfish one.

The boy reached into his pocket and brought out his pen. He stared at it for a moment and ran a finger across its length. Then he held it out. 'I would like you to have this,' he said.

'Your pen?' said Tom. 'No, I can't accept your pen. It was your father's. It's your prized possession.'

'I know, but I would still like you to have it.'

'I can't take it, Leo. It's too precious.'

'But I want you to have it, Mr Dwyer. You must have it. Please. You see, when you use it, you will think of me and the times we have had together, the good times.'

'Oh, Leo.' Tom sighed.

'Please.'

Tom took the pen. 'I will keep it safe until you come back and see us in Risingdale, and then I shall give it back to you. You will come back and see us one day, won't you?'

Suddenly the tears came welling up, spilling over. The boy began to sob, great heaving sobs. Then he put his arms around the teacher in a great hug, before rushing down the path without looking back.

All afternoon Tom spent tackling the garden, flattening the molehills on the lawn, pruning the long, overhanging branches of the trees, clipping the hedges, trimming the dead flowers and weeding the borders. As evening approached, he smelled of earth and grass and ached from his exertions. He went into his cottage, washed his hands and flopped into a chair. Soon he fell asleep. He was awakened by a loud knock on the cottage door. On the step stood Janette.

'Hello, Jan,' said Tom, rubbing the sleep out of his eyes.

'I'm here to take you out,' she said.

'What?'

'You are not going to sit here moping in the dark,' she told him, sounding like a strict schoolmistress chastising a sulking child. 'You are to come with me to the King's Head for a drink, where you can drown your sorrows and be amongst your friends.'

'I can't,' Tom protested. 'I haven't shaved and I'm not dressed for a night out. I look a mess.'

'Well, I have seen you look better,' she admitted good-humouredly, 'but you will have to do. Now come along, I can't stand out here all night.'

Tom stared at her for a moment. She was framed like a portrait, the woman with the flaming red hair and the jade green eyes.

He smiled. 'I'll get my coat,' he said.

A *Class Act*, the final installment in Gervase Phinn's charming Top of the Dale series, is available now.